ANU TARA TIKI

A BLACK STONE ON THE WHITE CONTINENT

Lorraine Saint-Hubert
&
Ludovic Des Leuques

GLRD PUBLICATIONS
BOERNE, TX

Contents

1

BLUE PLANET

Émile was walking in what they called the *Quartier Latin*, a neighborhood of Paris he loved. He'd hung out there a great deal in his younger days, back when he was a student at the École des Mines. Now that he resided in the western suburbs, he hardly ever came to the area, but today was different because the tour operator he was making for, *Planète Bleue*, had set up its headquarters there. He'd parked his car a fair distance from the agency, not only to enjoy a brief stroll but above all else to save himself the cost of the underground parking lot, which he found extortionate. It was the end of September and it was raining. Émile was sweating under his windbreaker as he wondered why Americans always thought Paris was so romantic. He remembered an Italian author who'd dubbed it "The Gray City". *He got that right, but what was his name again? Goddamn memory lapses… Tabucchi maybe?*

Émile reflected on the idea that Parisians seemed much attached to their city. It was no doubt down to the smell of hot croissants as one walks by a bakery in the morning, or the crowded bistros where regulars put the world to rights, leaning on zinc-topped bars, a glass of red in hand and a cigarette stuck between their lips.

The sporadically potholed sidewalk was riddled with unavoidable puddles, which made him grumble at the idea of mud splashing up onto his light-colored pants. *Romantic, right? It's the stuff of nightmares. Roll on Christmas so I can escape this awful place, if only for a short while.*

This was precisely the reason behind his visit to *Planète Bleue*: to find a destination for the epic trip he and his wife Monique always took during the Christmas and New Year holidays. The Delaportes, by now in their early sixties, had taken up this habit twenty years earlier, after their two grown-up children had fled the family nest to fend for themselves. From then on, spending Christmas on their own in their apartment on the outskirts of Paris became altogether unbearable. These vacations, tailor-made for the both of them, were the only luxury that the couple, whose lifestyle was fairly modest, ever allowed themselves. They'd almost traveled the entire globe and, with the impression that they'd already seen everything there was to see, finding a new place to go on their great annual voyage had become a real headache for Émile.

Here it is. Planète Bleue has certainly grown. It's nothing like the small agency it once was, Émile thought.

He was somewhat overwhelmed by the state-of-the-art design of the brand-spanking new building and the ubiquitous I.T. equipment that he spotted through the large store front. He entered tentatively, did what he could to escape a receptionist who'd come forward to meet and greet him, and rushed to the section of wall where the brochures were displayed. He idly flipped through around ten of them, without any of the suggested locations grabbing his attention, since he and Monique had already visited every last one of them. Eventually, his eyes were drawn to a spectacular photograph on the cover of one of the booklets, showing an immense colony of penguins on a snow-covered beach, framed by enormous blue-tinged icebergs.

Émile began to leaf through the pages of Antarctic cruises.

I never imagined there'd be tourism in Antarctica, he thought. *But why not Antarctica? It's an original destination at least. And seeing as it's the Southern Hemisphere, December is probably just the right season. Plus, Monique has always dreamed of going on a cruise. We could make the most of it and stop off in Peru and Bolivia along the way. It's worth looking into…*

Loaded down with stacks of literature and his head full of ideas proposed by the expert at *Planète Bleue,* Émile returned to his car and made his way toward Rueil-Malmaison, where he and Monique had lived since their wedding day forty years earlier. The journey home went much better than expected. He'd feared the worst, since it had become impossible to get through the recently pedestrianized *Bois de Boulogne.*

"Another whim from the mayor and his increasingly ridiculous initiatives", he muttered aloud. "A music festival that swamps the capital for a week, a man-made beach along the Seine that puts the river-bank road out of use all summer, and now the *Bois de Boulogne* closed to traffic. Time to draw the line! All this is to amuse the masses. It's bread and circuses - like in ancient Rome! We aren't making any progress. We'd rather go backwards. What a time to be living in!"

This last phrase was one of Émile's favorite expressions. He'd rattle it off about everything and nothing. Émile was fundamentally resistant to change and anxious about the idea of anything novel or unexpected. His annual trip was the only adventure he could afford, but everything had to be perfectly under control, organized to the nth degree well in advance and without room for improvisation.

At least there's one good thing about retirement, he thought. *Now I have all the time I need to plan my vacation.*

As soon as he was back from his Paris outing, Émile settled down in his office to take a closer look at the pile of documents he'd picked up at *Planète Bleue.* He had a good two hours ahead of him. Monique wasn't in, for she spent every Wednesday afternoon visiting her mother in a retirement home on the other side of Paris. After a great deal of umming and ahh-ing, he thought he'd managed to create the ideal itinerary and was starting to get very excited about it. They would combine an Antarctic cruise with a short stopover in Argentina and a tour of Peru and Bolivia. All he had to do was discuss it with his wife, hoping that her hard-to-predict reaction wouldn't put an abrupt end to this rather off-the-wall idea. He wouldn't talk about it with her tonight, because he was going to have to hear her out as she gave him all the usual gossip: his mother-in-law's poor health, how awful the caregivers are, how bright the head doctor is, the exorbitant hospital fees, ad infinitum... It was better to wait for a more favorable opportunity, perhaps next

Sunday lunch in the presence of the children and their respective other halves.

Against all the odds, Monique accepted Émile's suggestions for their next vacation with delight. She seemed particularly enthusiastic about Argentina, a country she had always dreamed of seeing, with its tall pampas grasses, its *gauchos* and its preponderance of lefties and sunny cities where they perform the tango. She loved the tango and had danced it quite well in her youth. Unfortunately, Émile had two left feet and she wondered whether she herself would get into the swing of it again. She decided that she'd take some classes before they left. At first, she felt somewhat reserved about Antarctica, until Émile explained to her that it would be a short cruise and they'd be staying in a luxury cabin. This completely changed her perspective: heading off on an original and adventurous vacation in conditions that only rich people tend to have access to would certainly impress her friends. She was already picturing her neighbor's face, a woman who was always in charge of taking in the mail and watering the plants when they went away, and just couldn't wait to tell her the very next day.

"That old gossip will be knocked for six with this!" she exclaimed.

As for Émile, the Argentinean part of the trip was just a stopover of little interest before they hit Peru and Bolivia. What fascinated him most were the ruins of former civilizations and age-old monuments, including the various types of pyramids they'd toured in Egypt, Mexico, Guatemala and even China. However, there was one main goal for him on this trip to Antarctica: it would mean they had really been to all four corners of the globe. After this trip, apart from a handful of insignificant and very isolated places, Émile would have seen the whole lot and he could sit back, browse through his photos and meditate on everything he'd discovered and learned over the years. At the end of an otherwise rather insipid life, he felt as though this would be a pleasant way to go. Émile could never have imagined that his escapade to Antarctica would turn that quiet little existence of his completely upside down.

***

The Paris-Buenos Aires flight seemed to pass pretty quickly in business class. Between meals and movies they barely slept a wink, but the excited anticipation more than compensated for how tired the journey made them. They'd taken off from Paris at five in the evening and landed in Buenos Aires at about the same hour due to the time difference. The black limousine waiting for them at the exit of the terminal saw them arrive at the *Gran Palacio*, a five-star establishment in the heart of the *Recoleta* district, in no time at all.

Once in their room, Émile couldn't help but immediately uncork the bottle of Argentinean chardonnay, a welcome gift from the hotel team, which was sitting on the coffee table in the living room and pour himself a small glass. In the meantime, Monique ran herself a bath, into which she emptied virtually the entire bottle of green tea-scented bath salts elegantly positioned next to the immense tub.

"It's funny how you never find *Perrier* in these palatial hotels!" shouted out Émile.

"What makes you say that? You've never even set foot in a hotel like this before," replied Monique, lifting her head from the cloud of foam that was starting to engulf her.

"Our globe-trotting son told me that! He recommended this place, you know. What do you think of it?"

"This bathroom is just beautiful. With the living space and bedroom, I'd say it's almost as big as our apartment! What are we doing tonight? We'll be tasting the famous grills, no doubt. And then shall we go dancing?"

"Oh no, not tonight, I'm too tired. I'd prefer a light salad somewhere local and then an early night."

"We didn't just travel five thousand miles to eat salad and spend our evening in a hotel room, did we? You could make an effort! We can't leave Buenos Aires without going to a *churrasqueria* for dinner and dancing the tango somewhere!"

"All right! I'll ask the concierge to book us a table in a cabaret bar where you can stuff yourself and dance the night away!"

Monique was delighted. She quickly got changed and they took a taxi to the address given by the man down at reception. Émile was pleasantly surprised by the welcome they received at the restaurant. They were taken to a comfortable little table next to the dance floor, before the waiter gave them descriptions, in impeccable French, of all the various meat dishes on the menu. A sommelier then arrived and advised them to order an excellent malbec from Mendoza, which was supposed to be the ideal accompaniment to the regional specialties. The combination of *churrasco* with *chimichuri* and malbec made Émile momentarily forget his desire to go to bed early and he agreed to share a *dulce de leche* tart with Monique to finish off their meal. As they were both relishing their dessert with a languid bandoneon playing in the background, a swarthy local rushed over to Monique and urged her to join him onto the dance floor for a tango. Monique didn't have to be asked twice and soon found herself in the middle of the room, glued against the individual with his slick hair and thin mustache. Alone at their table, Émile could do nothing but watch his wife's performance. She looked delighted as she shook her derrière and rubbed herself, without a shred of decency, against this stranger's muscular body. Monique seemed ridiculous to him, in her form-fitting, frilly yellow dress, perched on five-inch heels and wearing garish lipstick. *When I think that she's bought those shoes and dress just for tonight and that she'll never put them on again, it drives me nuts! We're going to be lugging that stuff around in our suitcases the whole way! I can't wait for the day after tomorrow. Let's get to Peru already!*

Monique would have stayed there all night. It was with regret, and upon seeing her husband's defeated face, that she agreed to head back to the hotel. *Thank goodness we're staying another day! We can come back here tomorrow evening,* she thought in the taxi as they returned to the Gran Palacio.

***

The atmosphere was quite different in Lima. The city seemed more foreign than Buenos Aires, which to all intents and purposes felt like a European capital. Émile pointed out to Monique that at least now, they felt far from home and that this little tour in Peru would be much more pleasant than their stay in Argentina. Monique didn't agree in the slightest. She'd loved Buenos Aires and her first impression of Lima was comparatively disappointing. Plus, she'd read in a guidebook that pick pocketing was common in Peru and so held her purse very tightly against her, watching anyone that approached them with a suspicious look. In the streets, there were a great many individuals with a very pronounced American-native look: small, poorly dressed men alongside plump women wearing large petticoats and black felt hats. Monique wasn't particularly reassured. Added to this was the fact that the hotel was much less luxurious than the *Gran Palacio de la Recoleta* and no one spoke French there. Monique managed to relax once in their room, which was, in fact, very comfortable. Her mood definitely improved when Émile suggested they go to dinner in a famous tourist restaurant overlooking the *Plaza Mayor*. She went on to totally forget her negative bias towards both Lima and Peru when, towards the end of the meal, a group of musicians in traditional folk costume began to play some local music. When one of the musicians, dressed in a large multicolored poncho, approached their table and asked Monique if she wanted him to play any song in particular, she felt touched. "*El Condor Pasa*, please," she asked. She failed to repress her tears when, accompanied by the Andean flute and charrango, the singer, with the most warm and melodious voice, sang the words she knew by heart, the only words she had ever learned in Spanish.

Émile was very embarrassed. He was the shy type and any sign of emotion, especially in public, made him very uncomfortable. He had the feeling that the whole dining room was staring over at their table. He wondered how Monique could possibly know the lyrics to this song and why it caused her to get into such a state. What did she know of South America and its culture? Nothing, as far as he was aware....

"Obviously, you're quite the fan of Peruvian music," he said once they were back at the hotel. "I had no idea you were such an expert on the Andean flute. I think you'll enjoy what I've got planned. We're going to see every single inch of the Andean mountains, top to bottom!"

"What do you mean by that? Aren't we staying in Lima?" asked Monique with a hint of concern.

"Just one more day. We'll be visiting the *Oro del Peru* Museum and the National Museum of Archaeology. Is there anything you'd really like to do while we're here?"

"Actually, I'd like to go to lunch in a restaurant I've heard about. There's a Japanese chef who set it up, Nobu, and I really admire him. He's invented a lot of very famous dishes. I'd love to sample his grilled octopus, one of his most well-known creations. I imagine the seafood must be particularly fresh here. I mean, we're on the Pacific coast, so I doubt we'd be served farmed salmon or frozen crab legs!"

"That's true enough. But I can't guarantee that we'll get a table at Nobu's tomorrow. If it's anything like Paris or Tokyo, we'd need to have booked several months in advance. Let's hope the hotel concierge knows what he's doing. Anyway, Nobu or not, I promise you, we'll fill up with grilled octopus, *ceviche* and *sashimi* of every kind before we leave the coast."

"And then, what's next on the schedule?"

"The day after tomorrow, we'll fly to Cuzco, where we'll stay three days. It's the heart of ancient Peru and there'll be so many interesting sites to visit. We're going to take a look at this spectacular place called Sacsayhuaman and then Machu Picchu, the lost city of the Incas. We'll be dropping in on two or three traditional native villages in the valley along the way. Then we'll head towards Lake Titicaca before passing through Bolivia and exploring Tiwanaku, where there are enigmatic ruins to be seen. Some say that they date back as far as Noah's Flood!"

"I've got a feeling I'll be seeing more than my share of old stones and hearing my fill of you and your incessant chatter about the origins of humankind, forgotten civilizations, Atlantis and all the rest of it. I mean, that's what you're passionate about! Actually, despite what you might think, I'm quite interested in it too."

"That's reassuring. I was getting worried you'd only be interested in dancing, eating… and the Andean flute!"

After their cultural and gastronomic day in Lima, Monique and Émile headed for the airport early the next morning en route to Cuzco. The plane flew over some stupendous snow-covered peaks before plunging into a wide valley, drowned in clouds. As they disembarked, a damp cold hit Monique and Émile, whose warmer clothes remained neatly tucked away in their suitcases. They quickly developed a painful and dizzying sensation in addition to a low-level yet persistent headache due to the sudden change in altitude.

"Let's hope the weather improves," said Émile, "I don't see myself trudging around the city and visiting a load of ruins in the bitter cold."

"Yes. You didn't plan for this, did you?" Monique grumbled. "It's going to be a real laugh if we're stuck here for three days in these conditions…"

By the time the private minibus journey to the *Casa del Inca*, a magnificent colonial period convent transformed into a five-star hotel, had reached its end, the cloud cover had begun to dissipate, and the sun had just started to show its face. After lunch, they left their room and ventured outdoors. The sky was now bright blue and the temperature almost summery. Émile, a map of the city gripped in his hand, led Monique to the main square, which was only a stone's throw away from their hotel in the historic center of the city. In front of the imposing cathedral dominating the square, Émile started to complain in an almost depressed voice:

"Just look what they've done to the Incan capital! From what I read, there was a magnificent temple here, made of enormous cut stones and walls covered with gold plaques. The Spaniards stole the gold, dismantled the temple and used the blocks to build the foundations for their homes and churches. It's exactly what also happened in Tenochtitlan, the capital of the Aztec empire. It was a beautiful city in the middle of a stunning lake, and they transformed into the filthy megalopolis they called Mexico City. I don't think there's been a worse colonization than the one perpetrated by the Spanish!"

"Well! It can't have been any worse than what the French or English did!"

"It was much worse, because not only did they enslave the indigenous people and impose their cock-and-bull religion on them, but they burned all the documents that could have told us of the history and culture of these peoples. Almost nothing is known of their civilizations!

And when you think they melted all those gold masterpieces to pay for the wars of Charles V! All that remains are a few oral traditions, which our European historians call legends and which only give a vague idea of what their world was like before the Spanish arrived. Feeling up to all this?"

"Of course, why?"

"Well, I just want to show you what the Inca world was like before the barbarians got their hands on it. If you're fine to walk a while, there's a really authentic little spot not far from here, called Sacsayhuaman. I'd rather see that than these churches and convents."

When they arrived in Sacsayhuaman, Monique and Émile were amazed by the gigantic size and enigmatic nature of the incredible buildings before them. Except for a small group of Japanese tourists in the distance, crowded around their guide who kept waving a small flag over his head, and who looked tiny at the foot of a cyclopean wall, they were alone on the vast esplanade, which gave them the strangest of sensations. It was as if they were entering the home of giants from some distant galaxy. Neither of them knew just how to feel or what to think. They remained speechless for several minutes, until Émile finally spoke up and broke the silence:

"It's just incomprehensible how these huge blocks of stone are so perfectly cut and assembled like this. We've never seen anything like it elsewhere."

"It reminds me a little of Stonehenge or the menhirs in Brittany," Monique ventured.

"No! Come on!" replied Émile, shrugging his shoulders, "it's nothing of the sort. The menhirs are huge megaliths, I know that, but the stone is rough, and they don't form an architecturally complex ensemble like this. It reminds me rather of some of the Egyptian monuments, like the Osirion that we visited in Abydos."

"Are there pyramids around here too?" continued Monique.

"Well, yes, from what I've read," said Émile. "We should see one in Tiwanaku, or at least what's left of it. Some archaeologists have recently discovered dozens of them all scattered along the Peruvian coastline. Too bad we didn't plan on going there."

"What does your guide say about Sacsayhuaman?" asked Monique, moderately satisfied with her husband's explanations.

"It doesn't give a clear picture," Émile muttered. "They claim that it was a military fortress built by the Incas shortly before the arrival of the Spanish. But I know that there are thinkers out there who suggest that it could have been a machine to extract precious metals, built by a very advanced antediluvian civilization, even aliens… Basically, nobody really understands anything…"

"And what are your own thoughts on it?" asked Monique with a mischievous look.

"In all honesty, it leaves me totally perplexed," Émile confessed. "The men who built something like this had to have reached a significant degree of technological development, but then I don't see the Incas, as described by the conquistadors, capable of such a feat. In this day and age, we remain incapable of manipulating blocks of stone of this size, despite all our modern contraptions."

After spending a good part of the afternoon climbing the gigantic walled sections and trekking back and fore along the Sacsayhuaman esplanade, Émile and Monique returned to their hotel with similar thoughts in their minds. Something wasn't right about official history…

The next morning, the couple made their way down to Cuzco station at dawn to board the little train that would take them to Machu Picchu. The atmosphere on the platform was almost clichéd: Hippies dressed in faded blue jeans and Peruvian lama wool hats, local peasants loaded with baskets and surrounded by a horde of chapped-cheeked kids, and street vendors harassing the *gringos*, trying to sell them postcards and brightly colored blankets. When the train entered the station, a lively crowd stormed the economy class carriages trying to secure a place. Fortunately, Monique and Émile had first-class tickets and didn't have to fight to find their reserved seats. Through the window of the compartment, Émile had plenty of time to take some snaps; full-length portraits detailing the picturesque costumes of the Andean peasants, close-ups of their angular and chiseled faces and panoramic views showing the incredible hustle and bustle that reigned in the small station.

Their discovery of the ruins of Machu Picchu was a truly dazzling experience. Up close to the sky, nestled on a narrow promontory surmounted by two elegant rocky peaks and surrounded by precipices at the bottom of which snaked the thin silver ribbon of the Urubamba River, lay the most enchanting abandoned city imaginable.

Monique and Émile sat on a stone bench of sorts, overlooking the central square. They stayed in situ for some time, contemplating the imposing sections of the walls of the now roofless buildings, the countless terraces running down the vertiginous slopes and the remains of temples whose significance had been lost over the centuries. Sitting a little further away, a small group of young Westerners had formed a circle around a musician and, lulled by the rasping yet warm sound of the instrument, by the serenity of the place, and by the large joint they were passing from one hand to the next, were smiling with ecstatic looks on their faces as they contemplated the majestic panorama. Normally, Monique and Émile would have disapproved of such behavior in a youth they might have described as degenerate, but here, not only were they not shocked, but they almost hoped they'd be invited to join in.

"This place really is quite magical!" said Émile, breaking the silence. "It's ridiculous that we don't know more of the origins and function of these buildings. The only thing we do know is that the last Inca took refuge in Machu Picchu to try to escape the Spanish conquistadors. The city was abandoned after the conquest and soon became covered in vegetation. They only found it again in 1911! I really can't fathom how so many big cut stones could have been brought to such an inaccessible place. How did they do it?"

"I'm sure there must be lots of places like this, still buried underground or in the jungle and waiting to be rediscovered," Monique said.

"It would be wonderful to find an equivalent for Latin America of the Rosetta Stone," added Émile. "Not necessarily in Peru, since there's not much evidence of ancient writing in this region, but in Guatemala, for example, where it would allow to better decipher the Mayan script and perhaps to see a little more clearly when it comes to all these pre-Columbian cultures."

Enchanted by their excursion to Machu Picchu and with their heads full of dreams of lost cities and forgotten civilizations, Émile and Monique returned to Cuzco and continued on Émile's impeccably planned journey. First, they took a trip around some of the native villages in the Incan Valley and then explored additional archaeological sites within the surroundings of Cuzco which they felt were perhaps less spectacular, but just as mysterious as Machu Picchu and Sacsayhuaman. They then took a train ride to Puno and a visit to the floating villages on Lake Titicaca. Monique, who was beginning to develop a taste for archaeology and extinct cultures, forgot her initial desires to stay by Lake Titicaca and had no objection to them heading straight for Bolivia.

In Tiwanaku, whose visit they combined with the nearby site of Puma Punku, Émile and Monique were once again stunned by what they found. On the vast and desolate plateau, perched at an altitude of twelve thousand feet, they were confronted with the intriguing ruins of a distant past that were beyond all comprehension. An incredible pile of enormous megaliths littered the site, testifying to the destruction of monumental archaic buildings by some dreadful cataclysm. The shape of the stones was surprising, as if they'd been designed to fit together like pieces of *Lego* and industrially shaped using sophisticated tools. Among the few buildings that had partially escaped destruction were a loosely pyramidal construction and a stone arch, the so-called *Puerta del Sol*. On its lintel they noticed traces of a figure whom the guidebook claimed to be Viracocha, the Inca god of the sun.

"There are just so many mysteries in South America..." Émile commented with a faraway look in his eyes. "There's no real evidence that it's actually a representation of Viracocha and there's nothing to say that it was the Incas who built these monuments. Do you know what they found buried in a field not far from here? A vase covered with cuneiform inscriptions that look Sumerian! Incredible, isn't it? There's really something we're just not getting about all of this. When I see these things, I can't help but think of Atlantis. And those increasingly popular extra-terrestrial stories don't seem too far-fetched after all…"

"Instead of wasting billions sending men to the moon or rockets to Mars," Monique suggested, "our governments should better invest in archaeological research so that one day we might understand the meaning of all these strange monuments. They're all over the world! It would definitely contribute more to the progress of humanity!"

"The problem is that people at the top don't care a bit about the progress of humanity," Émile deplored. "What they want is to keep the public in ignorance. They want us to swallow a whole bunch of nonsense. What a time to be living in!"

This exchange of ideas continued throughout the journey from Tiwanaku to La Paz. Émile talked of the remains of the primitive civilizations they'd seen in Central America, Asia and the Middle East and compared them with what they'd just discovered in Peru and Bolivia. He evoked certain similarities between all these places, which on the surface have little to do with each other. Common to all these sites, he noted, was the implausibility of the official explanations. At best, experts recognize that they have no idea who, when, how and why; at worst, they attribute the authorship of these incredible achievements to people who had only just emerged from the Stone Age, affirming that all this was to honor violent and tyrannical gods or to bury their leaders, whether they were kings, emperors or pharaohs.

"I really missed my vocation!" Émile concluded as they neared their hotel in La Paz. "Why did I study electro-mechanical engineering? I've wasted my time for forty years working for large industrialists exclusively interested in financial profits. I should have tried to become an archaeologist. I would have loved to have dug deeper, to have learned more about these lost people and the origin of humanity…"

2

A BLACK STONE ON THE WHITE CONTINENT

The long flight that took them to Punta Arenas, with a short stopover in Santiago de Chile, where the only thing they saw was the transit lounge at the airport, forced their conversations to return to more prosaic subjects, such as the poor quality of the food and the discomfort of the seats on the local airline.

They didn't expect much from Punta Arenas, just that it would be the starting point of their Antarctic cruise, but they fully believed they'd be seized by the freezing cold as soon as they stepped off the plane. They were surprised, therefore, by the relatively mild temperature, which wasn't that different from how it had been in La Paz despite the fact that they were now in one of the closest inhabited places to the South Pole. The journey from the airport to the *Aventura* Hotel gave them the impression that this was a small, clean and relaxing place. In the late afternoon, they walked along Cristobal Colon Avenue, on which their hotel was located, and then pushed on to Cerro Mirador, a kind of observatory overlooking the port from where one could enjoy a vast panoramic view of the entire city, the Magellan strait and beyond, the Tierra del Fuego mountains. As they made their way back to their hotel, they followed the historical route, along which plaques had been placed commemorating the exploits of some of the great names in South Pole exploration. The thought that they themselves would, the very next day, follow in the footsteps of Amundsen, Scott, Charcot and Shackleton made them both very proud as well as somewhat anxious.

This Antarctica cruise was in fact a big deal; until this point, they had only really considered the incredible spectacle of the adventure, but they now realized that the trip might still involve some risks: Many of these Antarctic explorers had not made it home alive...

Their Antarctic adventure began with a short flight from Punta Arenas to King George Island, the largest of the Southern Shetlands, bypassing the dreary Drake Passage and thus arriving much sooner at the coastline of the great Antarctic continent. Before they knew it, they found themselves comfortably set up in one of the best suites aboard the Thetis Adventurer.

Monique couldn't quite believe it. Who would have thought that she and Émile, modest French pensioners, would ever experience such an extravagant adventure, out there on the waves at the other end of the planet? She had never been on a cruise before and felt pleased that their cabin was so surprisingly spacious and comfortable. As they'd boarded, a hostess had informed them that the ship had an excellent restaurant, shop, spa and conference facilities. A small floating town of sorts. Instinctively, images from the film *Titanic* crossed her mind, and she hastened to ignore its tragic outcome so she could focus on the more romantic aspects. *It's a pity Émile doesn't look anything like Leonardo Di Caprio*, she thought.

Émile was busy uncorking the bottle of champagne that was resplendent in an ice bucket in the middle of the coffee table. He had completely neglected the envelope with the Thetis Adventurer stamp on it that lay beside this welcome gift. Monique grabbed it and ripped it open. On the cardboard inside the envelope, she was flattered to read: Mr. and Mrs. Delaporte, welcome aboard the Thetis Adventurer. We hope you have a very pleasant cruise. Best wishes for your wedding anniversary. Compliments of the captain and his crew.

My Émile really knows how to do things well, she thought as she pointed out the note to her husband.

"This is a thoughtful little message, but why is the captain wishing us a happy anniversary? It's not any time soon!" she asked.

"Actually, you're right, we did get married a bit later" confirmed

Émile. "But when I made the reservation, it stated somewhere that if we were taking this cruise to celebrate a special occasion, we'd get a discount and a few extras thrown in… like this bottle of champagne and a free spa session… and we could even have a renewal ceremony if we wanted. So, I said we got married on December twentieth."

"Good thinking! I'm so looking forward to the spa!" enthused Monique.

The clientele on the ship was very international. Monique and Émile got friendly with a Belgian couple, who were among the few people with whom they could converse in French. The Americans, besides saying: "Hi, how are you today?" at every opportunity, avoided speaking to them because they had little to no French and conversation in English with Émile and Monique was extremely limited. However, the captain spoke French to near-native level. *He's such a charming and educated man*, thought Monique. One evening, in the restaurant, while Monique was unsuccessfully trying to pick up her *spaghetti carbonara* with her fork, unaware that she was supposed to be using the spoon as well, the captain approached their table and asked them how they were enjoying their trip. Monique, slightly awkward and unfamiliar with the customs, embarked on a long speech in which she thanked him with effusion for the bottle of champagne, as if it had really been a personal gift from him, and praised him for his kindness and perfect French. Contrary to all expectations, the captain neither displayed annoyance nor a desire to quickly move to the next table. He found it refreshing to see that there were still simple, straightforward people around who recognized such small attentions and remained impressed by the quality of service on board… and the presence of the captain. This was vastly different from the majority of customers, especially Americans, who demanded maximum value for their money and threatened to sue at the slightest inconvenience. This is how, quite naturally, he got into the habit of coming every evening to speak with the couple.

Captain Mario Zampeze was Argentinean but, like a great many of his compatriots, he was the descendant of Italian immigrants who had fled their miserable lives at the end of the nineteenth century. At the age of fifty, he was a former naval officer, hero of the Falklands War, and now this new career at the helm of a cruise ship was allowing him to continue to indulge his sole passion: sailing, particularly around Cape Horn, which he knew like the back of his hand.

Their cruise on the Thetis Adventurer seemed to be flying by far too quickly to Émile and Monique. It was as if they'd never tire of admiring the majestic mountain ranges and immense, immaculate white glaciers that were scattered along the Antarctic coast. It often happened that entire sections of these ice facades broke away into terrifying creaks, crashing into the ocean and generating huge icebergs with tortured shapes and psychedelic bluish tones. Émile and Monique were surprised at the abundance of life in this seemingly inhospitable landscape. Contrary to what they had previously imagined, Antarctica was literally teeming with multiple species of birds and marine mammals. They spent long periods of the day up on the ship's deck, wrapped in their large parkas and huddled together, gazing in wonder at the silent appearances of peaceful, gigantic blue whales or the impressive feats of the more fearsome killer whales constantly on the lookout for some unfortunate sea lion. They were surprised to learn that the white continent also had its very own elephants and leopards - the sea versions, of course, but just as powerful and aggressive as their East African counterparts. Thanks to the explanations of the captain and crew members, they were able to quickly distinguish the majestic emperor penguin with its saffron yellow crop and black and white suit from the Magellan penguin, with two black stripes on its white belly, and the small gentoo penguin, with its red beak. Monique thought it inspired of Émile that he'd chosen to conclude their journey in South America with this captivating escapade to Antarctica.

One afternoon, as the weather forecast was ideal for the next few days, Captain Zampeze decided to steer his ship towards a deep cove, devoid of dangerous reefs and currents, which he'd spotted in the past and where he knew there was every chance of finding a colony of emperor penguins. He believed it would brighten his passengers' day. In addition to ensuring the safety of navigation, meeting the expectations of the tourists on board was one of the requirements of this new profession of his. The penguins were indeed there, and the show generated immense excitement among everyone aboard. Armed with powerful telephoto-lenses and binoculars, they were all fascinated by the enormous concentration of these strange, flightless birds which waddled in a bizarre manner on the icy beach and whose plumage made them look like butlers in their Sunday best. The captain dropped anchor, knowing that this spot was perfectly safe and that the display would be enough to keep his passengers occupied all evening. He thought he could organize a small zodiac expedition to the mainland the next morning for a group of hand-picked people. This type of trip would only be possible with a limited number of guests who could be trusted to strictly comply with the sailor's instructions and not behave in an inappropriate manner. And so, he proposed this excursion to the very pleasant French retired couple he used to talk to at dinner. Monique and Émile, who throughout their journey had gradually managed to forget their habitual lack of recklessness, hastened to accept this invitation from Captain Zampeze.

In the early morning, Émile and Monique, accompanied by another discreet couple of a similar age, and whom they understood to be Finnish, Captain Zampeze and his assistant, found themselves squeezed into a small inflatable zodiac boat that carried them at low speed to the coast about three hundred yards away.

Monique and Émile both felt their hearts in their mouths as they saw the hull of the comfortable cruise ship moving away. They suddenly understood that they were sailing on what was essentially a very frail vessel in the middle of a freezing ocean just a few hundred miles from the South Pole, without a great deal of people around to help them in the event of trouble. And who was to say that those penguins that looked so nice from the safe distance of the ship's railing wouldn't turn out, if they felt under attack, to be as formidable as crows out of a Hitchcock movie. Their fate was now in the hands of Captain Zampeze, whose apparent serenity was somehow reassuring. They were relieved, when the zodiac landed safely on a huge beach covered in large grey pebbles, to see that the penguins didn't appear to be bothered in the least by this intrusion into their territory. Monique and Émile, encouraged by Captain Zampeze, were even so brave as to approach at a distance where Émile could easily take a few close-up photos. Émile was pleased to have exchanged his old and bulky Pentax SLR with its multiple lenses and traditional films for a small Kodak digital camera with an integrated zoom function. He could take as many shots as he wanted, without worrying about running out of film as the memory card was so substantial and without having to change lenses according to the desired perspective. It also meant he could instantly aim and frame his pictures and ensure that his photos came out nicely. He had the most wonderful time snapping the magnificent animals from every angle. As he did so, he managed to stroll quite far from the shore and completely lost all sense of time. He was taken aback when he heard Mario's powerful voice along with that of Monique, who probably hadn't left the captain's side for more than a moment during the entire excursion, shouting at him and at the Finn, who had also ventured quite a way from the shore.

"Come on, gentlemen, we have to go now. The zodiac leaves in fifteen minutes!"

Émile looked at his watch.

Damn, it's already ten thirty! Time to go already. But I have to pee. How am I going to find a secluded spot here?

He looked around and noticed a mass of fallen rocks on the edge of the pebble beach where the cliff towered above it. He scurried over and hid as much as he could behind the pile of stones before relieving himself with a sigh of satisfaction. When Émile saw the large yellowish patch that his urine had produced on the snow-covered ground, he felt a little embarrassed. Even though there was little chance that anyone would pass behind him and notice the stain, he instinctively decided to try to erase it by covering it with fresh snow and stones using the tips of his sturdy hiking boots. As he kicked at the ground, his foot hit a large piece of black stone. He felt its resistance to move and noted that it was partially anchored in the icy terrain. He felt immediately intrigued by the appearance of this stone, whose shape and color contrasted with that of all the others around it. Without thinking, he bent over to grab it with both hands, pulled hard and managed to shift it out of its resting place.

This isn't your average pebble! It almost looks like it's carved out of marble. I'm taking it home. Something to remind me of this amazing day.

He slipped the stone into the inside pocket of his backpack, both to carry it away with greater ease because it weighed quite a bit but also to hide it because he believed that tearing something out of its natural setting was more than likely totally illegal. He recalled that in the United States, picking a flower in the Grand Canyon or collecting a piece of wood from the Petrified Forest National Park was punishable by a heavy fine and that, when he wanted to bring a peacock feather back from Rajasthan, he'd gotten into serious trouble at customs. Perhaps it was illegal here too - so it was better to play it safe…

For long enough, Monique was the only person who knew about the existence of the stone. She suspected something was up when Émile was climbing back aboard the zodiac. While she attempted to help her husband, who was naturally clumsy, to steady himself into the boat, by offering to take his backpack, he stopped her in a rather harsh manner.

"Get off my backpack! Get off it!"

"Come on, don't be stupid!" Monique rolled her eyes as she shouted back at him. "What could be so precious about your backpack? I'm not going to drop it! I can just see that it's going to knock you off balance!"

Monique tried to remove it from his shoulder and as she did so, she felt that the bag was unusually heavy.

"What the hell are you carrying in there?" she cried.

Émile, half-panicked by this point, tutted and held on to his bag.

"Hush, you'll attract attention! I'll explain later…" he snapped as he managed to climb into the zodiac, which brought them back safely back to the ship. It was only when they arrived in their cabin that Émile revealed his treasure and explained how he'd found it to Monique. She did not believe for a minute that the stone could be anything extraordinary and was convinced that it was a vulgar piece of granite and simply the natural product of ice erosion. However, she thought it a very good idea to have taken the stone, which was beautiful enough and would serve as a souvenir of their expedition to the end of the world.

***

The cold weather on their return to Paris seemed almost spring-like to Monique and Émile after their icy stay in Antarctica. Despite the grueling pace of their recent trip, Émile felt little fatigue; quite the contrary in fact, he felt almost rejuvenated. The images of the voyage jostled in his head and he was eager to think back through everything that they'd seen and print his photos to organize them into an album. The Rueil apartment was immediately transformed into a museum. Émile filled the dining room table with all the objects they'd brought back from the trip. Stamp collections, entrance tickets to all the archaeological sites visited, brochures collected in hotels, restaurant business cards, coins, an Aymara poncho and above all, enthroned in the middle of this vast mess, the large black stone, on which he could now clearly see engraved signs evocative of some sort of very ancient writing. Although she was not a tidying fanatic and their apartment had always been somewhat of a shambles, Monique found that Émile was crossing a line and demanded after two days that he find a home for everything, pretending to threaten, should he refuse, to throw everything out the window; especially that black stone, for she failed to share her husband's fascination with it.

Émile agreed with a grumble to archive all the material in his office, not without first having taken photographs of his stone from every possible angle, ensuring he took multiple close-ups of what he thought were engravings.

"I'm sure it's a form of writing," he kept mumbling while continuing to take pictures, triggering Monique's sarcastic remarks as she remained eager to regain full use of her dining room table.

"My poor love, thinking you're Champollion! You're going to end up in a mental hospital!"

After studying every which way, Émile was finally convinced that the stone he'd ripped from the ground of Antarctica undoubtedly originated in some distant and unknown civilization. He had the thought that perhaps deciphering the signs engraved on his stone might help to clarify the mystery of all those misunderstood ruins they'd visited in Peru and Bolivia.

Émile became even more passionate about the study of ancient civilizations. He started subscribing to several archaeology magazines and bought a number of books on the subject. He soon realized that there existed among archaeologists a movement of thought that totally challenged official history, affirming that certain monuments, such as the Sphinx in Egypt, Sacsayhuaman in Peru and Tiwanaku in Bolivia, were much older than claimed and that there had probably been a quite brilliant global civilization, Atlantis, Mu or another, several thousand years before the supposed beginning of modern history, in Sumer around 4000 BC.

Émile also became an avid viewer of programs broadcast by an American television channel, in which certain researchers went so far as to evoke an extraterrestrial origin to the development of the human race. He became familiar with the names of two experts in particular, who regularly debated each other on television panel shows and at specialized conferences.

One, Samuel Kahn, an American professor of archaeology at Harvard University in Boston, had significantly contributed to the better understanding of cuneiform and Sumerian writings. He supported the thesis that the civilization born in Sumer was the first (the first to invent writing and the wheel, the first to build cities - in short, the first to do just about everything) and that any subsequent civilization derived more or less directly from Sumer.

The other, Dorian Green, an Irishman, originally a priest, a former professor of archaeology at Oxford and all-round authority, was capable of understanding both cuneiform writing, Egyptian hieroglyphics, ancient Greek and Sanskrit. He had several spectacular archaeological discoveries to his name. Father Green, as many people continued to call him, was an ardent supporter of the concept of a distant, highly advanced antediluvian people, of which Sumer, the Indus, Egypt and all other ancient civilizations would have been lesser offspring.

When this American television channel decided to put out a

program on the theme "Is Atlantis just a myth?", on which Samuel Kahn and Dorian Green were invited to debate, Émile knew he couldn't miss it under any circumstances and convinced his wife to watch it with him. Throughout the show, Monique kept complaining that it was boring and that she'd have rather watched the funny movie with Christian Clavier which was playing at the same time on a French channel, but Émile persisted in watching the show.

"It's a pity it was in English. Subtitles aren't enough to fully understand," he acknowledged as it came to an end. This reflection had the effect of enraging Monique.

"Couldn't you have said earlier that you didn't understand anything? I missed a good movie because of your silly whims!" she shouted.

Three months passed and the memories of their trip and Émile's passion for archaeological research and the history of ancient civilizations started to fade. Spring was finally here and Émile renewed his passion for gardening and began to spend most of his time planting tomatoes and pruning his roses on the small plot of land he owned in Sarcelles, near his mother's house.

One April morning, while distractedly reading the *Rueil Hebdo* paper and drinking his coffee, he learned that Professor Samuel Kahn would soon be giving a lecture on Mesopotamia as part of the *Knowledge and Understanding* lecture series at the Rueil Municipal Theatre. As he and Monique were paid-up members of this theatre, he booked two tickets for the conference and immediately ordered Samuel Kahn's book. He would ask the man himself to sign it at the end of the session, which would also give him the chance to approach him and show him his stone. As an archaeologist and expert on Sumer, Akkad and Babylon, Samuel Kahn would be able to confirm if Émile was not out of his mind and that the stone found in Antarctica was indeed engraved with cuneiform characters.

3

UNDER THE SANDS OF MESOPOTAMIA

Samuel Kahn was feeling tired and melancholic despite the fact that he was only in his late forties and life was treating him rather well. He was a university professor, had had a prestigious academic career in the Harvard Archaeology Department, a problem-free family life and no financial worries. Since he had worked as a consultant for the mega oil group, TOTEXX, his financial situation had become very comfortable indeed. Ten years earlier, the company's managing directors had convinced him, for an extremely attractive salary, to help them obtain permission to drill their oil wells in Iraq, in the heart of an area potentially rich in ancient ruins. The renowned archaeologist and sumerologist had agreed to sign an expert report in which he attested that the land coveted by TOTEXX was completely free of any archaeological remains. In fact, Samuel Kahn knew very well that this conclusion was, if not certainly false, at least probably incorrect. Indeed, everything led him to believe that one of the Sumerian cities mentioned in the ancient texts but not yet exhumed might very well have been hidden under the sands and now surrendered to the formidable appetites of TOTEXX. His report had caused an outcry at the time, particularly from supporters of True Archaeology, a scientific society questioning certain official truths in archaeology and the history of ancient civilizations. True Archaeology had denounced the disreputable aims of TOTEXX, for whom the pursuit of high profits took precedence over humanity's right to understand its past.

"Under the sands of Iraq, which the illicit industrial activities of TOTEXX are about to irreparably contaminate, probably lie the ruins of Larsa, a jewel of the Sumerian civilization, just like Uruk, Sippar or Nippur. The so-called experts who claim otherwise are simply corrupt traitors. This is a milestone in the history of humanity whose memory TOTEXX is about to erase and every effort must be made to stop these criminals," Dorian Green, founder of True Archaeology, publicly stated.

In the end, the controversy was skillfully managed by the Communication & Public Relations department of the TOTEXX group and Dorian Green found himself preaching in a vacuum, both ignored by the media and treated as a pariah by university-level archaeological establishments.

Thanks to Professor Samuel Kahn's bogus report, TOTEXX had got its hands on a phenomenal oil field that had enabled the company to make some thirty billion dollars in profits over ten years. For his loyal service, TOTEXX had awarded him a *baksheesh* of three million dollars. For the first time in his life, Samuel felt rich. Without having to borrow a dime, he immediately bought the magnificent home he and his wife had always dreamed of in the upscale Wellesley neighborhood near Boston.

Over the years, perhaps since the whole TOTEXX episode, Samuel had become more and more cynical. The fact that he had knowingly contributed to the elimination of a Sumerian city whose existence some of his colleagues claimed to be true had never really prevented him from sleeping. That his opponents at True Archaeology, who were telling the truth, were subjected to all kinds of humiliation, while he'd made his fortune on the basis of a lie, made him laugh frankly. Archaeology no longer really interested him. Besides, had he ever really been truly passionate about the discipline? He'd chosen this path of studies because, at the time, archaeological research made it possible to obtain, without too much difficulty, the prestigious title of associate professor. This meant he could travel and bang random girls on archaeological digs. Speaking of girls, he recalled a particularly hot summer in southwestern France, where female apprentices in short skirts seemed much more excited by the study of the male anatomy than by the restoration of the Cathar ruins. It was one of the few times in his life when he'd felt really happy. Had that been down to the fact that his erotic partners were mostly blond and Christian? Had it been due to the climate and charm of the French countryside? Or had it simply been because he was still young back then?

Later, he went to Egypt, to Turkey and then to almost every country in the Middle East. The country that had fascinated him was Iraq, because of what remained to be discovered beyond Babylon, Nineveh and Ur. And so, he had learned to read cuneiform writing, then decided to specialize in sumerology and had become one of the few experts in the early history of Mesopotamia on the planet. But he had quickly become disillusioned. In spite of the pride of being able to boast a professorship and being qualified as a world expert in specialized circles, it didn't bring in a decent living, at least not much, and certainly not enough to offer a good life according to his criteria and to those of the family he had eventually gone on to found. So, he didn't hesitate for a second when TOTEXX offered to pay for his signature at the bottom of a bogus report. There was nothing to regret because his wife Dana, he, and their daughters now lived in what most would call a luxurious environment. The Wellesley house, vast and comfortably equipped, was located in a secure enclave near a nature reserve with a large lake around which they could go jogging and walk the family dog. The Kahns employed a gardener to maintain the lawn and flowerbeds that adorned the large yard surrounding the house. They regularly used the services of maids to clean windows, polish floors, shine woodwork and take care of the more menial and tedious household tasks. Recently, they had even invited an au-pair into their home, whose main task was to walk the dog and keep an eye on the children. Dana had been able to replace her old Ford with a brand new 4WD Range Rover, which, according to her, was necessary when it came to driving in the snow and ice that are very common in Massachusetts. Sam had continued to teach at the university, publish articles and books on Sumerian civilization and give lectures on Mesopotamia all over the world.

Everything seemed for the best in the best of all possible worlds, as the French philosopher Voltaire would have put it. So why was he so depressed? Samuel Kahn searched his mind for the possible causes of his discomfort.

It's not my family. I get on very well with Dana, who doesn't even notice my marital infidelities, or, if she suspects them, has the tact to never allude to them. Our daughters are adorable and don't cause us any problems. It's not my job. I'm the head of my department and the university administration team leaves me alone. Of course, conferences are sometimes tiring, but at least they allow me to see the country and they break the monotony. It's not money. Of course, the house expenses are quite hefty, but the building itself was paid for in cash and I still have some savings left. I think I'm bored...

Samuel was deep in thought when Dana's voice brought him back to reality:

"Sam, are you ready? Your limo is waiting for you! Please call me as soon as you get to Paris! " she shouted.

Samuel was going to attend a series of conferences on Mesopotamia in several French cities, organized for the *Knowledge and Understanding* lectures. This would allow him to promote his latest book *Civilization was born in Sumer six thousand years ago*. Although he was traveling in business class, he experienced airplane trips like living nightmares. Check your luggage, queue for security, take your laptop out of its case and place it in a tray, remove your shoes, belt, keys, coins and watch and place them in another tray so they can be scanned in the metal detector, face a line of security guards, each one more scary-looking than the last, wait in a crowded lounge and deal with almost systematic delays. It all got on his nerves.

This is what depresses me, he thought to himself. *A journey that should take six hours turns into twelve hours of shit! If only the hostesses were still pretty and attentive... But even that is extremely rare nowadays. Airlines employ aggressive, ugly people, who repeat themselves stupidly: fasten your seat belts, lift the back of your seat and your table, place your hand luggage under the seat or in the compartment above your head, blah, blah, blah, blah... Then they serve you crappy food. And there's little chance of the hostess being hot because the profession has become all the rage with men, especially fags. Like in hospitals, where there are fewer and fewer female nurses. They're all guys. What a pain in the ass it all is. Maybe this is what's getting me down - the degeneration of humanity. And you're not allowed to do anything anymore. Smoking is prohibited almost everywhere, even on the streets. Driving more than seventy-five miles an hour on a deserted highway is forbidden – even when your BMW can do one sixty without any problem. You can't even buy a bottle of alcohol on a Sunday. There'll be a ban on flirting any day now!*

Samuel's bad mood dissipated when he was put on the plane. He was pleased to see that he'd have a rather pretty neighbor next to him on the flight. Seeing as he'd stand little chance hitting on the hostesses, he'd have to have a go at this little charmer…

Using some of his favorite lines that had proved their worth many times, a subtle mix of banal questions, discreet compliments and humorous remarks, Samuel achieved his goal with little difficulty. Just before landing in Paris, the young woman, also traveling on business, had promised to meet him at his hotel the next evening so that they could have dinner together, a simple prelude, Samuel had no doubt, to enacting something more private in nature.

As soon as Samuel spotted a female to his liking, he couldn't help but try to come on to her. It was in his nature and he was very talented in this field. An assiduous practice of flirting, combined with his undeniable charm, generally ensured a very high percentage of success. One of his best hunting grounds was, of course, the Boston University Campus, where his number of conquests was impressive. His colleagues regularly warned him about the risks of his behavior: one of his victims, either out of regret at having fallen for his false charms or out of the hope of some financial compensation, might one day sue him for sexual harassment. To which Samuel replied with a laugh that flirting was not harassment, that compliments given to a beautiful woman was basic gallantry and that the women to whom they were addressed were always perfectly consenting or even asked for it…

In the taxi that took him from Roissy Charles de Gaulle airport to his hotel located at Porte Maillot, Samuel could not repress a smile of satisfaction when he recalled the mastery with which he had made a play for his new-found friend and anticipated their upcoming session in his room at the Latitude Étoile. He remembered that when he was still a student in New York City and living with the young Dana in a crappy apartment in New Jersey, where both were originally from, he drove the long and tedious daily commute between the faculty and their home. But quite frequently, he would call his wife from college and claim that hellish traffic jams were preventing him from getting home, which then allowed him to spend the evening in a motel with some girl he'd just hooked up with. At the time, he used to take his conquests to the Red Bull, a rather sordid Hoboken motel. *At least now they don't have anything to complain about! I give them a night in a four-star establishment these days!*

When he arrived at the Latitude Étoile after spending more than an hour in traffic on the ring road, shifting forward at a snail's pace between two grayish rows of gloomy buildings and breathing in stinking exhaust fumes, Samuel was no longer in such a good mood. There was obviously not enough staff to deal with all the guests at the hotel desk and the fifteen minutes he had to wait to even reach the receptionist put the nail in the coffin. He then had to argue for half an hour, initially with the receptionist and then with a supervisor, in order to get immediate access to his room. His night flight from Boston had landed in Paris in the early hours of the morning and it wasn't yet official check-in time. Finally in possession of the key, Samuel hurried to his superior suite on the executive floor where he threw himself fully clothed on the king-sized bed. He was exhausted. He'd slept very little on the plane because, at the end of his fruitful conversation with his neighbor, the combination of too high and too low temperatures in the cabin plus the indigestible nature of everything he had to eat and drink as well as the discomfort of his seat whose reclining angle did not allow him to obtain a perfectly horizontal position had prevented him from having a restful night.

He would have liked to remove the clothes he'd traveled in, which were now soaked in a sticky sweat, take a good shower and then slip into fresh sheets, but he still had to wait for his suitcase, which remained down at the reception desk, to be brought to his room. His first conference was scheduled to start at five that afternoon, in Rueil-Malmaison, in the western suburbs of Paris, less than an hour's drive from the hotel, which would give him time to take a nap, eat a light meal and review his presentation, if the damn porter would only get a move on.

Once his suitcase was delivered, Samuel was finally able to put his plan into action. Freshly shaved, showered and wrapped in a soft bathrobe, he had just fallen into Morpheus' arms when a violent knock on the door woke him up with a start. Without having had time to fully understand what was happening, he found himself face to face with a North African woman, who, in addition to her maid's uniform, wore an Islamic veil hiding almost her entire face. She muttered a few words of apology in an incomprehensible accent in which Samuel thought he recognized some French consonances and then simply stood there asking him if she could go ahead and clean the bathroom. Samuel looked up to the heavens and sent her away, cursing himself for forgetting to place the "Do not disturb" sign on the door. As soon as he'd gone back to sleep, after carefully hanging up the aforementioned sign, the phone rang. It was reception apologizing for the inconvenience caused by the cleaning lady. Incandescent with rage, Samuel almost hollered every hurtful insult that an American raised in New Jersey was able to formulate down the phone and had to use incredible inner strength to control himself. He simply requested, in the most chilling and authoritative tone possible, that he no longer be disturbed under any circumstances, pointing out to the extremely apologetic employee that all the harassment he had been subjected to since his arrival was not worthy of a hotel of this class and that he would make sure the Latitude Étoile ended up with one hell of a reputation on the Internet if it continued like this.

Samuel got to his feet, unplugged the phone, pulled closed the double curtains across the window, went to get some earplugs from his toiletry bag, which he pushed deep into his ears, and a blindfold that he adjusted over his eyes, before lying back down with a pillow over his head. But it was impossible to go back to sleep. The earplugs didn't do enough to shut out the noise: vacuum cleaners humming, trolleys rattling, hotel employees chattering in the hallway, cries from out in the street, police and fire department sirens, car horns... Nor did the blindfold completely prevent the rays of sunshine that crept in around the curtains from penetrating his eyelids. And the jet lag didn't help. It was now five in the morning in Boston, the time he usually got up to go jogging before breakfast...

Convinced that all his efforts to try to get any rest would be in vain, Samuel decided to get up, get dressed and head outside for some fresh air.

They call this a four-star hotel! What must it be like in some of the less glamorous places? I should have gone to the George V! Except I can't really afford it.... Even if I were Taittinger, the chairman of the TOTEXX board, or Rothschild, I could never agree to pay more than a thousand dollars for a night in a hotel! It would be indecent...

After leaving the hotel, Samuel took a deep breath of cool air and relaxed a little. It was rather mild for the end of April, though a little chilly, but the clouds were scant and the sun, when it made an appearance, warmed the skin pleasantly. Samuel crossed the street on which the entrance to the Latitude Étoile was located and headed towards a bar-restaurant that occupied the corner of a wide avenue that went up towards the Arc de Triomphe. They had a display where large oysters planted in crushed ice seemed to invite passers-by to taste them. Samuel went in and ordered a dozen of the fattest oysters, which the waiter told him came from the Arcachon area, adding that they were truly exceptional. In Boston, Samuel was a fanatic of Legal Sea Foods restaurants, which served the best shellfishes in the United States, including the huge cherrystone clams he loved. He was pleasantly surprised by the subtle taste of French oysters, a mixture of milky sweetness and mineral savagery. Boston clams had nothing on the flavor of these things. Samuel declined the waiter's offer of dessert, although the *tiramisu* and raspberry tartlet might have tempted him if he'd had more time and ordered a double espresso along with the bill. Satisfied following his delicious yet light lunch, Samuel returned to his room, where he set about reviewing the slides he'd planned for his conference and rereading the notes that accompanied them.

His first slide showed him at the age of twenty-five, climbing the flight of steep steps leading to the top of the great Ziggurat of Ur in present-day Iraq. He read aloud the sentence he would say in his introduction, in quasi perfect French:

"Hello, I'm Professor Samuel Kahn, Director of the Department of Archaeology at Harvard University in Boston and it's a great pleasure for me to be with you tonight in Rueil-Malmaison to talk to you about Mesopotamia, my life's passion. In this picture, you'll probably recognize me, albeit with less white hair and an obviously more athletic physique. I was still a handsome young man at the time I was doing my first excavations in Iraq."

I'll have to try to make the atmosphere relaxed from the beginning, he thought, *because the subject may seem daunting to this type of audience. Then I'll show them the map of the Middle East, because I'm sure most people have no idea where Mesopotamia is.*

"Mesopotamia means a place between rivers. It was here, between the Tigris and the Euphrates, roughly on the territory of present-day Iraq, that the first great civilization in the history of mankind started to develop. The words *History* and *Civilization* are crucial and must be perfectly understood. Let me therefore elaborate on these terms for a moment. Before we had writing, there wasn't much History to speak of and it was in Mesopotamia, in Sumer, that writing, in this case cuneiform, was invented and engraved on clay tablets. Before writing, the transmission of ideas and knowledge was oral and subject to distortion and often forgotten over time. Only writing preserves the traces of facts and thoughts and thus allows a reconstruction of History. We therefore talk about prehistory when we talk about the time before writing. And History only really began in Sumer. Without sophisticated means of social organization, we can't really talk of Civilization. However, it was in Sumer that all the fundamental elements of a true society appeared for the first time in History: cities, government, judges and lawyers, priests dealing with religious affairs, teachers in charge of education, and a number of activities that could be described as cultural such as festivals, literary works and theatrical productions. "

Then I'll show them on the map where the main cities are located, which they might have already heard of such as Ur, Uruk, Nippur, Agade, Babylon and Nineveh. I'll let them see some photos of the main monuments and artifacts that archaeological excavations have uncovered in the region: the great Ziggurat of Ur, the Ishtar Gate exhibited at the Berlin Museum, the famous statuette of the ram caught in the bush made of gold plated wood and lapis lazuli, visible at the British Museum, and finally a tablet covered in cuneiform characters from the Assurbanipal library, now displayed at the Louvre.

We'll then move onto the inscription on the cliff of Behistun in present-day Iran. I'll have to explain to them that this vast inscription was carved into the rock on the side of the mountain at a height of a two hundred feet and contains three versions of the same text to the glory of the great Persian king Darius, written in three languages: old Persian, Elamite and Akkadian.

"This inscription is to the cuneiform script what the Rosetta Stone is to Egyptian hieroglyphics. In 1835 AD, it allowed a certain Henry Rawlinson, like Champollion with the deciphering of Egyptian writing, to begin to decipher the ancient cuneiform writing of Mesopotamia. The understanding of cuneiform, the oldest known form of writing, has made it possible to take a major step forwards in terms of our knowledge of the history of humanity. Among the thousands of tablets stored by Assurbanipal in his royal library in Nineveh, one could read some absolutely fascinating stories such as the famous Epic of Gilgamesh. Gilgamesh was a king of Uruk, and the Epic tells of his adventures in search of immortality. We have learned that many of the themes, events and characters mentioned in the Sumerian texts have their counterpart in the Hebrew bible, such as the Garden of Eden or Noah's Flood. It is certain that the Hebrew, when they wrote their sacred book, between 800 and 500 BC, were very largely inspired by the ancient Sumerian, Akkadian and Babylonian writings, to which they had access during their captivity in Babylon."

At this point, I think I'll take the opportunity to encourage them to buy my book.

"Unfortunately, we won't have enough time tonight to explore in detail the content of these ancient pieces of Mesopotamian literature and I encourage you to read the translations that are now available in French and English. I myself have just updated, or should I say improved, the translation of the Gilgamesh Epic. You can find it in my latest book, which I will be happy to sign for you at the end of this presentation. "

His review of the conference slides eventually had the soporific effect on Samuel that he had so hoped for but no longer expected. He closed his eyes for a moment and didn't wake up until half past three.

"Shit!" he yelped after looking at his watch and realizing that he only had thirty minutes left to ready himself if he wanted to arrive at the scheduled time for the start of his lecture. He hastily reclassified his documents which were spread out in disarray across the desk, ensured that the correct version of his presentation was properly archived and easily accessible on his laptop, ran to check how he looked in the bathroom mirror and made a quick phone call to Dana before rushing out of the hotel.

"The theatre in Rueil-Malmaison" he told the driver of the first taxi he found parked near the hotel, handing him a brochure advertising the conference with his portrait on the front.

"OK! We're off!" replied the driver with a vulgar Parisian accent after carelessly looking at the brochure, revving up the engine of his old Peugeot, and turning towards the western suburbs.

$$4$$

KNOWLEDGE AND UNDERSTANDING

At the same time in Rueil-Malmaison, Monique was getting ready to go to the theatre in question. For the occasion, she'd decided to wear her nylon blue floral dress that she loved more than any of her others, not realizing that she was the only one who thought she looked pretty in it. She applied several layers of her favorite lipstick, a fuchsia pink, to her fleshy lips without worrying about the fact that she'd smeared it over the lip line. Then she gave herself a good few squirts of her favorite eau de toilette. Émile, who had been ready for quite some time and was now getting impatient, shouted at Monique from the next room:

"How much longer are you going to be?"

Monique appeared, feeling radiant.

"Look, I'm ready! We can go!"

Caught in the heady smell of the perfume, which tended to react badly to his wife's freckled skin and which he feared would cause her a serious allergic reaction one day, Émile barked at her, displaying a disgusted facial expression.

"You've put too much on again! It will bother people and give me a migraine."

Without feeling the slightest offense at the lack of tact on the part of her husband, Monique took a last look in the mirror of the entrance hall.

"No!" she retorted with a laugh. "In five minutes, most of the perfume will have evaporated and I'll smell lovely. All right, let's go!"

Monique wasn't the kind of person to doubt or question herself. She was always happy and convinced that she was probably the last wonder of the world in almost every area of life.

Émile put on his linen jacket, which always wrinkled horribly but had the advantage of not making him too warm, which was the case with most of his clothing from April onwards. He also took the small backpack, into which he had slipped the black engraved stone he wanted to submit to Professor Kahn's expertise and the couple set off.

It seemed as though half of Rueil had shown up for the *Knowledge and Understanding* lecture on Mesopotamia. There was the hospital's head nurse with her husband, the deputy mayor of the town; Mademoiselle Brandely, the beautiful pharmacist whose charms had quite an effect on Émile, Doctor Goldenberg, the physician and Madame Astruc, the dentist. There was also the Peugeot dealer with his wife and their two grown-up boys, the baker with her sister-in-law and the history teacher from the high school. Émile and Monique, reassured to find themselves on familiar ground, shook many hands and exchanged some small talk with their acquaintances. When a bell rang in the foyer, inviting everyone to take their place in the theatre, Émile and Monique rushed to the second row where two seats were reserved for them.

"Did you see who's there, right in front of us?" Monique giggled in Émile's ear as she craned her neck. "It's the mayor! We're in a really good spot!"

A few seconds after everyone was seated, the lights in the room gradually faded to an almost complete black, while on the stage, in the middle of the whitish halo diffused by a powerful spotlight, the theater director appeared. He wished the audience a pleasant evening, spoke a little of the purpose behind and activities included in the *Knowledge and Understanding* lectures and finally confirmed the subject of the day, Mesopotamia. He had the courtesy of not revealing any of the content of the talk and immediately turned to the right side of the stage, where the speaker was waiting in the shadows.

"I now have the great pleasure and honor to welcome Professor Samuel Kahn, Head of the Department of Archaeology at Harvard University in Boston, Massachusetts. Professor Kahn is a world-renowned expert on Mesopotamia and has come especially from the United States to illuminate the people of Rueil with his science," said the director enthusiastically, reaching out his right arm to the speaker and inviting him to join the lectern center stage. His introduction triggered a thunderous applause from the audience.

Samuel, smiling confidently, thanked the director for his introductory message, greeted the audience in near-perfect French and, to begin, took a sip of mineral water that had been provided.

Monique found Samuel Kahn very attractive. She was impressed by his height, sporty appearance and symmetrical face framed by very short grayish-white hair. Everything about him was appealing. The eyes, that she guessed were steel blue behind the pair of glasses with shiny black frames; the nose, fine and aquiline; the square jaw and especially the wide smile and the impeccably aligned bright white teeth behind it. She felt in this man a mixture of brutality and delicacy that made her heart skip a beat.

Samuel was well aware of the magnetism that his physique exerted on most women. Women liked him. He knew it and abused it. He was always good-to-go, hiding a fundamentally depraved nature behind polite appearances. As he slowly rested his glass of water on the surface in front of him, he thought of the pretty brunette he'd met on the plane. He couldn't wait to see her. This conference was the only thing that separated him from the object of his desire. He just wanted to get it all over with as quickly as possible, but he gave the audience the illusion that it was his greatest pleasure to be there.

In the midst of the attentive silence, Samuel began to project his presentation. From the second slide, he intuitively felt that his audience was already won over and that his communication tactics were working perfectly. He managed without difficulty, in just under an hour, to inform them of the most spectacular aspects of the ancient civilizations of Mesopotamia, beginning with Sumer and ending with Babylon via Akkad. He noted their fascination with everything he told them.

Monique, among many others, was drinking in Professor Kahn's words with excitement.

How cultured and interesting he is! She thought. When I think of all those ziggurats and treasures found in the sands of Iraq, I wonder why Émile never thought of taking us on a trip there. We've been to all the countries in the Middle East: Egypt, Israel, Jordan, Syria…We even went to Yemen and Iran! It's too bad and now it's too late. We can't go now… not with the war…

She made the decision there and then that if it wasn't possible to go to the site itself, she'd have to go to the Louvre Museum next week, where a collection of artifacts from Mesopotamia was on display.

The words "thank you for your attention" on his last slide, superimposed on a picture of Samuel in Boston with Dana, their two daughters and their dog, pulled Monique out of her daydream while bringing about an explosion of applause even more powerful than the one that had welcomed Samuel when he'd initially appeared on stage.

Great! All I have to do now is answer a couple of questions, spend thirty minutes signing my book and we're done, Samuel thought, while displaying his brightest smile and bowing to the audience, like a diva after a dazzling opera or a lead actor at the end of a successful play.

As all the lights came back on in the room, Samuel gave his listeners responses to some of their most burning questions.

Émile turned to his wife and encouraged her.

"Come on! Go ahead! I'm sure you have a lot of questions!"

Monique was just thinking she might ask Professor Kahn what the ziggurats were for. But she suspected he didn't know much about them; Of course, so as not to lose face, he would tell her with aplomb that they were religious buildings used by priests to observe the stars. It's like when you ask an Egyptologist what the pyramids were for. They always say that they were the tombs of the pharaohs. Plus, she feared that such a question, testifying to her ignorance and naivety, would expose her to ridicule in front of the crowded room.

"I have nothing to ask the professor, but I have a question for you. When are you planning on showing me around Iraq?" she muttered in her husband's ear.

"I knew it!" Émile whispered. "We'll discuss it at home. Let's listen to what everyone else has to say."

It was the history teacher who opened fire.

"First of all, I'd like to thank you for your brilliant presentation. My name is Bernard Duteil and I'm a history teacher here in Rueil. I'm no expert on ancient civilizations as you are, but I've read a lot on the subject and I'm surprised that you described Sumer as the oldest known civilization. What about the ruins that have recently been found in Bogekli Tepe, Turkey, which are believed to date back at least five thousand years before Sumer?"

My God, this might take a while, Samuel thought.

"Thank you, Bernard, for your very relevant question. You cannot compare the few monuments discovered at Bogekli Tepe with the many testimonies left to us by Sumer, especially entire cities, refined goldsmiths' work and above all a sophisticated writing. The Bogekli Tepe monuments certainly prove that a few individuals were able to build some sorts of temples around 10,000 BC, but these remains alone don't allow us to speak of civilization in the true sense. Some think that the people who nomadized in the region and built the Bogekli Tepe monuments could be the precursors of the men who would later found the Sumerian civilization."

It was the doctor who asked the next question.

"David Goldenberg, general practitioner in Rueil. Thank you, Professor, for your wonderful presentation. My question is this… The remains of the Mesopotamian civilization can be found in Iraq, Syria and Iran, all overwhelmingly Muslim and politically unstable countries. What impact does this have on archaeological research in the region? Are religious fanatics not in danger of destroying all traces of this glorious pre-Islamic past, as happened in Afghanistan with the destruction of the Buddhas on the Bamiyan cliff?"

Samuel, who instinctively felt sympathy for this French doctor whose surname was clearly of Jewish origin, replied benevolently.

"David, I'm not a diviner and I cannot tell you whether acts of barbarism such as those committed in Bamiyan might at some point occur in Iraq, Syria or Iran. But, like you, I'm very concerned. However, remember, Islamist terrorism isn't the only threat to our work. The bombings that took place during the Gulf War have left a great many after-effects. It's all very sad. This is one of the reasons why I travel the world giving these talks. I think that the more people are informed about what the ancient civilizations of the Middle East represent, the stronger public pressure will be to prevent this type of disaster."

An old bearded man then stood up at the back of the room and cried out.

"You've talked about the Gulf War and Islamist terrorism, but you forget to mention the devastation caused by the excessive exploitation of the region's subsoil by multinational companies! What can you tell us about the American oil group, TOTEXX? It's been accused of drilling wells in a rich archaeological area in southern Iraq and removing the remains of a large Sumerian city in the process, hasn't it?"

Samuel felt himself blush and, to hide his embarrassment, cleared his throat, grabbed his half-full glass of water and emptied it in a couple of gulps as if he were very thirsty. These few seconds allowed him to think of an appropriate answer to this embarrassing and unexpected question.

"I also read this story in the press a few years ago. As far as I know, a rigorous investigation was carried out at the time and it turned out that the rumor was unfounded. TOTEXX was the victim of a misinformation campaign from its competitors who had been ousted from this oil-pro-ducing area. Personally, I'm convinced that the area where TOTEXX drilled didn't contain any valuable archaeological remains."

Then it was the turn of one of the Peugeot dealer's sons, a young man of sixteen or seventeen with an acne-covered face who stood up rather defiantly to put his question to the professor.

"Why do you object to the supporters of True Archaeology, who claim that Sumer is only a pale copy of a much older, primordial civilization, such as Atlantis, Shambala or Mu, which was swept away by a cosmic catastrophe, like a giant meteorite or a massive flood?"

Kahn was fuming.

This is all I need. Some pimply kid who has the audacity to bring up this nonsense about Atlantis!

With the greatest hypocrisy and a touch of condescension, he made his reply.

"Let me first say that I'm very impressed by your intimate knowledge, at such a young age, of the darkest undercurrents of the archaeological discipline. Of course, everyone has heard of the myth of Atlantis and the wild ramblings that tell of a continent disappearing in the middle of the Indian or Pacific Ocean. It should be noted that these allegations are based on nothing more than a few lines in Plato's writing or a number of novels that have emerged from the fertile imaginations of some pretty marginal characters. Here again, you cannot compare what is only hearsay with what is visible and concrete. I'd love to see monuments, artifacts and, even more convincing, writings with evidence of the existence of Atlantis."

An elderly woman held up a wavering hand and Samuel encouraged her to ask her question.

You should be in bed by now, grandma, he scoffed internally.

"My name is Marguerite Dumas and I'm a retired public servant. I'm passionate about Middle Eastern civilizations and I've read your latest book. I noticed that there are as many different translations of the Gilgamesh Epic and the Enuma Elish as there are translators. Which version do you think is the most accurate? Do you think that those who call themselves experts in cuneiform writing today are really able to understand the deep meaning behind these ancient writings?"

You're not as dim as you look, Samuel thought to himself. He wondered for a moment how he was going to defuse this particular grenade. To top it all off, he could feel the signs of an episode of tenesmus coming on, perhaps linked to all the prolonged standing and the extra strong espresso he'd had at lunch. Samuel was prone to this type of unbearable anal pain, probably the result of a sphincter spasm triggered by an inappropriate position or food stimulant, which left him bordering on blacking out and caused him to drip with sweat. He knew he had to speed things up and finish this question session and more importantly, this visit to Rueil-Malmaison…

"Dear Marguerite", he managed to articulate with a kind tone, "you've put your finger on the most difficult obstacle to a better understanding of high antiquity. There are very few people in the world who have studied cuneiform writing. It's extremely difficult to know how the language associated with these signs was pronounced and what the cultural values of our ancestors were. The result, you are quite right, is that there is no absolute consensus among experts on how to translate these texts engraved on clay tablets, which by the way are often incomplete. So, when it comes to the best translation, you won't be surprised by my answer: Mine! I'm kidding, of course…"

Samuel had imagined that this question would be the last one and was about to leave the stage when a hirsute weirdo, sitting in the fourth row and looking like he belonged to a Hare Krishna sect, jumped out of his chair to ask another question.

"I imagine that, like most of us in this room, you were raised in a monotheistic religion. Did your research in Mesopotamia and the discovery of the Sumerian texts, including the Sumerian account of genesis and references to the Anunaki gods, have any impact on your religious beliefs? More precisely, does the concept of one god still have any meaning at all to you?"

Samuel, now being truly tortured by the pain of his tenesmus and in no way willing to elaborate on his Judaism, replied rather dryly.

"You will certainly understand that I don't wish to comment on my religious beliefs, which are part of my private life. But let me just tell you an anecdote. I have a colleague and very good friend who is a Muslim and who was for a very long time the curator of the Cairo Museum. I can tell you that, although he had a real passion for translating Egyptian hieroglyphics and spent more time with Isis, Osiris and Horus than with his wife and children, this man still goes to the mosque every Friday and hasn't yet converted to paganism. There, I think you understand my meaning."

Seeing that hands were continuing to rise and fearing that this Q&A

session would continue forever, Samuel, almost bent double by the amplification of his anal pain that was now radiating throughout his lower abdomen, turned a livid and sweaty face towards the theater director. The man took one look at the professor and wondered if he should not immediately call an ambulance. Perhaps Professor Kahn had diabetes and was in the midst of a hypoglycemic episode? Or worse still, maybe he had heart problems and was about to have a cardiac arrest? In any event, he felt it was preferable to immediately end the conference, so he rushed to the center of the stage and spoke to the audience.

"Ladies and gentlemen, I'm quite sure you would like to ask many more questions. However, it's getting late and we must now bring this conference to an end. "

He stepped towards Samuel and went to shake his hand warmly.

"Dear Professor, on behalf of the people here of Rueil-Malmaison, I thank you very much for your outstanding presentation!"

He turned back to address the room again.

"I now invite you to join us in the foyer where, in a couple of minutes, the professor will be at your disposal to sign his book, which you will find for sale near the front desk. Thank you and have a wonderful evening!"

Samuel removed his microphone and thanked the director, placing his hand on the man's shoulder as he did so. The latter asked about Samuel's state of health.

"Are you all right, professor? Are you feeling well? Do you need anything?"

Samuel, to whom the relief of no longer being bombarded with unwelcome questions already had brought some color back in his cheeks, reassured the director and managed to give him a tense smile.

"Everything is fine, thank you! I just need a glass of water. Also, is there a private bathroom somewhere? With all these people, I'm afraid there might be a long line in the public toilets."

"Of course, Professor, let me take you to my office, where you'll be more comfortable."

The theater director's office could be accessed through a discreet door behind the stage. The director showed Samuel where the very well stocked minibar and the large and comfortable adjoining bathroom were located. Samuel let the director know that he could now leave him to fend for himself:

"Perfect! I'll meet you in the foyer in ten to fifteen minutes for the signing session."

Samuel loosened the knot of his tie, unbuttoned the collar of his shirt and avidly swallowed the content of the two small bottles of sparkling water he found in the minibar. He then spent a good ten minutes sitting on the toilet, alternating deep breaths and shallow breaths while massaging his lower abdomen, a maneuver he knew from experience would accelerate the end of his tenesmus. When he was pretty sure that his difficulties had passed, he left the director's office and headed out towards the foyer.

At the sight of the long line that had formed in front of a small table with a huge pile of his books on it and quickly understanding that the signing session could still take him a good hour, Samuel glanced at his watch and made sure he wasn't likely to be late for the *rendez-vous* he had back at his hotel. He felt a mixture of satisfaction at the idea that he would sell a hundred books tonight, but also boredom at the prospect of having to deal with this horde of nincompoops eager to get a personalized dedication. He decided to put on a cheerful smile, sat on the rustic metal chair that was obviously intended for him behind the table, and asked the person at the front of the line her name.

"To Simone, with my best wishes. Samuel Kahn", he scribbled hastily on the blank space inside the cover page. Then he handed over his signed book with his left hand to the said Simone, while shaking her right hand and making it clear to her that she had to quickly move on to give way to the next person. With extraordinarily mechanical precision, he repeated the same exercise four times with a Maurice, a Christine, a Marie-Claude and a Jean-Paul. He reached out his hand to perform the very same gesture with the next individual but was amazed when the latter, instead of handing over his book, rummaged around in a small backpack and shoved a large black object under his nose. Disturbed by this interruption in flow, Samuel, who wondered if he could be dealing with some dangerous psychiatric patient, lost his smile.

"What is this thing and what do you want me to do with it?"

Émile was a little distraught by Professor Kahn's lack of enthusiasm for his stone but understood that he had to give a modicum of explanations.

"I found this and I think there are some cuneiform characters engraved on it. I'd like your expert opinion. What do you think?"

Samuel, so as not to upset this possible madman and expose himself to a violent reaction, reluctantly agreed to inspect the rock. Against all the odds, his initial disinterest quickly turned to astonishment. The object, *in prima facie*, looked like an authentic Sumerian artifact…

How can a beautiful piece like this be in the hands of this dwarf? wondered Samuel, who himself was very tall and treated anyone who was not at least six-foot with disdain. While continuing his inspection of the artifact, he asked without even looking up:

"Does this object belong to you? Where exactly did you find it?"

Émile was excited to find that the professor now wanted to know more.

"Of course! I found it on my last vacation during an excursion on the Antarctic continent."

This is ridiculous. I'm dealing with a mentally ill person. I hope he's not totally insane. He'd better not pull a gun. Perhaps I'd better call security… Samuel thought, while continuing to examine what was in front of him.

Émile, disconcerted by the professor's prolonged silence, resumed the conversation with apprehension.

"I'm sorry, professor, for bothering you with it. Forget about it. I'd just like you to autograph your book for me."

"Oh yes, that's right, my book…" Samuel replied, although remaining distracted, lost in thought. "So, what's your first name… and I'll sign it for you?"

While thinking about what to do next, he wrote out his dedication: "To Émile, to quench his thirst for knowledge of the ancient civilizations of Mesopotamia. Sincerely. Samuel Kahn."

"You're kidding me, aren't you?" Samuel suddenly said, staring at Émile with an inquisitive look. "You can't have found that stone in Antarctica. You probably mean that someone sold it to you during your vacation at the South Pole. Or are you confusing it with another trip?"

"No, no. I assure you," Émile said, feeling offended. "I really found it in Antarctica! I see it as my good luck charm and I thought that, by showing it to you tonight, it would make it easier for me to approach you. You know, it's a great honor for me to speak with a scientist like yourself! If it's just a common rock, you can tell me. I can take it."

"Look, Émile, I can't comment right now. I'd need to study this stone in depth… Unfortunately, the people queuing behind you are getting impatient and I can't keep them waiting any longer."

"I understand. Excuse me again," Émile stuttered in confusion.

"No, no, no, don't apologize! You've been really very pleasant with me, so here's what I'll do for you. If you entrust me with this, I promise to do a thorough analysis of it in person and ask the opinion of other expert colleagues if necessary. I can send it back to you with a free appraisal."

Émile couldn't believe it. He felt so very proud to be taken seriously, flattered to have made such a good impression on Professor Kahn and delighted to receive free expertise on his stone from a world-renowned authority. He rushed to accept Samuel's proposal and handed over his stone along with a business card with his address on it.

Émile had no idea he wouldn't see his treasure again anytime soon…

5

THE SACRED TERRITORY OF ANU

Samuel, blown away by the unexpected appearance of Émile's object now in his possession distractedly continued his signing session without even looking at the time. He was obsessed with the stone, to the point of forgetting the date he was supposed to be going on that evening. During the taxi ride back to his hotel, he couldn't help but caress its surface, evaluate its texture and validate his first impression that it was indeed an authentic find. When he arrived at the hotel, he rushed to his room, double locked the door, after hanging the "Do Not Disturb" card on the handle, and feverishly attacked the deciphering of the inscription engraved on the stone.

Armed with the large magnifying glass that he always carried with him in his suitcase when traveling, Samuel identified a total of around fifteen cuneiform characters on the surface, whose style signaled a very ancient Sumerian origin and which he reproduced in pencil on a notepad, drawing one character per page.

"Too bad the text is obviously incomplete, and the stone is broken in the middle of a word," he whispered to himself.

When all the symbols had been carefully recorded, he taped the pages to the wall of the room, ordered according to the arrangement of the characters on the stone, then stood back and contemplated the whole thing from his bed. Because of his long and intimate relationship with Sumerian writing, it didn't take Samuel long to be absolutely certain of the validity of his first translation, or at least to get a fairly accurate idea of the meaning of the symbols. He could see "ANU" quite easily, the name of the master of the Sumerian pantheon. He suspected that the next word was "TARA", which seemed to refer to a sacred territory, a capital perhaps. The following word was apparently "TIKI", possibly a reference to the people living there. There was little doubt about it: Samuel was in the presence of a fragment of a stele covered with Sumerian script and at least five thousand years old. At first sight, the part of the inscription he had just deciphered, ANU TARA TIKI, seemed to refer to the capital of the people of Anu or to the people living in the sacred territory of Anu. Perhaps the stele from which this fragment came was a milestone, indicating the boundary of a city or territory. What fascinated Samuel was the fact that, if Émile was to be believed, the rest of the stele was in Antarctica!

Amazing! In his head, Samuel was thinking about a possible solution to the enigma. *The more I think about it, the less I feel that Émile is a fraud or a compulsive liar. It's highly probable that he did find this stone in Antarctica. But in that case, what would a Sumerian stele be doing there, on a continent covered in ice, at the end of an immense and inhospitable ocean? The place was only discovered less than two hundred years ago. Could it be possible that Sumerian sailors landed in Antarctica at some point and left this trace behind? This would mean that the Sumerian people were capable of undertaking very long and dangerous sea voyages and that they were therefore even more technologically advanced than is usually believed. Moreover, they would have to have approached the Antarctic coast at a time when the ice was not yet completely covering the continent, i.e. well before the presumed date of the outbreak of their civilization in Mesopotamia… Or else, but this hypothesis is even more far-fetched, advanced people were living on Antarctica five thousand or even ten thousand years ago. They had cities, a writing and therefore all the elements of a developed civilization, and the Sumerians were either descendants or a colony… In any case, this piece of stone is likely to call into question quite a few respected theories…*

At this point in his thinking, Samuel shuddered at the idea of the True Archaeology supporters if they ever got their hands on this object. He already imagined himself being ridiculed by his sworn enemy, Father

Green, founder of the movement that detracted from the archaeological establishment, of which he himself was one of the main representatives. In his overloaded mind, the image of Father Green was clear to him, brandishing the stone in front of a gang of journalists during a press conference.

"As I've always stated, and contrary to what conventional archaeologists and official historians would have us believe, Atlantis did actually exist. Atlantis was based in Antarctica and disappeared under the ice some ten thousand years ago. This stone is proof of that!" he would say.

The worst part was that Father Green was perhaps right… It would be a blow to Samuel's career, who for years had dragged Atlantis supporters through the mud and shouted loud and clear that civilization was born in Mesopotamia.

Then another thought crossed his mind.

If the fact that extremely ancient remains have been found in Antarctica were to become public knowledge, it's likely that the whole continent would become a protected archaeological research area. This would seriously compromise the exploitation of the subsoil, which is apparently full of precious minerals and oil and seems to have been really whetting the appetites of a few large multinational companies. I believe that my friends at TOTEXX have very advanced plans for oil extraction there…

Samuel was confused. Shouldn't he, as the ethics of his profession required, disclose this incredible discovery to the scientific community at large?

After all, if I were to take the lead on this, it would show that I'm not completely rigid in my thoughts and that I know how to recognize my past mistakes. Maybe I could even direct this new path of research and exploration?

He took some time to imagine a destiny were he to choose this option, then decided to explore the second possibility.

Wouldn't it be more advantageous to keep quiet about this discovery and negotiate a new juicy contract with TOTEXX? If my information is correct and if TOTEXX does have oil projects in Antarctica, they would offer me a very good price for the purchase of this relic and my silence…

Samuel, who could not or would not admit too quickly that, between respect for ethics and prospect of financial benefits, the balance would most certainly favor a huge wad of dollars, concluded that the decision he had to make was fraught with consequences, that he had to carefully weigh the pros and cons of the various options and that the best thing was to go back home immediately as to continue with this series of conferences in France would be an absolute waste of time and energy in view of the stakes. He was going to cancel his commitments tomorrow morning and say that family reasons were forcing him to urgently return to Massachusetts. He would take tomorrow's first available Paris-Boston flight, tuck the stone away in his safe and quietly finalize his action plan.

Satisfied with his decision, Samuel carefully tidied up all the documents that were scattered about the room, placed the stone delicately on the bedside table, programmed the clock radio for six the next morning, hung a breakfast order on the door of the room, swallowed a light sleeping pill and went to bed.

He was woken up the next morning by the repeated knocks at the door by the waiter who had brought him breakfast. In addition to a croissant, orange juice and three strawberries, Samuel eagerly swallowed the entire contents of the large coffee pot he found on the tray, which dissipated the persistent effect of last night's sleeping pill. He then phoned the airline. Assured that a seat was now reserved for him in business class on the ten fifteen flight and realizing that he no longer had a minute to waste leaving the hotel if he wanted to get to Roissy Charles de Gaulle airport before check-in closed, he took a quick shower, got dressed and started packing his suitcase. The stone posed a problem that he'd failed to anticipate until this point. Was it a good idea to put it in his luggage? Given the size of his suitcase, he would definitely be prevented from taking it with him in the cabin. It would have to travel in the hold. However, he'd heard somewhere that in French airports, baggage handlers took a malicious pleasure in mishandling luggage marked *priority*. It was even said that they broke locks to steal any valuable items. Was putting the stone in his carry-on bag an option? If customs officials or an airport security guard spotted it during a search, they'd be able to force him to give up the stone there and then, just as they stupidly force people to get rid of their bottles of water, toothpaste tubes or metal nail files… Or worse, they would suspect him of trafficking, and he could end up behind bars.

He had no choice. The stone had to be entrusted to the suitcase. But how could he make sure it wouldn't break? Ideally, it would be wrapped in bubble wrap, but where could he get hold of some of that now?

There's no point even thinking about it. I won't find any, especially at this time of the morning, Samuel thought before deciding to put the stone in as many plastic bags as he could find in the closet, normally intended for dirty laundry.

He then wrapped his cashmere sweater, shirt and pants around the package, wedged it between his toiletry bag and a pair of shoes and made sure that it could not move in the tightly packed suitcase.

Everything went much better than he'd feared. He arrived at the airport in time to check in his luggage and the hostess didn't even ask him any questions about its contents. The rather nonchalant security guards didn't utter a word to him and let him through all the checkpoints without incident. He just had time to make a phone call to Dana to inform her of his early return and to ask her to come and meet him when he got in at Boston Logan. Samuel sighed with relief when he fastened his seatbelt and the plane took off without even a minute's delay. He now had seven or eight hours to think about what to do with his stone.

"A scotch, double or even triple, I really need it!" Samuel replied when a hostess asked him what he wanted to drink.

At ten in the morning? This should prove interesting, she thought.

As soon as he had his glass of whiskey and the assortment of peanuts and roasted almonds that accompanied it, Samuel opened his laptop and began to record the events of the previous day in a new file called ANU TARA TIKI. He wrote:

"During the book signing session at the end of my lecture on Mesopotamia at the Rueil-Malmaison theater in France, an individual named Émile (aged about sixty, nothing much to look at) handed me a stone so that I could assess it.

There's almost no doubt that this object, made of black diorite and engraved with cuneiform signs, is a fragment of a stele from the Sumerian period. The signs speak of the capital city of Anu, the great Sumerian god.

This is particularly troubling because Émile claims to have found this stone on the Antarctic continent. The presence in Antarctica of such an artifact, usually originating in the Middle East, raises a series of questions.

Did the Sumerians make long sea voyages over five thousand years ago?

When exactly were Sumerians (or men sharing the same culture with Sumerians) able to approach the then ice-free Antarctic continent?

Was there an advanced civilization, prior to the known Sumerian, and potentially at the origin of it? Might they have been based in the Antarctic? Is this an actual basis for the myth of Atlantis?

Could other remains be buried on the continent? Archaeological excavations on site would provide a clearer picture.

Samuel then set to thinking about it all a little more.

Excavations in Antarctica are all well and good, but where exactly would we be searching? Would it be possible to find the exact place where Émile found the stone? Unfortunately, I didn't think to ask him for clarification on that point. Anyway, before considering such a complicated, long and expensive research project, I think it'd be more useful to go down the TOTEXX route. I need to know what stage they are at in terms of their oil exploration in Antarctica, and to see if there's any way to make money from this discovery of mine.

As he was imagining how he'd approach the directors of TOTEXX, the combined effect of the whiskey and the fatigue of the trip led Samuel to fall asleep. He woke up with a start when a hostess tapped him on the shoulder and, leaning towards him, questioned him with a worried look on her face.

"Are you all right, sir?"

He realized he'd just been having a terrible nightmare. Although rather hard to remember now that he was awake, this bad dream had seen him back at the airport in Paris. He's been taken to one side by a customs officer, while he was trying to pass through security with his carry-on bag in which he'd hidden several gold bars. Strangely, the customs officer was dressed not in a uniform that was in keeping with his profession, but in the black cassock with a tight white collar of a traditionalist Catholic priest. He'd interviewed Samuel with a little smirk on his face:

"Do you have anything to declare?"

"No, Father," Samuel replied to the customs priest, whose face looked very much like Dorian Green's.

But the religious man had carried on with insistence:

"Are you sure about that? You look as though you have something heavy on your conscience! Give me your bag, follow me and confess your sins."

Samuel had found himself on his knees in front of Father Green's imposing stature and had finally confessed as he sobbed.

"Forgive me, Father! Indeed, I stole some poor fool's treasure. I hid the truth about something of vital importance to humanity; I used blackmail to get a lot of money unduly; I…"

Father Green then interrupted him with a hand gesture and a severe frown.

"Enough! Vade Retro, Satanas!"

Father Green asked him to recite the Hail Mary ten times, but Samuel didn't know it. Dripping with sweat, he simply mumbled a few words in Hebrew from the Mourners Kaddish, "*Yitgadal v'yitkadash sh'mei raba b'alma di-v'ra chirutei*", which made his torturer laugh loudly…

The hostess woke him up at that exact moment.

"No, I mean yes… How much further is it?" he replied, not yet fully recovered from the trials he'd just endured in his dream. "When do we land? I hope I wasn't talking in my sleep and disturbing anyone…"

"We'll arrive in an hour. We'll be serving snacks shortly. Would you like an assortment of cheeses or pastries? Maybe with a strong coffee to get over your bad dream?" the hostess asked, smiling at him.

Samuel felt almost nauseated by the idea of swallowing one of those

French cheeses with their filthy smell or one of those cakes dripping with cream.

"Just a coffee, no sugar please!"

The hostess went to join her colleague in the area cordoned off by a curtain behind which the flight crew prepared the meal trays.

"Have you seen that guy? He looks weird, right? He's been very nervous all the way through the flight and he said some unbelievable things when he was asleep. I hope he's not dangerous! "

"Of course he isn't! He's just a drunk, like most old businessmen. I bet the delirium tremens was setting in when you woke him up. If you ask me, you should have offered him a glass of cognac instead of coffee, so we could have had some peace! "

At Boston Logan Airport, Samuel was relieved when he picked up his suitcase which was one of the first to arrive on the conveyor belt. It was fine. The lock was intact; there were maybe two or three additional scratches on the surface, but frankly nothing really noticeable. Samuel almost regretted his prejudice against French baggage handlers. All this was probably nothing more than baseless slander... As agreed, Dana was waiting for her husband outside the baggage delivery area on the international arrivals side. When he appeared, she immediately noticed how rough he was looking. He was very pale and moving slowly, dragging a suitcase that seemed to weigh a ton with great difficulty.

I hope he's not sick, she thought. *That could be why he had to shorten his stay in France.*

She rushed to him to kiss him, asking him how he was feeling and whether or not he'd had a good trip.

"I'm fine! I'm fine! There's no problem," Samuel replied, adding, "I'll explain everything in the car."

He thought that, as usual, Dana would get on his nerves with the tedious questions and never-ending rants, but strangely enough, today, he wasn't all that irritated. He even had what might be described as pleasure in the idea of getting back to the routine of his mundane existence. As soon as they were comfortably settled in Dana's big SUV that she'd managed to park in the lot just in front of the terminal, she, seemingly no longer interested in the cause of her husband's early return, began to list every slightest thing that had taken place in the USA, Boston and their neighborhood during Samuel's short absence.

"Did you hear about the shooting at that school in Texas? We still don't know if it was terrorists who did it or a psychopath! This kind of horror seems to be happening every other day and I'm starting to get really scared for the girls! It could happen here too, you know!"

Then without even pausing for breath, she commented on the weather, saying that they had never had such high temperatures in April in Massachusetts and that global warming was most certainly a reality; on the price of gas, noting that it kept rising and she should have bought a Ford Fiesta; and on the dog, which was still not house trained and had peed on the living room carpet. But her main topic of the day was the au-pair, Kate Von Tardy. She went on to describe her every last move in the greatest detail.

"You'll never guess what she just did."

"I bet she burned my shirts again," Samuel replied in a malicious tone.

"No, because after that last time, I haven't given her any more ironing to do!" explained Dana. "It's much worse. She almost set fire to the house! Last night, I think she must have wanted to impress us by making us a French dessert: *crêpes flambées*. Of course, she poured a ton of liquor into the hot frying pan, causing a fire to start in the kitchen. Fortunately, she still had the presence of mind to turn off the gas and smother the flames with some wet dish towels."

"The girl is a walking disaster! I don't understand why you let her cook. Nothing she makes is kosher! Besides, do you really think that alcohol-soaked pancakes are an appropriate dessert for children? What a strange mother you are!"

"You're right, I never thought about it like that. The problem is that I have a hard time telling her off. I like her. In a way, I feel a little sorry for her. And I wouldn't want her to think that we don't want her because she's not Jewish."

"But the fact that she's a *Shiksa* has nothing to do with it! We can't let her get away with all her bull. She'll wind up thinking we don't give a shit! Besides, could you explain to me why you feel sorry for her? She's not an orphan as far as I'm aware."

"No, of course not, but I asked her a little bit about her past. She told me that she came from an old aristocratic, staunch Catholic family in eastern France and that she had spent her entire childhood surrounded by priests and servants. At home, there was a housekeeper to take care of the children, a cook to prepare meals, a laundry woman to clean and iron clothes, a maid and a driver! That's why she can't do anything with her own two hands! She can't even boil an egg! But when it comes to riding a horse, skiing or playing golf, she's a real champ."

"And that's why you pity her? Honestly, I don't understand you!"

"Of course not! But let me finish! From what I understand, she felt suffocated in her environment, especially since her parents wanted to completely rule her life and were planning, apparently, to make her marry some hot shot from their social circle. At the thought of not being able to choose her own destiny and having to imitate her parents' life-style to the last letter, poor Kate snapped and decided that it was high time for her to discover "real life", as she says, and to fend for herself. So, you see, when she wanted to get involved and do some cooking, I found it touching and didn't want to discourage her. Poor thing, she'll have a hard time when she has to face up to it…real life…"

"That's a very sweet story, but I don't want the Kahn family to be used as guinea pigs in Miss Von Tardy's life lessons! The less she studies real life in our house, the better! And what about the children? Is she taking care of them properly?"

"Oh, there's no problem on that front; the girls love her!"

"Considering where she grew up, we can at least hope that she'll teach them good manners… But tell me, by what miracle did this Kate find a position here? We're the exact opposite of a French Catholic aristocratic family. Isn't the cultural difference a bit too much for her?"

"I don't think so. She told me that she was very happy to live in a normal and simple American family."

"Great, I'm seen as some simple and insignificant guy! How pathetic! People are never happy, are they? Those who were born with a silver spoon in their mouths dream of a proletarian life, while people like us who came from the bottom of the pond are prepared to do anything to get out!"

As soon as Dana had parked her Range Rover in the double garage of their Wellesley property, Samuel rushed into the luxurious bathroom next to the master bedroom to take the long, hot shower he felt he needed after his mammoth trip from Paris. As he shaved, wrapped in his comfortable bathrobe, Dana came to ask him if sushi would be OK with him for dinner or if she should have Domino's deliver a mushroom pizza to them instead.

"Look," replied Samuel, "I don't think I'm going to eat anything tonight. I feel slightly queasy because I ate too much crap on the plane. And I'm very tired. It's been a really long day, not to mention that with the time difference, it's already one in the morning in my world. I'll unpack my suitcase and give you my dirty laundry to wash, take a look at the mail I received while I was away and then, if you don't mind, I'll head straight to bed."

"I understand. No worries at all," said Dana, who had learned never to upset her husband when he returned from a transatlantic trip. "You know, there's no rush for the laundry. I'm not going to put a machine on until tomorrow, so don't feel like you have to unpack your suitcase now, if you're too tired. Well, I'll go watch TV and try not to wake you when I come up to bed later. Go ahead, get some rest!"

Feeling clean and relaxed, Samuel put on his pajamas and ensuring Dana, the girls and the dog were all sitting in front of the television set, took the heavy object wrapped in various pieces of clothing out of his suitcase and locked himself in his office. He carefully removed the stone from its makeshift packaging and studied it again for a few minutes before placing it in his safe. He then began to sort through the pile of mail that had managed to accumulate during his short absence.

"Bills, bills and more bills; at this rate, we'll soon be completely broke!" he whispered aloud, disappointed by the absence of any interesting letters.

Turning to the now hermetically sealed safe and thinking about the value of the object inside, Samuel thought that this ancient artifact might be the perfect solution to forever freeing him of any financial worries…

6

REVELATIONS OF THE DRUID OF TARA

Emma Coffey, newly promoted to the enviable position of librarian at the famous Bodleian Library in Oxford, devoted a great deal of effort to getting to know her new clients. Most of them were students at the prestigious universities within the city and were easily recognizable by their age, general appearance and behavior, which was often disrespectful of others and the premises themselves. For Emma, the Bodleian Library was like a sacred temple of knowledge that should only be frequented when displaying a kind of quasi-religious reverence, so she usually frowned upon the noisy and pretentious young students who most of the time borrowed only the common and ordinary books whose reading was imposed on them by their tutors.

When a handsome older man, slim and hunched, with a long aquiline nose and pale blue eyes, slowly walked up to her and asked her very politely for Padraig O'Cróinín's Revelations - in Gaelic, Emma was momentarily stunned. Although she was rather erudite to say the least, she'd never heard of this author or title. She recognized the man for he always stood out among her usual clientele of dissipated kids and his style matched rather well with the profile she expected from a Bodleian client. He appeared courteous, distinguished, cultured... To avoid looking ignorant, she pretended to know this Padraig O'Cróinín.

"I'll check my records right away," she explained, "but I'm not sure we have it in Gaelic. If we can't find it here, I'll contact my colleagues at the Old Library of Trinity College in Dublin and they'll probably have a copy. Under what name should I ask for it? I've heard the students calling you Father or Professor, what title do you prefer?"

"That's an interesting question you ask," replied the man in a mischievous tone. "I haven't been a Father for a long time, but the tradition continues, and many people still call me Father Green. I've also been a Professor, but I've just retired, and I would find it rather pretentious to keep referring to myself thus. Then again, I don't want to just be called Mister, because I find it too commonplace and no one has ever called me that. Actually, I'd rather people just called me by my first name, Dorian. That's what my friends call me, and I think it makes me sound younger! And if you insist on adding a last name, put Green."

"I really like your first name," Emma replied with enthusiasm. "Dorian, it's original and also very poetic."

"Do you think so?" asked the old man with false surprise. "Dorian Green perhaps reminds you of Oscar Wilde's hero, Dorian Gray, but I can assure you that I have little in common with him. My portrait was never that of an Apollo. As for the immorality and vices of the character, I sincerely believe that I'm not afflicted by a single one of them."

"I would hope so. How could a priest, of Irish origin I imagine, have such defects?"

"Ex-priest, by the way…"

"At the risk of being indiscreet, may I ask you what happened? Why did you leave the priesthood?"

"Oh, that's easy enough to answer. I no longer believe in God, or at least I no longer believe in conception that the Catholic church's has of the Divine. And you'd understand why if you ever find the book I've asked you for, *Revelations* by Padraig O'Cróinín."

"Of course, excuse my banter. I'll see about that right now!"

Emma Coffey started to learn more about Dorian Green, a.k.a Father Green, a.k.a Professor Green. Their conversations went beyond those that usually took place between a librarian and her clients. She came to know a great many details about his past. Dorian Green was born in 1939 in a remote village in Connemara, to extremely poor and illiterate parents. One wouldn't say that his childhood had been a happy one, but unhappiness wasn't something the Green family allowed themselves to feel. They were satisfied to be sheltered from the harsh climate and to be able to eat the potatoes grown on their allotment around their cabin or the shellfish harvested on the beach. They also improved their lot by rearing a few sheep. During Dorian's early childhood, the Green family had barely even perceived the echoes of the war that ravaged the rest of the world. No one cared about Connemara. There was nothing interesting to appropriate, only peat bogs, forbidding cliffs, the raging ocean and an unceasing drizzle. The only forms of entertainment, the pub and the church, were both a fair distance from the family cottage. But the Green family, without exception, would walk a good hour every Sunday to get there. Mass to start the day and Guinness to finish it. Dorian, over whom the priest's sermons, the smell of candles and the songs of the faithful exercised a real fascination, became an altar boy. It was thanks to the village priest, an individual who was not fundamentally cultured but who was less ignorant than his parishioners, that Dorian developed a genuine taste for learning. The man taught him English, which his parents couldn't speak, and the basics of Latin. He also ensured that his parents did not take him away from the elementary education provided free of charge by the communal school. They on the other hand, would obviously have preferred Dorian to help keep the sheep, dig up the field and collect shellfish from the foot of the cliff rather than waste his time reading, writing and sitting all day in a school classroom.

Throughout his early school years, Dorian had become a brilliant student, by far the best in his class. The priest, tormented by the prospect that such an intelligent boy would have to put an end to his studies as soon as he finished elementary school to return to the farm and experience the same miserable life as his parents, offered to recommend him for admission to the seminary. And so, Dorian, who knew that this option was his only chance to continue studying and to discover something other than Connemara's peat, became destined for the priesthood. His parents not only didn't stop him but, conditioned as they were to fanatically revere Christ and his clergy, took immense pride in dedicating one of their offspring to the service of the Church.

One day, Emma permitted herself to question Dorian on the subject.

"When you entered the seminary, did you feel a real vocation or was becoming a priest just a way of escaping poverty?"

"If you mean the material misery of my family environment, I wasn't really aware of it at the time," Dorian confided. "We were poor, of course, but we weren't hungry! We ate as much as we wanted, especially mussels and cockles; they tasted so good! And there was no one around us with whom to compare our difficult work as sheep breeders. There was no contempt on that front. No, it wasn't material misery I fled, but stupidity and ignorance. I soon realized that my parents didn't know much of this world. And I've always wanted to learn. I can't deny that I became a priest to continue studying rather than due to an intense desire to serve Jesus Christ and the Catholic Church. At the beginning, I had one main goal - to perfectly master languages other than Gaelic, the only language spoken in my family."

"It's odd," Emma declared, "I thought you loved Gaelic! Didn't you ask me for a book in Gaelic?"

"It's simply because the original version of *Revelations* is in Gaelic and what Padraig O'Cróinín says in this book is fabulously interesting," Dorian explained. "As you probably know, he calls himself a druid, the last descendant of the druids of Tara, the religious capital of the Celts, and the holder of knowledge of the universe and the origins of humanity transmitted orally by his ancestors since time immemorial. I need *Revelations* in Gaelic in order to translate it into French."

"French?" asked Emma, surprised. "And why not in English?"

"Because," Dorian patiently replied, "I've already translated it into English. If you'd been more interested in the question when I asked you for the book in Gaelic, you'd have taken a look at the English version you certainly have at the Bodleian. You'd have noticed that I'm mentioned as the translator. Unfortunately, I still can't find the Gaelic original I had at home. I've lost it or it was stolen… And I don't want to write the French version from the English one, so I have to get my hands on a Gaelic copy. Of course, I was under the illusion that I would find it at the Bodleian but I forgot about the Anglo-Saxon contempt for the Celts…"

"What makes you think that?" objected Emma. "I myself am English, but I have absolutely nothing against the Celts!"

"And for good reason, you have an Irish name! You must know that Coffey is the English translation of Cobhtaigh, which means victorious in Irish Gaelic?"

"No, I didn't know that," Emma admitted. "But don't imagine for a minute that I have any Irish blood! Coffey isn't my father's name but my late husband's. He only married me because I'm Catholic!"

"Well, well, well!" Dorian looked amused. "An English Catholic is quite rare…"

"Maybe," Emma smiled. "I'd like to know more about your life, which is infinitely more interesting than mine. So, you became a priest only so that you could study. But why weren't you discouraged? What about all the renunciations it implies, such as mandatory celibacy and not being allowed to have children?"

"You know, with my dreadful physique and poor health, it would have been surprising if a woman had ever been interested in me. As for children, I've never really been able to stand them…"

"Why do you think your appearance is unattractive? Personally, I think you have a lot of charm and I'm sure that when you were in your twenties, you must have been very good-looking."

"You're too kind! In any case, women and family have always been the least of my worries. My only motivation in life has always been an immense thirst to learn, to know more and if possible, to understand who, when, how and why? When I think about it, it was almost pathological, in any case extraordinarily obsessive…"

"Why do you say it *was*? You're using the past tense as if you've lost your desire to learn? Or maybe you already know everything and there's nothing left to understand?"

"I'm talking about my state of mind when I was young… I'm sure I still don't know everything, but I've since learned a lot. Do you know that I have an excellent knowledge of a good ten languages? Not only living languages such as French, Spanish and Arabic; but also, languages that are said to be dead such as Latin, Ancient Greek, Sanskrit, Hebrew and Sumerian. Without wishing to brag, I believe that I'm one of the very few experts in the world who can read the cuneiform script used in Mesopotamia five thousand years ago… And I've been fortunate enough to travel extensively in Asia, Latin America, the Middle East… There are few places on this planet I haven't visited. The contacts I've had with so many different cultures have certainly changed me…"

"There's something I don't understand," Emma said, frowning. "I thought that the studies at the seminary would have been mainly about theology, sacred texts and liturgy. I can understand that you were taught Hebrew there, so that you could read the Bible in its original version, Greek, so that you could read the original Gospels and Latin, since Mass was said in Latin until not that long ago. But why Arabic and Spanish, Sanskrit and Sumerian? The Church must have sent you to the Vatican, since that is where the Pope resides. You must have been to Jerusalem and the Holy Land, so that you could walk in the footsteps of Jesus. That makes sense. But what led you to Asia and Latin America?"

"You're right," Dorian admitted. "I suppose, it does all sound a little odd, but I'll explain. At the seminary, I was somehow recruited by an apostolic order that I won't name. It wasn't the Society of Jesus, but it was an institution dedicated to research and teaching. This order encouraged me to pursue higher education, so much so, in fact, that I gained my doctorate. Later on, I was even appointed as a professor of archaeology here in Oxford, but that's another story… Throughout my studies, and as long as I was a priest, I had to go on regular missions for the Order, in places where it had, let's say, *interests*… And it turns out that the Order had interests all over the world."

Shortly after they'd met, Emma had welcomed Dorian to the library with a: "Hello, Father Green" and he'd replied: "Won't you call me Dorian? I think I've already told you that I'm no longer a priest."

Emma felt a need to question Dorian about this conversion: "Please forgive me, but… you mentioned to me that you renounced the priesthood because you'd ceased to believe in God. But you didn't really explain to me what led you to this apostasy?"

"Paradoxically," Dorian replied, "it was all the studies and missions that the Church and my Order had me complete. By studying the history of humanity, by visiting the remains of multiple past civilizations, by rubbing shoulders with people from very diverse cultures, I thought a lot, analyzed, compared, criticized… It would have been very short-sighted not to see that there existed or had existed something other than the Judeo-Christian world in which I'd grown up. The first dawning I had was in Egypt, after discovering the pyramids, the temple of Amun at Karnak and the tombs of the Pharaohs in the Valley of the Kings at Luxor. Clearly, the ancient Egyptians were a far cry from being barbarians and fools. They achieved so much and it's clear that their knowledge in many areas was at least as advanced as ours. However, their religious beliefs were very different from Christianity. In fact, they honored several deities rather than a single God. So, how can we claim that our ideas are truer or more advanced than theirs? One of my missions there was to teach Catholic dogma to Coptic communities. I couldn't help but think that the current condition of these communities represented a lamentable regression in relation to the glorious past of ancient Egypt. Another of my missions there was to try to convert followers of Islam to Catholicism. I had some difficulty convincing myself that my monotheism was superior to theirs: Our one common God, whether we call him Allah or Jehovah, was *a priori* the same and what differentiated the two religions seemed singularly futile to me. Incidentally, on a different note, the archaeological work in which I later participated in Egypt also opened my eyes to the imposture of official History. I can guarantee you that the theory, which no academic would dare to question publicly for fear of being castigated by the establishment, in which the pyramids of Giza are the tombs of Khufu, Khafre and Menkaure, is a massive fraud.

I had the very same doubts on my missions in Bolivia, when I taught pure Catholicism to the Aymara Indians, supposedly long since converted but in practice still faithful to the cult of their ancestors. I later participated in excavations in the ruins of Tiwanacu, which, once again, greatly undermined my confidence in History as told by our official experts.

The same happened in Cambodia, when I was sent to convert Buddhist populations and where I explored the temples of Angkor and Preah Vihear.

After a while, it became viscerally impossible for me to want to impose my religion and culture on others. Teaching vulnerable people in Asia or South America ideas born in Judea, dogmas established in Rome or Constantinople and rites practiced in Western Europe seemed to me to be a fraud. I refused to participate in it, especially since I was less and less convinced that what I'd been taught and asked to teach had the slightest basis of truth or credibility. So, there you are! That's everything! I don't know why I'm telling you all this… I barely know you… You must think me a madman!"

"Oh no, not at all!" Emma reassured him with conviction. "On the contrary, I find it admirable that you had the courage to question yourself and show such respect for others. I really appreciate that you felt you could tell me such personal things. But wasn't it all very difficult to give up? Didn't you suffer for it?"

"Suffer? No, not at all. Actually, I felt relieved, liberated… The most difficult thing was to face my ecclesiastical superiors. At first, I told them that all the missions they had entrusted me with in the most inhospitable corners of the world had led me to the point of exhaustion and that I needed rest."

"Then you said you'd burned-out or had a nervous breakdown?" Emma ventured.

"I could have… You know, these illnesses are very common among teachers and priests. But I didn't want to lie. Nor did I want to discuss the loss of my faith. You don't know bishops and cardinals. They would have claimed that I was possessed by a demon and taken malicious pleasure in trying to exorcise me! I simply asked to take a year off for personal reasons. Plenty of people did it at the time. It was very popular in private or public companies and was strongly encouraged by psychologists, human resources managers and officials from the Ministry of Education. Strangely enough, the Church willingly follows everything that is new among the laity in terms of people management and they found it acceptable that I too, just like everyone else, decided to take sabbatical leave."

"May I ask you what you did during that year?"

"I finally dedicated myself to my true passion," Dorian confided. "The study of ancient texts and archaeology. That sabbatical year was the first step towards my second career. I think I mentioned that, after being a priest, I became a professor of archaeology at Oxford, didn't I?"

"But how could you, as a priest, do that? How did that even happen?"

"It was all down to my meeting with Prosper Tabellion. Prosper is a French archaeologist whom I met during one of my missions as a priest. I'd been sent to Guatemala to re-educate Quiche Indians in the Catholic religion and I took advantage of my time there to visit the Mayan ruins of Tikal. By happy coincidence, I came across Prosper who was on a dig there and we started up a conversation. From that moment on, we remained in constant contact and, over time, developed a strong friendship. As a fervent Catholic, he was happy to have a priest friend who knew how to read Hebrew and knew all the biblical stories that obviously inspired him in his research. I, eager for new knowledge, was fascinated by everything he taught me about ancient civilizations. When I took my sabbatical year, I naturally turned to Prosper. I shared my feelings about religion, my wish to put an end to my career as a priest and my keen interest in everything related to ancient civilizations. At that time Prosper was digging in the Nasiriyah area of southern Iraq, and he suggested I join his team. He said something along the lines of: "You think being an archaeologist is wonderful. So… come and see what it's really like in the field. You have a gift for languages. So… learn Sumerian. It'll come in useful when we get our hands on some tablets in Uruk. We're completely surrounded by Shiites in Nasiriyah. So… you can say Mass to us every morning!" That's exactly what I did… At the end of my sabbatical year spent searching the sands of Mesopotamia, I informed my ecclesiastical superiors that I was returning my chasuble. Thanks to a recommendation from Prosper, I was able to enroll in the Faculty of Oriental Studies at Oxford University where I perfected my knowledge of Sumerian, obtained my PhD, and eventually became a professor of archaeology. A few years ago, Prosper and I founded a society called True Archaeology, whose mission is to lick this discipline into shape and to revisit a whole host of established dogmas that no longer hold water with regard to the origins of civilization. The headquarters of True Archaeology are located at Benson Castle, which in our jargon we call "The Manor".

"What a journey for a poor child from Connemara!" exclaimed Emma with an admiring tone. "Priest, professor, archaeologist, expert in Sumerian, founder of a learned society and now Lord of The Manor! It must come from your Irish genes. So many famous people are from Connemara…"

"I think a lot of it is exaggerated, you know," Dorian laughed. "James Joyce, certainly. But you can't compare James Joyce's fame to mine, which for the moment is practically non-existent."

"I have incredible intuition," Emma said ardently. "You will become very famous one day! The first time I saw you at the library, I immediately felt that you were quite extraordinary. You are so different from those posh types who go to Oxford because it's expected of them but don't care about studying and whose only interest is partying and sport. And not just any sport - it has to be golf or squash… something aristocratic…"

"I get the distinct feeling that you're not the greatest fan of our Oxford students," Dorian remarked with a mischievous tone. "What did they ever do to you?"

"Nothing," Emma replied with a pout, "but I don't really like them. They're snobbish and superficial. They don't contribute anything to society. They just eat, drink and make merry!"

"Like the best of us", smiled Dorian, as if trying to reconcile her with the student body. "I think it's just the times we're living in. It's very difficult not to be influenced by social norms, the media, fashion, advertising… You should be more forgiving."

"I think," Emma said to justify her poor opinion of Oxford's golden youth, "that we should all be capable of forming our own opinions and refusing what we don't like or what feels wrong to us. Look at you! You've freed yourself from your origins, you decided to become a priest in order to be able to study and you changed direction when you felt something wasn't quite right. No one forced you, and no one persecuted you for making your own choices. Fortunately, we no longer live in the Middle Ages! Gone are the days of the Inquisition when there was no such thing as human rights."

"That's what they want you to believe!" replied Dorian ironically. "But don't be under any illusions. Liberty, equality and fraternity are only words. They certainly sound magnificent, but they're lacking in objective content. The vast majority of men, and without any real change since the beginning of time, remain slaves. Of course, modern-day slavery no longer has the physically brutal character of slavery in Babylon, Thebes, Rome or Tenochtitlan. But the basic principle remains unchanged."

"Stop it! You're going to end up making me feel depressed!" Emma pleaded.

"I know. There's nothing more depressing than the sad reality of the human condition. It's always unpleasant to hear," Dorian insisted. "It's so much more comfortable to stay up on your little fluffy white cloud. I'm sorry: I shouldn't let my cynicism bring you down. I won't bother you with it."

"You're not bothering me at all!" replied Emma, fearing that she had given Dorian the wrong impression. "In fact, I find it very stimulating to be able to discuss issues other than the usual topics of conversation such as the weather, rising gas price or what's on TV."

"If you enjoy philosophical discussions," Dorian suggested, "you should visit us at The Manor one of these days. I could introduce you to the members of our society and explain what we do at True Archaeology in more detail."

"I would be delighted!" Emma replied immediately, with noticeable excitement in her voice.

"Very well," Dorian confirmed. "I'll send you an invitation for our next dinner-debate. See you soon then!"

Behind the wheel of his old Austin, returning to The Manor, Dorian Green was thinking back to the conversation he'd just had with the librarian. He almost regretted revealing so much of his past to her and sharing some of his more intimate beliefs. Usually, he did not give such information up so easily and would gauge his interlocutors at length before confiding in them. Was it wise to invite her to The Manor? Before sending her a formal invitation card, he would talk to Prosper about it.

Dorian didn't do much without first discussing it with Prosper. The two of them were like Siamese twins. The trust between them was absolute. They shared everything, starting with the direction of True Archaeology where their views on the world and life were surprisingly similar. Since they'd founded True Archaeology together, the strength of their relationship had been tested many times and had always come out that bit stronger. When you denounce the incongruity of pseudo-truths assailed by official History, when you put forward theories considered blasphemous on the origin of man and civilization, when you proclaim your mission to be to shake a structure firmly rooted within the university establishment, you inevitably make enemies, who will stop at nothing to destroy you. Prosper and Dorian had together had to face low maneuvers and intrigues from their archaeological colleagues, religious leaders and rulers of all stripes. Their solidarity in this turmoil was unshakable. On the other hand, they had learned to be wary of anything that fell outside their small circle of hand-picked friends. A stranger could be a spy tasked by the enemy to investigate True Archaeology or even do away with a member deemed too much trouble. Although this Emma Coffey didn't quite match the profile of a Mata Hari, one could never be too careful…

When Dorian arrived at The Manor, he told his friend Prosper about his meetings with Emma, the positive impression that this charming woman had given him and his feeling that the librarian could become of great use to True Archaeology. Prosper had no objection to him inviting this potential new recruit to their next meeting.

"It sounds like a great idea," Prosper enthused. "Firstly, she's probably not stupid if the Bodleian Library recruited her. Secondly, it could give us access to the rare publications we need for our research. Thirdly, she's a woman who, for you to have found charming, is probably not unpleasant to be around and it will make a change from all the old men in this place. And let's not be completely paranoid. Fortunately, the world isn't only made up of evil secret agents. We don't want True Archaeology to be transformed into an esoteric cult."

Relieved, Dorian quickly sent Emma an invitation card, asking her to attend the dinner-debate scheduled for the following week at The Manor.

7

CHALLENGES

When she received her invitation, Emma felt a strong rush of excitement. She was very flattered to imagine herself walking in through the doors of Benson Castle and meeting the eminent personalities who, she had no doubt, were involved in True Archaeology. However, she felt a sudden anxiety attack her when she realized that the invite gave practically no details about the evening. There was only mention of an informal dinner-debate starting at half past seven. What clothing would be appropriate? Was she expected to arrive empty-handed or bring a bottle or dessert, as was done for an informal event between friends? Should she arrive at exactly seven thirty or a little earlier and, if so, how long before? And then, talking with Dorian in the library had been relatively easy, but would she be able to contribute intelligently to the conversations with the other participants? Dorian had painted a rather reassuring picture of Prosper Tabellion, but she knew nothing about what the other members of the society would be like…

Emma opted for her salmon-colored silk blouse, gray suit and pearl necklace. The whole thing was elegant without being flashy and generally worked well no matter what the occasion. Initially, she thought it would be inappropriate to arrive empty-handed and that she should bake an apple pie, her specialty, that she always did perfectly well and that people were generally fond of. But not only was she afraid of being seen as ridiculous, arriving at the entrance of the castle with her hands encumbered with a bulky dish, but she feared that her clumsiness would lead to a disaster, such as dripping sticky apple juice down her clothes or, worse still, splashing it on a guest's suit. She finally decided to bring a bottle of eighteen-year-old single malt, which she easily found at the local liquor store and had packed in a gift-wrapped box.

The taxi took almost an hour, due to the heavy traffic, to travel the nearly fifteen miles from her house in central Oxford to Benson Castle. Upon reaching the property gate, Emma noticed that it was only a quarter past seven. She congratulated herself for not arriving late for the start of the meeting, while avoiding an early arrival that would certainly have been a cause of embarrassment. Between the gate and the main entrance of the building, while the taxi was slowly making its way across the screeching gravel of the long driveway lined with majestic trees, Emma took the opportunity to admire the architecture of the castle, its eighteenth century style and the manicured park that lay in front of its façade. *That little Father Dorian certainly knows how to live it up*, she thought. *I didn't know you could make this kind of money saying masses and digging up old stones!* Emma came out of her reverie when the mansion door opened before she'd even pressed the bell and was surprised when a woman of indefinable age and with a definite aristocratic air about her came into view.

"Emma Coffey, I presume? How lovely to meet you! I'm Edwina Tabellion, welcome to The Manor! Come in, please!"

Emma, who had imagined that she would be welcomed by Dorian and that he would make the introductions, remained confused for a moment in front of this somewhat intimidating woman despite her warm voice. She wondered if she should give the bottle of whiskey to her, but finally decided to keep it in her clasp.

"Is this the headquarters of True Archaeology?" she stammered, almost apologetically. "I received an invitation from Professor Green for a dinner-debate this evening. Is he here?"

"Of course," Edwina replied smiling. "This is the True Archaeology headquarters and you will see Dorian in a few moments. He's currently in the small sitting room, having a conversation with my husband and the other members of the steering committee. By the way, I'm Prosper Tabellion's wife. He's the co-founder with Dorian. I inherited this castle from my father and gave it to my husband, so that he could have somewhere to work on his society and complete the mission in peace. This evening is very important for us, as we're preparing Dorian's transition to television tomorrow, an exceptional opportunity for True Archaeology to become better known to the general public."

"I'm sorry, I didn't know," Emma blushed, "I wouldn't have bothered you. This is probably not the best time. I don't want to be disrupting your preparations. I'd better go home…"

"Not at all," Edwina said with reassurance. "We're counting on your participation. You can help us enormously by listening critically to the sentences and keywords we want to convey and making your recommendations on how best to formulate them so that they have maximum impact. For once we have the opportunity to explain our philosophy during a prime-time broadcast. We can't afford to make any mistakes!"

"But I'm not sure I'm qualified or competent enough to do that… I know almost nothing about archaeology and I'm not yet familiar with what your society does…"

"Well, that's just it, you're exactly the person we need! The audience will probably be, like you, quite ignorant in this field and the vast majority of them will have never heard of True Archaeology. You'll be able to react to our messages exactly as they might. If there are parts you don't understand, we'll have to change the wording and be more explicit! If Dorian says anything that shocks you, he will have to be more subtle and diplomatic! It'll be fun. You'll see! Come on, come with me to the formal sitting room and I'll introduce you to the other guests. Would you like me to relieve you of that?"

Emma realized that she still had the gift package she'd planned to give to Dorian in her hand. She hesitated for a second and finally gave it to Edwina, who took the bottle out of its packaging and nonchalantly placed it on a pedestal table without even looking at the label.

"That's very sweet, it will please our leaders, but you really didn't have to."

Edwina led Emma to a large room with walls covered with wooden panels and shelves fit to bursting with leather-bound books and where around a dozen people were already comfortably seated in large Chesterfield armchairs. Emma was introduced by Edwina to each and every one of them, among whom Emma retained there was a judge accompanied by his wife, a history teacher, a couple of doctors, a banker and a German geographer with a name impossible to pronounce for a born-and-bred British woman. As soon as she'd finished shaking all their hands, she noticed a general movement in the corner of her field of vision as a group of men entered the room, whose noisy conversation punctuated by laughter detracted from the hushed silence of the formal sitting room. Emma turned around and recognized Dorian, surrounded by four friends. These newcomers made it their duty, each separately and in the greatest disorder, to make a tour of the guests, whom they'd obviously known for a long time. Dorian noticed Emma's embarrassed look. She stood motionless in a corner and seemed lost in the middle of a sea of perfect strangers. He rushed towards her.

"Dear Emma! Thank you for coming! Let me introduce you to my friends and colleagues at True Archaeology."

One after the other, every member of the steering committee, starting with Prosper, was diverted from whatever conversation he was having and introduced to Emma.

"Emma, this is the famous Prosper Tabellion, my other half at True Archaeology, of whom I've previously told you a great deal and whose wife, Edwina, you must have already met. Prosper, meet Emma Coffey, recently appointed Senior Librarian at the Bodleian Library, who is very interested in our work."

Prosper, a giant of a man with a wide bald head and a jovial face, grabbed Emma by both shoulders, and without a second's warning, planted four big kisses on her cheeks that left her speechless and flushed with emotion. He spoke in a strong French accent:

"Good evening, Madam, and welcome to the club! Dorian told me a lot of good things about you and we're delighted to have you with us tonight! "

Dorian then introduced a Dr. Louis, a psychiatrist by profession, and head of public relations at True Archaeology. Emma found him to be very pleasant, and fortunately less demonstrative than Prosper. Dr. Louis was a man in his fifties, with ash brown, medium-length hair, a nascent beard and dressed in a denim and leather outfit that gave him a youthful appearance. Then came Alan Chamberlain, who Emma learned was a professor of economics at Trinity College and whose role at True Archaeology was to ensure the financial health of the society. Alan appeared to Emma much more reserved than the two previous gentlemen. He spoke little and she had to listen carefully to make out the sound of his voice. Finally, Emma met Bob Murphy, a police commissioner and the general secretary, responsible for all legal, administrative and logistical matters concerning True Archaeology. Bob was a medium-sized guy, rather rustic in appearance, dressed in beige cords and a tweed jacket with elbows adorned with large patches of worn-out leather, but whose inquisitive and icy look gave you the impression that he was suspicious or looking into your very soul… The formal sitting room, with its previously almost silent atmosphere, became, upon the arrival of the small group of True Archaeology's leaders, a buzzing beehive where conversations were flowing with ease, stimulated by the glasses of champagne that a liveried member of staff was circulating without moderation. After about twenty minutes, during which Emma had learned a little more about everyone, the ding-a-ling sound of the repeated blows of a teaspoon on a glass of champagne caught the attention of the room and Dorian took the floor.

"My dear friends, before we go to dinner, I have some important announcements to make. First of all, we welcome tonight a new permanent member of True Archaeology. This is Hans Diekirch, a geographer by training who has been interested in our activities since our inception. Hans is German, works at the Hamburg Institute of Oceanography and is about to travel to Antarctica, where he will study the impact of climate change on the continental ice sheet and pack ice. I would like to take this opportunity to remind you that no territory, however remote and inhospitable it may be, can be ignored by True Archaeology and, in Antarctica, Hans will be providing us with precious information."

Dorian then turned to the young man, whose identity Emma had previously struggled to understand, and, while initiating a round of applause, spoke to him with warmth:

"My dear Hans, welcome to True Archaeology and all our best wishes for your next expedition to the antipodes."

Hans, clearly moved, bowed his head several times towards the members of the audience, and answered with a pronounced Teutonic accent.

"Thank you, Dorian, and everyone here at True Archaeology. It's a great honor for me to be accepted into this extraordinary society and I hope to have the opportunity to contribute to your work as soon as I can. Thank you again!"

Once the applause had subsided, Dorian continued.

"I would also like to thank Emma Coffey here for her interest in what we do. I recently met Emma at the Bodleian Library, and I have no doubt that Emma, through her expertise in books and her enthusiasm, will provide us with significant support!"

Emma suddenly found herself in the spotlight and felt touched to be the subject of thunderous applause just as Hans had been - although he was now an official and deserving member of True Archaeology unlike her.

Edwina, who, as soon as Dorian's announcements had ended, had slipped away for a few seconds to make sure everything was ready for dinner, now reappeared to invite the audience to come to the table.

"Please follow me to the reception room for dinner. In fact, it will be a working dinner, or dinner-debate as we called it on the invitation card. Here's how it's going to work… You will be divided into groups of six per table; during the meal, Dorian will explain the subject of tonight's debate and the rules of the game, if I may call it that, and as soon as dessert is served, we will start working together on a number of issues. I'm not saying any more… Have fun and enjoy your meal!"

In the vast dining room, there was a podium and a large screen as well as four round tables, on which small cards with the names of the guests specified the seat each should occupy. Emma was placed to Prosper's right, with Dr. Louis to her left. As soon as the serving staff had brought the starters and served a first glass of wine to those who wanted it, Dorian moved to the podium to address the group.

"As you probably already know, tomorrow I will be the star guest on the television show *Challenges*, which is on every week at half past eight. For those who are not familiar with the show, I'd just like to point out that last week's guest was Prince William who was talking about the future of the British monarchy and the previous week's guest was Bill Gates who discussed the results and plans of his Foundation. You can probably guess that my head has swelled beyond measure (I'm kidding). This TV show has always been a huge success and the channel's management expects millions of viewers to be riveted to their screens tomorrow night. Needless to say, the stakes for True Archaeology are high and I can't afford to make a single mistake. For the first time in its history, True Archaeology will be in the spotlight, with the opportunity to explain its vision, mission and values to a very wide audience indeed. This is a unique opportunity for which I want to be impeccably prepared and that's where you, loyal members and supporters of True Archaeology, come in! While you enjoy your *foie gras* and *filet mignon*, I'd like to show you the kind of questions I expect from the journalist and the answers I plan to give. Please do not hesitate to intervene if you think of other possible questions. Once you are in the digestion phase, that is, when we're having dessert, and when a number of glasses of Bordeaux or Burgundy have allowed you to lose some of your inhibitions, I will ask you to discuss the quality of my answers in small groups. Be brutally honest and merciless! Please feel free to express your opinions on how best to communicate our key messages. When the coffee arrives, each table will share the results of their discussions with the whole group. I'm sure that by midnight, we will have defined the best possible way to go about this. Do you have any questions about tomorrow's show and the plan for the evening ahead?"

Edward, a doctor whom Emma had just briefly met and who, together with his wife, was sitting at the same table as she, raised his arm.

"Congratulations on your appearance tomorrow! I myself am a keen spectator of *Challenges*, which is always extremely interesting. I imagine that the journalist leading the debate will be Kimberley Cosby as usual. She's a formidable woman and has a gift, with that charming face of hers, for asking embarrassing questions and making her guests feel uncomfortable. Have you had the opportunity to speak in advance with Kimberley about the type of questions she might ask you and do you have a clear idea of her agenda?"

"Excellent question, Eddy," Dorian commented with satisfaction. "Of course, I discussed the content of the show and how it will work with Kimberley. She'll be doing some grilling tomorrow. Unfortunately, the rules of the game are that she can ask any question that she thinks will interest the public (and drive the audience numbers up, of course) and that I can't know them in advance. She wants to be direct and spontaneous! On the other hand, as far as her agenda is concerned, she's assured me that her goal is to make sure the public understands who we are, why we founded True Archaeology, what we believe in and what we do in practice. No real surprises there."

At the next table, the judge's wife, a woman named Cynthia, started posing some questions of her own.

"During this program, will it be all talking, or will you have the opportunity to show some slides or videos? Also, will you be alone with the journalist in a studio or can you bring guests with you?"

"Thank you for your questions, Cindy!" said Dorian appreciatively. "I'll be able to show some slides and short videos that will be selected in advance by Kimberley. I'll be alone with her on the set, but we'll be in a small auditorium and I can bring up to five guests, whom the camera can film briefly, if Kimberley so wishes, but who won't get the opportunity to express themselves on air. In practice, the members of the steering committee, meaning Prosper, Edwina, Bob, Alan and Dr. Louis, will be coming along to encourage me."

As no one wanted any further clarification, Dorian decided to get to the heart of the matter. He had prepared some slides that he now began to project, each containing key words or phrases that he intended to repeat throughout the program, whenever the issues raised warranted it. He gave his presentation with a powerful and confident voice, alternating scientific precision with passionate enthusiasm.

"At the outset, I need to expect a question along the lines of… Why is your association called True Archaeology? Isn't the name a little too presumptuous? Are you suggesting that archaeologists who disagree with your theories are all wrong? In that case, here's what I plan to say… The aim is certainly not to put a spanner in the works for our archaeological colleagues, the vast majority of whom are honest scientists who do an outstanding job. Far be it for us to say that we're the only ones who know the truth. The problem is that, in the fields of official archaeology and history, many theories, sometimes based on very weak foundations, are considered to be set in stone and therefore not open to debate. Let me give you a few common examples. Not a soul would dare to question the theory that the pyramids of Giza are the tombs of the pharaohs of the fourth Egyptian dynasty, would they? However, there are a great deal of arguments that conclude that the pyramids were never used as tombs. Another example is that we are assured that Sacsayhuaman in Peru was built by the Incas and was used as a military fortress. However, when you look at the enormity of the stone blocks and the technology that must have been required to cut them so finely, to transport them across mountains and valleys and to assemble them with such incredible precision, it seems clear that the Incas can't possibly have been behind the construction of Sacsayhuaman. When we talk about True Archaeology, all we're saying is that we must have the courage to question established theories when it becomes evident that they no longer hold water. We have to be capable of exiting our paradigm.

When asked who the leaders and members of True Archaeology are, here's what I intend to say… The two founding members and co-chairs are myself and Prosper Tabellion. We are or have both been professors of archaeology - Prosper at the University of Strasbourg in France and me at the University of Oxford in England. We have both carried out excavations at numerous sites around the world. We are also both, if not experts, at least enlightened amateurs in comparative religions, the history of ancient civilizations, and linguistics. To give you an overview, I was a Catholic priest in my former years, and I read cuneiform script with ease, as well as Sanskrit, Hebrew, Greek and Latin. The other members and leaders of the True Archaeology team come from a wide variety of backgrounds. We are an international organization, with our base in the United Kingdom. I believe around fifty nationalities are represented among our members, the vast majority of whom have university degrees. Almost all disciplines are represented in addition to archaeology. We have historians, philosophers, linguists, astronomers, physicists, economists, geologists, doctors and geneticists. This is one of the major assets of our society for it allows us to have a multi and interdisciplinary approach to problems and to remain very open to others rather than stubbornly centered on our own specialties and certainties.

I imagine Kimberley will also ask me to specify what information True Archaeology intends to reveal. At that point, I think I need to really lay it all out and establish our priorities. I'm going to say that True Archaeology is convinced that there was a very ancient and great primordial civilization from which all the ancient civilizations that we know of derive, starting with the supposed first, Sumer, followed by the civilizations of Egypt, Indus, China and the Americas. True Archaeology is convinced that there was, until about fifteen thousand years ago, a single language common to all humanity, which explains the strange similarities sometimes observed between the different languages spoken throughout the world today. True Archaeology believes that the great primordial civilization was based on the exploitation of the masses by a minority of superiorly intelligent beings, possibly belonging to a different humanoid species. We might even go so far as to say that the homo sapiens genus could be a deliberate creation by this higher humanoid species through genetic manipulation in the laboratory or hybridization… and that we were intended to serve as their slaves.

Logically, the next question might be… What evidence do you have that what you say is more credible than what you'd call "official History"? If this is the case, here's what I'll say… First of all, there's more than enough evidence to show that, on all the issues discussed above, official History is wrong. Let's look at Sumer. We've been told that this was the very first civilization, yet it is almost certain that the very people who established the Sumerian civilization came from elsewhere and only passed on to those living on the banks of the Tigris and Euphrates what they had learned from a pre-existing civilization. The Sumerians were either settlers or survivors from Civilization X. Some of the tablets found in Uruk tell of the arrival from the sea, in this case the Persian Gulf, of a certain Ea or Enki, who taught the natives agriculture and how to build temples and cities… basically all the elements of a civilization, which he therefore must have known before his arrival in Mesopotamia. On the question of the origin of modern man, Darwin told us that Man evolved from Ape, through a slow evolution due to the natural selection of mutants that were better adapted to their changing environment. The problem is that we have never found the famous missing link, which might confirm a gradual transition from Ape to Man. In addition to this, for hundreds of millennia, the Homo species hardly evolved, living by gathering and hunting and using only rudimentary stone tools. And suddenly, as if out of nowhere, what we call civilization appeared, representing a phenomenal qualitative leap that natural evolution fails to explain. Something abruptly transformed Homo into Homo Sapiens around 15,000 BC. Official History either ignores or refuses to admit this. This means that what we've been told is not the truth and we now feel it necessary that experts, such as the members of True Archaeology, point this out loud and clear and propose another narrative. I know you're about to say that this doesn't prove that True Archaeology knows or is telling the truth. We readily acknowledge that we don't yet have irrefutable evidence proving that what we assume is true. However, we already have a large number of solid arguments, first and foremost the myths common to all peoples around the globe and in particular, the written histories found in Mesopotamia. Let us note in passing that these famous gods, whose ancient writings from Sumer, Egypt, India,

China, Mexico and Peru all tell us that they educated, directed and often even created humanity, are most probably those superior humanoids of which I was speaking earlier and who are more than likely at the origin of the primordial civilization."

Dorian then stopped and drank from his glass of water before continuing.

"Now it's your turn to play! In small groups, at your tables, I'd like you to discuss the anticipated questions and proposed answers I've just presented. If you think my answers are either not clear enough or completely incorrect, please feel free to say so! If you can think of any other crucial questions for which we need to prepare appropriate answers, say so too! In about thirty minutes, a representative from each table will report back to the entire group on your discussions. Enjoy the rest of your meal and here's to some productive deliberations!"

Dorian then left the podium and joined the table where his seat awaited.

Throughout Dorian's presentation, the room had been almost eerily silent, occasionally disturbed by the noise of a fork hitting a plate, but now it suddenly began to buzz.

At Emma's table, Prosper volunteered to facilitate the debate. He turned to face her.

"Emma, this is all very new for you, so you're probably in the best position to comment on the clarity of the answers. Is there anything in what Dorian said that you didn't understand well or that seemed totally inconceivable to you?"

Emma, somewhat unprepared and embarrassed to be put in the spotlight, took a few seconds to think about what she might say, considering that everything Dorian had spoken of seemed clear to her.

"Although I'm a total newbie, I think I grasped everything. So, I don't think the listeners of the show will have any problem understanding Dorian's answers, if these are the questions asked. On the other hand, if I were the journalist, there are other issues I would raise..."

"Excellent!" encouraged Prosper. "This is exactly what is expected of us... that we anticipate all the questions that the journalist might come up with tomorrow evening. What questions do you have in mind, Emma?"

"Well, to be perfectly honest, when Dorian mentioned a great primordial civilization that was at the origin of all the others, I immediately thought of Atlantis. In fact, I was very surprised that he never even mentioned the word Atlantis. I wouldn't be surprised if the journalist asked him if True Archaeology believes Atlantis disappeared in some sort of cataclysmic event and if the discovery of traces of an ancient island continent in the middle of the Atlantic Ocean is part of True Archaeology's agenda."

At this point, Dr. Louis spoke up:

"You are absolutely right, and we've already thought about this. We don't want to talk pro-actively about Atlantis so as to avoid the overused image that the word already has in the public mind. We don't want it to be associated with True Archaeology. But I can tell you what Dorian plans to say if Kimberley brings it up. The fact that Plato mentioned the existence of Atlantis and that many scientists believed or believe that Atlantis really existed is another argument in favor of the theories of True Archaeology; but Atlantis is only one possible solution among others. There are also elements supporting the idea of an ancient continent submerged in the Pacific Ocean on which Mu's civilization may well have developed. Indian writings also suggest that there was a vast area now swallowed up somewhere in the Indian Ocean, called Lemuria. True Archaeology does not want to exclude or favor any hypothesis, provided that it has solid arguments supporting it. The problem with Atlantis, Mu or Lemuria is that the amount and strength of evidence is extremely limited. All in all, the only thing that True Archaeology is convinced of is that there existed, a very long time ago, before Sumer, before Egypt and before all the others we know of, an extremely advanced primordial civilization that was technologically and culturally gifted and which spread across the planet."

Prosper looked at all the participants at his table.

"Does this answer seem satisfactory to you?" he asked. "Do you have anything to add on the theme of Atlantis? No? Well, what else can you think of? "

The waiting staff took advantage of the calm following this lively discussion to quickly clear the empty plates and wine glasses that were cluttering the table, before placing in front of each guest a small plate containing a large portion of lemon meringue pie with a cup of Earl Grey tea as an accompaniment.

Edward, the doctor sitting across from Emma, continued where they'd left off:

"When Dorian talks about the superior humanoids that dominated primitive humanity, the journalist could well ask whether True Archaeology agrees with those who believe the earth was colonized by aliens, who have been recorded in history as gods. Have you thought about the best way to approach this question?"

"Again, that's a very good remark!" said Prosper. "Of course, we've talked about how to approach the issue of aliens. Here's what we think… The fact that more and more experts believe that it was aliens who brought civilization to earth, or even created the Homo Sapiens in their image, shows that the history we have all been taught is less and less credible and that there is a better explanation for the mystery of the origin of humanity and civilization. True Archaeology believes that the theorists of extraterrestrial origin are asking valid questions, but that their answers are not necessarily the best out there. For us, aliens are the easy option and would certainly solve almost all the riddles… but it requires too much faith: No credible witness has ever seen an alien. The ancient texts never explicitly state that the ancient gods came from another planet or galaxy. It seems simpler to consider that the superiorly developed beings at the origin of civilization appeared from somewhere on Earth itself, probably a large island, with a favorable climate and a fairly benign wildlife, rich in animal, vegetal and mineral resources. And probably these beings were a species of Homo that was simply more intelligent and industrious than the rest of the Homos of the time."

After half an hour of passionate debate and proposals from all sides, Dorian got up from his seat, walked to the center of the room and invited each table to nominate a speaker to report back to the group on the outcome of the deliberations. At Emma's table, Dr. Louis volunteered himself and shared the new questions and answers suggested by his group. Two other tables had reached very similar conclusions, and everyone seemed satisfied with the proposals communicated by Dr. Louis. Dorian thanked the group for which Dr. Louis had acted as spokesman and initiated a round of applause. The second group recommended anticipating a question on the geological and climatic changes that must have affected Earth in the more or less distant past and clarifying their influence on the evolution of humanity and civilization. In particular, clarifying True Archaeology's position on Noah's Flood would be appropriate, they ventured.

The third and fourth groups suggested that Dorian prepare himself for a question about his past as a priest and the state of his faith in a single, uncreated, eternal, universal and omnipotent God. True Archaeology seems to believe that the gods were not only plural but were the masters of the primitive world worshiped by their dominated humanoids: What about monotheism and the existence of God?

Dorian sensed that there was no way round this question.

"I'm afraid I won't be able to escape it! As you know, one of my fundamental values is honesty and it is viscerally impossible for me to lie or even try to ignore this question. At the risk of alienating many spectators, I will confess that I no longer believe in the God preached by the great monotheistic religions, whether that be Christianity, Judaism or Islam. I will repeat that, in our view, the common concept of god was originally applied to the first highly developed humanoids that dominated the rest of humanity. I will also state my feeling that men cling to the idea of God because they feel a sense of anguish when it comes to death and the afterlife and by the absence of satisfactory answers to the great existential questions such as: How was the universe created? Where does Man come from? What happens after death? In my opinion, rather than inventing things and having no possible way of proving them, we should become intellectually and psychologically mature, understand that certain great fundamental questions will remain eternally beyond our comprehension and reflect on the best way to make this short journey through life as happy as possible…"

When all the tables had provided their comments and recommendations, Dorian warmly thanked the participants for their contributions and declared the dinner-debate over:

"Wish me luck for tomorrow night! We'll meet next week to discuss the impact of the program and an action plan for the future. Have safe journeys home tonight and see you all soon. "

The guests began to leave The Manor, wishing Dorian good luck with his television appearance and thanking Edwina for her hospitality as they did so. Emma discreetly asked one of the domestic staff about the possibility of ordering a taxi and, having received confirmation that it would arrive within fifteen minutes, waited until the room was empty to approach Dorian and thank him for inviting her to this evening's event which had interested her very much. Dorian in turn thanked Emma for her presence:

"I'm so happy that you enjoyed it. If you're interested in the work of True Archaeology, I invite you to formally join us. You could contribute more significantly to our activities by becoming an active member. There's so much to do and we still lack motivated people. Think about it and let me know. Have a safe trip home and thanks again. "

Edwina then came to inform Emma that her taxi was waiting for her in front of the entrance.

"I do hope you had a good evening and that we'll see you again very soon. Feel free to call me if you want to know more about True Archaeology," she said as she handed Emma her business card and walked her outside.

In the taxi back to Oxford, Emma, whose head was spinning after the avalanche of surprising information she'd just heard about True Archaeology and the excitement of the discussions with the group, tried to calm down with a series of deep breaths. She wondered what would come next for her… Certainly, she had found all these stories of lost civilizations, forgotten times, ancient gods and primordial humanity absolutely fascinating and felt perfectly in tune with all the participants of the evening. However, would it be a good idea to officially affiliate herself with True Archaeology? Wouldn't there be some risks in establishing closer relations with those people whose lives she really didn't know much about… Undecided, she let herself dream of archaeological excavations in Iraq and Egypt, deciphering ancient manuscripts, discovering the Grail… She was surprised to find herself home so quickly. At this late hour and in the absence of any traffic on the roads, it had taken the taxi only twenty minutes to make the return trip from Benson Castle…

8

VADE RETRO SATANAS

Alone in his office, Samuel span around nonchalantly in his large leather chair and thought about how to convert Émile's stone, which was still sitting in his safe, into a huge wad of dollars.

I reckon I could definitely get several million… The only question is: Who would offer me the most? A dealer or TOTEXX? The problem with dealers is that they're going to throw a load of questions at me about the origin and the authenticity of the stone and then they'll try to convince me that it would be very difficult to sell and that they can't give me much for it. They're all scam artists! No, the easiest way to do this would be to negotiate with my friends at TOTEXX. If they've already invested billions of dollars to develop a huge oil field in Antarctica… and I think they have…, then they won't hesitate for even a second. They'll put a few millions on the table to buy my silence on the archaeological potential of their drilling area. It'd be a rerun of the Iraq coup, in a way, except that I won't even have to sign some bogus report… But they're going to take some initial convincing. They will certainly have a hard time to believe that Antarctica, a continent covered with a huge layer of ice since time immemorial, could, because of an unfortunate piece of black stone, become a protected archaeological zone prohibited to oil companies. That said, I can only imagine the schemes that TOTEXX has already had to engage in to obtain authorization to prospect in Antarctica as, officially, this continent is supposed to be prohibited to them already… They certainly won't want to draw attention to their barely legal activities in the region. It would be enough for me to inform them that I intend - if we are unable to agree on the price of my silence - to launch a major publicity campaign around the archaeological discovery of the century in Antarctica and the need to prevent its destruction by industrialists eager to profit from an exceptional human heritage... I have nothing to lose and everything to gain by playing this hand. I absolutely must pay a short visit to the CEO. I'll call him tomorrow to arrange an appointment as soon as possible. Perfect! On that note, it's time for bed.

At ten the next morning in Dallas, on the top floor of the TOTEXX Tower, Sissi, the CEO Jeff Fishman's secretary, gently knocked on the closed door of the huge corner office where he was working. She entered without waiting for an answer, knowing that Jeff would be alone at that time and asked him:

"Jeff, I have Professor Samuel Kahn on the phone; he's been harassing me since the early hours to set up a meeting with you. Should I put him through? "

"What exactly does he want?"

"I'm afraid I don't know," Sissi said apologetically. "He says that it's of the utmost importance, absolutely confidential and he can only talk to you about it."

"Samuel Kahn... Isn't he the archaeologist who worked for us in Iraq a few years ago?" asked Jeff, pretending to have only a very vague memory of the man.

"Yes, that's him," Sissi confirmed.

"His contract is long over, so I don't know what he would want to talk to me about! You can put him through, I suppose. But tell him to hurry because I'm in the middle of something."

Ten minutes had passed since she had patched through Professor Kahn's call to Jeff Fishman's private line when Sissi received a call from her boss:

"Sissi, you have to set up a meeting of the Executive Committee for me by the end of the week. Find a spot in my diary, preferably around two in the afternoon on a day when I don't have any travel plans. Tell all the ExCom members that this is about the ICEBERG project and therefore top priority and confidential. Their presence is mandatory. You must also invite Professor Kahn to the meeting. Send him the Company private jet for a same-day Boston/Dallas round trip. Offer him expenses for the day; eight hours at a thousand dollars an hour should be more than enough. Have I made myself clear? Hop to it !"

An hour later, Samuel received a call from Sissi, asking him if he could make it to the TOTEXX tower in Dallas for a meeting with the members of the company's Executive Committee that Friday at two. Samuel kept Sissi on the edge of her seat for several seconds, pretending to check that he had no other commitments that day, and then made up the fact that, in order for him to be in Dallas by the end of the week, he'd have to completely turn his schedule upside down and postpone several important appointments. Samuel was indeed free that day but he enjoyed the next few minutes during which Sissi used all the flattery and pleas she could muster to convince him to accept their invitation; it was obvious that she was worried about not being able to accomplish the mission Jeff Fishman had just entrusted to her. Samuel thought:

Just an hour ago, this bitch was treating me like a piece of shit on her shoe and trying to stop me from talking to her boss. And now she's making cooing noises and seems ready to do just about anything to make her life that little bit easier. It's funny how access to people in power can change so much.

After having had his fill of fun with the secretary and her anxieties and feeling satisfied that Jeff Fishman obviously considered his case to be both important and urgent, Samuel finally agreed to participate in the meeting.

Once he'd put the phone down, Samuel smiled to himself, savoring what seemed to be a sign of success to come. What little he'd said to Jeff Fishman on the phone had obviously struck a nerve and the CEO seemed to be taking very seriously any potential threat that might interfere with their activities in Antarctica. This confirmed that TOTEXX had, just as Samuel had guessed following rumors and indiscretions heard on the grapevine, a major oil development project on the frozen continent. He only had a few days left to prepare the presentation he'd need to convince TOTEXX to offer him several million dollars so as to avoid derailing their project and the huge profits expected. Samuel rubbed his hands together and locked himself in his office, thinking: *Come on, man! Get to work!*

He began by deciding that he wouldn't take the stone with him. Although putting this exhibit in front of them would be a very effective way to prove to TOTEXX that the Antarctic soil contained some fabulous archaeological remains, the multiple risks of removing the object from his safe were far too high. A shock could break it and it could even be stolen… They would have to be satisfied with photos and just take his word for it when he attested to the characteristics of the stone, its size and its mineral type. He would give an overall picture of the object, show photos of all its sides and close-ups of the cuneiform characters inscribed on it and explain their meaning. Of course, the team at TOTEXX would ask him where the proof was that this stone had been found in Antarctica. He'd have to paint a portrait of Émile (his social background, his psychological profile, his professional and personal history, his absence of any sort of criminal behavior) that would remove all possible doubts they might have about the origin of the artifact. Above all, he'd have to explain why this stone had exceptional value for the archaeological community and why its revelation to the public would be a huge bombshell with devastating effects for TOTEXX. He thought:

It would make sense for me to remind them what would have happened with their drilling in Iraq if I hadn't produced my report certifying the absence of ancient ruins on their exploitation site. Of course, they'll say that Antarctica is nothing like Iraq, that it's common knowledge that the ancient Mesopotamian civilizations were established in Iraq while no one believes that there has ever been anything but ice in Antarctica. In the presentation, I absolutely must refer to books about the geological upheavals that have affected the planet, maps of former navigators showing ice-free Antarctica and stories of sunken continents. I'll also have to tell them about True Archaeology, about the fact that these people believe strongly in the existence of an antediluvian primordial civilization, possibly in Antarctica, and that they would love nothing more than getting their hands on a stone like mine to justify their theories. I'll have to mention that they have great means to launch information campaigns and excavations.

Once the plan of his presentation was defined, Samuel started frantically rereading all the authors that wrote of a vanished civilization, a lost continent and the possibility that Antarctica could conceal the Great Book of Thoth, the Tables of Atlantis or the Archives of Mu…

Friday came around very quickly. Without revealing the existence of the stone and the maneuver he was using, Samuel had explained to Dana that TOTEXX was once again calling on his services and that he'd been invited by the CEO to spend the day at the Dallas headquarters to discuss the practical arrangements for their next collaboration. Dana, who remembered how her husband's previous contract with TOTEXX had improved their lot, literally jumped up and swung her arms around Samuel's neck:

"That's great! You're just the best! I hope that this new mission will be just as well paid as the last one. Make sure you negotiate the terms of your contract as well as always!" And she left it at that. No further questions.

As Samuel was getting dressed for his meeting, he asked Dana, whose judgment in this area always seemed on point to him, to help him choose the most appropriate outfit.

"Honey, what would you suggest? Tie and suit or something more casual?"

"Come on, Sam," Dana replied, rolling her eyes, "you're not going to a party with your friends! You need to show to the CEO of one of the world's largest companies that you're the best expert in your field and that you understand their business! You have to demand respect. You need a suit and tie! But at the same time, you have to look relaxed and confident, so don't just wear an ordinary black suit, with a white shirt and a non-descript tie. If I were you, I'd wear my gray suit, with a pink shirt and a light green tie!"

"What about the socks and shoes?" Samuel continued, going to grab the clothes she'd picked out, which he spotted easily in the vast and perfectly organized closet next to their room.

"Gray socks," Dana suggested, "dark brown shoes - your beautiful Italian ones…"

"Got it. Right, I have to hurry, my ride will be here any minute," Samuel said with impatience.

A few minutes later, he was settled comfortably in the luxurious black sedan that TOTEXX had sent to take him to the small airport where the company's private jet was waiting on the tarmac. It was a real pleasure for Samuel to travel in such conditions. There were no orders from aggressive security guards, no stripping or humiliating body searches, no uncomfortable waiting in a noisy and crowded passenger factory and not a single second wasted.

Door to door, from his home in Wellesley to the reception desk of TOTEXX Tower in Dallas, the journey took only four hours, which meant Samuel hadn't had a whole lot of time to revise his presentation. He reached the foot of the building and contemplated the impressive avant-garde architecture of glass and steel:

If I'd taken a regular flight, it would have taken me almost all day and I would never have been able to go home the same evening! It's amazing how much money can change your life! It's the kind of living I could get used to: A private jet, a chalet in Aspen, a villa in the Bahamas, the whole shebang…

Even the weather was better: Unlike Boston, where it was cold, wet and windy, it was very mild in Dallas and the sky was uniformly blue. Samuel had just finished hanging the name badge on his lapel, which the receptionist had given him at the entrance and which she had told him to wear in order to be able to walk around the tower, when Sissi appeared and headed over towards him. With a pronounced Texan accent, Sissi welcomed him to TOTEXX, asked if he'd had a good trip, offered him a glass of water and then invited him to follow her to the elevator reserved for "executive use" which whisked them away in a flash up to the top floor. As soon as they stepped out of the elevator and into the inner sanctum, Sissi led Samuel to what she called, in a tone that conveyed both admiration and fear, the "Board Room". Samuel saw before him a large room in the center of which was a huge U-shaped table, visibly made of solid mahogany and surrounded by high-back black leather armchairs. On the table and in front of each chair was a plaque with the name and title of the person whose designated place it was. Samuel felt a puff of pride when he noticed that his name was on one of the plaques, followed quickly by a shadow of disappointment when he realized that he would be sitting at the end of the table, far from the center, which appeared to be reserved for the big boss, and that the chair he had been given was different from the others, smaller and less luxurious… Clearly an addition intended to let someone know they didn't belong to the club. Sissi invited Samuel to take a seat, brought him a glass and a bottle of mineral water and asked him if he wanted to give her his memory card so she could help him project his documents on the big screen that covered one of the walls. Before leaving, the secretary assured him that he wouldn't have to wait very long before being joined by the ExCom members.

Now alone in this impressive meeting room, Samuel looked around at the furniture. Everything oozed opulence and power. On the paneled walls were hung photographs of the founders of TOTEXX and its main managing directors since the company's inception. In front of each of the chairs, a leather-bound notebook, file and pen with the TOTEXX logo, awaited each participant. Samuel was not surprised to count twelve chairs, in addition to the extra chair added for him and thought:

Nothing has changed in five thousand years. There were twelve great Anunaki gods who were the supreme masters in Sumer, Heracles completed twelve labors, Jesus Christ had twelve apostles and there are twelve constellations in the zodiac… and the Executive Committee of TOTEXX is obviously composed of twelve members!

After a few minutes, the huge double doors opened and Jeff Fishman appeared, flanked by an elderly man of impressive stature, whom Samuel had never met, and with whom the CEO was behaving with an obsequiousness that was hard to watch.

Jeff walked towards Samuel and shook his hand vigorously:

"Professor Kahn, I'm delighted to see you again! How are you? Welcome to TOTEXX! Let me introduce you to Mr. Taittinger, Chairman of the Board, whom I've asked to attend our meeting today given the importance of the subject." Then, turning to Taittinger, he continued, "Sir, I would like to introduce Professor Samuel Kahn, a world-renowned archaeologist who provided us with some services when we were prospecting in Iraq a few years ago."

Taittinger gave Samuel a haughty look and, without shaking his hand spoke with a hint of contempt in his voice:

"Ah, you're Kahn! I was told about your contribution to our activities in Iraq a long time ago… I found it intriguing when Fishman asked me to attend this meeting and I'm curious to know what you have to tell us this time."

Without giving Samuel time to make a response, Taittinger went straight to the presidential chair in the center of the table, took a look at his watch and pointed out to Jeff Fishman that he would appreciate it if the meeting could start precisely on time.

Jeff immediately turned to Sissi, asked her in an angry tone why the other ExCom members were not already in the room and demanded that she fetch them immediately. Sissi replied that they were just in the small adjacent chamber waiting for the Chairman and CEO to be seated, as the rule required. She hurried to get them. A few seconds later, the entire group of C-levels entered the room, each being careful, before taking their respective seats, to greet Taittinger with respect, before nodding to Jeff Fishman in a more informal manner. Nine males and one female marched past Fishman and Taittinger: the COO, in charge of commercial operations, the CFO in charge of finance, the head of the legal department, the head of strategy, the head of research, the head of technological development, the head of the ICEBERG project, the head of the risk management department, the head of human resources and the head of communication.

At one minute to two, Taittinger gave Jeff Fishman, sitting to his right, a small wave of his hand indicating that the meeting could start. Fishman immediately initiated the discussion.

"I have requested this ExCom meeting, at which I am very grateful to Mr. Taittinger, our Chairman, for attending, because I've just obtained some vital information that could affect the company's priority project and therefore TOTEXX share price. I invited Professor Samuel Kahn, the archaeologist to whom I owe this information and whom some of you already know, to explain what's going on here. Professor, please go ahead! Explain your discovery to Mr. Taittinger and the Executive Committee and share your recommendations with us."

Samuel rose from his seat and confidently delivered the introduction he had repeated at length in private and now knew by heart.

"Lady and gentlemen, first of all, I'd like to thank you for inviting me today. As Jeff just told you, I'm Samuel Kahn, professor and head of the department of archaeology at Harvard University in Boston. When it launched its oil exploration campaign in Iraq, TOTEXX called on my services to obtain the approval of the authorities to drill in an archaeo-logically-sensitive area. As you know, no company is allowed to extract oil from Iraq without first proving that no archaeological remains lie in the subsoil of the exploitation area.

If my information is correct, TOTEXX is currently interested in the oil resources that abound in Antarctica. I understand that you have already invested considerable amounts of money to start prospecting in this region. Moreover, in its report to shareholders, TOTEXX anticipates that huge revenues will come from new deposits in the mid-term. At this point in my presentation, you are most likely thinking to yourself… What is the relationship between our projects in Antarctica and the fact that in Iraq, we can only drill after excluding the presence of archaeological ruins? Isn't Antarctica a deserted continent? Hasn't it always been covered with ice? There can't be anything of archaeological interest there!

Well, think again. I'm about to show you that there are indeed archaeological treasures in Antarctica. It's clear that, if such information were to become public, TOTEXX would under no circumstances be able to continue its activities there."

Samuel then went through the presentation he'd carefully prepared, happy to see that the members of the audience were drinking in his words, fascinated by what he was teaching them about cuneiform writing, the great gods of creation, and the references to antediluvian civilizations in sacred texts around the world. They seemed frankly amazed by the history of the discovery of an ancient carved stone in

Antarctica. He paid little attention to Taittinger's increasingly red face, which he blamed on poor vascular circulation due to his old age, or to Jeff Fishman's growing nervousness, for whom his boss's non-verbal communication was perfectly clear…

"Now that I have this archaeological treasure from Antarctica in my hands, I have two options," Samuel explained in conclusion. "The first possibility is to disclose this discovery to the whole world. By being the archaeologist who discovered a piece of stele engraved with Sumerian characters in Antarctica, I would become a celebrity overnight. I could launch an excavation campaign at the site of the stone's discovery and become the new Howard Carter, because the discovery of an ancient city forgotten under the ice of Antarctica is on a par with the discovery of Tutankhamen's tomb! Better than that, I might become the initiator of the greatest upheaval in human history that the world has known since Darwin, proving that Antarctica was ice-free a few thousand years ago and that this is where Atlantis, or Lemuria or Mu, the great primordial mother civilization, was located! In such a case, it seems obvious that Antarctica would immediately become a no-go zone for TOTEXX.

The other possibility is that I keep my discovery to myself. You would remain the only ones to know this secret and no one in the archaeological and historical community would bother stopping you from drilling in Antarctica. I imagine that you've already taken measures to neutralize the ornithologists, oceanologists and all other conservationists and so won't encounter any obstacles on that front… I also assume that you've already secured the goodwill of the political world and the United Nations. Of course, if I were to take this second option, I would be making enormous sacrifices on a personal level. I would have to give up the satisfaction of making the discovery of the century. I would never see that renown and glory; I could not welcome the financial benefits of such a discovery. There'd be no best-selling books, no international conferences, etc."

Jeff Fishman, whom Samuel Kahn was beginning to bore with his long speeches and who was concerned about the impact of these revelations on his boss's mood, abruptly cut him off.

"We've got it, Professor! You'll make this stone disappear and in return TOTEXX would compensate you for your loss of opportunities. But what proof do you have as to the truth of your statements? You showed us a black object on your slides, you explained us how to decipher the Sumerian, you told us about Atlantis… all that is very nice, but we are industrialists, not dreamers. The first step for us would be to see what the damn stone looks like in reality. Why didn't you bring it today?"

Then, turning to Taittinger, he tried to gauge the man's thoughts on the matter.

"What do you think, Mr. Chairman?"

Taittinger sat up in his chair, cleared his throat and spoke in a deep and dark voice.

"I don't like your allegations at all, Mr. Kahn! And I'll tell you why! I'm a strong believer: It's thanks to Lord Jesus that I'm here today, at the head of one of the largest international companies. I'm not going to tell you my whole story; you can ask Sissi or Fishman later if you're interested. In short, it was after praying to Lord Jesus, when I was broke and in the depths of despair, that I miraculously discovered, on the small ranch I had inherited from my parents, the gigantic oil well that was at the root of TOTEXX success. So please understand that your speech about the existence of exotic gods, about the development of antediluvian civilizations and about the presence of remains in Antarctica deeply shocks me! Not only are you threatening me with not being able to drill in Antarctica, unless I buy your silence, but you dare to question the foundations of my religious beliefs. I simply won't accept it! "

Taittinger was then taken by a violent coughing fit that caused him to choke, his face turning a purplish hue. Sissi, who had faithfully served him for many years and knew all the details of his personal life, feared that, due to this sudden anger, the President would have an uncontrollable asthma attack. She rushed and whispered in Taittinger's ear that it might be a good idea to interrupt the meeting and resume the discussions later, once he'd had a few puffs of an inhaler, several of which she kept in reserve in her office closet. Taittinger, unable to speak and trying desperately to catch his breath, simply nodded. Sissi helped him out of his chair and accompanied him out of the meeting room.

The truth was that Taittinger was not at all worried about his ability to breathe and the meeting could very well have continued as far as he was concerned. But he preferred to take this opportunity to get rid of Kahn and give himself the time to calmly discuss the situation with his CEO and a small number of select ExCom members.

Sissi reappeared in the board room a few minutes later, informed everyone that Mr. Taittinger would be unable to resume the meeting today, requested that it be closed and that Jeff could reconvene a follow-up meeting in the coming days if necessary.

This announcement left Samuel totally stunned. He had not had the opportunity to defend his position after Taittinger's assault, none of the members of the TOTEXX Executive Committee had given an opinion on his presentation and no conclusion had been reached. He turned to Jeff Fishman and asked him if he was in a position to make a decision on the next steps to be taken in terms of his proposal.

"After Mr. Taittinger's reaction," Jeff asserted, "it's obvious that there is still no consensus within the management team and that I cannot commit TOTEXX to anything one way or the other. The best thing you can do now is to just go home. We know enough to discuss it internally and develop a strategy. I'll get back to you as soon as I've had a chance to validate the way forward with the Chairman. Anyway, thank you very much for your excellent presentation."

Fishman then turned to the secretary:

"Sissi, please kindly escort Professor Kahn to the reception and take care of the practical arrangements for his return to Boston."

He approached Samuel to shake his hand and gave him a hypocritical smile.

"Thank you again and safe trip back", he said before leaving the room, immediately followed by the other members of the Executive Committee.

Sissi led a silent Samuel to the elevator and, seeing his disgruntled face, tried to comfort him:

"On behalf of TOTEXX, please accept our apologies for this inconvenience. You know, Mr. Taittinger is an old and sick man. His asthma attacks are becoming more and more frequent. But don't worry. He'll see more clearly as soon as he calms down and I don't think he'll be forgetting you any time soon. In his defense, I must say that what you just told us is pretty hard to digest! For people our age, it isn't always easy to question ourselves... Personally, what you told us didn't particularly shock me. I've already read books on these subjects and I'm a keen viewer of the history channels. It's not uncommon for them to discuss new theories about the origin of humanity and civilizations on those history programs. Actually, they talk a lot about aliens and about how they might have built all the strange monuments on this planet of ours. Some even say that humans were created by aliens to serve as their slaves! So... an antediluvian civilization and a lost city in Antarctica... why not? But for the boss, it's a different story! He told you that he's a very religious man. Well, he got that right! The only truth out there for him is in the Holy Bible! He had "Faith in God and His Son Lord Jesus" inscribed in the company's values! It's at the top of the list. We now have non-Christian employees who have tried to have it removed, because they think it is discriminatory, but Mr. Taittinger wouldn't hear of it and reiterated loud and clear that it would remain so as long as he was Chairman of the Board of TOTEXX, so... until his death."

"He must have taken you for the Devil himself!" Sissi added as she proffered a little mischievous laugh.

This is my chance, thought Samuel. *TOTEXX must be the only public company in the world led by a fanatical Christian extremist! I never thought a place like this could still exist in the twenty-first century! I should probably consider myself lucky that he didn't give the order to have me crucified or burned at the stake for heresy or blasphemy...*

In the elevator, Sissi continued to chat with him:

"Fortunately for you, not all the ExCom members are like Mr. Taittinger! For example, our Director of Communications, Rachel, recently told me that this company value of ours, which is displayed on just about every wall of the tower, makes her very uncomfortable..."

Samuel, while watching the numbers of the floors scrolling at a dizzying speed on the screen of the elevator shaft, reflected on this news:

I'll have to get to know this Rachel better. And on the plus side, she seemed pretty hot. Too bad the meeting was over so quickly. She didn't even have time to open her mouth…

9

TRUE ARCHAEOLOGY

Two months had passed since the conference on Mesopotamia in Rueil and Émile had almost forgotten all about his meeting with Professor Kahn and the strange stone he'd entrusted to him. Major family worries had recently taken up every single ounce of the Delaporte family's attention. Monique's mother had died suddenly and under extremely suspicious circumstances in the retirement home where she'd been vegetating for over a decade. Monique had found her in good shape the day before when she'd gone on her weekly visit and was convinced that her mother had been abused by her caregivers. No sooner had the Delaportes settled Monique's mother in her final resting place, than Émile's own mother had taken a fatal fall down the stairs of the small Sarcelles house where she lived alone despite her old age and infirmities. Two funerals in the space of a few weeks had somewhat affected Émile's morale and pulled him away from his usual activities. The only thing that managed to get him out of his melancholy was the television… and only then on occasion.

It was time for *Challenges* on the English language channel, one of his favorite shows and, directing his attention toward the write-up in the TV guide, he saw that this week's episode was entitled *True Archaeology: Does Dorian Green really knows the truth?*

Émile emerged from his apathy and thought: *This will probably take my mind off things!* He had already read the French translation of a book by Dorian Green and remembered vaguely that his theories were not lacking in relevance. He prepared a quick bite to eat, opened a can of beer, turned on the TV and sat comfortably in his armchair. It was a good thing that Monique wasn't home tonight. First of all, it didn't much cheer him up when she repeated her suspicions in regard to her mother's murder, of which she'd never been able to obtain the slightest proof. Plus, she could never watch a show in silence. She always had to make comments, generally of no interest, for the sole pleasure of saying something. It was a blessing that she'd gone to the bedside of her best friend Jeannette, who was recovering from hip replacement surgery.

Challenges began with the show's generic music, followed by a view of the studio audience. The camera then zoomed in on the guest of the day sitting at the other side of a glass table to the star presenter, Kimberley Cosby, who, with her enticing face, began the dialog.

"How should I introduce you to our audience? Should I call you Father Green, or Professor Green, or President Green?"

"It is true," replied Dorian, who had anticipated this exact question, "that I was a priest and many still call me Father Green, despite the fact that I haven't been in the priesthood for a long time. It is also true that I was a professor of archaeology at Oxford, but I'm now retired. President is also not incorrect, since I, with my friend and colleague Professor Prosper Tabellion, chair the True Archaeology society, which we founded a few years ago with a view to making things happen and changing attitudes within this discipline. But you know, I'm not a big fan of formal titles. The easiest way would be for you to call me Dorian. Plus, I hope that the purpose of this show isn't to talk about me, but rather about True Archaeology!"

"You've just given me the perfect transition!" exclaimed Kimberley, happy that her show had started on such an easy note. "I was just getting to that! So, True Archaeology! True is a little pretentious, isn't it? You could have said new or even revolutionary, and we'd have understood… because it's clear that you want to put down traditional archaeology and rebuild it upon different bases. But what makes you think that conventional archeologists are wrong and that you and your society are the only ones who hold the truth?"

"One thing is absolutely certain," Dorian answered calmly. "Official archaeology and history tell us a lot of lies, especially about ancient civilizations. The most demonstrative example is the official theory of the pyramids of Giza. We are told that they are tombs, that the Egyptians designed their architecture to ensure the passage of the Pharaohs, true incarnate gods, to eternal life in the paradise of Osiris and that these monuments were built during the fourth Egyptian dynasty, around 2500 BC. I can tell you, and True Archaeology is not alone in saying this, that the pyramids were by no means tombs but rather kinds of machines and that they were built long before the fourth dynasty. The problem is that conventional archeologists and historians are terrified by the meaning behind these truths. Who were these people who eight thousand or twelve thousand years ago, were able to build such wonders that even our engineers today with all their incredibly sophisticated technology would find it difficult to reproduce? To admit such a truth would imply the collapse of the entire edifice of the beliefs on which many parts of society are now based. A major step toward the truth would be to acknowledge that a number of statements made today by so-called experts and leaders are false. Don't you find it disgusting that your children's heads are stuffed with rubbish from these so-called history books?"

"Aren't you being a little harsh?" said Kimberly, pretending to take offense and putting on a doubtful, almost worried look.

"I don't think so," Dorian said in a doctoral tone. "Imagine believing that the Earth is flat. Galileo was called a heretic for dismissing such baloney. Can't you see that what we thought were absolute truths in the Middle Ages were absolute stupidities! Fortunately, for our medieval ancestors, education was not accessible to all and nor compulsory! I'm convinced that no teaching at all is far preferable to teaching nonsense. I would prefer that our teachers tell today's children that we simply don't know who built the pyramids nor when, rather than stuffing their heads with false notions."

"Let's assume that what we're taught is not always perfectly accurate," Kimberley admitted, "but are you sure that what True Archaeology preaches is any more true? If I understood your last book correctly, which I imagine reflects the theories of True Archaeology, you say that it was the Anunaki who built the pyramids more than ten thousand years ago, that they had at that time more sophisticated technologies than ours and that these Anunaki developed the first great civilization… and that everything that followed was inferior. You even claim that the Anunaki, who were perceived as gods by the Sumerians, made Homo Sapiens by using genetic manipulation or hybridization from apes! Do you honestly think that all this sounds truer than the official teachings?"

"Wait a minute! Not so fast!" Dorian exclaimed, emphasizing his point with a wave of his hand in front of the camera. "We have never claimed that our theories, which are still only working hypotheses, represent the absolute truth! The only thing we're saying is that the answers that are now being given to a number of unexplained phenomena – that are presented as absolute truths - are in fact wrong. And we're not just making this up gratuitously. We have amply demonstrated why a number of official theories are clearly inaccurate. I've just told you about the mistakes concerning the pyramids of Egypt, but I could multiply the examples ad infinitum. I could tell you about the nonsense that is being put out there about the ruins of Tiwanaku in Bolivia, Sacsayhuaman in Peru, the statues of Easter Island or the alignments of Carnac in French Brittany and so on. But your show isn't long enough! After demonstrating how certain official explanations don't hold water, we make hypotheses based on facts that have so far been either ignored or misinterpreted and on the basis of new research we have been conducting. The Anunaki hypothesis is, among others, the one that solves the greatest number of enigmas. For those watching, I'd like to point out that we have Sumerian texts, engraved in cuneiform characters on clay tablets, which speak of the Anunaki. They tell us that these Anunaki made a hybrid humanoid to serve as their slave. Let me note in passing that most of us are descended from those slaves who worshipped or feared their creators as they migh gods… Sumerian texts tell us that it was the Anunaki who brought about agriculture, the construction of temples and cities, writing, laws, social and political organizations, in short, everything that makes civilization and that our human societies have then reproduced almost identically since time immemorial."

"What you're saying is that humans, according to you, were created by the Anunaki to be their slaves and interpreted their creators and masters as gods," Kimberley confirmed. "As a former Catholic priest, is that really how you see the notion of divinity? Does this mean you no longer believe in the one God of the Jews, Christians and Muslims?"

"If I were a hypocrite," Dorian replied with a sardonic smile, "I would tell you that my faith in one God is still as strong as ever, that the true God is much more than these Anunaki gods who were really only superhuman, and that my God, the God of Christians, exists and is by far superior!"

"But as you're not a hypocrite, you'll confess everything to us..." Kimberley said, interrupting Dorian, with an ounce of irony in her voice.

"At the risk of shocking some of you," Dorian continued calmly, "I will indeed give you the gist of my thoughts. I think that faith in one or more gods is actually a mental illness. Unfortunately, the vast majority of people suffer from this disease, without being aware of it, as is typically the case for most mental illnesses, and this disease makes their lives absolutely miserable, contrary to what they are led to believe. Let me explain my reasoning here. Modern man, possibly because of his altered genetic material, is an extremely anxious animal because he is capable of thinking... but his limited intellectual capacities prevent him from finding answers to certain great existential mysteries such as... How was the universe created? How could something concrete, such as a star or a planet, appear from nothing? How can space be infinite or even finite? Where do we come from? And above all... What happens after death? The invention of the whole concept of God is the most powerful anti-anxiety medication that man could find before the invention of modern drugs! God as an anxiolytic seemed to provide reassuring answers to all these questions and thus calm most of our anxious ways. It's a comfortable thing to be convinced that there is an invisible genius called God who created the whole universe, who sees and hears us, to whom we can turn for help, and whom we will join in

Paradise after our time is done here on Earth. But religion is actually a very bad remedy, which only masks the disease rather than curing it and is the cause of countless, serious side effects. I'm referring mainly to all the atrocities committed in the name of religion… In my opinion, the only way to heal from this anxiety is, first, to become aware of it and, secondly, to learn to dominate your fears and live as a liberated, dignified and courageous person."

"Are you telling us that True Archaeology is a therapy center for the mentally ill?"

"Kimberley," Dorian replied condescendingly, "don't try to confuse the public here by putting words into my mouth! True Archaeology is neither a cult nor some sort of charlatan enterprise! Its purpose is simply to help humanity free itself from its amnesia as to its origins, to awaken the consciousness of people about where they come from and how they became what they are and, ultimately, to help humanity out of the paradigm or out of the impasse in which it has locked itself. And this requires us to find the very first civilization, which, in our opinion, is neither Sumer nor Egypt, nor any of the great ancient civilizations officially recognized as such. As its name suggests, the main activity of True Archaeology is archaeology. We are convinced, on the basis of evidence that already exists, that one day we'll find irrefutable evidence of this primordial civilization, such as a manuscript or engraved tablet or even better… a lost city. That's why True Archaeology organizes excavations in all the places we believe this primordial civilization could have flourished. Let me give you some examples of the areas we feel are the most promising:

a) The Amazonian forest - There are several indications that the jungle may contain much more than wild tribes, piranhas and toucans. We've found some quite elaborate pottery there, we observed traces of ancient man-made canals and, of course, there is the amazing story of Eldorado…

b) The Gobi Desert - We've found very old mummies and strange metallic objects whose function and origin we don't yet understand…

c) The Antarctic continent - We know that ancient navigators witnessed this continent at a time when it was ice-free because they left us very accurate maps. Antarctica could very well have been a central starting point that could have spread both to America (hence the ancient remains found in Peru, Bolivia and as far as Mexico), to Africa (hence the Egyptian civilization), to the Middle East (hence Sumer and the Indus civilization) and to Asia / Pacific."

Upon hearing Dorian speak of Antarctica, Émile, who had been rather perplexed by the expert's words until now, jumped up:

This is unbelievable! To think that I was in Antarctica just a few months ago and found that stone! An engraved stone! I'd almost completely forgotten about it! I must write to Professor Kahn to get it back. It's odd that he's not been in touch…

Émile took advantage of the short ad break with its series of ridiculous commercials to get rid of his plate and his now empty beer can and serve himself a small glass of Cognac before returning to his seat and sitting back comfortably to enjoy the rest of the show.

"Imagine that True Archaeology manages to find evidence somewhere of a civilization older than the others," Kimberley continued. "What do you expect to find? I mean… who were these people you call the Anunaki and where did they come from? How did they disappear? Apparently, they didn't leave many traces… Were they aliens? And how did we arrive at the situation we're in today?"

"You are asking me to rewrite the entire history of humanity in ten minutes… Maybe that's why the show is called *Challenges!* I will nevertheless try to answer you, since I aspire to behave as a free-thinking, dignified and sensible man… This is how I suspect things must have gone… A humanoid species, different from Neanderthal, Denisovan, Lucian or Java man, developed and was initially self-sufficient, on a territory particularly favored by nature (neither too hot nor too cold, nor too wet or too dry and devoid of ferocious animals such as the T-Rex or the saber-toothed tiger). Physically, in all likelihood, they were individuals with white skin and light eyes and of large stature. This is how the Aztecs described Quetzalcoatl, the initiator of civilization in their region, the Mayans described Kukulcan and the Sumerians described the Anunaki. These people obviously had superior intellectual abilities. They asked themselves lots of questions, looked for solutions, experimented, analyzed results, reasoned and implemented what they thought made the most sense: They were the first scientists if you wish. Presumably, these people understood that they only were insignificant creatures in the vast universe, that great natural forces were at work around them and that, to live as pleasantly as possible, they had to adopt a certain number of rules in order to organize life as a society. I think they shared a collective vision: They aspired to happiness. To achieve this vision, they set themselves the mission of defining the conditions of their happiness and the means to be implemented in order to achieve their goal. For example, they thought about the best way to ensure basic living needs such as eating, drinking, sleeping and protecting themselves from the elements. They found that livestock, agriculture and the construction of houses and cities were excellent ways to achieve this. They also realized the importance of documenting and transmitting knowledge. They then codified language, invented writing and created an education system. They also found that a number of behaviors created problems in society and introduced prohibitions, laws and moral principles. Finally, they realized that a growing society required a government to which powers over others should be delegated. In my opinion, the first government was a group of elders who deliberated and took decisions together by majority vote."

"It's a perfect society you're describing here," says Kimberley mockingly. "Don't you think you're idealizing? Confusing your dreams with reality?"

"It's very possible," Dorian conciliated. "In the absence of tangible evidence, the things I've just been talking about are just totally gratuitous assumptions. But, in general, my impression is that this primordial society was respectful of its members, that citizens felt free and responsible, that overall there was a certain harmony and that people were probably more than satisfied with their fate. The civilizations that followed, on the other hand, showed all the signs of degeneration and decline."

"And then what happened to these Anunaki?" Kimberley asked.

"As a result of their scientific discoveries and technological advances," Dorian proposed, "they eventually were able to cross the oceans, most likely by ship and possibly even with flying machines and embarked on long voyages of exploration. Of course, after discovering new lands (South and Central America, Africa, India, Asia) they decided to exploit their resources and colonize them. Hence all these stories of great white men arriving by sea, sometimes described as half fish like Ea / Enki in Mesopotamia, sometimes described as flying snakes like Quetzalcóatl, who undertook major irrigation and construction work. The Anunaki, who had already mastered the domestication of many animal species such as cows, goats and sheep back home, domesticated the curious animals they found in their colonies. For example, llamas and alpacas in South America, which they used as draught animals and wool providers, donkeys in Africa, camels in the Middle East and horses in Asia. But also…they found in these places beings whom they considered to be animals but who had a disturbing resemblance to themselves. Great apes and primitive hominids. They decided to domesticate them as well and use them to carry out the most menial tasks. This is how slavery first started. But then sexual relations occurred between Anunaki and domesticated primitive hominids and it appeared that the two species were compatible. Thus were born hybrids, or half-breeds if you will, who appear in ancient writings as demigods or heroes.

Gradually, an increasing promiscuity between masters and slaves meant that Homo eventually became Sapiens, either because their genetic heritage was enriched with Anunaki genes, or simply because the masters initiated their slaves to the various elements of their civilization.

One day, probably about twelve thousand years ago, some sort of monstrous natural disaster destroyed the Anunaki homeland. Was this disaster the famous Flood to which all the traditions of the world refer? Did a giant meteorite hit Earth? Or was it the eruption of a mega volcano? It's impossible to know for sure. Few people on earth survived this disaster. And the pure Anunaki who survived in the colonies found themselves cut off from the base of their civilization and now in a minority among their Homo Sapiens slaves. Several scenarios could have then occurred. In some cases, the slaves massacred their masters and kept very little of the Anunaki culture; in other cases, the masters freed their former slaves and rebuilt alongside them on a relatively equal footing. It can be assumed that, in these cases, civilizations relatively similar to the primordial Anunaki civilization could have been recreated; in other cases, the masters simply disappeared little by little, overtaken by the Homo Sapiens population, the latter having had time to assimilate some scraps of civilization…

Following the disappearance of the Anunaki metropolis, the various colonies evolved without contact with each other for a very long time and thus were born the ancient civilizations we know of today."

"How do you explain, if your hypothesis is correct, that mankind has forgotten everything about its origins?"

"Many factors must have been at work to cause this amnesia," Dorian answered confidently. "Let's start with the psychological factor. In the wake of Freud's work, some psychiatrists have argued that mass psychology is surprisingly similar to individual psychology. Just as an individual is capable of repressing the traumatic events of his or her childhood in the depths of the unconscious, it is not too far-fetched to think that humanity may have repressed the very badly experienced events of their beginnings, such as the creation of Homo Sapiens from a higher humanoid species, the initial slavery of the Homo Sapiens, possibly the extermination of their masters, in other words the murder of the father, to paraphrase Oedipus.

In addition to this, the need to document events in writing and to ensure that knowledge is passed on from one generation to the next is a concept whose importance was only grasped by our ancestors at a much later stage. This is why the only snippets of information about prehistoric times that have come down to us have been via the oral tradition.

Above all, humanity has gone through countless periods of barbarism, during which all traces of the past were deliberately erased.

Some megalomaniac tyrants used to remove all references to what had preceded them and might have overshadowed them. A number of Egyptian Pharaohs erased the depictions, the statues and so forth of their predecessors from the temples. Each popular revolution has had its share of the destruction of the institutions of the past. Wars have often been accompanied by ransacking and the disappearance of important symbols of heritage. Unfortunately, I fear that the worst of this was committed in the name of Christianity. Christian fanatics burned what was left of the Alexandria library after the serious damage caused by the fire more or less voluntarily set off by Caesar during his war against Pompey. Later, anything that might remind us of paganism was systematically destroyed by the Church as soon as it was in a position of power. The conquest of the ancient nations of Central and South America by Spain and Portugal ended, at the instigation of the Church, in the destruction of millions of documents and artifacts that could certainly have shed light on the origins of the Olmec, Maya, Toltec and other Incas."

Through Kimberley's questions, most of which the True Archaeology members had correctly anticipated and for which he was therefore perfectly prepared, Dorian Green had the opportunity to communicate on more or less every subject that was close to his heart and that he wanted to address.

Émile, who regularly fell asleep in front of the television in the evenings, had managed to watch *Challenges* to the end. Rarely had a television show fascinated him so much. Monique returned home at around ten, after making sure that her friend Jeannette was comfortable in bed and had everything she needed. She found an Émile not only still awake, but in an unusual state of agitation.

"Gosh," she said, "you're not in bed? Are you not feeling well?"

"No, no, I'm fine," Émile reassured her. "I just watched a great show on TV. It was *Challenges*, you know, that show I watch regularly. Today, they had Dorian Green on. He's an archaeologist who founded a society called True Archaeology. I've actually read one of his books. He's said some incredible things about the origin of humanity and civilization. You'll never guess what he said tonight!"

"I don't know… Maybe that we all came from Orion or that True Archaeology has just found the Holy Grail?"

"No, no, much more interesting than that," Émile said without perceiving the nuance of sarcasm in his wife's reply. "They expect to find the remains of the very first civilization in Antarctica!"

"And that's what's got you all excited like this? That's why you're not asleep?" Monique asked in astonishment.

"Antarctica! A city lost under the ice! Doesn't that remind you of something?"

"Well, yes! We were there! But we only saw icebergs, seals and penguins!"

"Oh, yeah? And what about my stone?"

"That's true. That hunk of rock you made us drag home. But do you actually believe you've found a piece of the Rosetta Stone or something?"

"Well, not the Rosetta Stone of course, but the sort of remains that Professor Green hopes to find one day in Antarctica and that would prove his theories are correct! I don't know if you quite grasp the enormity of this! I probably found exactly what this famous archaeologist is desperately looking for. And if that's the case, it's the discovery of the century!"

"Oh, love, I think you're delirious… Besides, what did Professor Kahn think of your stone after you gave it to him at the theater? What did he say?"

"Well now that you mention it… He kept the stone! He never got back to me on the results of his tests. I'm going to write to him first thing tomorrow morning and ask him to send it back to me immediately."

10

A FAKE ANTIQUITY

In the private jet back to Boston, Samuel Kahn was doing his best to analyze the meeting with the TOTEXX executives, desperately looking for what elements might have caused such a huge fiasco…

Obviously, he had made a very bad impression on Taittinger, the Chairman of the Board and therefore the most senior person in the organization. The real question was whether this old fool actually had any real power at TOTEXX.

This guy is supposed to be an enlightened man, but he apparently believes very strongly that he owes his fortune to the intervention of Jesus Christ. It's terrifying to think that in the twenty first century, important decisions in a huge company like TOTEXX could be left up to a senile freak like him. Being extremely wealthy and owning the majority of the shares of a company means you can play with the future of the company and its employees just as you please! This really is the capitalist system at its worst! I hope Jeff Fishman brought him to the meeting just for show, and in practice, as CEO, it's him really running the show… As far as the other members of the executive committee are concerned, it's hard to know what they thought since they didn't get a chance to speak. But then, they did seem to be following everything I told them, and it looked like they might agree with my analysis. You never know, they may have more weight in the company than you'd think… I seem to remember Jeff mentioning that he'd have a debriefing with them after I left. Let's hope they can bring the old fool to his senses. Anyway, the ball is in their court. I'll wait for Jeff to get in touch. I'll call him back in a week if he hasn't contacted me by then. But in the meantime, I'd better think about a plan B…

Samuel spent the rest of the flight imagining what his future might look like if he revealed the existence of an antediluvian civilization in Antarctica. How could he ensure that the reputation he'd gain from such a scoop would generate substantial revenues as quickly as possible? He distractedly jotted down some ideas in his notebook. *Make a statement at the opening of the next World Archaeological Congress with a press conference, obtain a large budget to launch an excavation campaign in Antarctica, write a book, appear on television…* And he concluded with a note that he underlined to indicate its importance: *Ensure Émile's cooperation!*

Samuel was relieved when the limousine that was waiting for him in the small private airport dropped him off at the foot of his beautiful home. This little trip had been more challenging than he'd anticipated. He was happy to be warmly welcomed by Dana and the girls. The au-pair appeared in the entrance hall just as he was finishing his round of hugs with the family. Was her hair different, or perhaps she was dressed more elegantly than usual tonight? Samuel suddenly found himself paying attention to this girl for the first time since she'd arrived in their home. He looked at her insistently before giving her a broad smile.

"Hello Kate, how are you?" he asked.

This little one's very pretty. I could get into her… She looks like she has a nice ass… The fact that she burns my shirts when she irons them might not be that big a deal after all…

Dana, who had not missed her husband's lewd look at the au-pair, led Samuel to the living room and asked him about his trip.

"So, you didn't stay in Dallas for long! Is that a good sign or a bad sign? Tell me how your talks at TOTEXX went."

"I don't really want to discuss this right now," Samuel replied in an irritated tone. "I'm tired. I spent eight hours in a plane today. There's an hour's time difference. I have a little jet lag. It's not much, I know, but I'm feeling it."

"You seem to be in a really bad mood," Dana remarked. "You're not home often, so if we can't talk now, when can we? Let me remind you that you have a family and that family is the most important thing in life. So, you could make a little effort and make yourself more available to your wife!"

"You're not going to do this again!" Samuel replied in an angry way. "Trust me, I think about our family every day! Why do you think I'm working like crazy and trying to get a bit more money behind us by negotiating with assholes like the TOTEXX executives? You and the girls are the reason I'm doing all this!"

"I know. I'm sorry I'm being difficult... Obviously, it didn't go too well with TOTEXX."

"Since you want to know everything, you're right, it didn't go very well! I thought I'd be negotiating a new contract, mainly with the CEO, you know, Jeff Fishman, the guy I've been dealing with since my mission in Iraq. I get along pretty well with him. But they put me up in front of the Chairman of the Board, a completely senile Christian fanatic, who has somehow convinced himself about Jesus Christ and the miracles he'd witnessed. So, you can imagine how he treated me when he heard my last name and saw my Ashkenazi face! It was like going up against Himmler!"

Before joining his family for dinner, Samuel went to his office. He opened his safe, mainly to take a look at the stone but also to put in the material used for his presentation at TOTEXX and the few scribbled notes he'd made on the plane, then went through the few magazines and letters that had arrived that day.

Archives of Archaeology, that can wait; advertising for a credit card, as if I didn't already have enough; more advertising for some anti-aging pills (I must have appeared in their records as senile already. Nice.); Ah! Gold coins for my collection, I'll catalog them this weekend; and bills... of course! Telephone, electricity, water... They'll ruin me eventually! Well, well... what's this? A letter from France... Undoubtedly someone from the Knowledge and Understanding lectures. They'll want to reschedule my tour.

Samuel grabbed a letter opener and hurried to tear the envelope, taking care not to damage the beautiful French stamps: *My God! It's from*

Émile Delaporte! What a strange coincidence. I was just thinking about him this afternoon… Let's see what he want?

Émile's letter was short, polite and precise. He was obviously very disappointed that he hadn't received any news after several months and asked him to kindly return his stone as soon as possible. Samuel laughed to himself, put the letter back in its envelope and threw it carelessly into a drawer in his desk, treating the man's request with the utmost contempt.

Two weeks later, when he had resumed work back at the university, Samuel learned from his secretary that a guy, a Frenchman according to her, had been harassing her on the phone for two days and was insisting on talking to him. The secretary hadn't really grasped what the man wanted because his English was terrible, but she'd understood that his name was something like "Doulepoutre" and that he wanted some object back that he'd given to the Professor several months earlier. She told Samuel that, if this guy called again, she'd have to put the call through to him. Samuel thought that things may just be taking a turn for the worse, that it was absolutely necessary to stop Émile saying too much, especially to anyone working at Harvard, and that he would have to deal personally with this nuisance.

"Of course! I understand! Put him through next time he calls!" he said in a placatory tone to the secretary.

The very next day, within an hour of arriving at his office, Émile called. Samuel answered him in quasi-perfect French, with a feint of cordiality:

"Émile! Good to hear from you! I'm sorry things took a little longer than expected, but I wanted to be sure of my conclusions before I sent the stone back to you. In fact, I was about to pack it up and mail it to you when your letter came to me three days ago. Émile, I'm afraid I have some disappointing news. The stone has no archaeological value. The lines on the stone that resembled cuneiform symbols are in fact just the marks of the friction of the ice on the stone. You know, these things happen very often. When I first saw the stone, I must say that I had my doubts… You'll be receiving a package within the next few days. Even though it's not very valuable, it's still a wonderful souvenir of your trip to Antarctica!"

Émile was divided between an undeniable disappointment at the news that his stone had nothing remarkable about it in the eyes of Professor Kahn, and on the other hand an immense relief at the idea that his souvenir of Antarctica would soon be back home with him. He stammered a few words of thanks to the professor for his time spent appraising the stone and for the inconvenience caused by the shipment of the package to France and put the phone down.

Samuel sighed with relief as soon as Émile's call was over and began to think about the situation. He had managed to calm things down with Émile: The man wouldn't question his expert conclusions and would quickly forget the whole idea of the stone being an object of Sumerian origin. However, Émile was now expecting to receive his stone in the next few days, but there was obviously no question of him getting it back. An idea, which he found absolutely brilliant, sprang to mind:

All the best museums now have souvenir shops where one can find resin replicas of the most beautiful artifacts on display; I saw some fairly realistic ones in the Louvre of the Marathon Man and the head of Nefertiti in the Berlin Museum. I know a craftsman who does it for the Boston Museum. I'll have him make a resin copy of Émile's stone. The fool won't notice the difference!

When he showed the original stone to the craftsman, Samuel explained that he'd decided to play a joke on an archaeologist friend and give him a resin imitation of a Sumerian artifact, with the original text in cuneiform writing transformed into something much more fun. Samuel then handed the craftsman a sheet of paper on which he had drawn cuneiform signs which would look quite similar to a non-specialist but were actually pretty different. When the craftsman asked Samuel what the signs meant, Samuel claimed that the original stone said *Prince of the Kingdom* while, for his friend, he wanted *King of the Hot Dogs* engraved on it and they both laughed together with a knowing look.

After picking up the resin imitation, Samuel personally went to the nearest UPS store, packed it as if it were a precious work of art and instructed the employee to send it by express parcel to a certain Émile Delaporte, Rueil-Malmaison, France.

Alea jacta est, he thought, and smiled at himself as he thought of the trick he was pulling on Émile and how he and the craftsman had laughed about it. In fact, the text he had asked the craftsman to engrave on the resin didn't quite mean what he'd said. Instead, the cuneiform characters he'd had written on the resin for Émile could be translated into modern American as something along the lines of *Fuck you…*

***

Three days later, in Rueil, Émile was in a terrible mood. Someone had parked a car in front of his garage door and he'd had to drive around the neighborhood for more than half an hour to find a parking space. He was returning from his daughter's house where she'd asked him to help her son revise his history and geography classes. Nicolas was, according to his parents, a difficult child at home and a dunce at school. By the time he was sixteen, he'd already been kept back to repeat two years of high school. Apart from girls and computers, nothing interested him… His parents were hoping that his grandfather's support, both with his schoolwork and with his personal development during this difficult period, would be beneficial to him, especially since, by a happy coincidence, "it was fitting well" between Nicolas and Émile, as the teenager would say. Although clearly of benefit to Nicolas, playing teacher and social worker was taking its toll on Émile. The noise of the television startled him as he entered the apartment and served only to exacerbate his bad mood.

Monique always turns the volume up to watch those stupid shows! And she's just going to get all annoyed when I ask her to turn it down! What a time to be living in…

He went and locked himself in his office rather than argue with his wife. On his desk, on top of his mail, sat a parcel from the United States that he hurried to open as he temporarily forgot his foul mood, thinking: *Finally, some good news! I've got my stone back!*

Monique, who suspected that Émile had just opened the package she'd signed for that afternoon and whose curiosity made her impatient to know its contents, entered the office without knocking and came to stand over him.

"Is it your stone?" she asked. "I figured it must be when I noticed it had come from Boston! Did you see that there's an envelope stuck on the packaging? It probably contains a letter from Professor Kahn. Aren't you going to open it?"

"I'll look at it tomorrow when I've rested a little," replied Émile, who didn't much appreciate his wife's uninvited intrusion into his office. "The important thing is that I've got my stone back. Anyway, the letter is probably in English and so it'll take me a while to decipher it. Right now, I only want two things: to eat and then rest. Six hours spent with Nicolas, then the infernal traffic in Paris and finally a moron who parked his car in front of my garage: I've had more than enough for today!"

The next day also started very badly for Émile. As he looked closely at the stone that Professor Kahn had returned to him, his heart rate suddenly accelerated and large drops of sweat began to bead on his forehead.

"What the hell is this? It's not my stone! Oh, my God!" Émile said aloud as he rushed to the filing cabinet where he'd carefully archived dozens of photos of the stone taken before he'd entrusted it to the Professor. It clearly appeared to him that the symbols engraved on the object sent by Kahn were different from the characters on the original stone. Moreover, to the touch, the object didn't feel the same at all. The texture of this one seemed odd. There was no possible comparison with the cold and smooth hardness of his stone that he still held perfectly in his memory.

Émile grabbed the letter that accompanied the package and with a trembling hand, he opened it. On a single sheet of line paper from a standard notepad, without a heading, was a handwritten note in English that he managed to translate without too much difficulty.

Here's the object you found. After careful analysis, I confirm that it's a fragment of a contemporary resin object, without any value, probably from an imitation of a statue. I believe it must have been broken and abandoned by a tourist. Yours sincerely, S. Kahn.

"This guy's messing with my head!" Émile shouted, feeling angered beyond belief. "What a scumbag! What an idiot I was to have trusted this crook! I should have gone to Professor Green instead."

Monique, who had heard his exclamations and run to see what was happening, couldn't help but stick a knife in the wound:

"Too bad it wasn't your famous professor Green who came to give a lecture! You always get yourself into the most unbelievable situations! That piece of rock has caused us nothing but problems! You'd rather have brought a penguin feather!"

"That's all you have to say?" Émile cried out in outrage. "You think it's me and not that bastard Kahn who's causing the problems! I refuse to allow this to happen! Do you think it's somehow amusing that Professor Green hasn't been to Rueil? Well, keep laughing! I'm going to go and pay him a visit at his place!"

"Sure you are!" Monique said, shrugging her shoulders. "And how are you going to do that? Do you think that such a famous man has nothing better to do than waste his time with an nameless stranger?"

"I bet he'll see me! From what I know of him, he'll certainly be very interested in my story! I think he lives in London or Oxford, in any case in England, so it's not a million miles away."

Émile immediately set about obtaining an appointment with Professor Green. With the help of his grandson Nicolas, delighted to be able to demonstrate his computer skills and relative English proficiency to his grandfather, he found Professor Green's contact details on the Internet and wrote a detailed letter describing all the ins and outs of his adventure. He concluded his letter by begging the Professor to meet with him at a convenient place and time and sent it by registered mail to Professor Dorian Green, True Archaeology, Benson Castle, Oxfordshire, UK.

Just five days later, Émile received a positive response from Professor Green. He'd taken Émile's allegations very seriously; when reading his letter, Dorian thought that he simply couldn't afford the risk of missing out on what could be the chance of a lifetime… An artifact attesting to an ancient civilization in Antarctica; wasn't that the Holy Grail to which he'd devoted his entire life? Dorian therefore proposed a meeting ten days later in London, at the Grosvenor Hotel where he would be staying for the next European Congress of Archaeology.

These ten days were enough for Émile to organize his stay in London. Monique wanted to go with him, not so much to meet Professor Green as to take the Eurostar for the first time and thus impress her neighbor by telling her all about her experience in the Channel Tunnel. Both agreed to use this short trip to not only meet with Professor Green but to take a look at some of the main tourist attractions in and around London. As usual, Émile devised a very dense itinerary, leaving no room for improvisation. They would take a guided tour to Stonehenge and visit the British Museum, where Émile was absolutely determined to see the Rosetta Stone, the Parthenon frieze and anything they had related to Sumer, Akkad and Babylon.

11

THE MISSING LINK

Dorian didn't mind sneaking away from the archaeological congress to devote an hour of his precious time to Émile. He had agreed with the concierge at the Grosvenor to reserve a quiet corner of the large lounge space for the meeting, having told him that he was expecting the arrival of a certain Émile Delaporte. As he waited, Dorian had reread the letter that had convinced him to set up this meeting.

Dear Professor Green,

Although I'm not an archaeologist, I read your book Civilization X and recently watched you on Challenges. I'd like to request a meeting with you, during which my intention is to show you some photos of a stone I brought back from my trip to Antarctica last winter, on which, I believe, are engraved cuneiform characters and which may well be the remains of a very ancient civilization.

However, I must inform you that I entrusted the original stone to Professor Samuel Kahn of Boston, whom you probably know, in order to gain his expert opinion. The latter claimed that this stone had no archaeological value. Strangely enough, he kept my stone and, when I insisted on having it back, he returned to me instead a bog-standard resin object that I'm certain is only a pale imitation of my original.

I hope you don't think this too farfetched. I want to assure you that I am of sound mind.

If this letter seems sufficiently convincing to you and you agree to meet me, please indicate the date, time and place that would best suit you (ideally somewhere near London or Oxford, as I live in Paris) and you can be assured that I will be there.

Whatever your decision might be, I would be very grateful if you could answer this letter. This whole business has been keeping me awake at night and I have the feeling that only you can assist me in solving this puzzle.

Respectfully, Émile Delaporte

Upon receiving this letter, Dorian had made some notes in his journal.

Not only does this Émile not seem crazy in my book, but my instinct tells me that this stone could well be the missing link that True Archaeology is desperately seeking. Meet Émile as soon as possible (at the International Congress of Archaeology in London next week?)

Dorian had just finished rereading Émile's letter and notes about him when the concierge, accompanied by a man in his sixties who looked nervous, walked up to him:

"Professor Green, the person you were expecting has just arrived. Can I get you anything?"

Dorian thanked the man, introduced himself to Émile, shook his hand and asked him in almost perfect French if he wanted a drink. Émile looked embarrassed.

"Oh no, please don't bother yourself!" he timidly replied.

Dorian understood that he would have to take the initiative and said to the concierge:

"Please bring us two sparkling mineral waters, with some nibbles maybe? Thank you."

As soon as the concierge had moved away, Dorian asked Émile to sit in the chair next to his and initiated the conversation:

"Thank you for coming here to meet me, sir. I must say that your story certainly aroused my curiosity. If you don't mind, perhaps you could tell me everything - in detail - from when you were in Antarctica to today?"

Émile went right ahead and Dorian regretted having mentioned the words "in detail", as Émile spared him none of the insignificant and unrelated events that had punctuated his life in recent months.

Dorian nevertheless decided not to rush Émile and to let him tell of his whole adventure without interruption. He congratulated himself on his patience when Émile, after lengthy logorrhea, placed before his eyes the ten photos he had taken of the original object before entrusting it to Samuel Kahn. Dorian couldn't believe it. Even in the absence of the real stone and despite the amateurism of the prints taken by Émile, he was almost certain to be looking at a fragment of an ancient stele, engraved with magnificent cuneiform characters, most probably in the oldest known form of Sumerian! He immediately recognized the words ANU TARA TIKI, which probably meant the sacred territory of Anu and therefore referred to the great Sumerian god. The beginning of other words was also visible, but the fracture of the stone had cut them, and it was impossible to speculate on their meaning without further study.

Dorian could also clearly see that the object returned to Émile by Samuel Kahn was indeed only a derisory imitation made of resin. He had to make an enormous effort of restraint to remain straight faced when he deciphered the inscription that was engraved on it and whose meaning he was careful not to communicate to Émile, as the text was so vile and insulting. On second thoughts, it was the kind of hurtful humor that his "friend" Kahn was known for. In a way, such coarseness engraved in resin validated the story of Émile, a man Dorian now considered totally incapable of having invented such a scenario. After all, before this face-to-face meeting with Émile, Dorian had been on guard and couldn't rule out the possibility that Émile might have been a myth maniacal mental patient. But now that he had the individual in front of him, Dorian was sure that everything this good man had told him was a true reflection of reality.

Somewhat stunned by everything he had just seen and heard, and before speaking in full with Émile, Dorian swallowed down several gulps of sparkling water, invited Émile to do the same, and summarized in his head the quasi-certainties he had just acquired.

1) Émile wasn't some crazy person and his story was true.

2) A fragment of a stele engraved with extremely old cuneiform characters had been taken by Émile from the frozen ground of the Antarctic continent last winter. It was likely that the rest of the stele was still there, as well as other remains that might testify to the presence of civilized men long ago in Antarctica.

3) Samuel Kahn had stolen Émile's stone. Knowing Kahn, what he was planning to do with it was probably not very honest. In any case, his attitude towards poor Émile did not bode well….

Dorian, without yet being sure of the way forward, decided that the most important thing at this point was to gain the good graces of Émile, who, he was sure, would play an instrumental role in the coming weeks:

"Émile, first of all I'd like to thank you for trusting me and for coming to London to share your adventure with me. Know that, in view of the photos you've just shown me, I have no doubt that your stone is of inestimable value. From my initial deductions, I believe it is a fragment of a stele, possibly marking the boundary of a large city and at least five thousand years old. If I'm right, and I have every reason to believe that this is the case, you have put your hands, or should I say your feet, on the discovery of the century. As you probably know, since you've read my books, I've always been convinced that a great primordial civilization, at the origin of all others, remains to be discovered. And I've always thought that the Antarctic continent, which we know hasn't always been covered with ice, was one of the few unexplored places on this Earth where its remains could be found. First, it's paramount that you get back your stone as quickly as possible. I must confess that I know Professor Kahn quite well, that I don't have a high opinion of him and that his attitude towards you only half surprises me. I'm confident that he will have to return the original stone of which you alone are the legitimate owner. If you are OK with it, I'll handle the Kahn problem."

"Oh! Thank you very much, Professor!" cried Émile. "That's reassured me! I completely agree to you helping me with Professor Kahn! Would you like me to write to him and tell him that you're now dealing with my case?"

"Please don't! Don't give him any information about your plans! Pretend you've been fooled by his deception and don't go any further than that. Let me do it. I'll discuss all this with my colleagues at True Archaeology and we'll consider the best strategy to implement with regards to Kahn. Don't worry about that. I promise you; we'll do everything we can to recover your stone!"

"Well, all right… So, I've not to do anything? I should wait to hear from you?" asked Émile timidly.

"That's right. I already have all your contact details and I'll let you know as soon as I have something new."

Dorian then got up from his chair to signify the end of the interview:

"Unfortunately, I must leave you now. As you may know, we have the European Congress of Archaeology in London at this very moment and I have to go back to it to do some presentations. Let's keep in touch!"

Émile stayed in his chair and collected his documents scattered on the coffee table, before speaking.

"Do you know who I have to pay for the drinks?"

"Don't worry about that," Dorian said, indicating with a wave of his hand that the cost of the drinks didn't matter at all. "I had our drinks put on my hotel bill. I'm staying here during the congress. Enjoy your stay in London!"

"Of course. As you wish."

Émile finally understood that he had to be on his way and allow Professor Green to go about his business. He shook Dorian's hand warmly:

"Well, then, goodbye Professor, and thank you for everything!"

Instead of returning to the archaeology congress, where he would waste his time listening to scientific presentations of little interest or exchanging banalities with former colleagues in the corridors, Dorian, very excited by what Émile had just told him, decided to go to the calm of his room to reflect. Instinctively, he felt that there was an urgent need for action, otherwise this unique opportunity to advance the theories of True Archaeology could well slip through his fingers. Kahn had an exceptional treasure in his hands and he no doubt already had a plan to exploit it to the best of his advantage. A race against the clock was now underway between Kahn and himself and he intended to win it! The first thing to do was to bring together the leaders of the True Archaeology to share this news with them and to develop an action plan. Dorian phoned Edwina, explained to her without going into detail that something crucial in terms of the future of True Archaeology had just come up, and asked her to organize a meeting the very next evening at The Manor with as many members of the committee as possible.

Dorian spent the next hour lying on the bed, thinking about what he might do, if he were acting alone, with a case like this. How would he go about recovering the stolen stone from Kahn, which was undoubtedly the first thing to do? He saw three possible tactics.

Convince Kahn, using his persuasive power alone, to give the stone back to Émile.

It's probably naive to hope that a piece of work like Kahn has enough integrity to acknowledge his crime and accept to hand over an object of such value.

Threaten to expose his misconduct.

But what would stop Kahn from denying everything and suing me for slander? Émile could testify, but the word of some unknown Frenchie *wouldn't be worth much against that of a respected member of the university Establishment?*

Fight fire with fire, i.e. steal the object back.

The problem is that the stone is probably locked away in a safe and I'm no burglar, I have no links to the gangster world and I'd be unable to recruit a professional to do the job.

The more he mulled over the problem in his head, the more it seemed to him that the third option, although perilous, was the only viable one. He was glad that he didn't have to make such a decision alone and that he'd soon be able to share the burden with his friends at True Archaeology. And if everyone came to the same conclusion that stealing the stone from Kahn was the best solution, the presence of a police commissioner, Murphy, on their team would turn out to be a blessing! Having regained his serenity, Dorian, albeit without much enthusiasm, decided to head back to the congress. He had no choice, since he had to make a presentation in the evening at a symposium entitled *"Is there any archaeological evidence supporting alien presence on Earth? "* This would be the tenth time he would participate in such a debate and he could have recited his argument both by heart and in his sleep. This was a good thing, because he certainly had other things on his mind…

***

Dorian was relieved when, the following day, he was sitting in the first-class compartment on the train from Victoria Station to Oxford. Dorian preferred this means of transport to cars. On the one hand, his eyesight had decreased considerably in recent years and he was now rather afraid of driving; on the other hand, train journeys allowed him to read something light that didn't require any particular intellectual effort, unlike what he usually read. So, he leafed through a popular daily newspaper and had fun discovering the kind of gossip and news that regular people feasted on with delight. Of course, he found every possible and imaginable story about the English royal family, tales of dogs being run over, tips for keeping fit, and lots of articles on sports and show business… It was pathetic, a far cry from Sumer, from the gods and the origin of humanity… When he browsed through the classified ads, as he liked to do back when he was a student priest in order to find the basic necessities at the lowest prices, his attention was drawn to the number of people looking for au-pair girls.

That would be right up Kahn's street. Hire a young pretty foreigner, pay her pennies to take care of everything in the house and if possible get anything else out of her…

Lulled, as if hypnotized by the regular squeaks emitted by the carriages sliding over the rails, Dorian sank into half a sleep and began to daydream about the impact on the general public of the revelation of the existence of Émile's stone, and then of antediluvian vestiges in Antarctica:

If we find monuments that were precursors to the Egyptian pyramids, the Mesopotamian ziggurats and the Mayan temples, perfectly preserved mummies or writings illuminating the thoughts and activities of the first civilized beings, what a slap in the face it will be to official science! And what a fantastic opportunity will then open up for True Archaeology to come out of the shadows and be able to move its agenda forward. We would open humanity's eyes to its past and to all the mistakes made since the golden age. It might even bring about a surge of hope before the next apocalypse....

12

———

THE LAW OF TALION

When he got off the train at Oxford Station, Dorian was pleasantly surprised to see his friend Murphy waiting for him on the platform.

"So, has Isis appeared to you?" joked Murphy. "Did she talk to you in your sleep and tell you where to dig to find the Emerald Tables of Hermes or the Great Book of Thoth? If you've summoned us all urgently, something exceptional must have happened! So, tell me all about it!"

"Not Isis, but not far off!" replied Dorian, looking enigmatic. "Unfortunately, you'll have to wait because I'd rather not repeat the same story ten times. But I promise you, you won't be disappointed. In the meantime, talk to me. What's new in law enforcement?"

"It's the same as ever!" lamented Murphy. "An exponential increase in crime and a decrease in the resources made available to the police. It seems offenders are starting to get younger and younger and these days they are all champions when it comes to computers and new technologies, so my old cops who barely know how to use a mobile phone are completely out of it. Listen to this… I just caught a guy, barely twenty years old, who managed to extort several million just by hacking into a bank's computer system!"

"We live in interesting times!" sighed Dorian. "Technological advances are, in theory, supposed to make our lives easier, but we've found a way to turn everything into a nightmare. Modern man destroys everything he touches! But I bet it's nothing new: If we ever got our hands on the very first writings, I'm sure they'd tell of murders, rapes, robberies and every possible crime. The big question is: Where do all these failings come from? Are they related to our simian genes or are they of divine origin? When I say divine, I'm of course referring to the Anunaki, not to Jehovah…"

Murphy always remained silent when Dorian, whether it be a deep subject or an everyday conversation, rattled on with his endless philosophical rants. Fortunately, they quickly reached his car, parked just in front of the station, and the need to focus on driving and the dangers of the road relieved him of the need to elaborate on anything that he felt was totally beyond him. They arrived in a few minutes at The Manor where, even though Dorian had not yet revealed the purpose of the meeting, the excitement level was palpable. Edwina, Prosper, Dr. Louis and Alan Chamberlain suspected that Dorian would never have summoned them with such urgency if he had not had some extraordinary information to share with them. Dorian and Murphy found them in somewhat of a frenzy, glasses of Scotch in hand in the sitting room, trying to guess what Dorian might have learned at the archaeology conference.

Dorian was immediately besieged with questions. What happened at the European Congress of Archaeology? Did True Archaeology win the award for best presentation? Or is the existence of True Archaeology being threatened?

"Dear friends, calm down! Everyone take a seat, fill your glasses with more single malt and relax! What I have to tell you has nothing to do with what was said at the congress, where I certainly did my best with the presentation on behalf of True Archaeology, but where we unfortunately did not win any medal! Don't worry, the future of True Archaeology is not under threat. On the contrary, you're about to see that True Archaeology may be on the verge of achieving its main objective… But enough generalities with no substance, let me explain why I called you all here today. Here we go: It so happens that in London, I was visited by a man named Émile Delaporte, a nice enough Frenchman who read my books and watched me on Challenges. This is what Émile told me and I'm pretty sure that his story rings true: Last winter, he and his wife took a cruise to Antarctica. During a brief trip to the mainland, Émile picked up a piece of stone that he thought looked pretty odd. The black hue and the polish of the stone seemed off to him. Émile, who is not totally ignorant about archaeology and the history of ancient civilizations, believed that he could make out cuneiform characters engraved on the stone. So, he decided to take it home with him, in memory of his adventure at the end of the world. Back in France, Émile was able to examine his stone at leisure. He took pictures of it (I'll tell you later about these pictures for I've seen them) and he finally convinced himself that it could be a real antiquity, resembling, in a disturbing way, a fragment of some sort of Mesopotamian tablet. A few months later, quite by chance, the infamous Professor Samuel Kahn gave a lecture on Mesopotamia in the Delaportes' hometown. Émile thought it a good idea not only to attend this conference, but to show his stone to the speaker so that he could gain his expert insight. Kahn examined the object, appeared extremely disturbed by it and asked Émile to leave him the stone for further analysis, which the poor man naively went and did. Two months later, with no news from Kahn, Émile decided to send him a letter asking him to be so kind as to return the object. You'll never guess what Kahn sent this man! Well, instead of the original, Kahn returned a cheap resin imitation, accompanied by a laconic note stating that the stone had no archaeological value. To top it all off, Kahn had the audacity to have cuneiform characters engraved on the resin, the meaning of which, only accessible to an expert of Sumerian, is something along the lines of "fuck off". Émile noticed that the consistency of the object sent by Kahn was very different from that of his stone and, by comparing the signs engraved on the resin and the signs on his photos, he understood that it was nothing but a trick. Kahn obviously couldn't care less about him (which is quite the understatement). So, outraged and completely helpless, Émile wrote to me and I agreed to meet him. Let me now give you my conclusions and you can then share your own thoughts:

a) For me, Émile is not a forger… and his story is true.

b) According to the photos he showed me of his original stone, I believe Émile found an authentic fragment of a stele, at the latest from the early Sumerian period, but possibly dating back to before five thousand BC.

c) Kahn stole the stone and is fully aware of the priceless value of it and its significance. He refused to return the original to Émile and thought he'd fool him with some imitation in resin instead.

Before I stop, listen to your comments and answer your questions, let me really make myself clear here: I think that Émile has just discovered the evidence that civilized beings lived in Antarctica at least five thousand years ago and that this discovery is exactly the reason why True Archaeology was set up in the first place."

The True Archaeology team remained unvoiced for a moment. All were convinced that the story Dorian had just told them was no hoax, all felt that they were probably on the eve of some pretty extraordinary events, however none wanted to be overly optimistic and everyone was thinking about possible flaws in the story.

Prosper broke the silence first.

"What makes you think that this Émile isn't an obsessive liar? Assuming that his stone is indeed a fragment of an ancient stele, are you sure he really brought it back from Antarctica? And does this stone really exist? He could very well have photographed an artifact displayed in a museum! Maybe he's watched too many films, like Romancing the Stone and The Adventures of Indiana Jones?"

"Of course," Dorian replied, "I had the same suspicions before I met Émile. But, after seeing and listening to him, and although I don't claim to be an expert in psychiatry, I'm prepared to bet that Émile is a perfectly sane fellow and that he told me things as they really happened. Anyway, you're perfectly right to be cautious and one of the first things to do is to check that Émile and his wife did indeed take a cruise to Antarctica last winter. Murphy, maybe you could take care of that? It shouldn't be too difficult for a police commissioner!"

"No problem, I'll check that tomorrow," Murphy agreed. "I have another question though. If Professor Kahn has had the object in his hands for several months now and knows that it's a genuine find that he's refusing to return to its owner, why has he apparently not exploited it in any way so far? If, for example, he'd announced such a discovery at the congress, he'd have become a star overnight. But as far as I know, nothing of the sort happened."

"An excellent question that I also asked myself, but to which I still have no satisfactory answer" Dorian admitted. "I know this man and I think that, rather than seeking academic glory, which actually doesn't bring much in terms of cash, Kahn will find a way to exploit this in a much more profitable way. You should know that a few years ago, Kahn didn't think twice about selling his services to an oil company and writing a bogus report certifying the absence of ruins on a site in Iraq where this company was drilling oil wells. This man sacrificed the interests of the archaeological community and allowed the destruction of a site where I suspect one of the fabulous undiscovered Sumerian cities was buried, all for his own personal gain! Do you think a scoundrel like that would have the slightest qualms about selling the heritage of humanity to the highest bidder? I wouldn't be surprised if Kahn were negotiating a similar contract right now."

Alan Chamberlain, the treasurer of the True Archaeology, in his element now that the discussion had turned to big money, intervened at this point.

"The problem with an artifact found in Antarctica," he explained, "is that I'm not sure with which company Professor Kahn could negotiate a big check. As far as I know, Antarctica isn't anything like Iraq, where big companies are eager to exploit underground resources. I understand that Antarctica is an area protected by an international treaty, where no one can undertake oil drilling or dig any mines of any sort. And which museum or private collector would pay a handsome sum for an object whose provenance seems unlikely, to say the least?"

"My dear Alan," Dorian replied, "I'm not sure I share your optimism about protecting Antarctica from the ambitions of major industrial companies. It's true that an international treaty for the protection of Antarctica is in force, which formally prohibits any military activity on the continent. It's also true that a convention regulating the exploitation of Antarctic mineral resources has recently been signed by a number of states. But, on the one hand, I understand that not every country on the planet has yet ratified this convention. On the other hand, this convention allows scientific research activities, and this seems to me to have left the door open to a whole load of dubious practices under the guise of science. And I trust the big industrialists will find a way to get around a treaty as soon as they get a whiff of the smell of billions of dollars in profits."

Dr. Louis, who had remained silent during all these exchanges, now took the floor:

"I fully agree with Dorian about Émile's personality. Although I have not seen him, I can tell you, as a psychiatrist and for many reasons that it would be too tedious to explain now, that this case is certainly not myth mania. And so, I believe that Émile brought the stone from Antarctica and he actually showed Dorian pictures of it. I have no reason to doubt Dorian's expertise and accept without hesitation the fact that it is a very old stele fragment and therefore that the remains of the ancient primordial civilization, whose existence has always been affirmed by True Archaeology, currently lie asleep under the ice of Antarctica. I also believe that Kahn is a crook who'll seek to get a massive pile of cash for this piece. The logical conclusion is that it is the duty of True Archaeology to get that damn stone back. And this is where it gets complicated! How do you plan on getting this stone? Does True Archaeology have enough money to offer Kahn the price he wants? We're probably talking several million dollars. Or does True Archaeology intend to set up a commando-style operation to retrieve it?"

"My dear Louis," Dorian stated "I'm happy that you share my views on Émile and Kahn and very flattered that you trust me absolutely as far as my interpretation of this object is concerned. You think that the True Archaeology needs to get the stone back and I totally agree with you. But before discussing how we might proceed; I'd like to make sure that no one has any doubts about the solidity of this story and that everyone is convinced that we need to act on it. Prosper, Edwina, Alan and Bob, do you have any questions or objections?"

"If Dorian and Doctor Louis are absolutely certain that this Émile is not leading us on," Edwina said, "I think we need to get our hands on the stone. But I'm a little worried about having to steal it from Professor Kahn… Are you sure we couldn't just buy it from him?"

"If, as Doctor Louis thinks, we have to be prepared to hand over several million dollars, True Archaeology is quite incapable of doing so!" countered Alan Chamberlain. "As treasurer, I can assure you that the maximum that True Archaeology could offer, given its financial situation, is somewhere in the order of three hundred to five hundred thousand pounds… But perhaps the Tabellion family is ready to sell its castle for a good cause?"

"Let's be reasonable!" Dorian intervened. "I would find it absolutely immoral and indecent to give Kahn even five hundred euros as a reward for his crime! Even if Edwina were willing to sell her castle to make it easier for us, I would do everything in my power to stop her! Kahn is a thief and the application of the Jewish Law of Talion in his case seems perfectly appropriate to me. Don't Jews preach *eye for eye, tooth for tooth, hand for hand and foot for foot*?"

"Although a fervent Catholic," Prosper remarked, "I, like Dorian, am in favor of applying the law of retaliation in this case and I accept the risk of purgatory for this great sin! In fact, I'm willing to take every risk, except selling the castle of course. After all, we're unlikely to see such a promising avenue for True Archaeology for some time. So, if there is any hope that we can finally discover irrefutable evidence of the existence of Civilization X, we must go for it! In my opinion, the first essential step is to get Émile's stone, even if the only way to do so is to steal it from Kahn."

"Why are you all using the term stealing?" Murphy asked. "Let's not forget that the real thief is Kahn! To return the stone to its true owner is the right thing to do. Of course, ideally, we should follow the legal procedure, namely convince Émile to file charges for theft and then let the police and lawyers do their job. As a police commissioner, I'm supposed to recommend that you follow this procedure scrupulously… But as a member of True Archaeology, I can guarantee that if we follow this path, we can forget the stone, Civilization X and the archaeological discovery of the century! If we want speed and efficiency, our only option is to operate outside the system."

"Well," concluded Dorian, "I have the impression that we have a consensus, at least on the strategy. The first step for True Archaeology is to get the stone back. As for the tactical means to achieve this, we agree that buying it from Kahn is not an option, and it seems that we should resolve to take it from him. Does anyone have any other idea, besides bribing Kahn or organizing the break-in of the century?"

Faced with silence from his audience, Dorian continued.

"Am I entitled to conclude that everyone is voting for the Arsène Lupin method?"

They all looked at each other and nodded their heads as an acknowledgement.

"Once, twice, three times, sold! " Dorian concluded, turning to Murphy.

"Bob, I fear that True Archaeology will have to use your services once again... What action plan can the expert on organized crime recommend?"

"I already have an idea in mind..." Murphy replied with an air of mystery. "However, I think it's better if you all stay completely out of the loop and the less you know about the operation, the better. By the way, I hope it's obvious to everyone that nothing that has been said at this meeting should leave this room.... The only person I'll keep informed of the project will be Dorian."

"Thank you, my friend," said Dorian. "You're quite right to insist on the importance of keeping this discussion strictly confidential. I'm counting on you! Well, I think we can bring this meeting to an end. Thank you all for making yourself available so quickly. I hope you don't feel like you've wasted your time. Personally, my instinct tells me that we are about to set off on an exceptional adventure and that in the very near future we'll know what it must have felt like to be Howard Carter, Paul-Émile Botta, Austen Layard and all the others who've uncovered fabulous treasures and whose names have forever gone down in History!"

13

REDEMPTION

The next day, as agreed, Murphy verified that Émile and Monique Delaporte had indeed taken a cruise to Antarctica aboard the Thetis Adventurer last December. After also, without any difficulty, obtaining some details about Samuel Kahn's private life, in particular the address of his property in Wellesley, Massachusetts, Murphy made an appointment with Dorian in a pub to share with him his plan of how they'd get the stone back. Murphy had arranged to meet Dorian in a bistro, run by a retired police officer whose discretion he knew he could count on. When Dorian joined him, both had a pint of Guinness, and Murphy explained in a low voice how he might get his hands on the stone:

"Yesterday, when I picked you up at the station, I briefly told you about a young computer genius I had just busted for a series of scams. Well, I'm convinced he's the right person for this. He doesn't have a criminal record yet, so he'll be almost impossible to spot, unlike the other professionals I know. He has a proven track record of theft of all kinds. There aren't many safes that can get the better of him. He's no idiot. It would be a huge waste to send him to jail when his best years are ahead of him and, strangely enough, his participation in our operation would be a chance for him to get back on track. I intend to offer him the following contract: Either I send him to a judge to answer for his crimes and he gets ten years, or he agrees to do us a small favor and he stays as white as snow in the eyes of the law. I think this is the kind of very generous offer he's not in a position to refuse. This favor will consist in him spending a few days in Boston all expenses paid, in entering Kahn's house, in finding the stone and then in bringing it back to us. For a guy like him, it'll be a walk in the park, so between that and a jail sentence, he won't hesitate for a minute… For True Archaeology, there are no risks because I will be his only contact."

"Are you sure we're not about to set off a grenade that could blow up in our faces?" Dorian asked in a worried tone. "Are you sure your guy is reliable and able to do this without getting caught? If it goes wrong, I'd like to believe that True Archaeology will be safe, but are you sure you're not taking major risks for your career by getting into business with this man?"

"In the worst-case scenario," Murphy reassured him, "he could be arrested for burglary. He's English and so the FBI would contact me. I would have him repatriated to England and one botched burglary wouldn't really make a big difference to his legal situation. But quite honestly, as I know him, I think the risk of him getting caught is virtually nil."

"Well, if you're confident and willing to take on this responsibility, I have no objection. How will we proceed?"

"This very evening, I'm going to put our offer to Kevin (that's his name). Personally, I think I know enough about the purpose of the mission and, until there is a successful outcome, there will be no further discussion on this subject with our friends at True Archaeology… for safety's sake. I'll keep you informed discreetly, but it might not even be necessary. I'll simply ask you, once you have the stone in your possession, to reimburse me my expenses, which should be around ten thousand pounds."

Dorian and Murphy toasted as they finished their Guinness, exchanging banalities unrelated to True Archaeology before leaving the restaurant separately. Murphy immediately made his way to his police station, where the young offender awaited, in whose hands the future of True Archaeology would rest…

***

Kevin McKee was born in Oxfordshire twenty years earlier, to a father of Irish origin and a Scottish mother. His father, a bus driver, was a violent alcoholic - a real brute. The mother, initially a waitress in a pub, had fallen into drug addiction and regularly prostituted herself to pay for the ever-increasing doses she needed. Eventually, the traces of cigarette burns and bruises regularly visible on Kevin's little body attracted his teacher's attention and social services concluded that the child's physical and mental health would be threatened if he were to continue to be raised by such degenerates. Kevin was therefore taken from his family at the age of six and placed in care home. The child did not seem to suffer unduly from this separation, quite the contrary in fact. Once fed, properly dressed and freed from the abuse once inflicted by his parents, young Kevin became a handsome little blond boy who posed no concern to anyone. He certainly was very lonely, never participating in the team games and sports for which the other children were major fans. At the home, one of the supervisors had noticed that Kevin was often plagued by episodes of night terrors, which were frequent at the beginning of his internment, especially when the holiday periods such as Easter or Christmas were approaching. But it seemed quite natural for a child separated from his family and in need of maternal affection. His teachers also knew that Kevin often locked himself in the toilet to cry during recess, but a few comforting words were enough to make everything right again. In fact, the most common note written in the institution's files and school records were: *A gentle, calm and remarkably intelligent child.*

He was undoubtedly smart, since throughout his early school years he'd come top of his class almost every semester. So much so that the school principal helped him gain entrance to an excellent high school for his secondary education, where his intellectual gifts were confirmed. Kevin was interested in everything from literature to physics, chemistry and mathematics. He retained everything, without the need for long hours of revision and he understood things with an ease that impressed his teachers.

His educators and high school teachers were convinced that he was a good boy. Kevin knew how to have them succumb to his charms.

It must be said that with his beautiful wavy blond hair that he wore half-long and his green eyes and his lovely smile, it was hard not to find him charming. The few high school friends Kevin had deemed worthy of hanging out with also found him to be a nice person. On the other hand, the victims of the multiple petty thefts he began to commit discreetly in the tenth grade would probably not have called Kevin "nice"… Indeed, as soon as he was able to escape the supervision of his teachers and the staff in the home, Kevin turned into a kind of Janus with a double face, half angel, half demon. Kevin was very passionate about computers. He loved what the Internet allowed him to do illicitly and in complete discretion from the solitude of his room. He started by copying pornographic videos, which he managed to get for free on certain websites, to sell them to his acquaintances. He then learned to find and collect confidential information about the students in his school and their family members. As soon as he found any kind of compromising story, he blackmailed the person concerned, threatening to expose the embarrassing information if he or she didn't pay up. The amount, proportional to the seriousness of the case, could in the most serious cases reach thousands of pounds… Kevin quickly built up a hefty sum, which he decided, at the age of fourteen, to invest in drug dealing. He'd found a way to hide things behind an air vent in the ceiling of his room. He accumulated bars of hashish, bags of cocaine and countless ecstasy tablets, of which he became the exclusive supplier for half the students in his high school. He himself never touched a single one of these poisons. No doubt the memory of his mother's downfall was still firmly rooted in his memory and the prospect of ending up in the same boat was terrifying enough to keep the desire at bay. Operating his thriving small business didn't prevent him from continuing to deepen his computer expertise and mastery of programming, browsing the Dark Web and perfecting his piracy skills.

Despite his clandestine activities, Kevin maintained his status as an exemplary student throughout his high school education, accumulating top marks in almost every subject. So much so that the headmaster facilitated Kevin's obtaining a state scholarship so that he could pursue undergraduate studies at the prestigious Oxford University. Kevin chose archaeology as his discipline.

At Oxford, Kevin suddenly became aware of his origins and social status, concepts that had never bothered him too much in previous years. Almost everyone around him at the university was from the aristocracy or the upper class. They all drove in luxury cars, dressed at the best tailors in Savile Row in London and spent their money without having to count it. These pretentious and arrogant people made it clear to Kevin that he and they didn't belong to the same world and Kevin found himself more alone than ever. At best no one dared to speak to him, at worst, he was openly mocked as being a pariah without title and without fortune. His isolation reinforced his passion for computers and his interest in the clandestine activities he could carry out alone in front of his screen. His only friends were online. Thanks to his laptop, he would take revenge for the humiliations inflicted by his university colleagues, whose credit cards and bank accounts he fraudulently used. Kevin also further developed his small drug business, whose revenues, combined with the fruits of his electronic petty theft, allowed him to somewhat bridge the gap between him and other students in terms of financial comfort. The sale of coke brought him the intense satisfaction of seeing these daddy's boys sink into addiction and pay him a magnificent price for the dope they ended up begging him to provide. As he was about to finish his first year at Oxford, Kevin was invited to a party by a client-student and heavy cocaine user who wanted his guests to enjoy some of the good stuff. It turned out that this boy was the youngest son of a Lord, an Earl related to the Royal Family of England. The son had taken advantage of his family's stay in their villa in Mustique to organize a memorable party in the family castle in Oxfordshire. While the party was in full swing, Kevin took advantage of the general intoxication to break into the lord's office, where he found a safe, the combination of which he discovered without major difficulty, and a computer, the secret code of which he had no difficulty in identifying. Not only did Kevin relieve the owner of the bag of gold coins in the safe, but he carefully recorded all the personal information he could find on the computer that would later allow him to reduce the Earl's bank account by a few hundred thousand pounds. Suddenly rich, Kevin simply failed to resist the temptation to show ostensibly that he was not as cheap as the other students thought he was, and decided to buy himself a sports car as flashy as that of the Oxford aristocrats: A convertible Morgan in red. It was this *faux-pas* that landed Kevin in Murphy's office.

It had not been too difficult for Murphy, who was in charge of investigating the theft from the Earl's home, to identify Kevin as his number one suspect: The Earl's son had mentioned Kevin as being one of the more dubious guests at his party; Kevin's faculty chums reported his recent and surprising change of style, brutally turning him from a penniless barefoot to a loaded playboy. By carefully studying the young man's online activities and the identity of the holder of a number of suspicious bank accounts, Murphy had gathered enough evidence to be certain that Kevin McKee was not the uneventful bright student that everyone thought he was, but that he was in fact an accomplished con man. Murphy had him arrested one morning before classes started and placed in custody. Back at the police station after his discussion with Dorian Green, Murphy asked that the young McKee, who had been locked in a cell since that morning, be brought into his office. A policeman took Kevin, handcuffed, into the commissioner's office and asked if he should un-cuff the prisoner and stay to witness the interview. The commissioner replied that none of that would be necessary and the policeman slipped away, leaving a Kevin handcuffed and sitting very uncomfortably in front of Murphy. The latter spoke in a chilling tone.

"I'm Commissioner Murphy. I suppose you know why you're here?"

"I have no idea!" replied Kevin, feigning innocence. "There has clearly been a misunderstanding."

"Look, kid," Murphy continued mercilessly, "I have enough evidence to put you inside for twenty years for theft, concealment of stolen property, drug dealing and other similar illegal activities. So, either you cooperate with me and maybe I can find you some extenuating circumstances and spare you, or you play dumb, deny everything and you'll be going down."

Kevin was surprised by the mixture of cold brutality and kindness he perceived in Murphy's manner and wondered how to react. He was outraged that the commissioner had called him a kid and been overly familiar with him, and for that reason alone, he was eager not to cooperate with him. But this guy was offering to spare him from a terrible fate, and this deserved consideration, particularly given the critical situation in which he found himself. Could he afford to deny what he was accused of? Perhaps Murphy was bluffing and had no proof yet. In that case, admitting to it would really be shooting himself in the foot… But if he had the evidence he needed, why was he offering to help him? Without removing his imperturbable mask, his mind quickly evaluated the different options and, unable to make a definitive choice, he tried to save some time:

"Perhaps you could be more specific about these illegal activities for which I am accused? What drugs? Trafficking? Do you mean importing drugs? What exactly am I accused of stealing?"

"With all due respect, it doesn't work that way," Murphy replied with a sly smile. "I ask the questions here, and I expect you to answer them honestly. You see, if you want me to help you, you'll have to show me that I can trust you. The first step is for you to tell me everything that has happened and then… ask forgiveness. Just know that I've carefully studied your background and that I'm not insensitive to the fact that you're a brilliant student, whereas your birth environment wasn't particularly favorable. I think it would be a shame to screw all that up because of a couple of mistakes."

"Am I not entitled to call a lawyer and to remain silent until advised?" asked Kevin.

"Indeed, you have the right to speak only in the presence of your lawyer," Murphy replied. "The problem with this option is that, for a lawyer to handle your case, I would have to fill out a charge file. Once officially charged, you'll be on the judicial circuit, and who knows what might happen to you… On the other hand, until I formally charge you, you remain clean."

"And what do I have to do for you to not charge me?" asked Kevin, seeing an opening.

"Firstly, you immediately return the small fortune you, let's say, temporarily borrowed. Secondly, you get rid of your drug stock and promise you'll stop with the dealing. Thirdly, you have to discreetly carry out a short mission for me. Let me reassure you. It's not a question of sending you to the wall, but of making the best use of your many talents; the mission is definitely delicate in nature, but with little in the way of danger, and in my opinion, between that and twenty years in prison, there is really not much choice."

"This whole thing seems completely off to me! I don't even understand why you have me in custody and now you're asking me to do your dirty work… Frankly, it all seems a bit weird."

"I see… I think it's best to leave it at that for today. Go back to your cell where you'll have all night to think about what I've said. Think carefully about the choices in front of you: Either you acknowledge your mistakes, make amends by accepting my conditions and take the unexpected chance that I'm offering you to get back on track, or you can plunge into a vicious circle of delinquency - indictment - trial - prison and basically your life is over… I will see you again first thing tomorrow morning and you can tell me your decision. Here's a book that might interest you, should you have trouble sleeping. You're studying archaeology, so you should enjoy it. Plus, it's linked to the mission to which I referred. See you tomorrow!"

Kevin, although encumbered by the handcuffs that were blocking him, managed to grab Murphy's book before being marched back to the cell where he was going to have to spend the night. Free from his handcuffs but confined in the narrow space almost entirely occupied by a bed and a toilet bowl, Kevin collapsed onto his mattress, distractedly threw the commissioner's book down onto the cover, grabbed his head with both hands and tried to think about the best way out of this mess. He, usually so in control of his emotions and able to calmly analyze most situations, now felt anxious and unable to think clearly. The first thing to do was to try to slow his heart rate down and overcome the fear that was confusing him and causing a tense feeling. He therefore settled into a yoga position, and, with the help of deep breaths in and forced exhalations, waited to regain a minimum of control over his body and mind. Thirty minutes of these exercises were enough to restore a feeling of almost normalcy and he began to develop a strategy.

It quickly became clear to Kevin that refusing to admit to the crimes he'd committed was not the best plan. He had not been arrested by accident. The commissioner certainly had evidence of his unlawful actions and stubbornly denying the facts would result in his being charged with a whole series of misdemeanors. He'd have to stand before a judge, face a more or less lengthy imprisonment, have a tarnished criminal record, receive a dismissal from university and he'd just have to forget about any future social ladder climbing.

So, he was going to keep a low profile and accept the offer, but not without some negotiation... He'd unconditionally agree to return his loot and stop things on the drug front, which wouldn't really be a problem for him. On the other hand, he would not volunteer for this famous mission until he had all the details and, above all, guarantees regarding his safety and chances of success. He picked up the book, which, according to the commissioner, contained some clues about the nature of the mission and decided to take a look at it. The title of the book was *Civilisation X* and the author was a man named Dorian Green, who was described in the preface as an ex- priest and former professor of archaeology at Oxford.

Kevin thought: *Interesting! If the mission has anything to do with what I'm studying at Oxford, maybe it's not such a bad plan...*

So, he started reading the book, which only an irrepressible need to sleep at around three in the morning forced him put down. What Green was saying in that book was absolutely fascinating. According to the author, modern day man was created by a very advanced humanoid species, through hybridization between primates and members of this superior species, in order to serve as domestic slave. The higher humanoid species established the first civilization and reached a very advanced degree of technological development. Their civilization spread all over the planet and all the great known ancient civilizations, such as those of Mesopotamia, Egypt, Asia and America, were mere offspring of it. Their technological advances would have enabled them to build these fabulous monuments whose remains are still visible but whose significance is no longer understood by anyone, such as the pyramids of Giza, the monuments of Tiwanacu and the statues of Easter Island.

Kevin was woken up with a start by the sound of the key rattling in the lock of his cell door, followed by the guard shouting out to him while handing over a scrap metal tray containing what he called breakfast. Having only slept for four hours, Kevin felt semi-comatose with aches and pains brought about by the hardness of the mattress he had just spent the night on. He drank a sip of what looked like coffee in the cup on the tray and almost choked on its bitter taste. He was tempted to bite into the piece of bread that accompanied this disgusting drink, but finally gave up for fear that the quality being equivalent to that of coffee. He'd just have to do without breakfast. To try to wake himself up a little, he walked over to the small sink and sprinkled cold water on his face. The commissioner had said he would see him again first thing this morning, so he'd have to do his best to be alert throughout this decisive interview. After a few yoga exercises that did an excellent job in bringing him round, Kevin repeated in his head the key sentences that might allow him to convince the commissioner of his good intentions:

Commissioner, quite surprisingly after the discomfort of the cell and the stress caused by the situation, last night went a long way to opening my eyes! I'm ready to take the opportunity you offered me yesterday. I must say that the book you lent me and that I devoured (much more avidly than the horrible breakfast served to me) fascinated me. The fact that you encouraged me to read such a masterpiece has convinced me that you're a good person in whom I can have complete confidence. So, I will hand back everything I've acquired illegally, and I promise you that I've learned my lesson and will never again engage in illegal activities. I've also agreed to give your famous mission a go.

However, before we proceed, I need some clarification on what, why, where, when and how? Above all, I'd be very grateful if you could release me asap.

Kevin didn't have to wait long. At eight sharp, the guard came to pick him up, handcuffed him and took him back to Murphy's office.

"So, young man, I hope your night here has given you some food for thought!" Murphy shouted cheerfully. "In any case, it gave you a taste of what to expect if you carry on with your ways... Have you managed to have a think about my proposal? What's your decision?"

Kevin was trembling, unable to repeat the tirade he'd prepared earlier. In any case, the little ironic reflections and humorous nuances were probably not really appropriate and so he chose to speak more soberly:

"Look, I think you're right and I'm willing to accept all your conditions. The only thing I ask is that you explain to me the objective and practical details of the mission, so that I can tell you whether or not I can accomplish it successfully."

"Good answer!" exclaimed Murphy with a broad smile. "You won't regret your decision! The mission you'll be entrusted with isn't really dangerous. In fact, once you know what it is, I think you'll thank me for it! It's a real gift! Here's how we're going to proceed. I'll release you, but if you wanted to take off and not honor your commitments, I'd have no difficulty finding you and my revenge would be beyond belief. You will meet me tonight at seven at the Old Tavern, where you'll bring me a sports bag with everything you stole from the Earl and where I'll arrange for you to meet someone who'll explain all the details of what you'll be doing. Have I made myself clear? I imagine you don't need a drawing and you can find the Old Tavern without difficulty?"

"It's all very clear," Kevin answered quickly. "Tonight at seven at the Old Tavern. Don't worry: I have no intention of letting you down. Do I have to sign anything?"

"The only thing I ask you to sign is this slip where you deny being the author of the facts that led to your arrest and where you certify that you were treated correctly during police custody. After that, you'll be as free as a bird... More or less..."

As soon as Kevin signed the document, Murphy called a guard

to release the accused from his handcuffs and escort him out of the building. Kevin thanked Murphy for his kindness, shook his hand and confirmed that he would do as agreed, before breathing a sigh of relief once out on the street.

Kevin enjoyed his day of freedom after the agony of police custody and the anguish before knowing what came next. He suddenly realized that things could have gone very wrong and that the risks he had taken so far with his clandestine activities were just not worth it. After all, he was lucky enough to be able to pursue higher education at one of the most prestigious universities and he was young, handsome and intelligent. He'd put his unhappy childhood and revengeful behavior behind him. He spent the morning strolling the streets of Oxford, had lunch in a trendy fish and chips bar that he found delicious after the terrible breakfast at the police station, then spent the afternoon in his room at the university getting ready for his evening appointment.

At precisely seven that evening, Kevin entered the crowded Old Tavern, looked around the room to try to spot Murphy and, not seeing him, approached the bar to ask for help from the guy who seemed to be the boss of the place.

"Yes, the commissioner is waiting for you, follow me," he told him without hesitation before leading him to a small table surrounded by high partitions, far away from the hustle and bustle of the main room. Murphy was sitting at the table with an older gentleman with a distinguished appearance that sharply contrasted with the style of the pub's clientele. Both had obviously just finished their dinner and were now on the brandy, as two half-full glasses sat on the table.

Murphy, upon seeing Kevin, addressed the second gentleman:

"Dorian, this is Kevin McKee, the young man I told you about."

The old man smiled at Kevin, reached out his hand and introduced himself:

"Dorian Green, nice to meet you. Please have a seat. My friend Murphy had told me of your dealings with the police and your willingness to do us a small favor in order to clear your tab."

Kevin stared at him, his mouth open. This old man was the author of the book that Murphy had made him read last night in his cell, he knew everything about his past and he seemed to be pulling the strings here. He turned to Murphy.

"Isn't Mr. Green the author of *Civilisation X*? Or is he one of your fellow police officers? What does he have to do with all this?"

"I understand that all this may still seem very mysterious," Murphy agreed. "The best thing is to let Dorian tell you who he is, what our relationship is and what we expect from you."

"Kevin," Dorian continued, "would you like something to drink? Some Armagnac, like us? Or something else? It will relax you and the story I'm about to tell you will seem less odd."

"Armagnac," Kevin accepted, "I have no idea what it's like, but this will be an opportunity to try it!"

While Murphy went to order the drink, Dorian undertook to enlighten Kevin about True Archaeology, his and Murphy's roles in the organization, the story of the tourist's discovery in Antarctica of some archaeological remains extremely important to True Archaeology and the theft of the artifact by an indelicate American archaeologist. He concluded his long monologue by explaining to Kevin that the famous mission that Murphy and he wanted him to do was to hop over to the USA, find the object at the American archaeologist's home and bring it back to True Archaeology.

"That's it!" concluded Dorian. "I think I've told you everything. What do you think? Do you feel up to it? Maybe you have some questions?"

"This is just incredible!" exclaimed Kevin. "It's like a James Bond movie or the Da Vinci Code novel! If you hadn't been Commissioner Murphy's friend and if I didn't know that you were an archaeologist and had published that remarkable book on Civilization X, I'd have thought you were delirious and wondered what you were trying to get me into! But I trust you and I'm delighted you asked for my help in getting this stone back. I don't think I'll have too many problems and I look forward to getting down to work! I'd like to know more about the practicalities. When do you want me to leave? Where exactly am I going? Who am I stealing from? What about my travel expenses?"

"Commissioner Murphy will fill you in on all that," Dorian said. "He'll supervise you throughout your mission. As for me, until you return to Oxford with the stone, I'll be staying out of it. Do not try to contact me before your return. Not under any circumstances. And if anyone asks you anything, please pretend this conversation never took place. You never met me. With that, I'll let you continue the discussion with the commissioner, and I'll slip away. See you soon and best of luck!"

After saying his goodbyes to Murphy, Dorian walked out of the pub, leaving Kevin and Murphy alone.

"I hope you're reassured" Murphy continued. "As you can imagine, Professor Green isn't a common thief and getting back the stone is more about justice than mischief. The real thief in this case is the American archaeologist! So, you see that what we're asking you to do isn't too shocking."

"That's the way I see it," Kevin confirmed. "I'd like to leave as soon as I can. I'm feeling fairly motivated. When are you going to give me the name and address of the man who has it? How much time do I have to assess the site and surroundings?"

"The guy's name is Samuel Kahn; he works as a professor of archaeology at Harvard in Boston. He lives in the suburbs of Boston, in Wellesley to be exact, where he has a large and beautiful house, probably protected by an alarm system but with no particular difficulty in terms of access. It's in a residential area with a few neighbors, all at a safe distance. He lives there with his wife, who runs a fashion store in Boston, and his two daughters, who attend a local private school. The Kahns have a dog, but not a Doberman or a German Shepherd, only a harmless little Yorkie. It should be noted that they have been employing an au-pair girl, a French woman, for the past few weeks, who is staying on site. It seems that this au-pair walks the dog in the neighborhood both morning and evening and takes the girls to and from school. I suggest you leave for Boston in three days. I'll book your flight tickets. Ten days there should be more than enough, and a room will be reserved for you in a Boston hotel. You'll also have a rental car at your disposal. You can spend a hundred dollars a day on food or whatever you need. I'll reimburse you as soon as you get back. Please keep all your receipts. Any questions? No? Well, you know where to find me if you need me. We'll meet again the day before your departure, same place, same time, so I can give you your travel documents and a final briefing. This is all up to you now! Enjoy your evening and see you in two days."

14

A SIGN OF MARDUK

Kate was a little bored au-pairing for this American family. Not that the Kahns were unpleasant… She actually saw very little of them. The father had a big job at Harvard, spent long hours at university and traveled a lot. The mother owned a clothes boutique in Boston and was rarely at home. Their two little girls spent most of their time in school. Kate's job wasn't very demanding… She was to accompany the girls to the school bus stop at eight thirty in the morning and pick them up at three in the afternoon. As soon as they were back home, she had to give them a snack and then make sure that they did their schoolwork in their rooms quietly until Dana, the mother, arrived around six. She was also in charge of taking the dog, an adorable little Yorkshire terrier named Marduk, for a walk in the nature reserve near the house morning and afternoon. Other than that, nothing else was really mandatory. Dana had sometimes asked her if she didn't mind ironing a few things, but she hadn't asked again since she'd burned the husband's shirts. Every now and again, Dana asked her to go shopping in the village. The husband, Samuel, never asked her for a single thing. Apparently, he barely knew she existed… Kate had thought that her stay in the United States would allow her to perfect her English, but paradoxically, with this job with the Kahns, she actually felt like she was regressing. The idle chattering of the two little girls and the pidgin-English spoken by the local Mexican maids were hardly going to help her progress… Rather than the language of Shakespeare, she had only learned some basic Spanish at the school bus stop with Maria Rodriguez, Conchita Sanchez and Dolores Lopez, who all worked in neighboring houses. So, she was delighted to be able, one day while playing with Marduk, to engage in conversation with a charming young man who had come to jog around the lake on the reserve.

When Marduk, in pursuit of the ball that Kate had clumsily thrown at him, barged under the man's feet bringing him to an abrupt standstill, he approached Kate, who was horribly embarrassed, and reassured her that the dog had not bothered him at all and took the opportunity to introduce himself. His name was Kevin, he was English, studied archaeology at Oxford and was in Boston on a university exchange program.

"It's funny, my boss is a professor of archaeology at Harvard, no doubt you know him?" Kate, surprised by the coincidence, replied. "It's Professor Kahn."

"The name rings a bell, but I can't say I know him," Kevin admitted. "You know, I just arrived in Boston and I haven't met many people here yet. But, tell me... Aren't you French? I think I can hear a very slight accent?"

"Please don't make fun of my accent! I know very well that it is not a slight accent in the least, and it's to try to lose it that I'm currently living here. You're right. I am French."

"Ah, I love France. What the hell are you doing in Massachusetts? Don't tell me you're also studying archaeology at Harvard with Professor Kahn?"

"Unfortunately, not. When I say that Professor Kahn is my boss, it's because I work at his house as an au-pair. You see, little Marduk here is his dog, and my job is to walk him."

"I understand! And are you enjoying it? Do you have any friends here?"

"I only half like this job, but it's not too bad. So far, I haven't made any friends, but I don't mind. Friends, going out, it's not really my style."

"But maybe you could make an exception? Like you, I'm a foreigner here and I don't have any friends either. It would be nice if we could meet up some time."

"Why not? But you must be busy during the day, with your university internship. We'll see… Anyway, if you're interested, you know where to find me. I walk the dog here every day at the same time! Well, I have to get going now. Very nice to have met you! Maybe I'll see you around!"

The next day, Kevin was waiting for Kate in the reserve, at the same time. Kate was rather flattered to find that this young man was probably not insensitive to her charms and was obviously eager to develop their relationship. And he seemed really nice. Smiling, humorous and well-mannered. Kate was happy to be able to speak with him in English; without feeling any real sentimental impulse towards him, she found that their meeting created a pleasant diversion from the dull monotony of her daily life. For three days in a row, Kevin came to see Kate in the afternoon during the dog's walk. Marduk had quickly adopted Kevin as his favorite playmate.

On the fourth day, as Kate was about to leave Kevin after Marduk's walk to go home, Kevin told her that he would like her to show him where she lived, so he could learn a little more about her and her way of life. Kate refused at first, arguing that the Kahns had forbidden her from bringing anyone into their house in their absence. At Kevin's insistence, she initially agreed to let him take her home, but said she couldn't let him inside the house. By the time they'd made the short trip from the reserve to the house, Kevin had succeeded in convincing Kate that she could safely show him around her room, that the Kahns would never know and that after all she had a right to live her life as she wished…

Kevin expected Kate, after unlocking the front door, to hurry to disable the alarm system and was surprised that this was not the case.

"Is there no alarm system in this house?" asked Kevin in a surprised way.

"Actually, there is," Kate replied in a carefree manner, "but I never activate it when I'm alone nor when I go for a walk with the dog or pick up the girls after school. I'm too scared of making a mistake with the code, setting off the alarm and then having to explain myself to the security guards or the police. Anyway, this is a very safe area, and nothing ever happens around here."

"You're right," Kevin said, laughing inwardly. "Americans are completely paranoid with their security. In England, there are no alarms in houses and people don't even lock their doors half the time."

Kate let Kevin into the Kahn's empty house and he followed her up to her room on the first floor. The bedroom, covered with a pretty *toile de Jouy* wallpaper in pink tones, wasn't particularly big and its furnishings rather Spartan: a bed, a shelf, a desk with a lamp and a chair. On the shelf, about twelve French paperbacks were lined up between two bookends of the Eiffel Tower and the Arc de Triomphe, and there was one photograph, a black and white portrait of a middle-aged man, in a dark wooden frame.

"Here it is!" said Kate. "This is my room. Now you know all about me!"

Kevin scanned the room with his eyes before lingering on the objects on the shelf.

"It's a nice room. It's pretty well decorated. Who's the man in the picture?"

"He's my father, the only person I really love. I always take his picture with me when I travel. When I look at his picture, I feel less alone."

"I see you're a great intellectual who never goes anywhere without her book collection," Kevin noted as he inspected the titles on the shelf. "I guess reading is your favorite hobby?"

"You're a fine psychologist, I can't hide anything from you! Indeed, reading is my passion. There are a few books, like *Le Petit Prince* by *Saint Exupery*, which I always pack in my luggage; I know it almost by heart."

"We have that in common. I like to read too. But I don't think I've read any of these. I would have asked you to lend me some, but since I'm not good at reading French, there'd be no point."

Kate had sat on the bed in silence. Kevin, not finding much more to comment on in the room, came to sit on the bed next to her. Suddenly, Kevin leaned in toward Kate and kissed her. Kate, without showing any particular enthusiasm, didn't reject this advance. While continuing to kiss her, Kevin cupped her breasts and then, met with Kate's lack of resistance, began to unbutton the tight jeans she was wearing. Kate gently pushed back the hand that was now creeping into her panties and blushed.

"No, I can't. Not right away…"

Kevin realized that Kate was probably a virgin, which made him even more excited.

This mission is definitely far from unpleasant, he thought, patiently continuing his exploration of the girl's anatomy, without paying the slightest attention to her weak protests.

Kate, alone in a foreign country and far from her family, felt incapable of seriously opposing Kevin's desire. Although she didn't really feel any physical attraction for Kevin, she decided to let him go ahead, as she thought:

I can't stay a virgin all my life… waiting for love at first sight. It'll probably never happen. Kevin is quite nice and quite personable… I'll just let him do it…

In a way, Kate, who had come to terms with the idea that she was going to lose her virginity, was quite disappointed when Kevin suddenly stopped stroking her. He had just decided that before losing control of his impulses, it was time to return to his mission, which was not to deflower a virgin but to find an object of great value in Professor Kahn's home. As Kate seemed confused, Kevin talked to her in a very gentle tone.

"Why don't you show me around the house?"

"If you want," Kate conceded without much enthusiasm. "It's pretty big, where do you want to start? The billiards room on this floor or the gym on the ground floor?"

"Let's start with the billiards room. Is it a pathetic American pool table or a real English one?

"Is there a difference?" Kate wondered aloud.

"Of course! Just as there's a difference between the excellent real British whiskey made from Scottish oats and the pitiful fake American whiskey made from corn in Kentucky!"

Kate, now fully dressed and more or less recovered from her emotions, accompanied Kevin into a large room at the end of a hallway with a huge billiards table, which Kevin confirmed was indeed an American pool table.

"As you can see," commented Kate, "there's also a beautiful bar... and it's very well stocked with every type of alcohol you could imagine. Would you like to join me for a while in one of the big leather chairs?"

"I'd rather not. It's too tempting! I'm afraid, if I settle down, I'll enjoy more than my fair share of their impressive collection of bottles and still be here tonight when the Kahns get back home. Isn't there a less dangerous room in this house, like a library?"

""Yes, of course, but it's on the ground floor. If you've seen enough on this floor, we can go explore down there."

Kate and Kevin went down the stairs and crossed a vast, well-equipped kitchen and a large, richly furnished living room to reach a double solid oak door that Kate opened.

"This is where Professor Kahn works," Kate said, "and it's where Mrs. Kahn gives me my pay once a week. I always have to count it again because she systematically pretends to get it wrong and always tries to cut my salary by a good whack! I have to confront her every time. She then acts surprised and hurries to open the safe behind this painting. I think she does it just to show me that they have a safe and remind me how rich they are. She doesn't even make sure I'm not looking when she types in the code. It's the dog's name! How stupid can you get?"

Kevin couldn't believe this! He knew little Marduk well after their visits in the park together. The Kahns were naive enough to have made one of the most frequent mistakes made by people when it came to codes and passwords: They'd chosen the name of their pet! Between that and Kate not activating the alarm system when she was leaving, the alignment of the planets could not have been more favorable. His mission, so far so easy, could well prove to be more than that... Kevin pretended to completely disregard the safe and the secret code and made as if he were inspecting the many books that lined the walls of the office. Most of them were on the subject of ancient civilizations and their archaeological remains.

"I read most of these books as part of my studies," Kevin confided, "but unfortunately in much less prestigious editions than these… This book, for example, is a rare print of the original edition: It's Paul Botta's book on the discovery of the monuments of Nineveh. It's worth a fortune!"

"I'm sure there's enough in this room to make an archaeology student happy! But if you want to visit the rest of the house, you'll have to hurry things up in here because I'm going to have to pick up the girls soon."

"You're right. I wouldn't want to cause you any problems. I should just go back to my hotel."

He then hugged Kate and kissed her again on the lips; "OK I'm leaving. I've had a fabulous afternoon! I'll come back to see you tomorrow at the park, as usual. "

On the way back to his hotel, Kevin was thinking about the best way to get back into the Kahn house and explore the contents of the safe. The easiest way would be to try to do it the following afternoon, immediately after Kate went out for a walk. Normally, the house would be unoccupied, with the girls at school, the father at university and the mother at her shop. If the stone was not in the safe it would give him almost an hour to explore other places where Kahn could have stashed it. If, as expected, he found the stone in the safe, he would have completed his mission in less than a week. There was one thing that concerned him: Kate…

In theory, fulfilling his mission would require that once the stone was in his hands, he'd jump on the first available plane to London. But disappearing and abandoning Kate so abruptly without any explanation bothered him. Kevin had fallen for this adorable French girl and dreamed of completing an important task for which she was most willing: Taking her virginity! He couldn't miss his chance here. As soon as he had the stone in his possession, he would go to meet Kate at the reserve and ask her back to his hotel where he would stay another night.

The next day, Kevin went to park his rental Camry around a quarter to two in the afternoon about a hundred yards from the Kahn residence. As usual, exactly at two, Kate left the house and headed for the reserve; strangely enough, little Marduk was not with her… Kevin wondered if, given this anomaly, it was prudent for him to enter the Kahns house but decided to go ahead anyway. He waited until he could no longer see Kate's figure at the end of the street, jumped out of his car, walked to the Kahn house and then, after making sure no one was watching him, hopped over the low wooden fence that enclosed the yard. When he came to the French window through which he spotted a huge cardio-training machine, dumbbells and other weight machines, he thought back to Kate's remark about the gym on the ground floor. He quickly grabbed one of the two large flowerpots at his feet, threw it violently at the glass, which burst under the impact, and unlocked the door by passing his hand through the broken glass. He prayed that Kate, as usual, would not have activated the alarm system on her way out and was relieved that no loud noises sounded out as the glass shattered… Quickly, he walked down the hall from the gym, recognized the living room opening onto the kitchen that he'd briefly visited the day before and the door leading to the office. He entered it and rushed towards the painting behind which Kate had told him that the safe was located. Once the board was unhooked, he typed MARDUK on the keyboard and turned the lever, praying that the name of the little terrier would indeed be the right code. He breathed a deep sigh of relief when the door opened and couldn't contain a cry of joy when he discovered, sitting there alone in the center of one of the shelves, the famous black stone he'd so hoped for. He carefully grabbed the object, slipped it into the padded case he'd brought, inserted the whole thing into his backpack, closed the safe, replaced the painting and left the house as he'd entered it. After putting the backpack in the trunk, he started his car and headed for the nature reserve. When he arrived at the reserve parking lot and was about to join Kate by the lake, he thought that the Kahns would surely hold the poor girl responsible, if not for the robbery itself, then at least for not activating the alarm. He absolutely had to find a way to get her out of this mess…

15

MANIPULATION

When Kevin reached the lake, he saw Kate sitting alone on a bench. *She's really pretty,* he thought. *I can't just leave her like that. I have to invent something and convince her to come with me to Oxford…*

Kate saw him in the distance, waved at him, smiling brightly and rushed to join him.

"I almost didn't come today" she told Kevin. "The Kahns left for the weekend to go see their parents in Sea Girt, New Jersey. They offered to take me with them, but I thought of you and our usual appointment; since I couldn't reach you, I turned down their proposal and told them that I'd rather take care of the house while they were away."

"That's great! You're free as a bird! We can get to know each other better" Kevin exclaimed, pulling in the girl to kiss her.

Kate responded to his kiss with more enthusiasm than the day before and Kevin felt an overwhelming desire to make love to her.

"How about coming down to my suite at the Hilton Downtown? Then we could go for a walk in Boston and then have dinner in a nice restaurant."

"That's a very good idea," Kate replied with a radiant smile. "You won't believe me but, since I've been here, I've never even visited Boston!"

"Right, well, let's go," Kevin said. "My car is parked nearby."

It only took Kevin thirty minutes to get from Wellesley to his hotel in downtown Boston. "You'll see, it's not luxurious but it's quite spacious," he told Kate as he opened the door to his room. "Come in!"

Kate took a quick look at the place which was furnished in a very functional and unattractive way, walked towards the window and quickly turned away from it after seeing that the view of gloomy buildings below was of no interest. She dropped down on the little couch.

"Would you like a glass of Chardonnay?" Kevin asked her.

"A glass of what?" Kate replied with a bewildered frown on her brow.

"Chardonnay," Kevin repeated. "That's how they talk about wine in the United States. It is not like back home, where we mention the region like Bordeaux, or the area like Médoc or better still the production domain like Château Margaux. Here, they only mention the grape variety, as if that's all wine is about! That being said, I think their California Chardonnays are drinkable! Do you want a taste?"

Kevin took out half a bottle from the mini bar and filled two glasses, one of which he handed to Kate.

"Cheers! It's an Anglo-Saxon custom. We have to clink our glasses together and look one another in the eye, it's supposed to bring good luck!"

"Yes, thank you, I know. The French usually say *Santé*. In my region, Lorraine, we say *Prost*, like the Germans. In Scandinavia, they say *Skol*."

They toasted and swallowed a sip of Californian Chardonnay.

"Do you like it?" asked Kevin.

"Not bad," Kate replied without much conviction, "but it's nothing like my father's Meursault."

Kevin downed the rest of his wine in one, took the glass from Kate's hand and put it on the pedestal table, before hugging the girl and moving his lips to hers. He was almost surprised to feel her mouth open and her tongue seeking out his own. At the end of their lengthy kiss, Kevin dragged Kate onto the bed, undressed her, started out by nibbling on the tip of her nipples and then ventured down her belly with his tongue. He felt Kate shivering under his caresses and in turn undressed, his stiff penis now standing to attention under Kate's gaze, in which he could see a shadow of concern. Kevin realized that Kate had never had sex before and decided not to rush her. He lay down against her and waited for her to get used to the contact of his penis, first against her thigh and then in her hand. When he felt she was ready, he penetrated her gently, started a slow back and forth movement inside her, making sure that she felt no pain, and finally allowed himself to ejaculate only after she had made a small rasp of satisfaction. Kevin withdrew, lay on his back next to her and took her hand.

"Are you all right?"

"Yes, I'm very happy," Kate whispered.

They remained silent on the bed. Kevin thought about how he needed to return to Oxford without delay but was finding it hard to imagine leaving this young girl, to whom he was now very attached, in Boston. Kate was thinking about the delicious sensations she had just experienced, wondering if it was possible that such sensations could arise in the absence of any feelings of love. Before this carnal adventure, the idea that she might have fallen in love with Kevin had never crossed her mind. Suddenly, she was now convinced that they must in fact be in love with one another.

Kate would have liked to be able to prolong her sweet reverie indefinitely, but a discreet pain in her lower abdomen accompanied by a strong urge to urinate forced her to get up and head to the bathroom. Locked in the bathroom, she washed her vagina, which was burning a little and noticed a reddish stain on the washcloth. *That's it,* she thought, *I'm not a virgin anymore! Having sex isn't that big a deal when it comes down to it… It went quite well, much better than I feared.*

Kate and Kevin got dressed and agreed to go for a walk in Boston before heading out for dinner somewhere. They reached Boyslton Street, which they strolled along up to Boston Park. They browsed the storefront windows, walked around the small lake and then carried on to the harbour and the waterfront. Kevin, who felt stimulated after walking in the cold and windy air and who seemed fascinated by the story of the Tea Party and the leaders of the American independence struggle, would have continued to Paul Revere's house and the cobbled streets of old Boston, but Kate was exhausted and, although it was still early, she begged him to take her instead to dinner in a seafood restaurant. Kevin gladly accepted, having seen a Legal Sea Foods a few minutes earlier, a restaurant very popular with Bostonians and renowned for the freshness of its produce.

"The really nice thing about the USA is that you don't have to wait until late at night like in France or worse in Spain to have dinner," he said. It was only five thirty and they had no trouble getting a comfortable table at Legal Sea Foods and getting a dozen huge clams as an appetizer, then a grilled lobster, all accompanied by an excellent bottle of Sauvignon. Kate was thrilled. The setting was pleasant, rather classy but sober and unpretentious, the service was impeccable, fast and attentive, and above all the dishes themselves were delicious. At the end of the meal, after having declined the dessert suggestions given by the waiter, Kevin discreetly paid the bill.

"It's been a long time since I've had such a delicious lobster! And the clams, they were phenomenal! Excellent choice! We'll have to come back!" Kate said.

"I'd never been to Legal Sea Foods before, but this restaurant was highly recommended by the hotel staff," Kevin explained proudly. "I must admit, it was fantastic! Well, what shall we do now? Would you like to spend the night with me in my hotel?"

"I would…" Kate apologized, "but I left all my things in my room back in Wellesley. I'd like to change, so I'd rather you take me back to the Kahns house, if you don't mind. We can meet again tomorrow if you want and I can then spend the night at the hotel with you. I can pack a bag."

"OK. No problem," Kevin assured her. "But you have to promise me you'll be there tomorrow!"

"I swear!" Kate assured him enthusiastically. "It's great that the Kahns are away in New Jersey. I don't know how we're going to manage this when they get back."

After escorting Kate back to Wellesley and returning to his hotel room, Kevin spent much of the night thinking about the situation he was now in. Now that he'd recovered the stone, he shouldn't stay in Boston too long. By staying longer, he would be exposing himself to the risk that the robbery of the Kahns house would be investigated by the police and that it would lead them immediately to Kate and therefore to him. For the success of the mission, and for his own safety, it was therefore imperative that he return to England as soon as possible. However, he'd promised Kate that he'd join her in a few hours, and it was out of the question not to honor this. Beyond this next meeting, he'd have to leave and there was nothing he could do about that. He had to convince her to go with him to Oxford. What could possibly make her decide her to leave with him, without giving the Kahns due notice? Kevin had no doubt that Kate would be ready to follow him at some point: He had taken her virginity, and, like almost every woman with her first lover, she must have felt a close attachment to him, for now at least. But how could he justify an almost immediate departure? Kevin didn't think this girl was madly in love with him to the point of blindly following him anywhere and anyhow without the slightest hesitation. The best thing was to invoke a major cause. And what could be better than hospitalization of a loved one… It was decided: He would explain to Kate that he'd just learned that his mother had been admitted to intensive care following a stroke, that the doctors were very concerned about her chances of survival and that he was forced to return to Oxford urgently; he would tell her that he loved her, that he didn't want to leave her and that he wanted her to go with him. After eliminating all the other options he could think of, Kevin decided that he would call Commissioner Murphy as soon as he woke up to inform him of his return, in possession of the stone but also accompanied by Kate, and to ask him to arrange their accommodation in decent conditions upon their arrival. Satisfied with his plan, Kevin let himself slip into a deep sleep, studded with erotic dreams about Kate.

***

Commissioner Murphy was both delighted with the excellent news Kevin had given him about the recovery of the stone but also perplexed and even annoyed at the announcement that a young girl would be coming back with him to Oxford.

"Look Kevin," Murphy said in an embarrassed tone, "you certainly did a very good job. But bringing back some chick was absolutely not part of the plan. Why do you feel compelled to bring her back with you? It's an added complication…"

"I would like to point out that without this girl, your stone would still be locked away in Kahn's safe! The least we can do is showing her a minimum of appreciation. If she stays in her job as an au-pair with the Kahns, she may get into a lot of trouble when they find out they've been broken into. It would be disgusting to allow Kate to be blamed for this. Plus, through her, they could be traced back to me and therefore to True Archaeology. Also, to tell you the truth, I think I've fallen in love with this girl and I don't want to go back to England without her."

"Ah I see!" Murphy said. "You couldn't help mixing business with pleasure! And what are you going to do with the little bit when you get home?"

"That's where I'll need your help," Kevin replied. "I had to tell her that my mother was dying to convince her to jump on the first plane with me and leave her job at the Khans' place without giving notice. So be careful to stick to the story when you meet her… Also, we'll need a place to stay, at least temporarily, while I find suitable accommodation for us."

"Well, of course!" Murphy shouted. "You've got some nerve, haven't you? I'll see what I can do, but don't think I'm going to be your caretaker from now on! Anyway, the important thing is that you get the stone back to us as soon as possible. Keep me informed when you know your flight references and arrival time at Heathrow. I'll come and pick you up. Right, I have to go now. I have work to do. See you soon and congratulations on this great outcome!"

Kevin hung up and let out a sigh of relief and satisfaction for the call had gone better than expected. Now all he had to do was to convince Kate…

He went to meet Kate at the reserve at the usual time. She flung her arms around his neck as soon as she saw him, and they kissed lovingly. Kevin then put on a sorrowful expression as he spoke softly to her:

"I have some very bad news. I've just found out that my mother has been taken into hospital. She had a stroke and the doctors are not sure she'll survive… So, I have to get back to Oxford as soon as possible."

"Oh no!" Kate said, looking distressed. "I'm so sorry! When do you plan to leave? And when will you be back?"

"I'm going to take the first flight tomorrow" Kevin replied, feigning great sadness. "I don't think I'm coming back to Boston. I was only doing a short internship here, so I have no reason to come back to be honest."

"But then, does that mean we won't see each other again?" asked Kate in a voice tinged with sincere disappointment. "Life really does suck…"

"Not really…" said Kevin in a reassuring tone. "Listen. I want you to come with me!"

"What?" Kate asked, stunned. "Are you serious?"

"I'm totally serious," Kevin said. "I love you, Kate, and I want to see where this goes. I wouldn't want my mother to die without first meeting you. She'd be so happy to see that her son had finally met a nice girl."

"But I barely know you and I can't leave my job with the Kahns just like that without warning them! Besides, what would I do in Oxford?"

"I don't know you very well either, but I already know you're the one for me and that's the most important thing! If you feel the same way, it shouldn't be too difficult to give up your job. I mean, there's nothing special about it. I'm sure your ambition in life isn't to be some maid on a miserable salary! I can guarantee you that you'll have no difficulty finding a job in Oxford. And a better job at that! Besides, you'll really be able to learn English, the real one, the one that well-educated British speak, not this racket spoken by the uneducated barbarians of the American melting pot."

"OK, I told you I was here to learn English, but the truth is, I'm not all that bothered about English. My real interests are mainly painting and horseback riding or rather art and animals in general."

"All the more reason to come with me to Oxford! I don't think you do much riding here, whereas in Oxfordshire, there are plenty of opportunities. As for your artistic temperament, if you stay locked away in your small room in the Kahns' kitsch house, then it doesn't have much chance to flourish. Oxford is a magnificent, historic city and London, a magnificent capital city full of museums and cultural events, isn't far away at all."

"But if I agree to come and live with you in Oxford, it doesn't mean I have to take tomorrow's flight. I need some time to think and to be really sure that this is what I want to do."

"When you really love someone, you don't need time to think. I fell in love with you straight away. It was love at first sight, as they say. Am I wrong in thinking that it's mutual?"

"No, that's not the point. You've caught me off guard and I don't know what to do…"

"Well, if you don't come with me tomorrow, then I just won't go, even if it means never seeing my mother again. You are more important to me than that woman who, I have to say, until a few days ago, was the most important person in my life…"

Kevin's words seemed a little melodramatic to Kate, but he seemed sincere and very much in love with her. What did she have to lose? Her life in Massachusetts wasn't all that great, her job as an au-pair was objectively irrelevant and she was sure she'd probably learn English better in England. Plus, this story of a dying mother had moved her and staying by Kevin's side to comfort him seemed like an almost obligatory act of Christian charity. She knew from experience that the illness or the death of a loved one is always a very painful ordeal and that compassion shown by a loving family and friends can help to overcome it.

"That's ridiculous! You can't abandon your mother because of me!" Kate continued. "And you're right, there's not much keeping me here. *Alea jacta est*! I'm coming with you!"

Kevin was gloating inside. It hadn't taken much to convince Kate to follow him. At the same time, this invention of his of a dying mother was a little troubling. How could he have lied to her with such poise?

How could he have shamelessly abused the trust of this sweet girl? Was he fundamentally evil, cynical and manipulative? He reassured himself that he actually did have loving feelings towards Kate and promised himself that once his mission was over, he would never behave so dishonestly with her again.

"Terrific!" Kevin shouted. "I promise you won't regret it! I will leave my student accommodation and we'll find a nice place! If you want, we could rent a barge on the Thames? Lots of Oxford students do it. In the meantime, I suggest you spend your last night in the United States with me in my hotel. Let's go get your things from the Kahns and leave quickly, before you change your mind!"

"It won't take long," explained Kate, "because I have so few things. Isn't it a little rude to leave the Kahns without warning them? Don't you think I should try to call them?"

"Don't do that!" Kevin advised her. "They'll try to change your mind and it'll make you uncomfortable. Leave them a note on the kitchen table and they'll find it when they return."

And so it was done. Kate only needed fifteen minutes or so to pack her suitcase. Before leaving the Kahn family home, she scrawled a quick message on a sheet of paper and placed it prominently in the kitchen.

"I've decided to return to France. Sorry and thank you for everything. Best wishes, Kate"

Strangely enough, she felt almost relieved when she closed the door behind her as she left the house. She suddenly realized that her experience with the Kahn family, without being disastrous, had never satisfied her and that embarking on an adventure, even if it was a little crazy, now seemed really exciting.

16

LIES

After heading back to Legal Seafood for dinner followed by a hot night at the hotel, Kevin and Kate boarded a flight to London the very next day. The six-hour flight allowed Kevin to learn a little more about Kate and her family.

"Tell me about yourself, tell me about your family," Kevin asked.

"I think I've already told you pretty much everything there is to tell" Kate replied. "As for my family, there's not much to say really… I'm the eldest of five children, three girls and two boys. My parents come from aristocratic families in Lorraine and are rather wealthy. So, I never wanted for anything as a child. Actually, no, I shouldn't say that… There's one thing I sorely lacked: Freedom. Where I'm from, a child is supposed to follow the path set by his or her parents - no questions asked. After a while, I got tired of it and that's why I ended up with the Kahn family."

"You mean you took that job to escape your family? Was it so hard being the daughter of rich French aristocrats?"

"From the outside, I'm sure it looks like the ideal life. Half a dozen servants, skiing in Switzerland every winter, beach holidays on the French Riviera during the summer, horse riding, piano lessons, private school, haute couture clothes, regular pocket money… probably most people dream of such things. The problem is that I'm just not interested in any of that; I hate the piano and I'm not a big fan of skiing. I'd rather wear jeans and boots than haute couture suits and luxury heels. I'd have liked to have gone to a secular public school rather than the Dominican

Sisters' Institute where I spent most of my adolescence. The straw that broke the camel's back was when my parents stopped me from going to art school and demanded that I pursue traditional studies to become what was expected of a Von Tardy girl: To become a pharmacist or a doctor. Then I really freaked out and decided I had to leave home."

"But you must have had a boyfriend or friends! You just left them behind?"

"Ha! Friends! All the girls I knew who I would have loved to be friends with were vipers: They were jealous of me; they were mean; they did nothing but lie to me and try to manipulate me. And I just can't stand lies and manipulation. As for the boys, the only thing they ever seemed to be interested in was getting a touch of someone's tits or fucking them. A while back, I met a Canadian student and I fell madly in love with him. He was older than me and very different from the typical boys I knew. While I was used to being harassed by boys, he seemed to really respect me: he took me to the movies, he took me to restaurants, and he spent hours teaching me how to speak English well."

"I doubt you've got this Canadian to thank for your level of English! They make up their own words for things and have a terrible accent!"

"You're such a snob! Why do you think your way of speaking and your accent are the best? It annoys me when accents are criticized. In France, the Parisians laughed at me because I supposedly had a provincial accent from Lorraine. It's weird that people have this nasty habit of judging people simply on their accent."

"But I was kidding… So, what happened between you and the Canadian?"

"Absolutely nothing! In the end, it turned out he was gay! He wasn't a bit interested in girls."

Kevin almost burst out laughing but made an effort to hold back. He thought:

Poor Kate! She's so incredibly naive; maybe that's why I like her so much. It's weird that she went on about how much she hates lies and manipulation. It's as if she sensed something… Am I not doing exactly that, lying to her and manipulating her? If I want to keep her, I can't carry on like this for long.

Kate and Kevin continued to talk for a while before falling asleep.

When they arrived at Heathrow, two men were waiting for them in the international arrivals hall. "Great," Kevin whispered to Kate. "My Uncle Bob and my mentor Dorian have come to get us! We won't have to struggle trying to make our way to Oxford now." When he reached them, Kevin shook hands with one of the two men and greeted him in a curiously cheerful and exaggerated manner:

"Ah, Uncle Bob, it's so good to see you!"

The man opened his eyes wide, as if surprised, and then muttered his reply in a gruff tone:

"Kevin, how are you?"

Kevin then spoke to the second man in much the same way:

"Dorian! Thank you for coming at such a difficult time!"

Dorian smiled snidely before responding.

"But of course! It's in these difficult times that you learn who your true friends are."

Kevin then introduced Kate:

"Uncle Bob, Dorian, meet the woman of my life, Kate. We fell madly in love in Boston."

Turning to Kate, Kevin continued:

"Kate, this is Uncle Bob, my mother's brother who has been caring for her during her hospitalization. And this is Dorian, my mentor at Oxford and a very valuable guide in my archaeological studies. He himself is an illustrious archaeologist!"

Kate smiled at them as she shook their hands.

"Hello! Very nice to meet you!"

"How is my mother?" Kevin asked his Uncle Bob.

"Oh, Kevin," replied Uncle Bob, mimicking the most extreme embarrassment, "this is going to be so hard: Your mother died last night."

"My God, no!" shouted Kevin, pretending to be appalled by this horrible news and making a sign of the cross. "I didn't make it in time…"

"You did the right thing by coming with him," Uncle Bob added, turning to Kate. "He's going to need your support. He loved his mother very much!"

Kate, somewhat stunned by such a shock as soon as they arrived, took Kevin's hand. "I know the pain of losing a loved one. But I'm here for you. I love you and I'm going to help you get through this. "

Bob grabbed Kevin's surprisingly heavy suitcase and Kate's lighter one and placed them on a trolley. "Well, let's not just stand here; this terminal is a bit hectic! Let's head to the car. "

The four of them made their way to the airport garage and climbed into a big Land Rover, after Bob had carefully packed the luggage in the spacious trunk. Dorian took the seat up front next to Bob, who was at the wheel, while Kate and Kevin sat together in the back.

"I thought, given the circumstances, that you could move in, at least for the time being, to The Manor," suggested Dorian. "You'll be very comfortable there and you won't have to worry about anything. You'll also be close to the university and the center of Oxford."

"It's very kind of you to do this for us!" Kevin replied. "Kate and I would not have been able to stay in my university room. It's far too cramped and uncomfortable."

Commissioner Robert Murphy sat there grinding his teeth all the way to Oxford. That this little crook Kevin had gone and called him Uncle Bob and made him look like his mother's brother in front of Kate was beyond what he could handle! When Kevin had phoned him the day before to tell him that he was coming back, not only with the precious stone, but also with a girl to whom he'd told the dying mother lie, he had agreed to it all without much thought. Now he regretted having taken it so lightly. Immediately after Kevin's call, Murphy had contacted Dorian to tell him about the success of the operation and ask what accommodation might be provided for Kevin and his partner when they returned to Oxford. He had been both relieved and surprised, when Dorian, ecstatic at the prospect of soon being able to hold Émile's artifact in his hands, enthusiastically offered to house them at The Manor. That Dorian did not take offense at Kevin's ridiculous behavior and that he offered to welcome Kate, a perfect stranger, into the very private world of True Archaeology, without further question, was surprising to say the least… But Murphy didn't bother to raise his concerns... Dorian was at home at The Manor and he was the great power behind True Archaeology....

On the way to Oxford, Kate was surprised that Kevin didn't say much to his uncle nor his friend, particularly that he didn't ask for the specifics about the circumstances of his mother's death. But she put it down to psychological shock and grief and refrained from making any comments. She was quite impressed when the car drove through the high gates marking the entrance to the property, then made its way down the drive and along the impeccably manicured lawn and the magnificent trees that adorned the park and finally stopped at the foot of an elegant stately home. She was about to ask Kevin discreetly if that was where they'd be staying, but she didn't have time before Dorian spoke:

"Here we are! Welcome to The Manor! I'm sure you'll like it here. James, the butler, will accompany you to your apartments and explain a few points. I'm referring mainly to mealtimes, as well as all the practical and logistical aspects of your stay."

After James rushed to open the door, Dorian stepped out of the Land Rover, confirmed to James that Kate and Kevin would be staying at The Manor for an indefinite period and asked him to take care of them both.

As another servant, Tom, took care of the luggage, James helped Kate out of the Land Rover and invited her and Kevin to follow him inside.

"I imagine you're tired after your transatlantic flight," Dorian said to Kate and Kevin. "You may want to take a bath, change and rest. So, let's meet at seven in the small sitting room for drinks before dinner. However, Kevin, I'll need to talk to you for a few minutes: Can you step by my office around half past six?"

"Of course!" Kevin replied. "I'll be there. Thank you again for having us."

Kate and Kevin were taken to the first floor and shown into a large, beautifully decorated room, whose large window framed by heavy drapes overlooked the park. Adjacent to the room was an immense dressing room and a large private bathroom, equipped with thick, luxurious towels and white bathrobes. James pointed out to the cord they could pull if they needed anything and told them how to find the small sitting room where they were expected later which was on the ground floor, to the left of the main entrance, before withdrawing and wishing them a pleasant stay at The Manor.

Once James disappeared, Kate turned to Kevin and almost yelled.

"Whoa! You're really spoiling me! This place is beautiful, I mean everything, the park, the house, the bedroom… That mentor of yours is so nice! It's just so awful that your mother passed away and we can't really enjoy the moment… You must be so terribly unhappy… I'm really sorry. What are you going to do? I guess you'll have to deal with the funeral."

"I'd rather not talk about it" said Kevin, looking upset. "I'm the one who should be feeling sorry for you; I would have preferred a less gloomy arrival in Oxford, something less dramatic for the beginning of our adventure together. I'll see what needs to be done with Uncle Bob. In the meantime, let's settle in and relax. We don't have much time before I have to go down to Dorian's office, then it'll be time for dinner."

Kate found Kevin surprisingly serene for someone who'd just found out about his mother's death; she assumed that his attitude was simply a reflection of his great emotional maturity as a man, as well as his desire to spare her his morbid thoughts that could tarnish their intimacy; she felt all the more touched. They then unpacked their suitcases and put their clothes away in the dressing room. Kate then hopped into the large bathtub and Kevin the shower.

While Kate was still doing her makeup, Kevin put on the gray flannel pants and white shirt he'd pulled out of his suitcase and which were still quite wrinkled, plus a navy-blue blazer which hadn't suffered quite as much on the journey. He popped his head around the door of the bathroom door to let Kate know that he was going down to see Dorian as planned and that he would come back for her at exactly five to seven to escort her to dinner.

Before leaving the room, Kevin discreetly made his way to the dressing room and took out of his suitcase the large package that made it so heavy. It was laden down with this cumbersome load that he entered

Professor Green's office, where, in addition to Dorian, Commissioner Murphy and a very elegant woman he had never met were also waiting for him.

"Come in, my dear Kevin," Dorian said as he saw him. "Let me introduce you to Edwina Tabellion, owner of the house and a prominent member of True Archaeology. Her husband, Professor Prosper Tabellion, is the co-founder of our society. Edwina and Prosper were generous enough to make their home available to True Archaeology and the society is now based here. You should be aware that Edwina knows all our little secrets and she was briefed on what you did over in Boston."

"I'm delighted to meet you," said Kevin politely, bowing his head respectfully. "I assume you know I'm Kevin McKee."

"Yes, I have indeed been told about you," Edwina assured him in a kind tone. "I'm so pleased to meet you and I look forward to hearing how you completed your mission!"

"Ah! My *achievement*!" Kevin proudly said. "Well, the easiest thing to do would be for me to take the treasure out of its package and show you. I managed to snatch it out of Kahn's claws without too much difficulty. I don't think I need to go into all the details."

Kevin placed the package, well-padded in layers of newspaper held together by string, on the coffee table and began to tear away at the wrapping. Dorian, Murphy and Edwina kept their eyes fixed on the package and held their breath until they finally discovered the object of their desire. When the black stone was finally exposed, Dorian couldn't stop himself from shouting out. "Bingo! We've hit the jackpot! " He literally jumped out of his armchair to grab it, to turn it over in his hands, to appreciate its consistency and inspect the engraved signs. After several long minutes, Dorian came to his conclusion in a trembling voice that was full of emotion.

"There's no doubt about it! It's a stela fragment covered with Sumerian type characters, dating back at least five thousand years! Considering where Émile found it, I think we can safely say that this is the discovery of the century and the beginning of the apotheosis for True Archaeology! "

After delicately laying the stone on the coffee table and inviting Murphy and Edwina to examine it, Dorian turned to Kevin with foggy eyes and a wide smile on his lips, to congratulate him on the success of his mission and thank him warmly:

"My dear Kevin, True Archaeology owes you a great deal. Bob believed in you and convinced me that you could be trusted. Good work!"

"I don't want to be a killjoy," Murphy said, "because I have to admit that Kevin acted like a pro and managed to get the stone back to us without any problems. But, I would still like to point out that he went way beyond the scope of his mission, firstly by bringing the Kahn au-pair back with him from Boston, which may well put Kahn directly on our trail, and secondly by making me out to be his uncle and you Dorian, his mentor!"

"My dear Bob," Dorian laughed, "I understand that Kevin's little fibs are not really to your liking… But in Kevin's defense, as the popular saying goes, you can't make an omelet without breaking eggs, and I find that in this case, the broken eggs in question are minor problems compared to the triumph that is before us, thanks to what he's done. From my perspective, the fact that Kevin introduced me as his mentor seems to make a lot of sense: He's a young archaeology student that I, a former professor of archaeology at Oxford University, am pleased to be supporting in his studies and career! As far as you're concerned, obviously being an offender's uncle might be a bit of a worry for a police commissioner. But I understand that, in view of the perfect accomplishment of this mission you'll have to keep your promise and Kevin's record must now be expunged."

"Okay," Murphy conceded, "but he will have to promise me that he'll never call me Uncle Bob outside of this house. If he slips up, I'll put him away again!"

"I won't, Commissioner!" Kevin said, holding his hands together as a sign of penance. "You'll only be my Uncle Bob as far as Kate is concerned and only within these walls!"

"Speaking of Kate," Murphy continued, "we'll have to agree on a way forward. Are we going to leave her in the dark forever or will we tell her the truth at some point? And right now, what should we be saying about this dead mother?"

"I don't want to rush things with Kate," Kevin replied. "I don't want to lose her! Of course, I'll have to explain the whole story to her one of these days, but not right away. As for my mother, we can say that her last wish was that her body be cremated and her ashes scattered in the Thames, without any ceremony and without any witnesses other than her son."

"I suppose you have no idea how long you'll be staying at The Manor and how Kate will pass her time here," Edwina asked. "Kevin, I understand you'll be very busy pursuing your studies. But do you know what Kate wants to do? What's her background? Did she have a job before working as an au-pair with the Kahn family?"

"I don't think she ever worked before she left for the Kahn family," Kevin said, "but I'm not sure. In any case, don't worry about it. At worst, she could take up a job as an au-pair in Oxford; she might even be able to give French lessons. I know she's studied drawing and is a champion horse rider, so we could also look into these areas."

"Anyway, Dorian added, "there's no urgency for this young woman to get a job. Let us give her time to find her bearings in her new environment and see what her intentions are. When the time comes, I can investigate with my network of contacts to make it easier for her to find a job. I think that might be a good way to go. Well, it's almost time for dinner. Edwina, I'll let you find a safe place for our treasure here. We can lock it away in True Archaeology vault, whose secret code is less easy to crack than Kahn's safe, I believe! I think that's the wisest thing to do! We'll need to convene a new extraordinary meeting of the True Archaeology steering committee tomorrow to discuss next steps. Having Émile's stone in our possession is certainly a huge step forward, but I don't believe that it is enough to confirm our theories. We'll have to find the stela from which it came… which means organizing an expedition to Antarctica. But this isn't a topic of conversation for today. Kevin, once again, congratulations! To avoid alarming Kate, perhaps it would be prudent to no longer refer to what happened over in Boston. Come on! Go and get Kate and bring her down for dinner."

Kevin found Kate waiting for him in their room upstairs, now carefully made up and very elegantly dressed in a green silk outfit that looked like it came from some great *Faubourg Saint Honoré* couturier. It matched the color of her eyes just perfectly. He had never seen her look so radiant, as the clothes she'd worn in Wellesley had been much more casual. She was so lovely, even more desirable than when he'd first fallen for her. He rushed to kiss her lovingly, which Kate couldn't refuse but which forced her to go back to the bathroom to touch up her lipstick. She came out with a tissue that she handed to Kevin and gave him a mischievous smile.

"You will have to remember that in the future, you are formally forbidden to kiss me when I'm all dressed up and ready to go out in public! It's all right this time, but rub this tissue over your lips or they'll think you're a transvestite! "

Kevin did just that and they went down the stairs together to join their hosts. James was waiting in the hall and took them through to the small living room, where Edwina, Dorian and Bob were already enjoying a drink. When she laid eyes on Kate, Edwina's eyes lit up:

"You look absolutely lovely!" she said to the young lady with kindness. "Welcome to The Manor. Let me introduce myself. I'm Edwina Tabellion, the owner of this place, which I make available to Professor Green and True Archaeology. My husband, Prosper Tabellion, co-founded the society with Dorian. Unfortunately, he can't be here to-day as he spends the week in Strasbourg where he teaches archaeology at the university and only stays here on weekends, unless he's digging in some far-flung corner of the world."

"I'm delighted to meet you" said Kate. "My name is Catherine Von Tardy, but people call me Kate. It's really very kind of you to welcome Kevin and me into your home. Given the way Kevin rushed me out of Massachusetts, where I was still living just a few hours ago, I imagine you didn't really expect to see me here!"

"You're right," Edwina laughed, "but it's a wonderful surprise!"

"Well," Dorian intervened, "now that the introductions have been made, let's have a glass of champagne in honor of Kate and Kevin, and wish them much happiness and an excellent stay here with us!"

James circulated a tray of Champagne glasses and everyone took a glass before raising them to the young couple's health.

Kate was thrilled. She had rarely been so warmly welcomed by complete strangers; everyone was taking care of her, especially Edwina whose presence and style put her in mind of her own mother, Sonia Von Tardy; the setting was fabulous and the Champagne deliciously chilled and almost soothing. She'd probably made the right decision by giving in to Kevin's advances and following him to England no questions asked. This boy obviously came from an excellent background, and his acquaintances seemed rather upscale to say the least…

After a few minutes during which Dorian, Murphy and Edwina continued with the small talk, mainly with Kate, while enjoying their Champagne, Tom announced that dinner was ready to be served and everyone sat down to eat. Tom pointed Kate to a chair between Dorian and Edwina and Kevin was placed between Edwina and Murphy. The whole conversation over dinner revolved around two topics: Kate, who she was, where she came from, what she was doing; and True Archaeology, mainly to explain to Kate its purpose and activities.

17

DAMNATION

Samuel Kahn was beyond exasperated. The trip to his parents' house with Dana, the girls and the dog was as big a nightmare as he'd anticipated.

Unfortunately, faced with his sister Rebecca's pleading insistence, he hadn't dared refuse to participate in the bar mitzvah celebrations of one of Rebecca's many offspring; indeed, his mother had taken the trouble to call him a good ten times over the previous few weeks to remind him of his obligations as a member of the chosen people and to threaten him with all forms of condemnation should he not attend his nephew's big day. Samuel, although he never had the slightest intention of denying his Jewish origins, abhorred all the rites and customs of Orthodox Judaism, especially when they were practiced in the ultra-fundamentalist environment to which his brother-in-law belonged. His sister Rebecca hadn't managed to find anyone better than a Hasidic Jew, a rabbi of his Brooklyn community, and she now scrupulously followed all the most archaic and grotesque customs of her adopted cult. She'd even shaved her head and now wore a horrible wig all the time. All she ever wore were old, scruffy clothes that made her look like a peasant woman living in Eastern Europe in the 19th century. When she menstruated, she lived almost like a pestiferous woman, taking care to stay well away from her husband to avoid defiling him. Not to mention the food bans, and strict liturgical obligations she imposed on herself…

The Kahn family had planned to spend three days at Samuel's

parents' oceanfront property in Sea Girt, New Jersey, and Samuel's bad temper had settled in as soon as they arrived mid-afternoon on the Friday. Every conversation had revolved around a single subject: Judaism and the importance for every Jew to respect traditions. Samuel's mother had developed an unbounded admiration for Shlomo Finkelstein, her Hasidic son-in-law: He at least was proud of his origins, he at least knew the teachings of the Talmud, he at least did not live the dissolute life of the goyim and he at least raised his children in the true religion… Such reproaches were given to Samuel in equal measure to the praise rained down on Shlomo: He rarely went to the synagogue, his daughters were not educated in a yeshiva, he accepted that his wife showed her legs, her arms and almost everything else to anyone who wanted to look, and maybe he no longer even ate kosher!

Things got worse when they went to Shlomo and Rebecca's home in the far reaches of Williamsburg, a district of Brooklyn almost entirely made up of the Hasidim. Samuel's parents had formally forbidden him to drive his own car there, on the pretext that it was sacrilege to drive on Sabbath day. To get around this ban, Samuel's parents had felt obliged to rent a minivan, with a goy driver of course, into which the whole family had been forced to squash themselves.

The show this Saturday morning in Williamsburg was beyond belief. The streets, almost devoid of traffic, were overrun by individuals wearing long beards, dressed in black frock coats arriving halfway down their calf, wearing black shoes with white stockings and wearing either a totally outdated black felt or oversize fur hat. Most appeared to be nearsighted and wore bifocal glasses. From their ridiculous headgear, long curls of frizzy hair escaped and fell down each side of the face. A number of them also displayed the tallit, a large white wool shawl partially striated with dark blue stripes, above their clothing.

The pathetic little house where the Finkelsteins lived was itself invaded by these maniacs and was buzzing with the strange sounds of the Yiddish language. Upon entering, Samuel had to remove himself from Dana and the girls, who followed Aunt Becky in one direction, while he and his father were invited to join the men, a strict gender separation being required among the Finkelsteins. All the men present were fussing around the 13-year-old Emmanuel, who was busy demonstrating to his rabbi father that he now knew how to use his pair of tefillin.

Samuel had to sit through the speech that Emmanuel had had to prepare for his transition to adulthood, then listen to him read a passage from the Torah and then finally show his appreciation for the whole performance with a resounding Mazel Tov. He then had to endure the traditional meal and comply with the ritual of gifts to the new full member of the community. Shlomo couldn't find anything more beautiful to offer his son than a luxurious version of the Mishnah and the Talmud, over which the whole assembly marveled. Most of the guests flooded the young Emmanuel with bundles of dollars bills, to his great joy and with the grateful smiles of Shlomo.

The last thing on the to-do list was to participate in a whole series of traditional dances. Two guys forced Samuel to bind himself to them and gesticulate in an infernal circle to the spitting sound of violins.

Samuel almost kissed the minibus driver's feet when he showed up at the Finkelstein household to escort the Kahn family back to Sea Girt. As soon as they'd crossed Williamsburg boundary line, Samuel heaved out a sigh of relief as he abruptly ripped the yarmulke off his skull to give his irritated scalp a break. Dana made a face of disapproval and encouraged him to put it back on his head, so as not to provoke his mother's temper. Dana and the girls didn't seem to have suffered as much in the women's group: They had danced a lot and seemed as though they had all enjoyed themselves.

When he arrived at Sea Girt, Samuel explained to his wife that he really needed to recover from the whole ordeal and that he was going to go for a walk, alone by the ocean. As he moved away from his parents' house and regained some serenity, and as he wondered how to permanently escape this kind of trap in the future, Samuel suddenly thought about the black stone locked in his safe in Wellesley and TOTEXX's failure to respond to his offer. Why not make a little phone call to Jeff Fishman? He may as well ruin his Sabbath too…

"Hello, Jeff. This is Professor Samuel Kahn from Harvard. I haven't heard from you after my recent trip to Dallas and I'd like to know if your company intends to give some consideration to my proposal regarding the archaeological remains found in Antarctica. If, it turns out, you don't attach any importance to this discovery, I might just feel obliged to immediately inform the scientific community and the general public. So I need to know what TOTEXX intends to do."

"Ah, Professor, I was planning on calling you!" Jeff answered. "I'm sorry I didn't contact you again earlier, but after your presentation in Dallas, I had to discuss the matter first of all with our Chairman, Mr. Taittinger, and also with the various members of the Executive Committee. As you can imagine, given Mr. Taittinger's reaction, it wasn't easy to reach a consensus on what strategy to adopt. But I'm now in a position to give you some very good news. TOTEXX is convinced that the disclosure of this discovery could definitely be harmful to the company's interests and we are therefore prepared to follow your recommendations. We will now have to agree on the practical arrangements of our collaboration and the terms of the contract to be established between you and TOTEXX."

"I'm glad that you've understood the importance of the issue and agree with me on what to do," Samuel said in a satisfied tone. "Can I ask you exactly what TOTEXX expects from me and how much the company values my services?"

"Look, it's not really the kind of thing you can talk about on the phone like this," Jeff said. "What I can tell you right away is that we obviously expect you to give us the stone. Beyond that, it will essentially be a question of supporting TOTEXX, if the need arises, by fighting, using your scientific means, any allusion to the existence of traces of an ancient civilization in Antarctica."

"Of course, I understand. But when exactly will I know how much I am to expect for these services?"

"It would be best if our legal counsel came to see you to bring you a preliminary version of the contract that TOTEXX plans to enter into with you. You could then show him the original object, of which we've only seen photos so far. You could then reach an agreement on the financial terms of the transaction."

"Couldn't you send me this preliminary version of the contract by e-mail or registered delivery instead? It would save us time and I don't see any point in your legal counsel traveling to Boston if it turns out there's no way we can agree on the terms of the contract."

"We prefer to avoid circulating such confidential documents by e-mail. And I can reassure you: I would be very surprised if you were disappointed by the offer! If I remember correctly, you didn't come to regret your mission for us in Iraq… But if you prefer, you could always come to Dallas! This would have the advantage of allowing us to eliminate all potential areas of disagreement, with all TOTEXX decision-makers present on site, and therefore we'd probably be able to finalize all the details the very same day."

"I think I prefer that idea," Samuel said. "And to tell you the truth, it would be most convenient for me to leave for Dallas tonight and to spend as much time as needed with anyone you think necessary Monday at the TOTEXX tower. If we could agree on a final contract as early as Monday, that would be perfect."

"This Monday?" Jeff asked in surprise. "That seems a little short notice to me! Couldn't you come over towards the end of next week? That would allow us to be better prepared. And I don't know if my financial expert and legal counsel will be available on Monday…"

"For reasons I can't explain to you, this Monday is the only possible day for me for some time," Samuel lied with aplomb.

"Well, I'll figure it out then. Agreed for Monday, but not before two in the afternoon. You must understand that I won't have time to get you the private jet today and so you'll have to travel on a regular flight."

"Getting to you won't be a problem. But perhaps you could reserve the private jet for my return? I'll be heading back on Tuesday and so that'll be three nights at the Ritz Carlton."

"All right. That works for me. So, see you soon," concluded Jeff.

"Monday, at two, in the tower," Samuel confirmed, smiling inside. "Have a great weekend!"

By the end of this conversation, Samuel had regained his optimism. Within minutes, he was going to be able to escape the nightmare of his family reunion by heading to Newark airport. He was going to be able to forget these mentally retarded Hasidim by spending a few days with the Texan oil kings. He was soon going to sign a fantastic contract with TOTEXX which would definitively put him out of harm's way in terms of his finances. He hurried back to his parents' house to inform Dana that he had to go to Dallas immediately for an urgent meeting. Faced with Dana's irritated astonishment and repeated requests for explanations, he got angry:

"Look, you need to know what you want: Go back to medieval obscurantism and mental retardation with Rebecca, Shlomo and my mother, or live in the greatest possible luxury in the twenty-first century! I choose luxury and modern life and there's no way I'm going to let this opportunity pass me by. I want to leave behind the misery I knew in my childhood with that family of mine! I'm going to pack my suitcase and take a taxi to Newark. All you have to do is take my car to Boston with the girls. And since I don't want to hear my parents' whining, you can apologize to them for my early departure. I'll let you give them whatever explanations you see fit… Well, come on, I have to get ready now and then I'm out of here. I think I'll be back to Boston on Tuesday night. I'll call you and let you know at what time to expect me."

***

Comfortably settled in a luxurious suite at the Ritz Carlton in Dallas, Samuel was about to have a club sandwich delivered by room service when the phone rang.

"Shit, I just want to be left alone!" he cursed as he went to pick up the handset. "Yes, what is it?" he shouted in an unpleasant tone, even before learning who was on the other end of the line.

A languid female voice answered him:

"Professor Kahn, this is Rachel Schwartz. Maybe you remember me? We met briefly some time ago at TOTEXX when you made a presentation to the steering committee on the obstacles the company might face with some of its oil exploration. I'm the Director of Communications.

Jeff informed me of your visit and asked me to contact you as soon as you arrived in Dallas to discuss the details of Monday's meeting. Are you by any chance available tonight? I could meet you at your hotel and we could talk over a drink..."

Samuel quickly tried to remember this Rachel and thought he recalled a rather pretty young woman sitting to Jeff's left, who was dressed very conservatively and looked rather stern. He concluded that spending this evening with her could be interesting...

"Yes, indeed, I remember you, the lovely young woman who sat next to Jeff at the meeting! I would be absolutely delighted to see you again. Unless you know a better place nearby, I suggest we meet at the Ritz Carlton bar. Call me as soon as you get here. "

"The Ritz bar is perfect," Rachel confirmed. "I don't live very far away, and I should be able to be there in about fifteen minutes. See you shortly!"

Samuel felt very excited as he waited for Rachel's call. This little stay in Dallas was definitely off to a great start! With a little luck, he would be able to convince the young Rachel to come up and check if the reputation of the Ritz Carlton's comfortable beds was justified...

Rachel hurried as fast as she could to get to the Ritz. Jeff Fishman had phoned her a few hours earlier to ask her if she could take care of Professor Kahn, who was due to arrive in Dallas that same evening for a contract negotiation on Monday. Rachel had participated in the discussions following Professor Kahn's recent visit to the tower and was aware of the company's position on the stone discovered in Antarctica. She knew that Jeff was willing to give Kahn a big check in exchange for this stone and his support if needed in the future. Jeff had given Rachel a delicate assignment: She had to build Kahn's trust and persuade him to accept minimum payment for his services. Jeff had explained to her that the big boss, Taittinger, had provided him with a maximum budget of around ten million dollars to make this whole problem with possible archaeological sites in Antarctica go away, but Jeff wanted to minimize the portion of that budget that would go to Kahn to keep a margin of safety in the event of unexpected issues. Jeff told her that Kahn had received two million when he helped them in Iraq in a similar context a few years earlier; he expected Kahn would be greedier this time and might expect to receive four or five million this time. Rachel had to bring Kahn to his senses and make him understand that three million was the very maximum he could hope for. Jeff had told Rachel that any tactics were fine by him ("if you know what I mean…" he insinuated) in order to achieve the right result and that her end-of-year bonus would depend largely on the success of this mission.

"Given Professor Kahn's personality and his interest in women, you're the only one of us that can make this happen. Don't spare your efforts and you'll be rewarded for your good and loyal service," Jeff whispered to her in conclusion.

Samuel almost choked to death when he saw Rachel at the Ritz bar. What had happened to the prim little employee he'd barely noticed a few days earlier at TOTEXX? The transformation was barely believable! She now looked like a sex bomb with sensuous lipstick, long jet-black hair floating freely over her shoulders, her legs sheathed in outrageously tight jeans and thigh boots and her chest partially covered with a black leather jacket showing glimpses of an impressive cleavage.

Rachel walked over, staring at him with her big brown eyes and giving him a cheerful smile.

"Professor Kahn, I'm very happy to see you again!"

"But the pleasure is all mine!" replied Samuel in a sweet tone. "I hope you don't mind me saying: You look stunning tonight! I prefer you like this, rather than stuck in that tailored suit you were wearing the other day… What would you like to drink?"

"A dirty Martini, please!" replied Rachel without hesitation.

"Bring us a Dirty Martini for my charming friend and a Daiquiri for me!" Samuel immediately called out to the bartender, showing him the chairs where he and his friend were planning to sit.

While waiting for the cocktails to be served, Rachel started the conversation stating that, although she had often come to the Ritz for business lunches, she had never had the opportunity to spend the night there. She asked Samuel if this was his favorite hotel in Dallas and if the rooms were as luxurious and comfortable as she'd heard. Samuel took the bait.

"I also like the Fairmont and the W, but I have a slight preference for the Ritz. It's true that the rooms here are very comfortable. If you want, you can just come up and have a look later and decide for yourself."

Rachel winked at him in a naughty way, flashed him her most attractive smile and declared:

"I didn't dare ask… But I'd love to…"

"But let's get back to the serious stuff," Rachel continued after delicately taking a small sip of the Dirty Martini that had just been brought to the table. "The sooner we finish the job, the sooner we can think about how to relax. So… I wanted to see you tonight so that Monday's meeting would be productive and you can leave with a contract that would satisfy both parties. TOTEXX has of course already thought about the terms and conditions it wants to see stipulated in the contract, but it wants to be sure that an agreement with you is possible and wishes to know your expectations in advance. To facilitate the discussion, be aware that we see two main aspects to our collaboration: Firstly, the transfer to TOTEXX of the object in your possession for an amount to be specified; secondly, and also for an amount to be specified, the production of an expert report, of the same type as the one you provided to the company at the time of its oil drilling in Iraq, attesting to the absence of any archaeological remains in the area of interest. You will only be required to provide this report at such time as TOTEXX deems appropriate. Does this seem to you to adequately cover all aspects of your collaboration with TOTEXX or do you have any objections or recommendations?"

Samuel had only listened absentmindedly, obsessed as he was by Rachel's promising cleavage, which he hadn't stopped staring at while sipping his Daiquiri.

"No objections. It all seems fine to me," he said distractedly.

"As for the expert report," Rachel continued, "it seems to us that it should be much easier to formulate than the one you wrote in Iraq. Indeed, no one has yet found a single ruin in Antarctica and the general opinion is that there can be no archaeological remains there. Therefore, we plan to offer you one million two hundred thousand dollars for the development and delivery of your signed report, payable in three installments. Is that what you were hoping for?"

"It doesn't sound like much to be honest!" Samuel exclaimed, pretending to be indignant. "I find that the simple act of signing this type of document and committing my credibility as an internationally recognized expert deserves at least two million. That's what I asked for ten years ago with the Iraq contract, and I should actually be asking you for a lot more taking into account inflation and the increase in my notoriety."

"You're making things difficult for me, Professor." sighed Rachel, pretending to be very concerned. "If I give in to you, my boss will be furious... But because it's you, I'll try to get him to agree to one and a half."

"If you get me one and a half, I'll offer you a dream stay at the Ritz Carlton in Cancun... with me of course! But don't tell anyone!" exclaimed Samuel with a laugh.

"For a week in Cancun with you, I think I'd do just about anything!" giggled Rachel, with her most mischievous smile. "It's a deal! Let's see if we can agree on the stone now..."

Samuel, for whom the amount he'd get for the stone was by far the most crucial part of the negotiation, suddenly swallowed what remained of his daiquiri, ordered a second one as well as a second Dirty Martini for Rachel although she had barely touched her first glass, and decided to take things more seriously. His saucy tone suddenly disappeared:

"Ah, the stone! Giving TOTEXX something of such immense value is much more difficult for me than writing a report!"

Rachel understood that Kahn was about to set the bar very high and knew she'd have to move up a gear in her seduction offensive. She took off the leather jacket to reveal the weapons she planned to use to achieve her goals: Under her almost transparent white blouse, Samuel could now see the curve of two voluptuous breasts, at the end of which he could clearly distinguish her appetizing pink nipples in the center of large brown areolas.

Rachel, pretending to readjust herself, ran her hands through her hair, arched her back and looked into Samuel's eyes.

"I must admit that I have trouble understanding your passion for this piece of stone... You surprise me, Professor! Isn't there anything else in life that excites you?"

Samuel felt his penis hardening with impatience. He needed this negotiation to be over so that he can explore Rachel's promising anatomy in the privacy of his room.

"Actually, yes," Jeff whispered as he leaned towards Rachel, "there are things that excite me much more than archaeology... The sooner we finish with the business side of things, the sooner I can tell you what really interests me... Offer me three million for my stone and we can move onto something else."

"Three million!" Rachel sighed, simulating amazement, "you'll never get away with it, Professor! If you really want to reach an agreement, you will have to be more reasonable... In reality, the stone has no value in and of itself. Perhaps it would if it were proven to be a fragment of an antediluvian ruin discovered in Antarctica, but that's unlikely to happen... As far as we know, no one else but TOTEXX would be willing to buy it from you... At most, TOTEXX can offer you a million, which is already a considerable sum for what is essentially a worthless piece of rock!"

"I can concede," Samuel argued, "that today, the value of such a stone out there on the market, as an archaeological relic, wouldn't be enormous... But that's not how TOTEXX should be reasoning this out. You must understand that if I disclose this discovery to my archaeological colleagues and publicize it, TOTEXX will lose a lot of money: At worst, you'll have to say goodbye to your oil drilling in Antarctica, at best, TOTEXX will waste a lot of time and spend a lot to demonstrate the absence of prehistoric ruins down there. So the issue for you guys is to minimize the loss of revenue, and I think billions of dollars are at stake here! Three million is a drop in the ocean compared to the sea of profits that you plan to make from Antarctic oil!"

"Professor, I believe your perception of how a company like

TOTEXX operates doesn't quite match reality. The people who run my company don't think like you. For the time being, our oil explorations in Antarctica aren't yielding any results; on the contrary, it's just a huge cost that's driving our annual profits down. We can't afford for these costs to increase any further, do you understand?"

"What I understand is that TAITTINGER and his clique of shareholders want to continue to fill their pockets and refuse to give up even a few crumbs to a guy like me who's not in the club… If TOTEXX is really that stingy, I might consider handing over the stone for two million. But not a penny less…"

"Gosh," sighed Rachel, "you're going to ruin this evening! And there was me thinking it might turn out to be quite pleasant! I don't know what to tell you, except that neither I nor Jeff has two million dollars… If you really want that kind of figure, I think I should just go home right now and I'm afraid your meeting on Monday might be very frustrating…"

"There's no need to get angry," Samuel replied, worried that his one-on-one with Rachel might be about to come to an abrupt end. "Let's keep talking… I'd like us to stay good friends and perhaps I'm willing to make concessions… How about one and a half million?"

"I can't promise you that much just for the stone, but I have an idea: Earlier, we agreed on a fee of one and a half in exchange for your expert report. Normally, we would give you a third of that on the day TOTEXX asks you to start work, i.e. not for several months, then a second third in the middle of the contract and the final third when the report is submitted. I can probably get you the first third, that's five hundred grand, right now, along with a million for the stone; so you could put your hands on one and a half million immediately. I think I can even work it so that the total amount for the stone plus the report is three million, by increasing the second and third installments for the report to seven fifty. How does that sound?

"Let me see if I understand you correctly" Samuel summarized. "You're offering me one and a half million right away, as soon as I give you the stone and another one and a half million in two installments, later, for the report. Since I don't really feel like haggling with you all night, I can live with this arrangement... Do we have a deal?"

"Deal!" confirmed Rachel with relief. "You know what? You're a formidable negotiator; we should hire you as Chief Financial Officer! Well, I'll notify Jeff and the legal department so they can have your contract prepared accordingly by Monday! You've exhausted me; I think I'm going to have to head off home now."

"Oh, you can't leave me like that!" Samuel insisted, looking like a beaten dog. "Take some time to relax after all that strenuous exercise! And you promised me you'd come up and visit my suite... I know we didn't sign a formal contract for that, but still!"

"Fine, but very quickly, because I'm tired..."

"Let's go!" cried Samuel as he turned to the waiter hurriedly, "Put all this on my bill: room 69, please."

Rachel put on her jacket, grabbed her purse and followed Samuel to the elevator. Once the doors had closed, Samuel grabbed Rachel and tried to kiss her. She pushed him back: "Not here! There'll be a camera." It was enough to temporarily calm Samuel until they reach the door of his room. Once they were both inside, Samuel threw himself at her like a horny animal, demanding that she undress. Rachel let him touch her breasts and kiss her brutally on the lips before pretending to be offended by his behavior:

"Come on, Professor, calm down! I think there's been a misunderstanding. I'm not the kind of woman you imagine! I would like to remind you that I'm here for work. I acknowledge that I probably made a mistake in agreeing to come up to your room to satisfy my curiosity and I apologize for giving you a false impression! I think I should leave you alone now."

"Come on, this is ridiculous!" Samuel muttered in confusion. "You've done a good job and now you are entitled to kick back a little."

"I'm exhausted and my fiancé is waiting for me," Rachel lied.

"If not tonight, then when?" Samuel insisted. "Tomorrow night? Monday night? You're just so desirable and you are driving me crazy!

We could go out together to a good restaurant and then come back here for dessert."

"OK," Rachel seemed to give in, "but let's make it Monday evening, after the meeting, so there'll be something to celebrate."

"Great idea!" exclaimed Samuel, reassured after the cold shoulder that Rachel had just inflicted upon him. "Is that a promise?"

Rachel smiled at him and declared that she'd keep her promise, but only if Samuel accepted the terms of the contract. Then, with a sensual perversity, she walked up to him and pressed her pulpy mouth on Samuel's for a long time, while caressing his penis through his pants. As Samuel began to regain hope and tried to unbutton Rachel's jeans, she stopped abruptly and laughed. "You're such a rascal! See you Monday! " and she rushed towards the exit.

Once she'd gone, Samuel rubbed his hands together with an air of satisfaction, before lying down on the bed and thinking back over the events that had just unfolded: He had reached an agreement with someone high up at TOTEXX on the terms of a new contract with the company; if everything went according to plan, he would soon receive the nice sum of one and a half million in exchange for a piece of stone stolen without any effort from some poor fool just a few weeks earlier; and then he'd be getting the same again at a later date for the production of a bogus report; finally, the icing on the cake, unless he somehow messed it up, was that he could add the beautiful Rachel to his long list of conquests!

Today has certainly ended much better than it started! I was so pleased to just get away from those freaks in New York and New Jersey and now this! I hope this Rachel is reliable and that there won't be any nasty surprises on Monday…

***

The meeting at the tower didn't bring any unpleasant surprises for Samuel: On the contrary, he had the impression that he was welcomed as if he were the Messiah by TOTEXX employees and Taittinger didn't show up to pollute the friendly atmosphere that prevailed from his arrival until his departure a couple of hours later. He was greeted by

Sissi, who inundated him with compliments on the presentation he had made a few weeks earlier and that, according to her, had made a big impression on the Executive Committee. Then Jeff came to meet him as soon as the elevator reached the top floor of the tower, thanking him for coming back to Dallas so quickly and agreeing to work with Rachel to help prepare the contract. He first led Samuel to his office where he invited him to talk for a few minutes before starting the meeting: He offered him a drink, inquired about how his flight had gone and the comfort of his room at the Ritz, and confirmed that the company's private jet would be at his disposal to take him back to Boston the following morning. He verified that Samuel was satisfied with the terms and conditions previously discussed with Rachel, who, he insisted in passing, was an outstanding collaborator, intellectually brilliant, endowed with great interpersonal skills and promised a great future in the company. Finally, after making sure that Samuel had no concerns or final questions, Jeff invited him to head toward the meeting room. There, Samuel immediately recognized, although her appearance differed vastly from the woman who had excited him so much two days earlier, the beautiful Rachel, sitting in front of several piles of documents. Sitting beside her were two men in their forties, dressed in black suits, white shirts and black ties, whom a layman would have thought at first sight to be FBI agents but who were actually a legal adviser and a financial manager. All rose when Jeff and Samuel entered the room and the two strangers in black came to introduce themselves ceremoniously to Samuel.

Jeff made brief introductions, reminded everyone of the day's objective, invited the legal and financial managers to explain the details of the contract, requested that Rachel take Professor Kahn back to his office at the end of the meeting before his return to Boston and then slipped away. Rachel then gave Samuel, as well as each participant, a copy of the draft document. The financial advisor went on to review, paragraph by paragraph, the multiple clauses of the contract. As soon as a sum of money was mentioned, he gave the floor to his financial colleague, who simply clarified the amount and specified the terms of the payments.

Samuel, who had brought a copy of the contract drawn up a few years earlier for the services rendered to TOTEXX in Iraq, was reassured to find an identical structure in the new document and simply nodded in approval. He regularly sought to capture Rachel's gaze, who simply pretended to keep her eyes fixed on the document. From time to time, however, the young woman responded to his insistent looks with a furtive, vaguely mischievous smile during which she discreetly passed the tip of her tongue over her fleshy lips, which completely destroyed Samuel's desire to argue with her two colleagues.

After two rather tedious hours, during which no significant objections were raised by Samuel, everyone smiled with satisfaction and congratulated each other on a "job well done"! The legal counsel asked that he be given thirty minutes to have his secretary incorporate into the final document the few minor corrections that had just been agreed upon and to give Samuel two copies signed by TOTEXX, one of which he would have to co-sign and hand back to the company. Rachel then invited Samuel to follow her to Jeff Fishman's office. During the short trip along the quiet corridor of the top floor of the tower, Samuel managed to work on Rachel. "I think I was very well behaved, and I deserve my reward… Is it still on for tonight? You'll meet me at the Ritz at seven and we'll have dinner together? "

"Yes, Professor!" Rachel replied with a smile. "I always keep my promises! I'll meet you at the reception of the Ritz. I hope you won't disappoint me…"

Rachel knocked gently on the door and received an enthusiastic "Come in!" from Jeff.

"So, everything went well?" asked Jeff. "No last-minute difficulties?"

"Everything went very smoothly" Samuel said.

"When can you give us the stone?"

"Whenever you want!" Samuel replied in a confident tone.

"Could Rachel stop by Boston and bring you your check… say next Thursday or Friday?"

"That's entirely possible. But the transaction would have to be done in the evening, because I'm afraid I won't be available during the day.

Maybe Rachel could visit me in Boston on Thursday night? Of course, she'd have to spend the night there, for example at the Four Seasons, which I think is the best hotel in Boston."

"What do you think, Rachel?" Jeff asked her. "Could you do that for us?"

"If that's what you want, Jeff," Rachel replied deferentially, "I have no reason to refuse."

"Well, that's how we'll do it!" exclaimed Jeff, rubbing his hands together with apparent satisfaction. "Professor, you will have the pleasure of continuing to work with Rachel, from next Thursday. Well, I guess the final contracts are now ready and we'll be able to let you go and get on with your day! Rachel will walk you out. I think there's a limo waiting for you at the entrance to take you back to your hotel. Thank you very much, Professor, and have a safe trip back to Boston!"

18

UNDER THE ANTARCTIC ICE

Since the arrival of Kate and Kevin, there had been an unusual level of excitement at Benson Castle. The mere presence of the two young people had brought an air of enthusiasm to the house. When he was not at university, Kevin, eager to be taken into the inner fold of True Archaeology, took every opportunity to talk with Edwina about the history and activities of the society and to question Dorian about his theories. Edwina, who often felt lonely because of her husband's constant business travel, was delighted. She appreciated the young man's keen intelligence and was happy to be able to play the role of teacher and initiator. Dorian, initially reluctant to waste his time talking to someone he considered a turbulent kid, had softened when he'd observed in Kevin traits similar to those he exhibited in his youth. He had even come to consider that this astute archaeology student might one day become his successor as the head of True Archaeology. Kate was equally thrilled in this environment: Being surrounded by servants reminded her of the comfort she had always enjoyed back home. Edwina, this very elegant and distinguished woman, put her in mind of her mother, Sonya Von Tardy. Dorian, this old, erudite and charismatic gentleman, reminded her of her grandfather, Célestin Von Tardy. Edwina, Dorian and the servants quickly fell in love with Kate, whom they all found to be very pretty, kind and well-mannered. Kate spent every morning exploring the park surrounding The Manor, its century-old trees where many birds and squirrels nested, its magnificent flower beds and its fishpond. In the afternoon, she loved to hide herself away in the impressive library, with its hundreds of books, most of them old leather-bound editions, almost all devoted to the history of civilizations, archaeology, mythology or philosophy. After choosing a book whose title grabbed her interest, Kate fell into one of the big leather armchairs and read of a world she did not yet know, populated by unknown gods, monstrous chimeras and impressive buildings. Sometimes, Dorian Green, would come in to fetch a book, startle her and pull her out of her reverie: Moved by the obvious passion that the girl showed, Dorian sat down with her, gave her some useful information for a better understanding of whatever book Kate had just immersed herself, and then usually stayed a good hour to tell her about some unusual episode in his life.

But, more than anything else, Émile's stone had turned the Manor's rather peaceful routine upside down. Upon Kevin's return in possession of the precious object, Dorian had, with Edwina's help, convened another meeting of the leaders of the True Archaeology. The phone kept ringing and it was clear, upon capturing snippets of conversations between Edwina and the people on the phone, that an exceptional event had just occurred, that True Archaeology was about to be on the global stage and that the steering committee had to meet as soon as possible to adopt a strategy and an action plan.

One day, just a week after Kate and Kevin had moved into The Manor, the two young people were informed by Edwina that there would be an important and confidential meeting of the True Archaeology leaders in the large sitting room at the end of the afternoon, followed by a dinner in the dining room. Kate and Kevin, not being members of True Archaeology, could not attend and Edwina asked them to find other arrangements for the evening. Before leaving The Manor for dinner in downtown Oxford, Kate and Kevin were able to witness, from their bedroom window, the more or less simultaneous arrival of several limousines and the half dozen or so guests that stepped out of them. When Kevin and Kate walked past the large sitting room on their way out, they could hear through the heavy closed doors the sound of lively conversations, interspersed with bursts of laughter. They glanced at each other with an interrogating look on their faces.

"It's a pity we weren't invited: The subject is probably very interesting and, moreover, they seem to be having a good time... I absolutely have to convince Professor Green to introduce me to these people!" exclaimed Kevin.

In the large sitting room, the True Archaeology members were eager to know what great news Dorian had to tell them. As usual, Edwina had remained very mysterious on the phone, and they had to comply with the rite of champagne, *petits fours* and the exchange of friendly banalities before getting down to business. And they did so with good grace. Silence met Dorian as he invited his guests to take their seats and listen to him. Dorian directed the participants' eyes towards a dark green velvet sheet covering some invisible object, sitting on a table in a corner of the room. He allowed the suspense to linger before speaking solemnly. "Under that piece of fabric lies the reason why you're here tonight. I'm sure you remember our last meeting when I showed you pictures of a black stone found by a French tourist in Antarctica and subsequently stolen by Professor Samuel Kahn in Boston. I assured you that this object was of priceless value to True Archaeology and we agreed that everything possible should be done to get our hands on the original artifact. Well... mission accomplished!"

In a theatrical gesture, Dorian lifted the veil and revealed to his friends and colleagues at True Archaeology the stone recently brought back from Boston by Kevin:

"I invite you all to approach and examine this treasure. There is no doubt in my mind that it is indeed a fragment of a diorite stele, engraved with cuneiform characters of an archaic Sumerian style. The fact that this stone was found in Antarctica by a good man who cannot be accused of exaggeration or machination proves that there are ruins under the ice that are at least 5,000 years old. Recent satellite images seem to show the presence of pyramids in Antarctica and the fact that there is probably a large city where the stone was found leads me to believe that Antarctica could well be the cradle of this great primordial civilization whose existence True Archaeology seeks to demonstrate. It wouldn't be at all surprising: Let's not forget that the Ottoman admiral Piri Reis left us a map showing an ice-free Antarctic continent…"

Dorian paused for a few seconds to enjoy the excitement that shone in the eyes of his audience and continued:

"We now have in our hands the key that should enable us to further our theories. Unfortunately, this is not sufficient in itself and it would probably be premature to claim victory now. We will firstly have to find the door, insert the key into the lock and enter the Holy of Holies! Only then can we reveal to the whole world that the history of humanity is very different from what they are trying to have us believe. We now need to work together to develop our action plan. This is why I have gathered you here this evening! "

The leaders of True Archaeology had all gathered around the artifact and were marveling at the polished surface of the diorite and the finesse of the cuneiform signs engraved upon it. Prosper, co-founder with Dorian of True Archaeology and archaeologist emeritus, picked up the object to stroke it and appreciate its texture: "How beautiful! The cuneiform characters are of exceptional quality: They seem almost purer to me than those I examined on the tablets of Uruk and Lagash! This reminds me of the superior perfection of the hieroglyphics of the first Egyptian dynasties compared to the rather degenerate hieroglyphics of the later dynasties. Perhaps the writing practiced in Sumer is in fact only a pale imitation of the writing practiced by Civilization X in Antarctica…"

Dorian gave everyone the opportunity to touch the stone and make their comments. When the general excitement had subsided a little, he invited everyone to return to their seats.

"I'm sure that none of you now has any doubt whatsoever about the authenticity of this and its meaning. In my opinion, there is now an urgent need for True Archaeology to mount an expedition to Antarctica to identify the exact location where Émile found this artifact and to conduct preliminary excavations to find the rest of the stele. Do you all agree with me? "

Dr. Louis raised his hand.

"I fully agree with the need to go to Antarctica. But, from what I understand of the history of this stone, there's only one person who knows exactly where it came from: The famous Émile. Without Émile, the expedition seems doomed to failure. What are you going to do about him?"

"Indeed," replied Dorian, "Émile's participation is absolutely vital to our project! Persuading him to return with us to the scene of his discovery is certainly the first step. As I think I have a pretty good understanding of the man, I have my own ideas as to how to convince him. First of all, I'm going to tell him that True Archaeology has managed to get his stone back. I'm sure he'll jump for joy and be eternally grateful to us for what we've done for him. This should make him available to continue to work with us. I'll simply tell him that when he came across this fragment of an ancient stele, he made a discovery as extraordinary as that of Tutankhamun's tomb by Howard Carter. The day his discovery is revealed to the general public, he'll become an overnight celebrity. But fame can be difficult to manage, especially for someone like him, without experience of this kind of situation. The best way for him to have all the benefits of it without the disadvantages is to be guided, surrounded and protected by a team of professionals, such as the team here at True Archaeology. I'll also explain to him that the stone, on its own, is not enough to start a successful communication campaign. For the stone to have a full impact, it is absolutely essential to uncover at least the rest of the stele from which it comes and, at best, the remains of the city to which it marked the boundary. Since Émile is the only one who knows the precise location of his discovery, it's essential that he return to Antarctica with us to guide us and participate in the excavations. Finally, something that should help him to overcome any hesitation, I would like to offer him a round sum for the acquisition of his stone. And it goes without saying that True Archaeology will cover all his expenses for this second trip to Antarctica and will pay him a good salary for his participation in the expedition. I can't imagine Émile refusing any of this."

"I imagine you want True Archaeology to buy Émile's stone for quite a sum!" intervened Alan Chamberlain, the society's treasurer. "Do you have any idea of the value of such an object? how much, at most, do you intend to offer Émile?"

"Estimating the value of the object is no easy task," Dorian conceded. "If we had to offer it today to a museum or a dealer, we would probably have the greatest difficulty in finding a buyer. Indeed, with the current state of official science, the fact that it comes from Antarctica, where no one thinks it's possible to find such a thing, would immediately provoke reactions of skepticism and rejection. On the other hand, the day we find the rest of the stele and the remains of the city sunk under the ice and when evidence of an antediluvian civilization on Antarctica is clear, the value of the stone is likely to reach dizzying heights. But in my opinion, that's not really the problem. This good man is neither an antique collector nor a profit-seeking speculator; for him, the important thing is that we take him seriously and show him gratitude. A sum which, without transforming him into a billionaire, would constitute a significant addition to his modest assets would certainly be likely to satisfy him. I was thinking of something between fifty and a hundred thousand Euros."

"That's reassuring!" exclaimed Alan. "I was worried that the reference would be the Rosetta Stone or the Hammurabi Code and that we'd be talking millions of dollars… Under these conditions, I think we can't begrudge him a hundred thousand Euros. If it were me, fifty thousand wouldn't budge me, but I'd start salivating at the idea of a hundred grand!"

"That's exactly what I thought," Dorian confirmed with a little smile.

"And as for the expedition," Alan continued, "how much will it cost us?" You know, at the moment, we don't have much in the pot and we'll have to involve all our members and generous donors. When do you think the expedition will take place and when will we start incurring significant costs?"

"I'd like us to go to Antarctica this winter," Dorian said, "so as not to miss the next southern summer, which will make work there more feasible. Ideally this December or January next year. The total cost should be around two hundred thousand and we'll have to book plane and boat tickets for all participants as soon as possible."

"Oh, OK…" Alan said with a heavy breath. "If I understand correctly then, all I have to do now is get to work immediately."

"That's exactly right," Dorian replied. "And if you need secretarial assistance, our new recruit, Emma Coffey, will certainly be happy to help you. As soon as I've confirmed that Émile is ready, I'll give you all the details you'll need for the logistical organization. In practice, apart from the climate, this shouldn't be much different from our previous expeditions."

Prosper raised his hand to ask his question.

"Apart from Émile, have you thought about who else will be going?"

"I was thinking a very small group," Dorian replied, "because I don't want to draw attention to our activities until we've achieved significant results, and secondly because we won't be undertaking heavy and extensive excavations at this stage: At first, the only really important thing to do is to dig up the stele and we don't need hundreds of coolies to do that. In addition to Émile, in my opinion, we'll need a senior archaeologist and perhaps two or three assistants. We'll be counting on our friend Hans who, and this is really a blessing, will be on a German base in Antarctica at the same time. As for the archaeologist, I can only think of you, my dear Prosper!"

"Me?" Prosper asked in surprise. "I'm very flattered! But don't you want to be part of this heroic expedition?"

"I would love to," Dorian replied with a slightly sad look, "but we have to be realistic: At my age, I don't think it's reasonable to embark on such an adventure. But I'll be following the progress of your expedition very closely from the comfort of The Manor!"

"I see I'm going to have to spend my New Year's Eve at The Manor again with Dorian! As usual, my husband will be having a good time on the other side of the world, while I play Penelope at home…"

"Edwina, why don't you go with Prosper? He'll need experienced assistants, and this would allow you to celebrate Christmas and New Year's Day with your husband."

"Don't be ridiculous!" Edwina replied "I think I'd rather wake up with you… Seriously, the idea of being stuck in the middle of an icy ocean, at minus fifty degrees, makes me feel ill. I'm sorry, but I'm past the age for that kind of thing!"

"I know someone who would make an excellent assistant explorer for Prosper," Murphy said. "A young archaeology student from Oxford who has proved that he has resources and talent. In my opinion, he'd say yes in a heartbeat. I think you know who I mean?"

"Yes, and it seems like a great idea," Dorian replied resolutely, "especially since I'm supposed to be his mentor and what better way to train an archaeologist in the field than on an expedition like this! Besides, Uncle Bob, how could I not give your nephew a little help? But joking aside: For those who have no idea what we're talking about, we're referring to a certain Kevin McKee, a young archaeology student from Oxford, to whom we owe the return of Émile's stone. I don't want to go into the details, but I can assure you that the young man accomplished this delicate task with the greatest of skill. You'll be able to meet him very soon. Are there any other questions?"

Dr. Louis then intervened:

"If, as we all hope, the expedition succeeds in uncovering the remains of Civilization X in Antarctica, I imagine that True Archaeology will have to communicate its discovery to the scientific community and the general public. As the person in charge of communication, I would like to know what I need to prepare: When, what, how and to whom will we address ourselves?"

"You're absolutely right" Dorian said. "True Archaeology will have to implement a communication plan that's not only very ambitious but also very cautious. It's obvious that the announcement of the discovery of a city under the ice of Antarctica will have an enormous effect. If it is powerful enough and reaches our target audience, the triumph of True Archaeology will be assured. But, if handled recklessly, this could all blow up in our faces! With our detractors in the academic establishment, we'll have to play it very carefully. They have always tried to ridicule our theories; they will feel threatened and will probably spare no effort in trying to bring us down. Even with the general public, it won't be easy to convince them. The major traditional media, television, radio, newspapers, are all controlled by the authorities in power and, if they receive instructions to minimize this, they are perfectly capable of manipulating public opinion by distorting the message or even by discrediting True Archaeology. Remember the case of the pyramids in Antarctica detected by satellite and then confirmed on the ground by explorers? Has official science mentioned this? No! Did it modify its theories accordingly? No! Did the mainstream media race to tell the world about this extraordinary discovery? No! Apart from a few marginal nut-jobs and a few obscure websites, no one has given this discovery the importance it deserves… So, I recommend the utmost caution. In particular, nothing should be declared by True Archaeology until we have found the rest of the stele. That being said, Dr. Louis, as I hope this will be the case by next January, you can start preparing a media plan."

"If we return from Antarctica in January with enough material to launch our media statements," Prosper added, "another problem we must anticipate is the risk of being overwhelmed by other teams who'll want to head out there for further excavations. How can True Archaeology be assured of exclusivity, or at least leadership, for future research on the site?"

"Excellent remark!" said Dorian. "We'll have to check which nation is sovereign over the Antarctic region where Émile found the stone. I suspect that it's either Great Britain or Chile, which in both cases should not cause too many problems. As soon as I have confirmation and know which ministry is in charge of authorizing excavations, I'll have to enter into discussions with national academic archaeologists, even if it means forging an alliance with the most influential local team. This is the kind of political and administrative obstacle that can turn into a nightmare… Bob, your contacts in the secret service and your diplomatic skills will be welcome here."

As the flow of questions had dried up, Dorian decided to conclude the meeting by summarizing the decisions taken and those responsible for their implementation.

"Let me summarize things:

Step one, the positive result of which is a necessary condition for the continuation of the project: I will call Émile and convince him, firstly, to sell us his stone and secondly, to head back to Antarctica with us.

Step two: Bob and I will make sure Kevin is on board for the expedition.

Step three: Alan will prepare a budget and find the necessary funds to carry out our operations. And I will ask Emma Coffey to provide administrative support.

Step four: Dr. Louis will develop a communication plan, for full implementation as soon as the success of the expedition is confirmed, which should be sometime next January.

Step five: Bob and I will prepare the political and administrative groundwork for obtaining the necessary permits for True Archaeology to obtain exclusivity or at least leadership for future excavations on the site. Above all, I will contact Hans Diekirch, so that he can facilitate our access to the German base in Antarctica where he is currently on an oceanographic research mission.

Finally, Prosper will have to be extra nice to Edwina so that she can handle spending the holiday season on her own with me. More seriously, he will have to prepare physically and psychologically to become the Heinrich Schliemann of Civilization X, or if he prefers the Paul-Émile Botta of Antarctica!"

He had barely finished his conclusion when a round of applause broke out and everyone headed back to the stele fragment to admire it again and superstitiously pray that it would bring good luck to True Archaeology and its polar expedition. They then all headed for the dining room where a sumptuous dinner awaited them.

19

A UNIQUE OPPORTUNITY TO MAKE HISTORY

Implementing the first step of his action plan without delay, Dorian called Émile the next morning.

"Hello, Émile? This is Professor Dorian Green. Do you have a few minutes to talk?"

"Ah, hello Professor," replied Émile, pleasantly surprised. "I have plenty of time for you!"

"Émile, I have some great news! Are you sitting down?"

"Yes, yes, I'm all ears!"

"True Archaeology has managed to get your stone back! It's currently safe with us and you will be able to see it again very soon."

"Oh, that's wonderful! I don't know how to thank you, Professor! How did you do it?"

"I don't think you need to know all the details of the operation," Dorian said mysteriously. "The only thing I can tell you is that True Archaeology put significant resources into play and that the work was carried out smoothly, without having to resort to methods that neither you nor I would have supported. So, you can rest easy! You just said that you don't know how to thank True Archaeology, well, I have an idea... and I have a feeling you're going to like this plan. But these aren't things we can talk about on the phone, so it would be nice if you could come and visit us as soon as possible at Benson Castle, near Oxford, where the headquarters of True Archaeology is located. Anyway, I imagine you're looking forward to being able to touch your precious souvenir from

Antarctica. Could you come early next week? Of course, all your travel expenses will be covered by us."

Émile, who felt very flattered to be invited to the headquarters of True Archaeology and to whom an all-expenses paid stay in an English castle sounded just the ticket, was about to immediately accept without discussion, but he held back, not wanting to appear too excited but thinking that he might be better off playing hard to get:

"Early next week? It's very short notice... And I have to ask my wife if we're available."

"All right," Dorian continued quite dryly, "but Monique's presence will not be necessary or even desirable. Your visit to the True Archaeology headquarters is serious stuff; it will be a business trip during which we will discuss important topics, such as the impact of a major archaeological discovery and the follow-up to such a discovery, if you know what I mean... Under these circumstances, your wife's presence might be an unwelcome distraction. I therefore would prefer that you come alone, and I hope that you'll have no difficulty explaining this to your wife."

Émile felt very embarrassed and terribly anxious at the prospect of telling Monique that she wasn't to be included on a trip to England. She had loved her recent crossing on the Eurostar so much and had found her shopping sessions in London too short by far...

"Look, Professor, I'll try to convince her, but I can't promise you anything. I'll give you an answer tomorrow. You know, we always travel everywhere together, so I don't know how she'll react."

Émile was rather taken aback when Dorian, who knew how to manage such impressionable and inconsistent people, suddenly took on an authoritarian tone:

"I don't care what your wife thinks! True Archaeology does you a great honor by inviting you to its headquarters. We have already done a lot for you, so we expect more from you than dithering around, indecision and fearful procrastination. You can take it or leave it. You either agree to this now or you'll hear no more about it."

"Well, then, all right," said a stuttering Émile, rather sheepishly. "I can be in Oxford on Monday."

Dorian, relieved that the bluff he'd felt compelled to use had worked so perfectly, even though he hated playing the bully, used a much kinder tone to conclude their conversation:

"Excellent! I'm sure you won't regret your trip and that your wife will have every reason to be proud of you when you tell her about all this. You know, Émile, you have to know how to seize opportunities when they come your way. As the popular saying goes, *once bitten, twice shy*, but not everyone is as dishonest as Professor Kahn and you should be congratulating yourself on your collaboration with True Archaeology. Émile, I'll be delighted to see you again next Monday! Bye for now!"

Confident in his chances of obtaining Émile's full cooperation and successfully completing the first step of the plan, Dorian immediately moved on to the second step and asked Bob to come to The Manor in the late afternoon, so that both could assess Kevin's motivation and his ability to play a major role in the expedition to Antarctica.

When James, the butler, informed Kevin that Mr. Green and Mr. Murphy wanted to have a meeting with him at five in Mr. Green's office, Kevin felt both very excited that he would finally have the opportunity to ask Dorian to open the doors of True Archaeology to him, but also somewhat worried about having to confront Commissioner Murphy. He feared that the Commissioner, who obviously didn't like playing the role of Uncle Bob, might have decided to make him pay for it. Upon entering Dorian's office, Kevin was afraid he'd be told that he and Kate were being asked to leave the sumptuous residence and that they'd now both have to quickly descend from the little cloud on which they'd both been sitting since their arrival. He was relieved to note the relaxed look of Commissioner Murphy and the radiant expression of Dorian Green.

"Ah Kevin!" exclaimed Dorian with a broad smile. "Thank you for giving Bob and me a few minutes of your time. I understand you'd more than likely prefer to be in Kate's arms right now than in the presence of two old fools like us! About Kate, I must tell you that everyone here finds her absolutely charming and that you really must take good care of her. Are you enjoying your time here?"

"Oh, everything is absolutely perfect!" Kevin replied gratefully. "What you're doing for us is really great! Allow me to apologize for making up that mentor story about you, Dorian, and the Uncle Bob tale about you, Commissioner. But, please understand, at the time, I couldn't think of anything else to say to explain to Kate that you were there when we arrived at the airport."

Together, Murphy and Dorian reassured Kevin that they understood that it had actually turned out to be a very harmless and clever little lie to get out of a difficult situation and that no apology was necessary.

"In fact, Kevin," Dorian continued, "we would like to know if you'd be interested in participating further in the work of True Archaeology. You've already done us a proud service, but perhaps you would be willing to do more? After all, as an archaeology student, being aware of Émile's discovery in Antarctica should mean something to you."

"It's funny!" Kevin laughed. "Do you know that I was planning to ask you how I could be initiated and fully integrated into your society? Of course, I'm interested! This story of an antediluvian vestige discovered in Antarctica is fascinating! In fact, my dream would be to go there to find more ruins that must be hidden under the ice. To experience an adventure just like the great explorers of the nineteenth century: Champollion, Layard, Botta… It would be so thrilling!"

"You must have a good idea," Dorian continued, "that True Archaeology has no intention of stopping at the discovery of Émile's stone… The next and essential step is to go to the place where Émile found it and to exhume the stele from which it comes, and possibly other monuments that accompany it. True Archaeology has therefore decided to organize an expedition to Antarctica this winter, the only season where it might be possible to see some of the ground cleared of ice. If you feel up to it, you could be part of this!"

"Wow!" Kevin exclaimed, looking ecstatic. "That's great! I'm hundred percent ready for this!"

"Don't get too excited, boy!" Murphy said, cutting him off. "What makes you think you're ready? Do you have any experience of excavations? Do you have any idea how harsh the environment is in Antarctica? Are you able to work in a team?"

"It's true that I've never actually participated in archaeological excavations before," Kevin admitted, "but I learned all the theoretical aspects on my course! It's also true that I don't have any experience of such a climate, but I guess with the right equipment, I mean a warm anorak, mittens, shoes and a hat, I'd able to survive! After all, lots of people who live on bases in Antarctica do just fine. Émile isn't exactly a young athlete, he went there last winter and didn't die. As for my ability to work in a team, it will depend on the team. If I have to work with a bunch of idiots or insane people, there might be sparks. But I know you'll choose the best scientists for an expedition like this, so I'm not worried!"

"I can already tell you," Dorian revealed, "that the team leader will be Prosper Tabellion, Edwina's husband, whom you've not yet had the opportunity to meet. There is no better man for the job. He's a professor and director of archaeology in Strasbourg and has a wealth of discoveries and publications to his credit. As for his character, the fact that he is Edwina's husband says a lot about his charm and kindness. For the time being, the other members of the expedition have yet to be identified, but it will be a very small team in any case."

"All right!" Kevin nodded. "In practice, what exactly will my role be and what can I do now to prepare myself?"

"The first thing to do, Murphy explained, "is to keep this information highly confidential. This is no time to be bragging to your friends at university. You can't even talk to Kate about it. We don't know how Kahn will react when he finds out the stone has gone and the later he finds out that True Archaeology is planning an expedition to Antarctica, the better!"

"Bob is right to insist on the secrecy of our project at this stage" Dorian confirmed. "We will only publicize it once our exploration has confirmed the existence of ancient remains on Antarctica. As far as your role is concerned, we thought you could supervise Émile. He's the only person who can identify the exact location of his discovery but Émile isn't the kind of ambitious, energetic and adventurous type who can be left to fend for himself on such a mission. You will have to be there with him, guide him and stimulate him. In addition, you will assist Prosper as soon as it comes to scientifically evaluating the site and digging according to best practices. As for your preparation, you should read everything you can find on Antarctica… But more than just the accounts of the great explorers of the past: Amundsen, Shackleton and the rest! You need to study the geopolitical environment and the living conditions on the permanent bases maintained there. I will have to put you in touch with our friend Hans Diekirch, who will be on a German base in Antarctica at the time that True Archaeology will be leading its expedition and whose full cooperation I hope to obtain."

"No problem!" Kevin enthusiastically agreed.

"As soon as I'm absolutely certain of Émile's participation, I'll ask Prosper to organize a series of team meetings. The first of these meetings, during which Prosper, Émile and you can get to know each other, will have to be held very shortly. After that, it will be up to you! Any other questions?"

"I have no further questions at this time," Kevin answered. "I expect you'll let me know about the first meeting. I'm so excited about this project!"

"Try to be as effective on this one as you were with Kahn!" Murphy added. "If you do so, you'll definitely have earned our trust and affection! Maybe I'll even consider having you adopted by my sister so you can publicly call me Uncle Bob!"

Everyone laughed and then went their separate ways after shaking hands. Kevin joined Kate, regretting that he couldn't share with her his extreme excitement but determined to scrupulously respect the confidentiality instructions and thus not disappoint Professor Green and Commissioner Murphy.

Murphy went to the police station thinking that he had definitely been well advised to help young Kevin enter the fold of True Archaeology. Dorian was very pleased to see that his project was on track and that his vision for True Archaeology seemed to be on more solid ground. All that remained for him to do was to convince Émile, who was the weakest link in the chain of success.

***

When he arrived at Benson Castle, or "The Manor" as his host Professor Green called it, Émile felt very intimidated. To begin with, he was very impressed when a driver holding a sign with his name on it welcomed him to London as soon as he stepped off the Eurostar and invited him to sit comfortably in the back of a beautiful dark green Jaguar, with soft beige leather seats. He was even more impressed when the car drove through the high gates marking the entrance to the property and then slowly slipped down a gravel path between two rows of majestic trees, allowing him to enjoy the view of a huge park with impeccably mowed grass and beautiful flower beds. When a servant came to meet him and show him into the castle, he felt his legs wobbling.

If Monique were here, she'd be lost for words, he thought while following the servant into a luxuriously furnished room.

Émile contemplated the height of the ceiling, the draperies framing the windows, the paintings and the shelves saturated with books with leather bindings.

To make it this far on his own, Émile had had to show unusual authority over Monique. When he announced his invitation to the True Archaeology headquarters, stating that the condition imposed by Professor Green was that he go there alone, she was beside herself:

"What's all this? I really don't see why I can't go with you! Why don't you just admit that you're having an affair and want to go to London and have a good time with your mistress! Don't even think you're going to get away with this!"

Émile tried to reassure her, but she started screaming.

"You must think I'm an idiot! Do you really believe I'm going to swallow this stupid story? Why would an archaeology professor be interested in a nobody like you? You're going off to be the big playboy and it's just humiliating! I'm telling you now: if you don't take me with you, I won't be here when you get back. You'll see!"

Émile had to resort to screaming back at her.

"Since there's no way to talk calmly, and since you're so stubbornly delusional, you can leave whenever you want! For once in my life, I have important people take me seriously and I'm not going to miss this opportunity! I've been vegetating all my life and it's high time it stopped. My decision is final. I'm going to see Professor Green on my own, just as he asked me, and come what may!"

The servant knocked on a second door on the far side of the room and opened it without stepping inside.

"Sir, your visitor has just arrived. Should I ask him to wait or do you want me to bring him in?"

Émile heard a powerful voice responding to the servant:

"Thank you, James, you can bring him in."

Professor Green stood up from behind his desk to greet Émile in French:

"Dear Émile! I'm so happy to see you again! How are you? Did you have a good trip?"

"I'm very well, thank you," replied Émile timidly, "and my trip was just fine. Thank you for the car and driver! I didn't have to worry about a thing!"

"Think nothing of it," Dorian said with kindness. "Ensuring your comfort and good mood is a priority for us here at True Archaeology! Please, sit down and make yourself comfortable. Would you like something to drink? Tea? Coffee? Or whiskey if you prefer?"

"Oh no, no whiskey, it's far too strong!" objected Émile, raising his hand and shaking his finger as a sign of refusal. "As I'm not a tea lover, I'll have a coffee, if you don't mind."

Dorian rang a bell, which immediately made the servant reappear, and asked for coffee and cakes.

"Émile," Dorian said dramatically, "we have some extremely important things to discuss today. But I imagine you only have one thing on your mind: to see your stone. But your vision should go far beyond this. Nevertheless, let's start by doing just that."

Dorian got up from his chair, walked to a small pedestal table near his desk and lifted the piece of cloth that was hiding the object in question.

"Here's your treasure!" he exclaimed as he opened his arms toward Émile. "What you see here is not a dreadful resin copy, and the signs engraved on it are not some odious contemporary joke. In ancient Sumerian, they mean something quite a bit more interesting! Come on, touch it and inspect it more closely, just to make sure you're not dreaming and that you recognize it! You see, as I told you on the phone, True Archaeology managed to tear your stone out of the clutches of that dreadful Samuel Kahn!"

Émile felt very emotional. He approached the object but hardly dared touch it now that Professor Green had authenticated it as a true Sumerian antiquity.

"Oh yes, that's it! There's no doubt about it! It's my stone! I recognize it! It's incredible! It's so strange to see it again!"

"Émile," Dorian continued, "do you realize that you have found something absolutely extraordinary? You know, don't you, that I have a fairly long history as a professor of archaeology, that I've been on many excavations all over the world, particularly in Mesopotamia, and that I'm one of the few experts in Sumerian writing. Well, I can assure you that, contrary to what that scoundrel Kahn tried to make you believe, this stone is at least five thousand years old, possibly much older, and the signs on it look much like the earliest Sumerian writing. According to my analysis, it is a fragment of a stele, the type of monument that the ancients used to plant at the entrance to cities or large religious complexes to mark their borders. If you'd found this object in Uruk or Eridu, no one would be particularly surprised. It would certainly be recognized as an interesting find and a museum like the British Museum or the Louvre would be happy to add it to its collection of oriental antiquities, but it would not change the history of humanity... What is unbelievable here is that you found this in Antarctica! However, I don't know if you really fully understand the situation. If there is an engraved stele in Antarctica, it means that people set foot on this continent a very long time ago. If these people wrote in Sumerian, it is probably because they had a connection with the Sumerian civilization. If people related to the Sumerians managed to cross the hostile oceans between Antarctica and Sumer, it's because they were much more technologically advanced than the Mesopotamians we believe we know. If Antarctica was habitable at the time when these people planted their steles there, it means that all this happened before the glaciation of the continent, i.e. before 5000 BC, perhaps even before the famous Flood! In other words, Émile, it wouldn't just be a pity, but a monstrous pity, if you kept your stone to yourself and if we couldn't follow-up on it. It deserves that much. Do you have a good understanding of the issues and do you have any comments about what I've just said?"

"No, no…" Émile stuttered, feeling intimidated. "I think I understand the situation well… You know, I found this stone by pure chance. I had no idea that this would cause so many problems. I don't want any trouble, so I understand that, under such circumstances, I can't keep it. But who should I give it to? If it has to be given to a museum, I would prefer it to go to the Louvre."

"Émile, I'm so impressed!" exclaimed Dorian with a loud laugh. "I congratulate you on your honesty and generosity! The fact that you're ready to part with your stone for the benefit of science is worthy of admiration! But that's not exactly what I had in mind. In fact, I have a much better offer. Firstly, it would seem fair to me that you should be able to derive some benefits from your discovery. So rather than giving your stone to a museum, I suggest you sell it to True Archaeology, and you'll immediately understand why our acquisition of it makes a lot of sense. Secondly, rather than sink into oblivion yourself, I propose that you come on the excavations that True Archaeology has decided to carry out this winter in Antarctica, on the basis of your discovery. So, once we've discovered the rest of the stele and perhaps the ruins of an antediluvian city in Antarctica, you can become a global celebrity, just like Howard Carter when he discovered Tutankhamen's tomb, and you'll go down in History with a capital "H"! What do you think of my offer?"

"This has come as a surprise," Émile stammered, stunned. "My head is spinning! Money for my stone! Excavations in Antarctica! This all seems incredible! When you say you want to buy the stone, how much money do you have in mind? I don't know the value of it at all!"

"What would you think would be a fair sum," Dorian asked, "for a piece of stone brought back from a tourist trip and that people like Samuel Kahn consider insignificant?"

"I wouldn't want to say anything stupid," Émile apologized. "If I could refund the price of our trip, I'd be pleasantly surprised!"

"All in all, how much did your trip cost you?"

"About twenty-five thousand Euros," Émile confirmed. "But I suspect it's probably too much."

"Émile, I think True Archaeology is about to make you an offer you can't refuse!" said Dorian in a confident tone. "We're prepared to give you a hundred thousand Euros! The check is right here in the desk drawer. You can leave tonight with it if you wish. Also, if you accept, you can always come and see the stone every time you come to visit us at The Manor, and you'll soon see that there'll be plenty of opportunities! So, do we have a deal?"

"A hundred thousand Euros? asked Émile in amazement. "But that's unreal! I never expected that… Are you serious?"

"I could not be more serious!" said Dorian. "I'll show you the check. All that remains is to write it out to you. I can put Émile Delaporte on it right now if you wish!"

"Well, as you say, I really can't refuse!" admitted Émile, laughing. "Deal!"

Dorian reached out his hand:

"Émile, you've just made an excellent decision! Congratulations!"

He went to sit behind his desk, signed the check after writing the name of its recipient and gave it to Émile.

"Do you understand that our mutually beneficial cooperation has no reason to stop there, Émile? How about doing a little work for the True Archaeology? When I say work, I'm not talking about having you do painful digs in the field or doing eight hours a day, five days a week in our offices… I just want you to participate in the mission that True

Archaeology plans to accomplish this winter in Antarctica. Of course, you'll be paid for this, in addition to all your travel expenses. The main part of your job will be to go back to Antarctica, first class of course, to go on the same comfortable cruise you went on last winter and to tell us the exact place where you found the stone. If you succeed, as I'm sure you will, you will have helped True Archaeology to discover the rest of the stele and perhaps even the ruins that are hidden in the area. We will become the authors of the archaeological discovery of the century, and, believe me, there will be some buzz! And, but only if you wish, a lot of lucrative activities can result from such fame: You can give interviews to journalists, you can appear on television, you can write a book, what else... Imagine your wife's pride and the faces of your friends when they see you on TV and learn that you've become an international hero! What do you think of that?"

"Well, we'll have to see..." Émile muttered, as if stunned by the enormity of everything he had just heard. "I have to talk to Monique about it, I don't know if she's going to want to go back to Antarctica... And when you say I'll be paid for my services, how much exactly?"

"To compensate you for the inconvenience, the time spent on the mission and the fatigue of the trip, we plan to offer you twenty-five thousand Euros, in addition to all your expenses."

"Twenty-five thousand Euros is about what our last vacation cost us... We could pay for another trip of a lifetime, maybe to Tibet this time... It's one of the few places we've not yet visited. And that's probably the kind of argument that could convince Monique!"

"Émile," Dorian interrupted in a peremptory tone, "let me give you some advice. I just have the feeling that you let Monique decide everything for you. I understand that you two are a strong couple. But in a situation like this, which is a unique opportunity for an incredible experience that almost never presents itself, I think you must decide what you want to do. Is an adventure like this one likely to satisfy your deepest desires in life? Does it excite you to break free of your anonymity and routine? Do you dream of leaving a legacy? If the answer to these questions is "yes", don't let Monique stop your ambitions! So, what does your gut tell you, Émile?"

"Oh, it would certainly be the highlight at the end of what has been a pretty ordinary little life! I'm tempted!"

"Well, Émile, go for it!" exclaimed Dorian with enthusiasm. "And don't forget that True Archaeology will be by your side and that, as you can see, we always do things well! So, do I have your consent?"

"Well, OK then!" Émile agreed, unable to offer the slightest resistance to Dorian's charisma.

"Émile," concluded Dorian with a grin, "this was meant to be! We are made of the same stuff, you and me! Passionate, adventurous, enthusiastic! This has been a fruitful meeting. I think I can leave you to go about your other business and head back to Rueil-Malmaison where you will have some very good news to share with Monique. In a few days, you will be contacted by your team leader and we'll get ready to prepare the expedition. A first meeting will probably be organized in the coming weeks and you will have to attend. That's crucial. Feel free to call me if there's anything on your mind. Anyway, we will have the opportunity to meet again very soon. Thank you for your contribution, see you soon and have a safe trip back!"

Dorian got to his feet and accompanied Émile to the entrance of The Manor where James then took over. Émile was in something of a daze, still under the influence of the incredible decisions he'd just made under the influence of Professor Green. Before leaving the house, he turned back to speak to Dorian again. "Thank you again Professor! Thank you for everything! And I hope to see you soon!" He was then asked by James to climb back into the green Jaguar that would take him to Saint Pancras International station in time to catch his Eurostar back to Paris.

As the car made its way towards London, Émile had to pinch himself to make sure that he hadn't dreamed all that had just happened. As Benson Castle fell into the distance, he couldn't help but take the check out of his pocket. It was true, there was a one followed by five zeros, it was made out to Émile Delaporte and issued by HSBC, whose name and reputation were vaguely familiar to him. *I think I must have a real gift for business,* he thought as he decided to give in to the temptation of taking a little nap in the comfort of the back seat of the luxurious sedan.

20

THE HEIST OF THE CENTURY

When Samuel surfaced at home again, two days after mysteriously slipping out of their family reunion, Dana Kahn knew right away that his escapade to Dallas had fulfilled all her husband's expectations. He had kissed her too eagerly when he arrived and his arms were full of gifts: a beautiful silver and turquoise necklace for his wife and pretty cowgirl boots and Texas blouses for his daughters. Samuel, exceptionally, didn't complain about being exhausted by his trip. On the contrary, his eyes were sparkling, and he seemed to be boiling over with excitement. Dana suspected that her husband had used the pretext of a meeting with TOTEXX to go and meet one of his mistresses, but preferred to keep her fears to herself, knowing full well that he would deny any extramarital affair and that the only result would be a swift return of his bad temper. She preferred to pretend to be totally ignorant of his infidelities.

"I get the feeling that your discussions with the TOTEXX executives went much better than last time!" Dana remarked. "How did it go in Dallas?"

"Wonderful!" exclaimed Samuel. They took me to a rodeo! It's amazing how those cowboys manage to control those enraged bulls. The poor animals are driven mad by the straps squeezed around their testicles, you know. That's here I got the souvenirs for you three. Texas is really something else!"

"Apart from that, did you manage to sign a great new contract with them?" asked Dana innocently, suspecting that in fact the rodeo with the old TOTEXX guys must also have included less admirable, though just as sporting, activities with some young local beauty.

"I'm pretty pleased with myself! I just came back from Dallas with a done deal! They're offering me several million dollars to provide them with an expert report certifying the absence of archaeological remains in Antarctica, which will allow them to quietly begin their oil drilling there. This mission will be much easier for me than the one in Iraq. I don't know of any credible archaeologist who believes in the existence of ruins in Antarctica which means my report in no way risks creating controversy. TOTEXX may find that they have problems with ecologists and ornithologists, but not with archaeologists. It's a good job I left you to deal with the Finkelsteins and my parents, isn't it?"

"You're right!" admitted Dana. "Of course, your parents were furious when they found out you were leaving, but it doesn't matter… Anyway, it was just a bar mitzvah, it wasn't the coming of the Messiah!"

"Well, it's the last time I'm going to that kind of circus, I can tell you that much. If it amuses my sister and my parents to dress up like idiots, to talk in Yiddish and to believe in all those archaic superstitions, good for them, but I'm not doing it. Already, having a name like Kahn and being Jewish by birth isn't exactly easy when you live in Boston, so I'm not going to add to all that with particularism and bigotry! Let's forget all about it for now. How did it go here while I was away? Any drama?"

"Oh, everything's fine," said Dana. "Except the au-pair has left us!"

"Oh, really? And why?" Samuel asked in an indifferent tone. "Wasn't she supposed to stay until the end of the year?"

"Well, yes… It's weird…" replied Dana. "I found a little note from her on the kitchen table. It just said that she had decided to go back to France. There was no explanation."

"I'm only half surprised," Samuel muttered. "What do you expect from a young French aristocrat who's used to being served by a horde of servants and going to mass every Sunday? Given this Kate's poor cooking and ironing skills, it's no big loss! You should use an American service company instead, especially now that we don't have to worry about the cost anymore."

"Yes, but it won't be the same," said Dana regretfully. "It was great to have full-time help in our home and she was practically part of the family. The girls are going to miss her. Kate was really good at taking care of them. But… as she would say: *c'est la vie.*"

"What else. How's work?" Samuel asked, interrupting her.

"It's pretty quiet at the store right now… But I'm sure it'll pick up soon again with Christmas and New Year coming up. I always make more money towards the end of the year."

"Oh yes, I had forgotten the holiday season" sighed Samuel. "We'll have to put up with Christmas carols all day long on every radio channel and on every street corner for a month. Thank God it helps you make sales!"

"I almost forgot! Something strange happened while you were away" Dana added. "Nothing serious, but a total pain! When I went to the gym on Monday morning, I noticed that the window was broken. I was worried because I thought maybe there was a burglar in the house. So, I called the police. They came right away and searched the house with me from top to bottom. There was nothing out of place. I checked everywhere and I don't think anything was stolen. The cops think it was probably a stone that was thrown into the glass by the gardener when he was mowing the grass."

"I don't believe it!" Samuel said, looking up to heaven. "Are you absolutely sure nothing was stolen?"

Suddenly, Samuel became livid. Dana thought he looked like he was about to faint.

"Are you all right?" asked Dana, worried. "What's the matter with you?"

"It's nothing…" Samuel replied without conviction. "I just have to go make sure my safe hasn't been broken into."

Samuel rushed like a madman to his office, lifted the painting hiding his safe off the wall and punched in the secret password: MARDUK. Dana followed and stood behind him as Samuel opened the door.

"Don't worry! I checked and nothing was missing," she said.

As soon as she'd finished her sentence, Samuel let out a loud scream.

"Oh, fuck! I can't believe this! Fuck me! Fuck!"

Dana failed to understand what could have caused such an explosion of filthy language from her husband:

"What's the matter? Has something important gone?"

"You idiot," Samuel shouted, "of course something important has gone! Millions! Damn it! Fuck it! What the hell did I do to deserve this?"

"What do you mean, millions? How could you possibly have that much in the safe?"

"Well yes!" Samuel erupted. "I put an object worth a hell of a lot of money in that safe and it's gone! That was what my contract with TOTEXX was all about!"

"What was it?" asked Dana. "I hope you kept some pictures of it. It is probably not too late to file a report for theft and to claim on our insurance."

"Unfortunately, it's not that simple," Samuel confided, looking devastated. "I certainly have pictures of the object, but I have no way of proving its value… The insurance company won't touch it."

"Look, Samuel, you need to be clearer," Dana said. "You're telling me that TOTEXX was ready to offer you all that money, yet you're also telling me that you can't estimate the value of this thing, so what exactly is it?"

"Since you want to know everything," Samuel explained in an angry tone, "it's a Sumerian antiquity that a tourist found in an area where TOTEXX plans to dig oil wells. This guy gave it to me and I offered a deal to TOTEXX - either I reveal the existence of this artifact and they lose any chance of exploitation in the region, or they buy the object from me, I keep it quiet, TOTEXX can continue its activities and everyone is happy."

"Wait a minute!" said Dana with a note of suspicion. "You told me that TOTEXX offered you several million dollars in exchange for a report on Antarctica. But actually, these millions were to buy the object and your silence. This business doesn't seem too honest."

"Oh, don't come on to me with your moral lessons!" Samuel replied, irritated. "If honesty paid off, then most people would be millionaires! Just remember that you don't get really rich without getting your hands a little dirty! And nobody died, you know?"

"So, nobody died," replied Dana, "but someone out there broke our window, sneaked into our house and opened your safe to grab that thing. So, your little deal was actually not totally harmless!"

"I know!" admitted Samuel. "Those who know about the existence of this object are obviously willing to take some risks to appropriate it… But then… Only a few people know about the existence of the stone. The tourist, me and TOTEXX! So, the thief, or the person who ordered the theft, has to be one of those people… Now I really don't see TOTEXX getting up to this kind of stuff, especially at as they've signed a contract with me allowing them to acquire the object legitimately… So, it has to be the guy who gave it to me! But how did that asshole manage to pull this off? He's just some pathetic little French pensioner who struggles with his English. Plus, I convinced him that his stone had no archaeological value."

"Really?" Dana remarked. "He's French? Kate was French, too! It's a strange coincidence that she left suddenly without warning right after your stone was stolen by a fellow citizen!"

"God, you're right!" exclaimed Samuel. "There has to be a connection. For all we know, Émile (that's the name of the French guy) is in cahoots with Kate! If that's the case, I've got a chance of getting my stone back…"

"What exactly are you planning to do?" asked Dana, vaguely worried.

"I don't know yet," Samuel replied. "This whole thing has completely screwed with my head. I'm going to take the dog for a walk in the park and then go straight to bed… Don't wait for me for dinner."

Samuel headed for the nature reserve, where Kate walked Marduk when she was with the Kahn household, sat on the bench where Kevin and Kate usually sat to talk, let the dog play around by himself and put his head in his hands while he thought about the situation.

Now that the idea of collusion between Émile and Kate was firmly rooted in his brain, he couldn't even conceive of any other hypothesis - only minor differences in the scenario:

- Maybe Kate had been sent as an au-pair to the Kahn family by Émile, so that she could recover the stolen stone? This was unlikely, since Kate had arrived at their home in early July and Émile didn't know at this point what Samuel would do.

- Maybe Kate was related to Émile? Perhaps Émile had asked her to spy, identify where Samuel kept the stone, and then take it back to Émile in Paris. Again, such a scenario was eminently flawed, because the probability that Émile's relative would be living with the Kahns precisely when he needed her was infinitesimal.

- The most credible scenario was probably the following: Émile, with the help of a private detective, had managed to learn of Kate's presence as an au-pair with the Kahns. The private detective then contacted Kate and took care of the robbery with her help.

Whatever the practical arrangements of their collaboration, Kate and Émile appeared to Samuel as the only possible perpetrators of this act. He would have to find them if he wanted to get his hands on the precious stone and not see the millions promised by TOTEXX disappear down the drain.

When Samuel thought about TOTEXX, he wondered what attitude he should adopt towards them:

- Could he leave TOTEXX in ignorance of this dreadful mishap? In that case, he'd have to find the stone pretty quickly. Indeed, although the deadline stipulated in the contract was a month away, TOTEXX expected to take possession of the stone much earlier than that. In fact, he would have to postpone Rachel's visit to Boston. The fact that Samuel wanted to delay the transaction would certainly look odd.

- What would happen if he informed Jeff Fishman about the theft? Most likely, Jeff would find the whole story extremely suspicious, doubt the reality of the existence of the stone and be tempted to cancel the contract. For such a disaster not to happen, Samuel would have to convince Jeff that the threat to TOTEXX remained real, at least until the fate of the stone was known, and that it was therefore crucial to solve the mystery of his disappearance. He'd have to soften Jeff by coming up with a credible plan to identify the perpetrator and neutralize him.

Samuel concluded that it was probably more prudent to be transparent with TOTEXX. The problem now was to find a way to track down Émile and Kate, the only two people able to lead him to the stone. Samuel then experienced a glimmer of hope: His brother-in-law, Naomi's husband, Dana's younger sister, was French, was living in Paris and was the kind of guy who could carry out this kind of investigation. His name was Maurice Paoletti. He said he was a journalist, but no one had ever read anything by him in any French newspaper, no one had ever heard him on any radio show, and no one had ever seen him on any television program. Originally from Corsica, he boasted of being connected to a network of thugs and mercenaries who carried out clandestine operations in former French colonies in Africa or the East for the secret services and the French army. Samuel was on much better terms with Maurice Paoletti than with Shlomo Finkelstein, his own sister's husband. He saw him quite regularly, especially when he was in Paris, and strangely enough he didn't hate the guy, who treated him as if they had been brought up together in the dregs of Ajaccio or Bastia.

Samuel left the bench, satisfied that he'd found the beginning of a solution to his problem and eager to call Maurice first thing in the morning. He went home, didn't say a word to the girls or Dana who were having dinner in the kitchen and ran straight up to his room. After quickly taking off his clothes, he swallowed two benzodiazepine tablets and threw himself into bed. As soon as he woke up the next morning, he rushed to his phone.

"Hello Maurice? This is Samuel from Boston. How are you? I hope I'm not disturbing you?"

"Hey, Samy!" Maurice replied, obviously happy to hear from him. "It's been a while since we've had a chat! It's going very well here! And how are you guys doing over there?"

"Well enough" Samuel explained, "In fact, it could be better and that's why I'm calling you!"

"Oh, my God! Nothing serious?" Maurice asked in a worried tone.

"Nothing too serious," Samuel reassured him, "just a juicy bit of business that will go tits up if I don't find a solution!"

"Oh well, I can probably handle that" Maurice said, with a sigh of relief. "As long as you're healthy, money issues can always be dealt with!"

"Let's hope you're right... In the meantime, if you could do me a little favor, I'd really appreciate it."

"It'd be a pleasure to help out. Tell me what I can do?"

"Thank you, Maurice; I was sure I could count on you! Of course, you'll get your share of the profits if I get back on my feet! Let me explain what this is all about."

Samuel gave Maurice just enough details for him to understand what was expected of him:

- First off, he would have to find a certain Catherine Von Tardy, an eighteen-year-old French girl who'd been their au-pair until a few days ago and had suddenly disappeared, probably returning to her family in Nancy, Lorraine. He would have to get her to fess up about what had happened to the black stone in Samuel's safe. If the girl has been involved in its disappearance, he would have to get it back from her.

- Secondly, he would have to spy on a certain Émile Delaporte, who was living in Rueil Malmaison. He would have to try and find out what role he'd played in the stealing of the stone. Again, in the event that Émile had the object in question, he would have to force him to return it.

"None of this seems too complicated to me," Maurice said. "With the names and addresses of these people, I should be able to fix this. I do have a quick question though... Can I use any means necessary to get them to spill the beans? Because sometimes we come across people who need quite a lot of convincing, if you see what I mean..."

"Do whatever you usually do in this kind of situation," Samuel stated decidedly, "but please avoid using extreme measures that might get us in trouble with the police."

"Understood, boss!" Maurice agreed. "I'll take care of this right away! Don't worry, everything will be fine. Give a big hug to Dana and the girls for me. I'll call you in the next few days to let you know how I'm getting on. Ciao!"

"Thank you again Maurice," said Samuel. "You're the best brother-in-law ever! Right, bye!"

Samuel, now assured of Maurice's cooperation and confident that he would find out what had happened to the stone, prepared to confront Jeff Fishman on the telephone. He was going to have to be particularly convincing if Jeff were to believe that the stone had been stolen, be satisfied with his plan to get it back and not decide to terminate their contract…

"Hello Jeff? This is Samuel Kahn. Do you have a couple of minutes? I have something a little worrying to tell you."

"Really?" Jeff asked with concern in his voice. "Nothing too serious I hope… Go ahead, but hurry because I have a meeting with Taittinger."

"I'll try to be as brief as possible," Samuel announced. "Here it goes: The stone I promised to sell you, and kept locked away in my safe, has been stolen. I wanted to inform you immediately of this unfortunate development, so that you wouldn't be surprised when I failed to deliver it to you as quickly as initially planned."

"What in the hell is this?" Jeff screamed. "I'm going to end up thinking you're either completely insane or a licensed scammer! First, you come to tell me some incredible story about the discovery of a Sumerian artifact in Antarctica; then, you make sure you never show me the actual object, you just give me pictures of it and you ask me to take your word for it; Next, you threaten to overturn TOTEXX and our plans by revealing the existence of archaeological remains in Antarctica and then blackmail the company by demanding that it pay you several million dollars for the stone and your silence; and now you're saying it's been stolen. You really must think I'm very gullible… or stupid even!"

"Look, Jeff," Samuel explained in a conciliatory tone, "I understand perfectly well that all this may sound absurd. But I promise you, I'm neither a con man nor a liar. Everything I've told you is the absolute truth. The fact that this stone has been stolen from me actually proves that people know its value and surely you'd be concerned if we didn't find it quickly."

"And, assuming it exists other than in your imagination, how do you plan on finding it again?" asked Jeff with an irritated tone. "Did you tell the police? Do you have any idea who took it? How can I be sure that this whole thing won't make the news?"

"I don't think it would have been a good idea to get the cops involved" Samuel said. "Especially as I think I know the identity of the culprit or culprits and I think I can solve the case myself. The thief can only be the Frenchman who found the stone in Antarctica, or the au-pair girl I employed at home, who's also French, and who strangely went and disappeared just after the incident. I took the liberty of using the services of one of my contacts, a private detective who works in France, to get these two individuals to talk. I think that with a little luck all will become clear very soon and you'll have your hands on the stone in less than a month. I know this setback is annoying, but I ask that you trust me and not change the terms of our contract just yet."

"Let's talk about that contract of ours!" said Jeff. "Can I remind you that there's a delivery deadline as far as that stone is concerned. There's no way that TOTEXX will extend it. I can guarantee you that if I don't have the item in my hands by the end of the month, you can kiss your millions goodbye! I don't know if you realize what a mess you've gotten me into! To think of all the work I put into getting Taittinger to swallow this crap and that I had to scramble to get the necessary budget to eliminate this so-called threat to the ICEBERG project… You need to realize that I promised Taittinger that I'd manage the case smoothly and that he'd never hear the story of a mysterious civilization in our oil exploration area again. What am I going to say to him when he asks me how everything is going? It's my position of CEO that is at stake here!"

"I know Jeff," said Samuel, "and that's why I called you. I think it is in our best interest to stick together through this rough patch. Help me find this object and make sure none of this gets out. If we pool our resources and do this together, we should be able to keep control of the situation."

"It's easy for you to be cool and collected," Jeff grumbled. "It's not your job on the line. I have to go now. Do your best to get us out of this mess and keep me in the loop. Goodbye, Mr. Kahn."

Phew, it didn't go too badly, Samuel thought with relief. *in any case, the bridges aren't burned… He has almost as much to lose as I do, and I was right to get him on my side. TOTEXX is neutralized for now; all we can do is hope that Maurice will live up to his reputation…*

21

THE END JUSTIFIES THE MEANS

It was easy enough for Maurice Paoletti to get hold of the information he needed about the Delaporte family. He decided to send Sarah (his secretary, colleague and sexual partner) to Rueil-Malmaison so that she could find a way to get in touch with Monique. Maurice suspected that it might be easier to get Émile's wife to talk as she was definitely a chatterbox from what he'd seen on several forums and social networks, and probably less paranoid than her husband about Antarctica and what they'd found there. As she arrived in front of the building where the Delaportes lived, Sarah was pleasantly surprised to find that there was a concierge on the ground floor. Madame Lopez was a fat, rude woman of Portuguese origin, who didn't hesitate to tell Sarah, who introduced herself to her as a possible future tenant of the vacant flat on the Delaportes' floor, everything she knew about the Delaporte family, including a great deal of information on their private life. Sarah forced herself not to interrupt Madame Lopez, whose accent made the conversation difficult to follow, and whose attention to the nitty-gritty details of no importance threatened to drown out the crucial information sought after. But Sarah soon congratulated herself on her patience when, after about fifteen minutes, Madame Lopez told her that Monique went every Thursday afternoon at half past two to the local hairdresser for her blow dry. The concierge took the opportunity to make a pejorative comment about Monique's hair style, that had not changed for at least twenty years and she found frankly outdated. Sarah claimed that she might have trouble with her boss if she didn't return to work immediately and left Madame Lopez after having warmly thanked her for her kindness.

Sarah immediately made an appointment at the very same hairdressers for three in the afternoon the following Thursday. She would arrive at a quarter past two, insist that she was happy to wait her turn in the waiting area and thus wouldn't miss Monique's arrival with whom she might then manage to start up a conversation.

When Monique entered, Sarah, who had been waiting quietly for a few minutes, immediately recognized the plump redhead, who she's studied from the photos found on the Internet and the description painted by Madame Lopez. Monique had to sit next to Sarah, the limited number of chairs available in the waiting area leaving her no other option. Sarah, pretending to be distracted by the arrival of a new customer, let her purse fall at Monique's feet with a clumsy thud. A travel brochure rolled out, the cover photo of which showed an ice floe covered in emperor penguins. Monique, leaning over to help her neighbor pick up the contents of her bag, couldn't help but notice it:

"Oh, it looks like Antarctica! I've been there! It was the trip of a lifetime!"

As Sarah had predicted, the conversation between the two women began with minimum difficulty.

Later this evening, as soon as she returned from Rueil-Malmaison, Sarah was delighted to be able to tell her dear colleague/lover/ boss that, for the cost of a particularly unpleasant scalp massage and a terrible haircut, she had managed to learn the basics about Émile and the fate of the stone.

"Good job, cutie!" exclaimed Maurice with a big smile. "That hairdresser made a real mess of you, but don't worry, you're still fuckable! Come on then, tell me everything!"

"Well," Sarah explained. "Dear old Monique told me everything! Did you know that it was your very own Professor Samuel Kahn who stole Émile's stone in the first place? In fact, poor Émile gave it to Kahn so he could have his opinion as an archaeological expert. And Kahn decided to keep it because he knew it was worth something! As soon as he realized that he wasn't getting his stone back, Émile turned to another archaeologist, a certain Professor Grym, who lives near London where he runs a company they call *Trou Archeologique* or something like that… In fact, it was this Grym who set about retrieving the stone from Kahn's house. This Émile doesn't have that stone anymore! He sold it to Grym for a lot of money! And wait for it, there's more… This winter, the *Trou Archeologique* people are going off on an expedition to Antarctica and Monique and Émile are planning to go with them!"

"You're awesome, my little one!" exclaimed Maurice. "You've done me a massive favor here because we now know who broke into Kahn's and we know what Émile and his new friends at *Trou Archeologique* or whatever intend to do with it. I don't even have to bother with that au-pair girl, Catherine Von Tardy, who is nowhere to be found. Despite what Samuel thinks, I'm almost certain that she hasn't even set foot in France since she left Boston. I've no idea where the little bitch is! But I'm sure we've now got enough on Émile for Samuel to forget all about her and be grateful to us for what we've managed to do here. So, why don't we go and celebrate our success in a nice restaurant?"

***

Monique, after her afternoon at the hairdresser's where she'd had, in her opinion, a very nice cut, returned in a happy mood to her apartment where an Émile was waiting.

"Your hairdressing sessions are getting longer and longer," Émile complained. "I hope dinner won't take long to get ready because I'd like to eat quickly! I'm starving!"

"I'll have it on the table in less than ten minutes" Monique reassured him, without taking offense at her husband's unpleasant tone. "I knew I might be late, so I prepared everything earlier. I just have to heat it up into the microwave. I have a nice cottage pie! Does that sound good?"

"Fine!" replied Émile. "But how come that a haircut of yours takes a whole afternoon? When I go to the hairdresser, it takes me fifteen minutes!"

"But you can't compare a couple of snips to your half-bald head with the work that goes into my hair," joked Monique. "And we ladies know how to take our time and it's true that we talk a lot when we get together. In fact, I met a charming young woman who's about to make a trip to Antarctica and who was very happy to talk with me about it. We became very friendly and we went for a coffee together afterwards."

"Really!" said Émile with concern in his voice. "And what exactly did you tell her about Antarctica?"

"Well, a little bit of everything!" admitted Monique. "She was very surprised when I told her about your stone and that the ruins of an ancient civilization were probably sleeping under the ice! When I said that you and I were going to go back there this winter on an archaeological dig, she was really impressed!"

Émile, devastated by his wife's naivety, or rather stupidity, replied in an angry tone that Monique blamed on his urgent need for food:

"You couldn't help but brag, could you? I told you to keep this Antarctic excavation project strictly confidential! Professor Green insisted that we had to be really careful because people like Kahn would probably take a negative view of the whole project and might try to scupper it!"

"Oh, you and your Professor Green! Don't you think you might be a little paranoid by any chance?" Monique replied as she rolled her eyes. "What could the clients of some little suburban hair salon do to you?"

"But you don't know who she is!" snapped Émile. "She could be a journalist and put your story in the newspapers! Professor Green would be furious! It would be a disaster! I'm going to have to tell him as he needs to know about leaks like this! Actually, he invited me to Oxford next week to prepare for the expedition with the rest of the team. Given your inability to hold your tongue, I'd rather go alone."

Monique, biting her lip and now conscious of her blunder, didn't dare object and went away to the kitchen to prepare dinner…

***

In Wellesley, Samuel Kahn was delighted when he received a phone call from his brother-in-law Maurice, less than a week after asking for his help.

"Maurice, great to hear from you! So, do you have good news?"

"It's twenty-five percent not so good, and seventy-five percent pretty positive," Maurice warned. "Where do you want me to start?"

"Give me the bad news first," Samuel replied somewhat concerned.

"Right," said Maurice. "So, the bad news is that I couldn't get my hands on your Catherine Von Tardy. But I'm sure of one thing… She isn't back here in France. Neither her close relatives nor the few friends she had here before leaving for Boston have seen or heard from her. My contacts at customs assured me that there was no trace of her in their computer system and that means she didn't enter the county by plane. So, I can't tell you where your au-pair is hiding."

"Shit, that's irritating…" stated Samuel. "Where the hell did that little tramp get to?"

"Look," Maurice reassured him, "it may not be that big a deal. When I tell you the good news, you'll see that finding Kate is probably no longer a priority."

"If you say so…" Samuel conceded. "So, tell me about the good news."

"I know who stole your stone!" Maurice announced proudly. "It wasn't Émile who did the job itself, but he found someone to do it for him. I'm not sure I've got the names quite right, because it's some English guys who robbed you. The leader is a man named Professor Grym, or something like that; it seems he is an archaeologist, based near London and he runs a company called *Trou Archeologique*. He's not the one who personally opened up your safe, but he's the one who sent a team of professionals to Boston."

"Incredible!" Samuel shouted out with amazement. "The guy's name actually is Dorian Green and I know exactly who he is. He's one of my sworn enemies, a completely crazy archaeologist who never misses an opportunity to piss me off. His society is called True Archaeology. They're opposed to academic and conventional archaeology. They are capable of doing just about anything to put their delusional ideas out there. I never thought that Émile was bright or resourceful enough to involve Green and True Archaeology in this… Well, life's full of surprises… So, I guess those bastards gave the stone back to Émile… Can you get it back off him?"

"Wait," Maurice said slowly, "it's a little more complicated than that. The *Trou Archeologique* bought it off him for a large sum of money! So, your stone isn't at Émile's, but in some safe somewhere in England. I don't know anyone who operates there, and so there's not much more I can do for you on this front."

"Oh God! What a mess!" exclaimed Samuel in confusion. "What can I do?"

"Well, I'm not sure I can help you," Maurice apologized. "Listen, there is something else you need to know, because it might give you some ideas on what to do next. Apparently, the *Trou Archeologique* people are preparing an expedition to Antarctica and they're taking the Delaportes along for the ride."

"Jesus!" Samuel yelled. "They don't waste any time, do they? I know exactly what they're planning on doing with Émile in Antarctica! This is getting out of hand."

"Listen Samy," Maurice pointed out, "for me, these people, this stone that apparently is worth a fortune and that everyone is fighting for, what is happening in Antarctica, all this stuff sounds really weird to me and I don't think I want to know more. I believe I did what you asked of me and now the rest is down to you."

"You're right, Maurice," Samuel admitted. "You did a terrific job. It's not your fault that the case has taken this turn. I have everything I need to start thinking about what strategy to take from now on. I'll call you back to let you know how it goes and if I need to use your services again. Thank you so much. See you in Paris soon, I hope!"

Now that he had this precious information about Émile and True Archaeology, Samuel wondered what his options were:

- Did he have any hope of getting the stone back? Obviously, obtaining it from True Archaeology now seemed beyond his capabilities. Dorian Green would never agree to sell it to him, even for a considerable sum. Only an expert criminal of the highest order would be able to defeat all the protection systems that the True Archaeology team must have put in place to guard the treasure they'd just acquired. But neither he nor Maurice Paoletti had such a contact.

- Was there any hope of getting any money from TOTEXX now? Without being able to give them the stone, this part of his contract had certainly lapsed. However, the Antarctic expedition planned this winter made the threat to their operations more imminent and serious than ever. How could he make himself indispensable to TOTEXX to counter this threat and thus remain in a position for which he might be paid?

Samuel remained deep in thought for several minutes. Finding no simple and realistic solution, he decided to call Jeff Fishman to share the results of his investigation, praying that he might recognize the value of the information and agree to pay him handsomely, even if it only meant a fraction of the millions he'd previously hoped for.

"Hello Jeff? It's Samuel Kahn. I have some very important information to share with you about the ICEBERG project and my collaboration with TOTEXX."

"Yes, I'm listening," Jeff Fishman replied sharply.

"My private detective has done some outstanding work," Samuel announced in an optimistic tone. "It cost me a fair amount of money, but I think you'll agree that it was a good investment in terms of protecting your interests. Everything I said about the risk of a major archaeological discovery in Antarctica seems to be coming to light. Let me tell you about it. It was the guys over at True Archaeology who stole the stone from me and now have it in their possession. They've decided to launch an excavation expedition to the site where it was discovered. They'll be going this winter. I don't know if you realize what all this means. It means that there are some extreme activists, I'm talking about True Archaeology, who loudly and clearly go on and on about the existence of some sort of fabulous antediluvian civilization whose trace remains to be discovered and who now have proof that evidence of it might very well lie in the subsoil of Antarctica. If ever, during their expedition this winter, they succeed in finding the stele of which the stone is a fragment, no doubt they will trigger some real media noise before arranging to start large-scale excavations. There is every reason to believe that it won't be all that difficult for them to obtain from the scientific community and the political world further protection of Antarctica. It may make things much more difficult for TOTEXX. In other words, any obstacles encountered by TOTEXX within the region will be increased tenfold to the point of becoming absolutely insurmountable. You can say goodbye to the billions in new revenue expected in the medium term… Just imagine the effect of this type of announcement on TOTEXX share price!"

"This is a disaster!" whined Jeff. "You should have been more careful with that freaking stone! You've got us into a hell of a mess! So, how are we going to limit the damage on this?"

"I have some ideas," Samuel said, "but we need to talk about my contract first. As it stands, I'm only supposed to get my money if I hand over the stone. But it's obvious I'm no longer in a position to do that, which means you could terminate our agreement. Even though the situation isn't as simple as it once was, I've done you a great service by providing you with information that's crucial to the future of TOTEXX and I should be compensated!"

"I can't believe you have the audacity to ask me for millions of dollars when all you've done is failing to stop a disaster heading our way? You really have some nerves!" Jeff yelled.

"I'll readily admit that I can't ask you for the amount we initially agreed" Samuel stated. "But I think a check for five hundred grand would be perfectly justified. It would be impossible for me to continue working with you if you refuse me a decent amount! And you still need me."

"Well, we'll see…" accepted Jeff. "In the meantime, tell me what we can do to prevent your worst-case scenario!"

"In my opinion, there are several possible options, but their implementation would be delicate and would require significant support from TOTEXX. I can't do them on my own. For example, I learned that True Archaeology plans to take the French tourist who discovered the stone with them on the expedition. He's the only person who knows exactly where the object was found. Without Émile, it would be almost impossible to know exactly where to dig. If Émile were prevented from returning to Antarctica for some reason, True Archaeology's hopes would vanish and TOTEXX would no longer have anything to fear. The other solutions are a little more difficult: True Archaeology could be tackled directly, either by derailing their expedition, or by discrediting or even threatening them…"

"As you say, it's delicate…" Jeff commented with a worried look. "Let's assume that neutralizing Émile is the easiest thing to do. Is that something you could handle? When I say you, of course I mean that private investigator you use…"

"It's possible," Samuel considered. "But I'd need to receive an advance. Let's say two hundred and fifty grand right now, with a promise to pay me the same again if we can stop Émile from heading off on the True Archaeology expedition."

"All right," agreed Jeff. "That's how we'll proceed. I hope you'll be up to it this time! As for your fees, please submit a bill claiming that you've carried out an analysis of the archaeological context in Azerbaijan, with a view to TOTEXX obtaining an operating permit. Good luck and keep me informed of your progress!"

Samuel thought that even though he'd missed out on a massive contract, pocketing a quarter of a million just for getting rid of Émile wasn't such a bad deal. Of course, Maurice would have to do the dirty work, but if Maurice succeeded and True Archaeology made no progress in Antarctica, he'd be getting a second cheque and be better off that when he started. He decided to call Maurice immediately.

"Hey, Maurice. It's me again. I have another little favor to ask you. It's about Émile and True Archaeology. Listen… It would be much appreciated if Émile were unable to return to Antarctica with True Archaeology this winter. Do you have any idea how that could be made to happen, and would you be willing to do it?"

"I don't really understand what's going on down there in Antarctica, but it must be very serious for you to want to prevent this poor Émile guy from going there at all costs," Maurice pointed out.

"It'd take too long to explain," sighed Samuel with embarrassment, "but basically it's my entire scientific credibility that's at stake. If True Archaeology discovers something interesting where Émile found that stone of his, when I publicly ridiculed them and called them a bunch of idiots, it's my career at Harvard that could go down the drain! So, you see, for Dana and the girls, it would be just awful, and I don't want to see that happen."

"I get it," Maurice said, "and anyway I was just joking. If you ask me to do something for you, I do it without question if it's within the realms of my capabilities. Stopping Émile from returning to Antarctica is entirely feasible. The only question is how far you're willing to go, because we have quite a few options here… For example, there is the final solution option, if you know what I mean… But that may be a little excessive, right? Otherwise, this Émile could be caught in some sort of traffic accident… Or he could have a chance encounter that would mean he'd have to go to hospital with two broken legs… None of this is particularly hard to do. And there are other possibilities…"

"To be honest," Samuel clarified, "I prefer not to go too radical on this. I like the idea of the broken legs or the traffic accident, if it means Émile could recover in three to six months. I just need him to be very scared and physically unable to make the long and painful trip this winter. How much would you need to set that up?"

"I'm glad you ask," Maurice said, laughing, "because something like this is going to set me back. The normal rate for this type of contract is between thirty and fifty grand."

"No problem. I'll send you a check for thirty right away and you'll receive an additional thirty when you're done. It goes without saying that the utmost discretion is required, and that the operation must under no circumstances have too serious an impact on Émile's health or wellbeing. I don't want us to go too far. I trust you! Do the best you can! Thank you again, Maurice, you're saving my ass here!"

"Don't worry, you can trust me!" Maurice said in a reassuring tone. "Well, I'll get to work right away. Speak soon, Samy!"

After concluding his conversation with Maurice, Samuel was overwhelmed by a sharp feeling of anguish. Wasn't he on a very slippery slope and was it worth it? When this had all started a few months earlier, all he'd done was steal a piece of stone from a nobody. It was not even really a crime… Then he negotiated a big contract with TOTEXX which could have earned him several million dollars without much effort. Not very honest, but nothing fundamentally wrong… But things had just taken a completely different turn. Hadn't he just paid for, if not a real blood crime, at least the physical harm inflicted to an innocent man? And he wouldn't be making several million dollars, but a half million dollars at best and nothing was absolutely certain… What if things went wrong with Émile? Of course, Maurice could be trusted to do things right and not take any ill-considered risks… But nobody was ever completely safe from mistakes or unexpected events… Samuel was about to call Maurice back to cancel the whole operation. However, the idea of being seen as someone who changed his mind at the drop of a hat, or worse, a coward, held him back.

"It's too late to go back on this one," he whispered to himself. "But after this, I have to stop… It's too dangerous and there's not enough money in it… Jeff Fishman and TOTEXX will have to manage without me… Better than that, if Green finds his Civilization X in Antarctica, I can be the first to congratulate him and praise him on television. With a little luck, I may even be able to get a place on the excavation campaigns that come after…"

22

THE BLUES

At Benson Castle, preparations for the expedition to Antarctica were in full swing. As agreed, Prosper had summoned the members of the small team whose mission would be to find the spot where Émile had discovered the engraved stone and to exhume the stele from which it came. Prosper and Kevin had finally been able to meet Émile, recently convinced by Dorian to return with them to Antarctica, mainly if not exclusively to show them the exact location of his discovery. Prosper and Kevin, who had already developed a solid relationship and whom the challenges of the expedition stimulated rather than inhibited, had some difficulty accepting Émile in their small circle. Although Prosper could communicate with Émile in French and therefore the language barrier had nothing to do with it, Émile had to be told the same things ten times and given endless explanations on every detail before he confirmed that he understood and endorsed the plans proposed by the rest of the group. Everything was a source of concern and hesitation for Émile and he never ceased to question his right to be there by constantly expressing doubts about his ability to meet the expectations of True Archaeology. Above all, Émile simply didn't share the sense of humor that Kevin and Prosper had in abundance and remained stony-faced or seemed horribly embarrassed when the other two swapped jokes. They had to force themselves to put on a smile for Émile, without whom unfortunately their expedition was inconceivable. It was a huge relief when all the issues on the agenda of the first team meeting had been worked out and they were able to leave Émile in the late afternoon, wishing him, with honeyed hypocrisy, an excellent trip back to Rueil-Malmaison.

Kevin and Prosper had become great friends. First of all, Prosper had, as far as Kevin was concerned, the aura of a renowned archaeologist, both a university chair and an expert in his field, with an impressive number of excavations in some of the most exotic corners of the planet. Prosper was the kind of person Kevin wanted to be: distinguished while enjoying a laugh and joke, intelligent while being approachable, simple and relaxed while living a life of luxury in his Oxfordshire castle. Since Dorian Green had offered him the opportunity to be part of Prosper's team for the Antarctic expedition, Kevin had promised to do everything he could to deserve Prosper's consideration and even friendship, both for the positive impact such a relationship would certainly have on his future career as an archaeologist and for the psychological comfort of having the father figure he'd never had. Kevin's energy was increased tenfold; as well as his Oxford courses, he knew he had to put in hours of study to become an expert in the history and geography of the Antarctic continent. He also ensured that he devoted enough time to Kate, whose search for a job had so far been unsuccessful and who spent most of her days learning about ancient civilizations in the Manor's incredible library.

As his departure date approached, Kevin realized that his situation with Kate was becoming more and more untenable. He had felt obliged to respect the confidentiality guidelines imposed by Dorian and had therefore not yet informed Kate of his imminent departure for the antipodes. However, he was concerned that any delay in this announcement might well be misinterpreted by Kate. On top of that, the idea of going to Antarctica without Kate and abandoning her in England for an extended period of time was making him very upset. It was clear to him by this point that he was madly in love with her and exposing himself to the risk of losing her was just unbearable.

He had been blinded by both the euphoria of his romance with Kate and the excitement of his prospects for a dazzling career as an archaeologist, but Kevin had ignored the possibility that his two passions might prove mutually exclusive. Obviously, neither Dorian nor Prosper had suggested that Kate could be part of the expedition. Could he ask that Kate accompany him to Antarctica without risking a clash with them and thus jeopardizing his own participation? But could he leave without Kate and risk seeing the woman of his life disappear? If he had to choose between Kate and the expedition to Antarctica with True Archaeology, what would his decision be?

This dilemma obsessed Kevin for several days, until one of the numerous plans he'd come up with in his tormented mind seemed suddenly to make the most sense to him. He would break the confidentiality clause, explain the whole project to Kate and beg her to go with him. He would then present Dorian and Prosper with a *fait accompli* and ask them to forgive his audacity. He realized then that there was little chance that Kate would be jumping for joy at the thought of a trip to Antarctica. He had to find a way to convince her. And he knew what it was. He was going to ask her to marry him and the expedition would be their honeymoon! All that remained for him to do was to find the right moment.

During his last class of the day, Kevin found himself sitting on a bench at the back of the amphitheater deep in thought when he suddenly realized that Kate was short for Catherine and that today was November twenty-fifth, Saint Catherine's Day. He knew that Catholics in France made a big deal out of this. He left the lecture in a hurry and rushed to buy a dozen beautiful red roses from the local florist. He wrote on the small card that accompanied the huge bouquet the words "Happy Saint Catherine's Day, my lovely Kate," and hurried back to The Manor.

Kevin knocked gently three times on their room door and was happy to hear Kate's voice inviting him in. He handed her the bouquet and gave her a broad smile as she read the card. Kate, pleasantly surprised, threw herself at him to thank him.

"Kate, I want to take this opportunity to tell you about an important decision I've made!" Kevin said. "Listen… I'd like us to get married!"

"Sorry? What a strange idea!" Kate said without the slightest sign of joy.

"What's strange about it? When two people really love each other, they want to spend their lives together and so they get married, right?"

"Of course," Kate admitted, "but don't you think that, as far as we're concerned, we've missed out quite a few essential steps? First of all, I don't think you've ever even told me you love me."

Kevin hadn't been expecting such a lack of enthusiasm from Kate in response to his proposal and, caught off guard, responded in a rather dry tone:

"Of course, I love you! Otherwise, why would I ask you to marry me? Happy now?"

"Oh, you feel obliged, at my request and without any spontaneity, to tell me that you love me, and I'm supposed to swoon!" laughed Kate mockingly. "Don't you even care if that love you say you have for me is mutual?"

"Wait, are you kidding me or what?" asked Kevin, feeling shaken. "I'm sure you love me!"

"Really?" asked Kate. "And what makes you say that?"

"You've been very happy since we've been living together here. I know you and you'd have been long gone if that wasn't true. And I'm sure you'd be heartbroken if I left without you!"

"Are you considering leaving?" Kate asked, her eyes wide open.

Kevin realized he'd just made a mistake and that, given the way the conversation was going, lying to Kate now would only make things worse.

"I might be going to Antarctica. But I won't leave without you…"

"Antarctica?" Kate noted, surprised. "And you want to take me? Couldn't you have chosen a warmer, more enjoyable place, like Phuket or the Caribbean Islands? And what are you going to do in Antarctica?"

"Look," Kevin apologized, "it's supposed to be strictly confidential and I swore I wouldn't tell anyone. I've already said too much, and because it's you, I'm going to be frank… Dorian and the True Archaeology team want to send me there on a top-secret research mission. It's quite complicated to explain… You probably don't need to know any more than that."

"On the contrary," Kate replied furiously, "I need to know a lot more than that! I really think I should have a say in this! A marriage proposal, a trip to Antarctica behind my back, a secret mission for True Archaeology, don't you think that's quite a lot to swallow? I need to understand what's going on in that head of yours…"

"What's going on is quite clear," Kevin said. "I've just found the woman of my dreams and I want to marry her; secondly, True Archaeology has offered me the opportunity to participate in the adventure of a lifetime, which might just allow me to become one of the most famous archaeologists of the twenty-first century, and I can't miss out on it!"

"And why have I been kept out of all this?"

"It was Dorian's decision. There was nothing I could do about that. But do you know what I'm going to do? I'm going to be straight with him. Either he accepts that, after we get married, we both go on the expedition and that's fine; or he refuses to let you go with me… In that case, they'll have to go without us, and we'll just move on and live somewhere else."

Kate couldn't really see the connection between the secret expedition to Antarctica and Kevin's need to marry her, didn't understand the need to risk creating a conflict with their hosts who had been very accommodating so far, and frankly found Kevin's attitude bizarre.

After these few restful weeks at The Manor, in an environment that felt naturally familiar to her, Kate had regained some of the pride and confidence she'd felt in her childhood and adolescence and which she'd somehow lost when she left her family and went to stay with the Kahns. She was definitely not the naive and impressionable thing that Kevin thought he'd met in Wellesley and she was determined not to let herself be led by the nose by this young English student, who was certainly intelligent and nice enough, but didn't hold any power over her. She wasn't going to give in so easily to Kevin's demands, even though she didn't absolutely hate the idea of marrying him.

"And when do you plan to challenge Dorian? And how will I come into all this? Follow you blindly without saying a word?"

"I think I'll let Dorian know right away and it's certainly not my intention to keep you in the dark" Kevin assured her in a conciliatory tone. "If you want, we can go and see Dorian together. But do you at least agree that we should get married and both go to Antarctica?"

"Of course, I agree!" Kate shrugged, "but I don't like people deciding for me."

"Great!" exclaimed Kevin. "Let's go see Dorian right now!"

Kevin and Kate quickly made their way to the Manor's library. Dorian was sitting at a small table with a laptop in front of him, grumbling to himself:

"There's just no way to get this thing to work properly! Computers are supposed to make our lives easier… But it's all just getting more and more complicated… Or I'm too old to keep up… I don't like getting old…"

Kevin and Kate, whom Dorian had not heard entering the library, looked at each other and felt embarrassed that they'd overheard the elderly professor's remarks. Kevin coughed gently to signal their presence. Dorian jumped a little, sat up in his chair and put on the confident look he usually gave to others.

"Kate! Kevin! To what do I owe the pleasure?"

"Kate and I need to talk to you urgently," Kevin said. "There's been a development in our relationship. We've decided to get married! So, I felt compelled not only to tell Kate about the project, but also to ask her to come along with me."

Dorian almost choked.

"I'm very disappointed in you, Kevin! I thought I'd been very clear in demanding absolute confidentiality. You obviously didn't think it was necessary to honor your commitments and I wonder if I was right to trust you to carry out this project. You know that this is of vital importance to True Archaeology… Now that everyone knows, the smooth running of the expedition could be seriously compromised! Besides, taking Kate on this mission is not the best idea."

Kate was angered by what she'd just heard.

"Are you talking about me? Am I everyone? Is this how you're going to treat me? Like someone unworthy of belonging to your little club? Let me remind you, Mister Defrocked Priest, that I am a Von Tardy, that I come from an illustrious family belonging to the very best French nobility, and that I am therefore NOT everyone! I accepted Kevin's proposal and if he has to go to Antarctica this winter, I'm going with him! I really don't see what could be so special about Antarctica that my future husband wouldn't have the right to talk to me about it."

She then turned to Kevin and declared:

"Let's get out of here! I've heard enough! Let's go and prepare our wedding instead!"

Kevin didn't dare to disagree with Kate and they both left the room.

Dorian remained in his chair for a moment, completely stunned. What was happening to him? Earlier, it had been his computer that stubbornly refused to obey him, now it was Kevin who hadn't respected his instructions and Kate who had been just plain insulting! Was the dreaded passing of time not only diminishing his physical capacities, but also depriving him of all his intellectual and mental faculties one by one? This would be absolutely unbearable… Obviously, learning to use IT equipment was perhaps beyond the limit of his ability, managing problems was becoming increasingly difficult and the respect he used to naturally impose on others no longer seemed self-evident… He was thinking about the monstrous decline that awaited him if these small failures were the precursors of some sort of Alzheimer's brain degeneration, when his mobile phone started ringing. Hearing Émile's voice on the phone immediately forced him to put his dark thoughts to one side.

"Ah, my dear Émile! What's new in Rueil-Malmaison? How are your preparations for the great adventure going?"

"Well enough, thank you," replied Émile with a pitiful sound to his voice. "But I want to report a little problem. The expedition hasn't been kept perfectly secret. I inadvertently told my wife Monique about it and, instead of keeping it to herself, she couldn't help but tell the whole story to everyone she knows. She even told some stranger she met at her hair salon. I hope it's not too serious! In any case, I thought I should let you know…"

"All this is obviously very unfortunate" Dorian said wearily. "This just goes to show once again the need to keep your wife completely out of our business. Is there anything else you have to tell me?"

"I also want to tell you," continued Émile, "that the first team meeting went well and that I I'm feeling quite reassured about the expedition. Of course, it's going to be difficult to explain to Monique that I'll be going off on my own over Christmas."

"Look, Émile," Dorian shouted in anger, "we can't start up with this again! "There's no way Monique is going with you! And after she told our secret to anyone who'd listen, you have a good reason to exclude her. When someone can't respect the team leader's instructions, it's basically unforgivable and you're going to have to pay the price for that."

"Yes, yes, I understand… "Émile mumbled, feeling somewhat nervous.

"Alright", concluded Dorian dryly. "See you soon Émile and take care."

After hanging up, Dorian took his head in both hands and sighed:

"This is a disaster! First Kevin and his Kate, now Émile and that Monique. This is what happens when you work with *amateurs*. They're going to mess this up…"

Dorian was starting to wonder who he could really count on right now. Prosper was probably the only one he could talk to about all this, but he didn't want to alarm him by highlighting the weakness of the team they'd put together. He needed Prosper optimistic. Bob Murphy, his other real friend, could actually understand and advise him usefully under these circumstances. Dorian decided to invite him to have dinner at their favorite tavern.

When Murphy joined Dorian at their usual table, he immediately noticed Dorian's tired face and hunched shoulders. Suspecting that his friend might be suffering from a depressive episode, he decided to immediately sort this out:

"Dorian, what's the matter with you? You know you can't crack now! Your life's dream is about to come true, you have a whole team behind you whose mood depends totally on the solidity and drive of its leader, so there isn't time for this…"

"I can't hide anything from you" Dorian sighed. "You are right, I think I am cracking up if the truth be told and only you can help me get a grip!"

"Just tell me what's bothering you," Murphy said empathetically.

"I have a feeling we're running into massive difficulties" Dorian confessed. "This is turning out to be a nightmare and the expedition to Antarctica may well sound the death knell for True Archaeology… I fear that, apart from Prosper, the team we chose to go find the Holy Grail is totally unable to carry out such a task."

"Come on, Dorian, what makes you say such things? Kevin can move mountains if necessary to achieve his goal!"

"Don't talk to me about Kevin!" exclaimed Dorian. "This idiot went and told Kate about everything, despite our confidentiality agreement! And he's decided to marry her so that he can take her to Antarctica! She's just a kid! So, as you can tell, I have every reason to be very worried about how all this turns out. If Kevin's main goal is to go and have a nice time down at the South Pole with his little girlfriend, I don't think there's much hope of us finding Civilization X…"

"And that's what's making you feel so down?" Murphy asked. "I really don't see how Kevin's marriage to Kate and the fact that she might be going along with him to Antarctica is a threat to the success of the expedition! You've just called him an idiot; but I think it's a very good sign that he wants to marry Kate. It shows that he loves and respects this girl, and that he is ready to assume his responsibilities. If he's reliable and honest with Kate, he'll be reliable and honest with us too! As for Kate's participation in what we're doing, it can only be beneficial! The presence of a charming and intelligent young woman in a team of three males will certainly be a source of balance and comfort, and with the remoteness, isolation and harsh climate, they'll need this!"

"Do you really think so?" asked Dorian. "But Kevin didn't respect my instructions! How can I trust him after such behavior? Can I trust anyone?"

"You should know that, generally in life, you can't ever trust anyone…" Murphy said. "The only person you can trust is yourself! Your ideas, your theories, you have always known they were right and you're about to show the whole world that the history of humanity is very different from what we've been told for millennia… So, the fact that Kevin didn't follow your instructions is something you're just going to have to drop… In fact, maybe you should ask yourself if your instructions really have to be followed to the letter… After all, mentioning this expedition to Kate, which he would have had to have done at some point anyway, isn't exactly posing a serious risk to the mission. I'm sure Kate will keep it to herself! You need to learn to accept the fact that not everyone, especially not a smart and proud young man like Kevin, is ready to blindly follow whatever you say. I suggest you be more flexible and cut the people to whom you've entrusted this important mission some slack!"

"I might have guessed you'd put your finger on exactly where it hurts the most…" Dorian admitted. "Well done, Doctor! Excellent diagnosis! I know, I've always had a tendency to be a dictator and keep everyone on a tight leash, and it doesn't get any better with age… I'll try to think about what you've said and tone things down a little…"

"That's what friends are for," Murphy pointed out, "to hold out a mirror and help you erase everything that's wrong with the picture! I feel like my little psychoanalysis session is bearing fruit and you're already feeling better! Is there anything else on your mind?"

"More of the same to be honest, except that this time, I was expecting it… Émile has told that wife of his more than he needed to. And she's gone and spread it throughout the entire neighborhood, boasting of her husband's discovery, of True Archaeology's interest in the object and our expedition plans! Apparently, Émile hasn't dared tell his wife that she will have to stay home quietly while he plays the adventurer and poor Monique still thinks she's going along for the ride!"

"Well, see, that confirms what I've just told you! So, the fact that

Kevin talked to Kate about the expedition is really not a problem as, thanks to Émile and his wife, the whole world will soon be aware of our project! I think you can definitely draw a line under all this. There's nothing to make a big deal about… As far as Émile is concerned, I really think you should be more patient and forgiving with him. Don't forget that, without Émile, there would be no stele fragment and it would be absolutely impossible to identify the exact location of its discovery. True Archaeology's only hope of finding the remains of Civilization X in Antarctica rests exclusively on Émile. Of course, he's neither Einstein nor Rambo, but we still need him! Besides, we can't hold him responsible for what his wife does. He married an annoying little gossip, but what choice did he have? It was probably that or staying a bachelor all his life or becoming a priest like you! Not many people can live like that! All jokes aside though… You know very well we have to tolerate others in life, with all their faults… So, you're just going to have to accept Émile for what he is and adapt."

"You're a good philosopher tonight, Commissioner! You usually can't stand any flaws in anyone!" Dorian replied. "I still think you speak too quickly when it comes to Émile…"

"Not at all!" Murphy argued. "Actually, you're the one who's a bit slow! Remember that the expedition leaves in less than a month! There's no time to procrastinate! All hands on deck and ahead full speed!"

Murphy was pleased to see that his words had given Dorian a burst of energy and that he'd lost the pitiful look he'd had at the beginning of their meeting. He thought that a good meal with plenty of wine to wash it down would certainly help Dorian out of this melancholy.

"Listen, I didn't come here tonight just to play Dr. Freud; I came here to eat and make merry! Why don't we order veal kidneys in mustard sauce and a couple of glasses of red?"

23

___

WORTH IT

Having arrived at *Paris Gare du Nord* after participating in a team meeting, Émile felt uneasy. The meeting had exhausted him mentally. Although Prosper and Kevin had been kind enough to him, it was clear that the three of them just weren't playing in the same league. The archaeologists used the same academic jargon, were always on the same page and understood each other very well, frequently using innuendo and shortcuts to communicate. He was not at all familiar with their terminology and, unless he asked for long explanations and multiple repetitions of basic notions, he had great difficulty following their discussions. Kevin was young and lively, whereas he felt introverted and aging. Prosper, familiar with all the practical and logistical aspects of an expedition of this kind, was confident and excited about what lay ahead, while he tended to get anxious for nothing and wanted to always put the brakes on. Émile feared that he would become a real liability for these two and that the atmosphere aboard the Thetis Adventurer might quickly become tense if he didn't manage to keep pace with them and meet their expectations. Had he not feared Professor Green's anger, Émile would probably have given up on the whole idea; unfortunately, it was now too late to turn back. True Archaeology needed him to locate the archaeological site and he'd already received an advance for his part in it all. All this was weighing on his mind… In fact, before he'd left The Manor at the end of the meeting, he'd been given a bundle of twenty-five hundred-euro notes, the first installment of the money promised by Professor Green. This too made him anxious. Wandering around this unfamiliar part of Paris with so much cash was really not a good idea. He now had to go to the *Châtelet-les-Halles* subway station and all he could see around him were dodgy looking people. Instinctively, he placed his hand over the inside pocket of his jacket where he'd stuffed his money. As he glanced behind him to make sure that no one suspicious was following him, he lost visual contact with what was happening in front of him for a second, before turning and seeing a black fist hurtling towards his face. He was thrown backwards onto the cemented ground and lost consciousness.

When he woke again, he was lying on a stretcher in a small room with white walls lit by a screaming neon light. Émile saw Monique's face leaning over him and he heard her saying:

"Ah, finally, you're coming to your senses! I'm so relieved! How are you feeling?"

He wanted to get up, but his wrists and ankles were strapped to the stretcher and he couldn't move.

"I think I'm OK," he grunted, "but I have a headache… I would like to be untied and for someone to let me off this stretcher! Where the hell am I?"

"You're in the emergency room at *Lariboisière* hospital," Monique explained. "I'll check with the nurse to see if it's possible to untie you, now that you're awake. It shouldn't be a problem since the doctors didn't see anything serious on the MRI scan."

"How long have I been here?"

"The police called me around five, so it's been about two hours… But do you remember what happened?"

"Yes, I think so," replied Émile. "Some black guy beat me up! Where's my jacket? He didn't steal it, did he?"

"No," Monique reassured him, "it's there in this closet, but it's in a sad state and I shall have to take it to the dry cleaner."

"You will not!" Émile got angry. "Go get it quickly and check if my wallet and money are still in the inside pocket!"

Monique immediately walked over to the closet and pulled out the dirty, wrinkled grey jacket and searched the inside pocket.

"Your wallet still looks like it's there," she confirmed. "What the hell is all this? What were you doing with so much money on you?"

"Put that away," Émile hissed. "I'll tell you about it later. Come on, get me out of here and let's go home!"

After multiple negotiations, first with a nurse, so that she would agree to remove the straps on the stretcher, then with the resident physician on duty, so that he would confirm, after a thorough neurological examination, that Émile was able to leave the hospital, and finally with a secretary so that she could check that no information was missing from Émile's administrative file, the Delaportes were allowed to jump into a taxi and return to their apartment in Rueil-Malmaison.

Thanks to the gram of aspirin and the sleeping pill he swallowed as soon as he got home, Émile had a peaceful night and woke up the next morning without even the slightest after-effects. During breakfast, after making sure, as recommended by the emergency room doctor, that Émile wasn't displaying any worrying symptoms, in particular headaches or behavioral disorders, Monique asked about the accident the day before:

"Tell me again exactly what happened before you passed out."

"Well," explained Émile, "I'd just got off the train and was walking towards the subway station. I had a large amount of money on me and I kept thinking to myself that a lot of people in the station looked like criminal types and I was afraid I'd get pick-pocketed. So, at one point, I turned around to make sure that no one was following me. Then I just had enough time to see him coming right at me. He was massive. He had to be at least six foot nine, he was black, probably Congolese or Ugandan, and on top of that he was wearing dark shades and a black cap… Maybe he was running because he was chased by the police or he was afraid of missing his train. Maybe he didn't hit me on purpose. In any case, it was a head-on collision, and I was thrown back… and then I don't remember anything…"

"People these days respect nothing and no one!" Monique spat. "But at least he didn't steal anything from you. By the way, where did all that money come from?"

"True Archaeology gave it to me. It's part of my payment! I told you I would get paid to work with them. See? Professor Green keeps his promises. I shall have to deposit all that cash into the bank first thing this morning. We can't have cash lying around like that."

"They're pretty legit at True Archaeology! You've never made money so easily in your life! But are you sure you're ready to go out and about after what just happened to you?"

"Of course!" said Émile. "I'm feeling just fine. Come on; let's forget about it all now."

The bank where the Delaportes had their account was located at Mont Valérien, and it only took Émile about ten minutes to get there by car. The parking lot reserved for clients was deserted. Émile, after carefully parking his Renault Mégane in the spot closest to the entrance, grabbed the bundle of notes he'd locked in the glove compartment, glanced at all the mirrors to make sure that no suspicious individuals were hanging around and pulled himself out of his vehicle. As soon as he'd closed the door, he felt a horrible tear in his right calf and screamed out. From nowhere, some dreadful mutt, a pit bull type, was chomping down on his leg. Throughout the assault, Émile remained totally paralyzed by the fear he'd always had of dogs and could only watch the carnage. It didn't even come to his mind to try to push the animal away. After about fifteen seconds, which seemed like an eternity to him, Émile thought he could hear the sharp sound of a whistle and watched as the animal abandoned his torn flesh and sped off towards a van parked out on the street, about fifty yards from the bank's parking lot. The van's side door opened, the animal jumped inside, and the vehicle rushed off, its tires squealing across the tarmac. Émile couldn't make out the driver's face, nor did he have the reflex to memorize the plates, as the van quickly disappeared into the distance.

Émile, twisting in pain, stared at the bottom of his tattered pants and the big red stain that stretched over the fabric. "Help!" he shouted. But no one seemed to hear him. The few pedestrians around were too far away and the employees of the bank were separated from him by the thick glass of the front door. When he tried to walk towards the door, a terrible pain struck him, his right leg refused to support him, and he collapsed to the ground just in front of the entrance. An employee of the bank, who had finally noticed from her counter that something unusual had just happened, rushed to open the door.

"Are you all right, sir?" she asked stupidly.

"Of course not! "Émile yelled in an explosion of tears. "Didn't you see that I was attacked by a rabid dog and now I'm bleeding to death? Call an ambulance! And call the police too! I'm Émile Delaporte and I've been a customer of this bank for thirty years. Here: You have to take this money and deposit it in my bank account before help gets here."

The emergency services arrived quickly and took Émile to Rueil hospital. As the nurse and doctor were busy at work on his swollen and bloody calf, a police officer showed up. He had to explain to him every detail of the assault and to sign the official report that he had been advised to file, although he was told that it was futile to hope that the police might find the owner of the dog. Despite the local anesthetic that had been injected around the wound and the efforts of the caregivers to minimize the pain, Émile almost fainted as the wound was cleaned and disinfected and he was injected with an anti-rabies shot. After the whole ordeal, the stitches seemed almost pleasurable to him. Émile didn't actually believe he was going to survive until he realized that his calf was completely bandaged and he was able to put his foot down. Of course, he felt a tug of pain every step he took, but walking was still possible. After about two hours in the hospital, Émile, with a prescription for painkillers and antibiotics and a medical follow-up appointment in a week, took a taxi back to his car at the bank and then managed to drive home. As soon as he entered the apartment, Monique began by asking him why the trip to the bank had taken so long; then, noticing his limp and torn pants through which a big white bandage could be seen, she yelled out:

"Oh, my God! Oh, my God! What the hell happened to you? Were you attacked again? This is like something out of an horror movie!"

"I was attacked by a rabid dog in the bank's parking lot," said Émile, "and I had to go to the hospital for stitches! Can you believe it?"

"Why wasn't the dog on a leash?" asked Monique. "Couldn't the owner stop him from attacking you?"

"Apparently not!" explained Émile. "The little shitbag escaped from a van. I don't think the owner had any control. I didn't even see whose dog it was! When he saw that his dog had maimed me, he got it back and drove off! I didn't even have time to spot the plates on his van! I couldn't even tell you what type of van it was."

"How awful!" Monique protested. "I hope you filed a report with the police! That dog could have killed you!"

"Yes, I filled out a form," Émile said with a doubtful tone, "but the policeman admitted that the chances of finding the dog and its owner were very slim!"

"Where exactly did it bite you?" asked Monique. "Is anything broken? Are you sure it didn't have rabies?"

"No, there's nothing broken, it's just the muscle and skin that took the brunt of it! We don't know if the dog was rabid, but anyway, the doctor gave me an anti-rabies shot to prevent any risk of contamination."

"You're never going to be able to go on your expedition to Antarctica now," Monique remarked, with an ounce of satisfaction in her voice.

"I'm not going to give up on True Archaeology because of a little calf injury! As long as I can walk, I can't see anything stopping me from getting on that plane!"

"But how can you be sure that you'll be feeling better by then?"

"We don't leave tomorrow," Émile argued. "It doesn't take a month for a wound to heal…"

The idea that two incidents happening so closely together was perhaps not just an unfortunate coincidence did not first occur to either of them. Monique carried on with her usual routine without thinking much about what had happened and Émile, who would tend to his wound every day, focused on preparing for the expedition. Émile had no doubt that he would be completely recovered within two weeks and had decided not to share his misadventures with either Professor Green or his teammates at True Archaeology. A few days had passed since the attack, when Émile, still limping, but eager to prove to himself that he could lead a normal and active life, decided to take the garbage to the dumpster out on the street, just a few yards from the entrance to their building. He had no trouble carrying the bag outside, which reinforced his belief that his calf would soon be back to normal. After making sure that the street was clear of traffic and stepping off the sidewalk to open the lid of the dumpster, Émile heard a car turn into the street at speed and turned around to look. He saw that a gray van, similar to the one the Pitbull had run into after biting him, was heading straight for him. He had the reflex to drop his garbage bag, the contents spilling on the asphalt, and step back onto the sidewalk where he would be safe behind the dumpster. The van swerved towards him, clearly trying to hit him on purpose, but missed before continuing on its way at full speed. Émile shivered as he saw the driver's silhouette. He could have sworn it was the same guy who'd hit him at the train station.

Madame Lopez, who had witnessed the scene from the window of her small flat, ran out of the building and towards Émile.

"Are you OK? He could have killed you! What kind of driving was that? And you're still recovering from that dog! Don't worry about the garbage! I'll clean it up. These dumpsters just aren't practical at all; people shouldn't have to step off the sidewalk… You OK?"

"Thank you, Madame Lopez… I think I'll be fine," replied Émile. "I just want to get back to my wife."

"Of course! We can't have Monique worrying about you. OK. You try to have a nice day now."

Émile headed back up to his apartment, panting. Monique was waiting for him by the door. She'd seen her husband chatting with the concierge from the kitchen window and was wondering what it might all be about.

"So, what did Lopez want with you?" asked Monique.

"This brave woman came to my rescue!" explained Émile. "Someone tried to run me over with a van! And you won't believe this: it was the same van, the one that rabid dog jumped into the other day! And the son-of-a bitch behind the wheel, I'm sure it's the same guy from the train station! There's someone out there trying to kill me!"

"No!" shouted Monique, as skeptical as she was frightened. "The van didn't hit you, did it?"

"A stroke of luck!" Émile congratulated himself. "I saw it coming at me and jumped behind the dumpster!"

"But who would want to hurt you? You haven't got into some sort of trouble, have you?"

"The only thing I can think of," Émile suggested, "is this stone business with True Archaeology. They managed to steal the object back from Kahn, didn't they? I don't know how…"

"But you didn't do anything wrong!" replied Monique. "Kahn is the thief! And that's no reason to go about killing people, is it? Anyway, if that's the case, we'll have to end things with Professor Green and True Archaeology! I was already thinking that it wasn't very safe to go to Antarctica with this leg injury of yours, but after this business, I think we should just forget all about this crazy expedition! There's no way I'm going back to Antarctica with those people!"

"Well, that's very convenient," Émile replied, "because True Archae-ology told me they don't want you there anyway! The only person they want down there is me, because I'm the only one who can show them where I found my stone!"

Monique turned scarlet and Émile thought her face reminded him of one of those red, translucent lanterns that people take onto the streets of Shanghai for the Chinese New Year. Émile regretted having been so brutal with her and was

"There's no need to get so upset! Come on, sit down. Do you want me to bring you a glass of water?"

"I think I'd rather have a Cognac!" replied Monique, already a little calmer. "So, you're still determined to embark on this adventure, despite all the trouble those people have already caused you! And now you've just admitted that you're going without me? Is that right?"

"I didn't want to worry you until the plans were certain. First things first, I need to contact Professor Green and tell him what's been going on."

***

Dorian was just finishing lunch with Prosper at The Manor when he received Émile's call on his cell.

"Hello, Émile, what's new with you? Is Monique pleased with your first payment?"

"Oh, there's no issue with the money! But we have a lot of other problems! First of all, Monique almost had a fainting fit when I told her I was going to Antarctica without her and I'm not too pleased about leaving her alone in Rueil. But that's not really a big deal. What I'm really scared about is that I've been the victim of three attacks in the past week, and I fear someone is out to get me."

"Really?" Dorian asked. "But what makes you think that?"

"Listen," explained Émile. "The first time was at the *Gare du Nord*, just as I was returning home from one of my meetings with you. This man threw himself at me and I had to be taken to hospital. Two days later, someone ordered a pit bull to attack me when I was going to the bank. I was back in hospital for stitches and a rabies shot. Thankfully, I didn't break anything, and I can still walk… And then today, when I went down to my street to put out the garbage, I was almost run over by a van. It was coming straight for me! I saw the driver and I'm sure it was the same guy from the train station. And his van was the one from the bank! It means that the same man has tried to kill me three times now! The only possible explanation is that someone is angry about the stone. So, it's all well and good, this expedition to Antarctica, but I'm not sure I want to be part of it anymore. I'm willing to help you, but I'm not ready to die for it!"

"Émile," Dorian argued, "I agree that these three episodes in a row are quite astonishing! But don't you think that interpreting them as assassination attempts is perhaps a little excessive? Have you talked to the police about this? What do they think?"

"The police don't care!" moaned Émile. "They probably think I'm paranoid! But I swear I've not gone crazy. Nothing that happened to me was by chance! I saw the assassin with my own eyes!"

"Excuse my questions, Émile" Dorian said in a conciliatory tone. "You're probably right, someone is probably after you for some reason… But why do you think it has something to do with the stone?"

"Because," Émile snapped, "nothing like this ever happened to me until True Archaeology got my stone from Professor Kahn and because I never did anything wrong in my life and because I don't know anyone around me who has the slightest reason to hurt me! You're the one who should know if my working with your organization is likely to upset anyone! For example, Professor Kahn might have a grudge against you and therefore against me!"

"I just can't imagine that Kahn would be capable of such a thing," Dorian admitted, "but now that you mention it, I can't rule it out. He's a crook and he'd do anything to prevent us from succeeding… There's a chance you might not be safe in Rueil… Listen, Émile, I don't want to put you at risk. What would you and Monique say to coming and living at Benson Castle for a while? I'd like you to come as soon as you can. It would mean you'd be on site to get ready for the expedition with the team. Monique could stay with you during the preparation stage and then she'd stay here with Edwina and me until you are back from Antarctica. I'm sure you'd be absolutely safe with us! And we'll see how to proceed at a later stage because the situation is likely to change. I'm hoping that your expedition to Antarctica will give us the archaeological discovery of the century and transform you into an untouchable world celebrity!"

"Perhaps it's a good idea…" stammered Émile. "I just hope Monique will agree to it."

"Émile," Dorian said, "don't tell me you can't stand up to your wife! After all, if your assumption is correct, then your life is at stake! And I'm quite sure Monique could imagine nothing better than living in a castle in Oxfordshire, surrounded by servants and cared for by the soon-to-be-famous True Archaeology team. Come on, Émile, I'm sure you'll manage to convince her! We'll be expecting you! You need to get out of Rueil as soon as you can!"

"Right! I'll follow your advice," said Émile. "I think we'll fly to London, this time. Do you think someone could pick us up at Heathrow Airport?"

"Of course, Émile" Dorian concluded. "Let me know your flight number and arrival time in Heathrow and someone will be waiting for you. See you soon, then!"

Prosper, who had been sitting in front of Dorian while he was talking to Émile and had heard some of his answers and comments, asked him for some clarification:

"What's happened to Émile? It must be serious if you're bringing the Delaporte family over here?"

"He says he's been attacked three times this week. He's convinced that someone wants to kill him because of his involvement with us."

"Isn't he freaking out over nothing?" asked Prosper, unable to believe what he'd just heard. "I get the impression that he has difficulty coming to terms with our big adventure and that he doesn't really want to go back to Antarctica with us. All this is too much for him!"

"Yes, I had the same reaction at the beginning of the conversation" Dorian confided. "But I must admit that the details he gave me lead me to believe that he may not be wrong. I wouldn't be surprised if Kahn, driven mad by his loss, commissioned someone to find out who was behind the robbery and when he learned of our expedition, tried to put a stop to it. There's something else too… I didn't tell you about it, but some time ago, just after Kevin brought the stone back to us, some random woman made friends with Émile's wife. She managed to get her to talk about Antarctica and… Monique ended up spilling the whole story. There's a concierge in their building too; I think she's been told all about True Archaeology and the expedition. It's quite possible that Kahn, for reasons that I can only assume, may want to prevent Émile from returning to Antarctica."

"Wait a minute!" exclaimed Prosper. "Do you really think Kahn would go so far as to have Émile killed, just to put obstacles in our way?

I know he's an awful man, but there's a big difference between writing false reports and committing murder."

"Émile is convinced that they want to kill him," Dorian reasoned. "But maybe they're just trying to scare him or cripple him just enough to make him give up on going on the trip. I'm sure Kahn is capable of that much! Besides, he may not be the only one involved. Imagine that he negotiated his silence on the existence of archaeological remains in Antarctica with some sort of powerful industrial group whose interests would be threatened by such a revelation… We know that Kahn has already done this at least once with TOTEXX. Who knows if TOTEXX or a similar company has interests in Antarctic's underground resources?"

"Well, that could be true…" Prosper conceded. "But do you really think it was absolutely necessary to bring Emile and his wife over here? We already have Kevin and Kate on our hands and it's not as if it's a hotel!"

"I know," Dorian apologized, "and I beg you and Edwina to forgive me… But this campaign will probably end in a triumph for True Archaeology and I think we need to get ourselves every chance we can here! I should also point out that, if Émile doesn't go with you, either because he's physically incapable or so petrified that he pulls out, True Archaeology can just forget about discovering Civilization X in Antarctica. I know that having Émile and Monique here breathing down your necks isn't going to be the best of situations, but I think it's worth it. As for Kate and Kevin, it's a good thing we have them on hand at the Manor: When Kevin told me he wanted to marry Kate and take her on the expedition, I was so angry and I think we almost lost them… If they hadn't been staying here at the castle, I don't think I could have gotten them back on board. But the wedding is just a few days away now and then they can celebrate their honeymoon in style on the Thetis Adventurer!"

Prosper and Dorian hastily finished their lunch and agreed to go together to tell Edwina of the impending arrival of the Delaportes.

***

A few hours later, in Boston, Samuel Kahn received a phone call from Maurice Paoletti, giving him some very bad news about Émile. The specialist recruited by Maurice, despite three perfectly executed attempts, had not succeeded in damaging Émile enough to make him no longer operational. Maurice had even learned that the Delaportes had just taken a plane to London.

Samuel, both disappointed by the failure of Maurice's mission but at the same time relieved to learn that nothing truly serious had happened to poor Émile, decided to keep Jeff Fishman immediately informed of the situation.

"Hello Jeff? Just to let you know that my agent, despite all his efforts and professionalism, has failed to stop Émile. Although the poor guy had to spend some time in hospital, he soon got back on his feet. Plus, he must have realized that he was under threat; he got scared and took refuge with his wife at the True Archaeology headquarters in Oxford. As far as I can see, he's now out of reach and I have no way of stopping him from going to Antarctica with True Archaeology. I suspect that their departure is imminent. It'll soon be summer down there… What do you suggest I do?"

"Nothing! I don't want you to do anything else! I think you have amply demonstrated your inability to solve this problem! I gave you a lot of money without any result! From now on, I'm going to have to deal with this personally…"

"Can I ask you what you plan to do?"

"I'm not sure it's any of your business, but…" Jeff replied. "I think TOTEXX will have to keep an eye on True Archaeology down in Antarctica and find a way to track and monitor them there. Everything will depend on their failure or success on the ground. There's a chance Émile won't be able to find the exact spot he found that stone in; if so, TOTEXX probably doesn't have too much to worry about… If unfortunately, Émile manages to guide True Archaeology to a promising archaeological site, I fear that it will be breaking news almost immediately; and so, there'll have to be some headlines about the heinous financial malpractices of the True Archaeology cult and the disgusting depraved behavior of its leaders… At this point, I can't tell you much more… I'll contact you again if TOTEXX ever needs your services. Goodbye, Mr. Kahn."

Jeff summoned Rachel Schwartz to his office as soon as he'd put the phone down.

"As expected, that asshole Kahn failed his mission and True Archaeology is about to head off on its expedition with the moron who supposedly found Sumerian remains there. I need two things from you: First off, you have to find a journalist who's prepared to work for us and who will follow them to keep us informed of their progress. Secondly, if True Archaeology ever gets its hands on anything down there, you need to create a real fireworks display… I'm speaking of a whole bunch of disgusting stories about True Archaeology and its leaders. So, I need you to rake through their pasts: You will have to find something that will discredit them forever and then throw it at all your contacts in the media; or if you find nothing usable, go ahead and make it up. Come on, Rachel! Get to it! You have to justify your exorbitant salary here at TOTEXX!"

24

HONEYMOON AT THE SOUTH POLE

An electric atmosphere reigned at The Manor. The hushed ambience and order that usually characterized the place had given way to a permanent effervescence and relaxation of protocol that exasperated the staff.

One of the factors that triggered this change had been the arrival of the Delaportes. Monique and Émile, totally unaware of what was common practice in the Anglo-Saxon aristocratic world, had great difficulty behaving appropriately, towards members of staff, their hosts and other guests. Sometimes ridiculously sycophantic, sometimes excessively uncomfortable, they had the gift of never feeling quite in their place and accumulating blunder after blunder. In addition, they made no effort to communicate in English, as if everybody around them should have been fluent in French.

The preparation for the trip to Antarctica was also a source of frenetic excitement. Prosper had taken a leave of absence from the University of Strasbourg and was now staying permanently at Benson Castle. As the leader of the expedition and seeing as they were now only a few days away from the big start, he imposed daily meetings on the team, which now included Kate in addition to Kevin and Émile. Prosper wanted to be absolutely certain that the three newbies were perfectly trained. He needed to ensure they would scrupulously respect a number of rules relating to the functioning of the team and the principles of archaeological research. Prosper also wanted to ensure that everyone had what was required in terms of personal belongings and search equipment in their luggage. Nothing superfluous should be taken, as any unnecessary load could hinder their movements, but above all, nothing essential could be forgotten including clothing adapted to the extreme cold, whose absence could prove dramatic in the event of bad weather conditions, and excavation equipment, the lack of which would jeopardize the success of the research. Emma Coffey, who had formally become a member of True Archaeology and had just been promoted to "Administrative Assistant of the Antarctic Expedition", now spent a lot of time with the team, documenting all topics discussed, writing the minutes of the meetings and taking care of any logistical details. The Manor's large living room had been transformed into the team's headquarters and was no longer available for any of its usual functions, to the great displeasure of those who worked there.

Finally, the major event that involved not only all the staff but also a host of external service providers was Kevin's imminent marriage to Kate. When Kevin informed Dorian of his intention to marry Kate and take her to Antarctica with the team, Dorian's very negative reaction initially caused a rift in his relationship with Kate and Kevin. However, Dorian, on Murphy's and Prosper's advice, apologized to them for his outburst and everything quickly returned to normal. With a view to erasing all traces of bitterness following the row, Dorian had even convinced Edwina that it would be appropriate to make the castle available to the couple on their wedding day. This had had the desired effect, especially on Kate, who in turn apologized for the violence of her words and warmly thanked both Edwina and Dorian. Edwina had found the idea of Kate and Kevin's wedding at Benson Castle absolutely wonderful and swore to herself to organize a memorable event. Especially since it was set to take place on December seventeenth, the day before the departure for Antarctica…

Kate and Kevin's marriage lived up to all expectations. Well over a hundred guests, all active members of True Archaeology, gathered together at The Manor. Everyone thought Kevin had been orphaned following his mother's recent death, so it came as no surprise that no one in his family attended. On the other hand, some were surprised at the absence of the Von Tardy family. Kate, certain that her parents would have disapproved of her marriage to Kevin and still not ready to reunite with this family which, only a few months earlier, she had decided to leave permanently behind her, hadn't seen fit to invite them, or even to inform them of her nuptials.

All congregated first in the castle chapel to attend the religious ceremony, celebrated according to Catholic rites by a priest friend and former colleague of Dorian. Kate was resplendent, dressed in white, her head adorned with a crown of orange blossoms holding back her long golden hair, and wrapped in the splendid white fur coat Edwina had given her for the occasion. Kevin also looked magnificent in the pearl-gray suit he had rented from Oxford's best tailor, which highlighted his blue-green eyes and mid-length fair hair. A few tears fell gently from Kate's eyes and Kevin's face bore an expression of great pride in marrying the woman of his dreams.

Everyone then headed back to the main castle, pleased that all preparations for the impending expedition were behind them and that they could now enjoy this day together. There, a civil registrar legally recorded the union, for better or for worse, of the two young people in the presence of their witnesses: Dorian for Kevin and Edwina for Kate.

A sumptuous lunch was then served, followed by an afternoon of dancing.

Monique was thrilled. It was as if she'd been invited to the Prince of Wales' wedding. Upon their arrival at Benson Castle, Professor Green had explained to the Delaportes that the owner, Edwina, came from a prestigious branch of the English aristocracy and was related to the royal family. And while talking to Kate from time to time in recent days, Monique had learned that the girl also belonged to a noble family in eastern France. Never before had Monique had anything to do with such an illustrious caste, who, although officially deprived in France of their former privileges, continued to arouse envious and admiring respect from most people... And then there were the members of True Archaeology, all holders of impressive academic titles, who were now treating her as if she were part of their family. Prosper Tabellion, Edwina's husband and professor of archaeology in Strasbourg, was not reluctant to have a conversation with her in their common native language; Emma, the principal librarian at the Bodleian Library, was absolutely charming. Commissioner Murphy always greeted her kindly; Dr. Louis, a psychiatrist, had even asked her to dance! Monique was also impressed by the fact that everyone seemed to like Émile and to show him such consideration.

In the late afternoon, the young spouses asked Dorian to conclude their magical day with a speech. Dorian climbed onto the small stage where an orchestra had been playing all afternoon and grabbed a microphone. "Dear friends, thank you for coming in such numbers today to witness the union of Kevin and Kate in holy matrimony and to wish the two newlyweds the very best of luck for the years ahead. As you who support True Archaeology know, the honeymoon of Kate and Kevin, which will begin tomorrow, will also be the most extraordinary expedition ever undertaken by True Archaeology. Under Prosper's leadership and accompanied by Émile Delaporte, Kevin and Kate will leave for Antarctica, where they will try to confirm the presence there of the remains of a very ancient civilization and thus prove our theories. I have fought all my life to make this happen and I am convinced that they will contribute to the most phenomenal archaeological discovery of the century. I truly believe this expedition is the most beautiful wedding gift I could give to Kate and Kevin. I hope with all my heart that they will have a fabulous honeymoon at the South Pole and that luck will smile upon them with the discovery of Civilization X! I ask you to pray for Kate and Kevin's success, both in their relationship and in their research! "

After a round of applause, the guests rushed to congratulate Kate and Kevin one last time and wish them good luck in Antarctica, before leaving.

When the last guest had left, Kate, Kevin, Dorian, Edwina, Prosper, Émile and Monique found themselves in the small sitting room. The wedding had been wonderful, but everyone understood that it was already necessary to turn the page on the carefree festivities and to now focus on the heavy responsibilities of what lay ahead.

The next day, when Bob Murphy, who had wanted to accompany the four explorers to Heathrow Airport, arrived, emotions were high. Dorian hugged Kevin for a long time. "Know that I think of you as the son I never had! Take good care of yourself and try to do as well as you did in Boston! " Edwina, after kissing Prosper and crossing her fingers as a sign of good luck, hugged Kate and, with her eyes fogged with tears, wished her much happiness in her new status as a married woman, while recommending that she take good care of herself throughout the expedition. Monique, in tears, had great difficulty in letting go of Émile's hands. "Be very careful! Don't forget that you're not in your twenties anymore and don't overdo it! And promise to call me every day! "

Bob pointed out that missing the plane might not be the best of plans and encouraged his passengers to get in the car. The Land Rover moved away, while Monique, Edwina and Dorian waved farewell. A kind of melancholy could be seen on Dorian's face, as he regretted that his old age no longer allowed him to participate in such an adventure. Once the vehicle was out of sight, Monique just stood there, as if lost, and Edwina had to take her by the shoulder to push her gently back inside.

"Come on, Monique, let's go in and find something to cheer us up! I forgot just how difficult goodbyes are!"

"This is the first time I'll have ever been separated from my husband," Monique sobbed. "It feels very strange to me… In fact, I'm scared half to death! How do you feel when Prosper goes away?"

"Well," Edwina replied, "I'm used to it. As you know, my husband works in Strasbourg and only comes here at weekends. And not every weekend… He often goes off on a mission for months somewhere at the other end of the world… It's true that at first, I was worried about what might happen to him and that I might never see him again. But now I've decided that there's little use worrying about it and I force myself to stay calm and optimistic! I advise you to do the same!"

"Well" Monique said, "I feel very relieved to be here with you.

I couldn't have coped alone in Rueil-Malmaison, especially after everything that's been happening recently. Maybe that man who went after Émile might have decided to come after me while he was gone!"

"You're right" Edwina agreed. "You can never be too careful! In any case, you are perfectly safe here!"

On the way to Heathrow, no one said a word. Kevin's insistence on sitting so closely to her was starting to annoy Kate. She noted the impassive faces of Émile and Prosper and understood right there and then that they belonged to a generation that was not hers. She found them remote in fact. The two men didn't really look all that bad, but she had little to say to them and probably they too had nothing to share with her. Hadn't she agreed a little too quickly to marry Kevin? She knew so little about him… Would they ever be able to truly communicate? Thoughts raced through her mind: *What have I got myself into? I'm going to be trapped with these three men for weeks, without a chance of escape…*

"You're not saying anything… Are you alright?" Kevin asked her.

Kate decided it was better to keep her thoughts to herself and answered with a forced smile:

"Yes, yes, it's just that I have a headache… I must have had too much champagne yesterday… Don't worry…"

The trip to Punta Arenas in southern Chile, with a stopover in Houston, then a second one in Santiago de Chile, took them about thirty hours and they didn't arrive at their hotel until the middle of the afternoon the next day. Kevin and Prosper didn't seem to have suffered at all, while Émile and Kate appeared to be on the verge of exhaustion. The group was scheduled to take a small plane the next morning to King George's Island where the Thetis Adventurer awaited. An information session, followed by a welcome dinner for all cruise passengers, was set to start in three hours at a nearby hotel in Punta Arenas. Émile, under the pretext that he had already been on the exact same cruise the previous year, refused to go and insisted on going to his room. Kate, claiming that she was now suffering from a terrible migraine, decided to follow Émile's example and also went to bed. Kevin and Prosper decided to take a quick tour of Punta Arenas before going alone to the welcome dinner.

Their night at the Jose Nogueira Hotel was restorative and, at breakfast, everyone had forgotten the horrors of the long flight from London and all were eager to continue on to Antarctica. The charter flight to King George Island in the Southern Shetlands seemed almost pleasurable after their two-day ordeal. Kate and Kevin were a little disappointed to see that the Thetis Adventurer was more like a floating low-rent housing project than the intimate pleasure boat they'd naively dreamed of for their honeymoon. Émile, recognizing the ship on which he and his wife had previously had quite a memorable adventure, felt that he was on conquered ground. Prosper was totally indifferent to the aspect of the boat because all he cared about was the hope that this vessel would carry him as quickly as possible to the precise place where Émile had found the fragment of the ancient stele. Kate and Kevin's mood improved when they entered the double cabin reserved for them by Emma, from which they could enjoy stunning ocean views. Émile found his cabin much smaller than the one he remembered, which had been magnificent. Prosper made no comment as to the quality of his accommodation on board the ship. After settling in their respective cabins, the four friends met up in the conference room where the captain and crew members had planned to give an introductory presentation. As they sat quietly waiting for the speakers, a young man came to sit next to Kate and engaged her in conversation.

"Hi there! I'm Aymeric Verhaeren, I'm a journalist for CNN and I'm doing a report on cruises in Antarctica aboard the Thetis Adventurer. May I ask you a few questions while we wait for the conference to begin?"

Kate rolled her eyes, exasperated at being approached by an unwelcome stranger as she was just beginning to feel well again, but nevertheless smiled politely:

"Of course, go ahead."

"Perhaps you could start by telling me your name and where you come from?"

"I'm Kate Von Tardy and I'm French."

"And what brings you to Antarctica on the Thetis Adventurer?" asked Aymeric.

"I'm actually on my honeymoon!" Kate replied with a laugh. "My husband, Kevin, here, and I were married three days ago and thought it would be more exciting to come to Antarctica than to go sunbathing on a Caribbean beach!"

Kate was relieved when the captain burst into the room and ended the pointless discussion with the reporter. Before the speech started, Kevin leaned over to Kate and whispered in her ear.

"What did this guy want with you?"

"Nothing," Kate replied. "He's just a journalist doing a report on cruises."

Émile felt rather emotional when he recognized Mario Zampeze, the captain of the Thetis Adventurer, who a year earlier had taken him ashore in a zodiac and thus allowed him to make his big discovery.

"That's Mario Zampeze, the captain… I'd know him anywhere!" whispered Émile in Prosper's ear.

"Good!" Prosper replied discreetly, "I'm so glad he hasn't found a job elsewhere! Well, you know what you have to do as soon as he's finished up there!"

As soon as the presentation had come to an end, Émile rushed over to join Mario Zampeze.

"Captain, perhaps you remember me? It's Émile Delaporte… I took the same cruise last year with my wife Monique?"

Mario stared at Émile whose face was vaguely familiar, though he didn't have a precise memory of it, and smiled at him.

"Yes, of course, Émile and Monique, I remember you both very well. Well, welcome aboard your second cruise on the Thetis Adventurer!"

"I have a favor to ask you, Captain," said Émile. "But first let me introduce you to the people I brought with me this time."

Prosper, Kevin and Kate, who had joined Émile to ensure the discussion with the captain went smoothly, introduced themselves one after the other by shaking hands with the perplexed Mario, who was beginning to worry about the type of special request this band of tourists might have.

"So," continued Émile, "last year, you took my wife and me ashore in a zodiac to a most magnificent place where there was a huge colony of emperor penguins. I would like to be able to do the very same excursion with my friends! I have such amazing memories of that extraordinary experience and I'd like to be able to share it with them. Are we going to follow exactly the same route as last year and, if so as I hope, would you be able to take the four of us to the mainland… to the very same spot?"

"It shouldn't be a problem" Mario Zampeze assured him. "Of course, everything here is subject to the changes in the weather and you can't always do exactly what you want. But I know precisely the spot you're talking about and it's on our itinerary. So, if the weather permits, I can arrange for you to head over there with the zodiac when the ship anchors in that area."

"Oh, if you could, that would just be wonderful!" exclaimed Émile. "When do you think we'll get there? Does it actually have a name that can be found on a map?"

"It's called Paradise Bay," Mario said, "and we'll be there in four days barring any major storm."

"Could you at some point perhaps show us a detailed map of the coastline and point out where it is?"

"Of course," confirmed Mario. "Come and find me tomorrow or the day after. Look, I'm sorry, but I have to leave you now. I have to get back to my post. I'll see you all tonight at dinner. Have a good day, everyone!"

As soon as Mario was out of sight, the four friends smiled with satisfaction.

"Things are looking pretty good." said Prosper. "Congratulations Émile, you did a good job. Let's all go together to find the captain tomorrow morning and ask about the map so we can try to get the exact coordinates. The hardest part is going to be having to wait four days! I suggest that until then, we play the tourists and try to make the most of these few days of forced holiday!"

Prosper had just finished his sentence when Aymeric approached their group.

"You seem to know the captain well! Is he a family member, friend or colleague? Perhaps one of you is also a naval officer?"

Kate, Kevin, Émile and Prosper looked at each other with embarrassed smiles, surprised that this stranger would interrupt their conversation and wondered what the best way might be to politely get rid of him.

"Not at all," said Kevin, "but we wanted to congratulate the captain on an excellent presentation and get more details on the itinerary. But to whom do we have the honor?"

"Forgive me" apologized Aymeric. "As I had already introduced myself to the lady at the beginning of the conference, I had forgotten that not all of you know who I am. My name is Aymeric Verhaeren and I'm a reporter for CNN. I was wondering if you would be willing to answer a few questions that would allow me to better define the profile of the participants on this type of cruise. For example, I already know that you and your wife are here on a honeymoon, but I don't know why your two companions are here with you."

"It's quite simple," Kevin stated. "Prosper is retired. He's my godfather and my only family. Émile, also retired, is Kate's godfather and also her only family. Kate and I are both very attached to our families and so we asked them to come along with us on our honeymoon. I'm sure your audience will think this is such a nice story! Real family attachment! Unfortunately, we're going to have to leave it at that for now because we have an urgent phone call to make. See you later."

Kate, Émile and Prosper followed in Kevin's footsteps towards their cabins and just left Aymeric standing there.

Before locking himself and Kate away in their cabin until dinner, Kevin had a word with the group.

"I don't trust that Aymeric. He managed to initiate a conversation with Kate, then he joined our group while we were talking to Captain Zampeze and I just find that a little suspicious. We should be careful of this guy."

"You're right, Kevin," Prosper added. "Given the strange attacks on Émile, it's quite possible that Kahn and his accomplices haven't given up creating problems for us; let's be careful, let's keep an eye on this so-called journalist. Above all, let's be careful not to give him any information about our mission if he asks any more questions. Well, on that note, I'm going to rest in my cabin until dinner. Let's meet at half past seven in the restaurant."

25

A SPY IN PARADISE

Aymeric had also returned to his cabin to call his employer and keep her informed of his progress.

"Hello, Rachel? It's Aymeric. I hope I'm not disturbing you. As agreed, I am calling to tell you what's happening on the ship."

Rachel Schwartz, who, in order to protect TOTEXX and execute the plan she had agreed with Jeff Fishman, had commissioned Aymeric Verhaeren, a penniless freelance journalist who had helped her in the past, to work on the Thetis Adventurer, was happy to hear from him.

"You're not disturbing me at all, Aymeric! On the contrary, I'm looking forward to hearing the results of your investigations. I'm listening!"

"First, of all," Aymeric began, "your information was correct! Émile Delaporte boarded the Thetis Adventurer today. He's here without his wife, which seems to confirm that this isn't a holiday. There are three people with him. For the moment I only know the identity of one of them, a very cute young French woman in her twenties called Kate Von Tardy."

"Well, well! I've heard of this young woman, but I didn't have any proof that she was in collusion with Émile! Very interesting… And what do you know about the others?"

"The only thing I've been able to learn so far," Aymeric explained, "is that there's a young man named Kevin, with an English accent, also in his twenties, who's this Kate's husband. Unfortunately, I don't know if Von Tardy, the name mentioned by Kate, is Kevin's last name, which seems unlikely to me, or if he is called something else. As for the fourth man, also French I think, I know that his first name is Prosper but I don't yet know his last name."

"Bingo!" exclaimed Rachel. "I can tell you what his last name is! His name is Tabellion. He is one of the founders of True Archaeology and a great friend of Dorian Green. Nice work, Aymeric! There's no doubt now. True Archaeology is on the trail of the exact location of Émile Delaporte's intriguing discovery last year."

"Do you have any specific instructions as to what to do for the rest of the cruise?" asked Aymeric.

"Keep it up," Rachel confirmed, "you're off to a great start! Try to confirm this Kevin's last name, because I don't have any Kevin in my file, and I'd like to know more about him. He's probably a member of True Archaeology. Above all, carefully monitor how these four individuals behave. Carefully note whether or not they go off on any excursion and then note exactly where they go. If they seem excited or happy after seeing a particular piece of Antarctic coast, note the coordinates of the place in question. I don't need to draw you a picture. These guys are looking for a particular place where True Archaeology thinks it will find some sort of treasure, and if they find it, it will probably show on their faces! Feel free to call me if you find out anything interesting! Nice work! Speak to you soon!"

The first three days of the cruise were unremarkable. Émile, wrapped in his large goose down jacket, was stationed almost permanently on the ship's deck and scanned the coast to make sure the boat did not pass the part of the coast he had been to twelve months earlier. He was delighted to see these landscapes again for his memory of them had partially faded. Kate and Kevin spent most of their time in their love nest, enjoying their honeymoon, while occasionally admiring the amazing views from the large bay window of their cabin. Prosper alternated between sessions on deck with Émile and work in his cabin.

The day after departure, all four of them went to see Captain Zampeze to ask for all the details they wanted regarding the itinerary of the Thetis Adventurer, the planned points where shore excursions were possible and above all the coordinates of the famous Paradise Bay.

On the morning of the third day, Captain Zampeze saw Émile heading towards the bridge after breakfast and told him:

"We should reach Paradise Bay by late afternoon, the place that impressed you so much last year. I hope that the weather won't get too bad and that I can take you ashore in a zodiac, with your friends, as planned tomorrow morning."

At around four in the afternoon, Émile, who, except for lunchtime, had spent the day at his observation post on the bridge, felt his pulse accelerate. The mountainous formations he was beginning to see in the distance seemed familiar to him. When he was pretty sure that the ship was approaching the cove where he'd found his stone, he rushed like a madman to go and knock frantically at the doors of his friends' cabins:

"Come quickly! I think the boat is approaching Paradise Bay! ".

His three companions hastily put on their warm clothes and followed Émile up to the deck.

"Look over there!" Emile shouted. "I recognize it! You see the huge ice-free beach at the bottom surrounded by high mountains, I'm sure that's where I found my stone!"

Kevin, despite his own excitement, felt compelled to moderate Émile's enthusiasm.

"Calm down, Émile!" he whispered. "We're not alone here and we don't want everyone to know our business. We don't want other passengers convincing Captain Zampeze to take them along for the ride on the zodiac tomorrow morning."

"Sorry," Émile whispered. "But I thought you'd be happy to know that I had found it!"

"Of course we are!" Prosper intervened. "We're all very excited to be so close to our goal. True Archaeology will owe you a debt of gratitude if we manage to uncover the ruins of Civilization X here. But I agree with Kevin. We must all control our emotions, at least until we have dug up the stele from which your stone must have come."

Then, turning to Kevin and Kate, Prosper continued to lecture the group:

"I advise everyone to act as if everything is normal. This isn't the time to go chatting to that shady journalist. We don't know anything about his intentions. That Aymeric, with his weasel-like manners, might realize that something unusual is going on and get us into trouble."

They all remained silent for the next few minutes, during which time the Thetis Adventurer made a long turn to enter between two rows of mountain peaks covered with blue glaciers, then headed for a huge pebble beach bordering a deep bay, before finally dropping anchor a few hundred yards from the shore. From a loudspeaker then came the voice of Captain Zampeze, announcing to all passengers the arrival of the Thetis Adventurer at Paradise Bay, where the ship would stop overnight. Mario encouraged the passengers to admire the thousands of penguins that colonized the beach, which immediately triggered an invasion of tourists onto the bridge, eager to capture as many snaps of the picturesque animals as possible with their powerful telephoto lenses.

Later, during dinner, Captain Zampeze approached the table where Émile, Kate, Kevin and Prosper had felt authorized to share a bottle of champagne to celebrate their arrival in Paradise Bay, in order to validate some of the practical details of the zodiac expedition the next morning:

"We'll have to leave the ship very early tomorrow morning, because I'm afraid the weather might have some tricks in store for us and it's not safe to be on the zodiac after nine. The winds have shifted and a major drop in temperatures is forecast with possible severe weather in the region in the coming days. So, if you want to go ashore, we'll have to set off at six at the latest. Is that going to work for you all? "

Kevin, anticipating an objection that might accidentally fall out of Kate's or Émile's mouth, rushed to say that there was no problem and that the whole group would be ready to board the zodiac at six. Once Mario had moved away and towards another table, Kevin did not wait for the complaints that he knew would come from Kate:

"We can't afford to upset Captain Zampeze. If it's true that bad weather is approaching and waiting longer would compromise the whole expedition, we have no choice but to get up early and be ready to board that zodiac. We're not going to blow it so close to the goal for the sake of a few hours' sleep!"

"Kate, if you think leaving at six tomorrow morning is too much for you, you don't have to come," Prosper added. "You can stay warm in your cabin while we explore ashore. On the other hand, for you Émile, there is no other option. You have to come with Kevin and me."

Émile stated clearly that he had no problem leaving so early and Kate had to admit that participating in such an expedition was well worth the small sacrifice. They then all toasted to the imminent success of their adventure.

Aymeric, sitting at a table a few feet away with another group of tourists, noticed that Kate's mood at the table was more playful than usual and that something special had to have happened if there was champagne around. He had also witnessed Kate, Kevin and Prosper running behind Émile on their way up to the bridge as the boat entered Paradise Bay. Earlier in the day, he'd questioned one of the hostesses and learned that a zodiac trip was to take a small group of passengers to the beach the next morning and had been able to extract the identity of the lucky guests from her. He decided to leave the dinner table before dessert and to go to his room to give Rachel his daily report.

"Hello, Rachel, this is Aymeric! I have interesting news from Antarctica!"

"Go ahead!" Rachel encouraged him.

"I managed to get the names of Kate Von Tardy and Émile Delaporte's two companions" explained Aymeric. "You were right! One of them is called Prosper Tabellion and it seems he's a professor of archaeology in France. The other is registered under the name Kevin McKee and is an archaeology student at Oxford. Does that name mean anything to you?"

"Kevin McKee? No, it doesn't ring a bell, but if he's really an archaeology student, I can easily check it. On the other hand, it confirms my thoughts that he could be a member of True Archaeology. True

Archaeology has obviously put in some serious effort into uncovering something down there."

"Also," continued Aymeric, "I have a strong feeling that where we're anchored right now may well be the site that you're interested in. The place is called Paradise Bay. I'll send you the exact coordinates by email. Obviously, our friends were all really excited when the boat arrived here… Better than that, they're going ashore in a zodiac tomorrow morning!"

"In that case, what I was afraid of seems to be happening…" Rachel replied with a worried tone. "These people are smart. They'll probably be able to find what they're looking for… Will you go with them?"

"Unfortunately, not" Aymeric replied apologetically. "There's only room in the zodiac for four people in addition to the captain and another crew member. I tried to ask the Captain if I could go, but he refused to take a fifth passenger for safety reasons.

"Here's what you're going to do" Rachel decided. "Make sure they board the zodiac, check that they get ashore and follow all their movements with binoculars. Welcome them back aboard the Thetis Adventurer and ask them as many questions as you can, especially Émile who is certainly the weakest link in the team. They won't tell you what they found, but the off-the-cuff explanations they will give you may still shed some light on the situation. This will be the most crucial part of your mission, so be perceptive! Keep me informed as soon as they're back. If you are convinced that they hit the jackpot, I'll be forced to activate my plan B. Do you have any questions or anything else you'd like to share with me?"

"Nothing else," Aymeric said. "I think that's quite enough to be getting on with. I'll question them to the best of my ability and get back to you as soon as I can. Have a great day, Rachel, and speak to you tomorrow."

26

CHRISTMAS IN HELL

In the middle of the night, whilst still sound asleep but subconsciously waiting for the alarm clock to sound at five, Kevin was awakened by unusual noises followed by movements of the ship. He realized that the boat's engine had just started and, looking out of the window, noticed that the ship was beginning to move. He noted that a strong wind was blowing with clouds of ice flakes smashing into the glazing. He put on some clothes hurriedly, left the cabin without waking Kate and ran to the bridge where there was a lot of excitement.

"Can you explain to me what's going on?" Kevin asked Captain Zampeze, whom he thought looked unusually tense.

"What's going on," Mario replied, "is that the weather is getting worse and we're having to retreat out of this area!"

"But that's just awful!" Kevin exclaimed. "We were supposed to go ashore in a couple of hours!"

"I know! It's such a shame," sighed Mario, "but it's out of the question to go out in a zodiac in weather like this!"

"But why leave the bay?" Kevin insisted. "Couldn't we just stay here and wait for the clouds to pass?"

"Listen," Mario explained, "it's obvious that you have no idea what bad weather can mean in these parts! I'd like to point out that the temperature has dropped sharply by forty degrees, that the storm could well last several days, and if we stay here, the boat will get stuck in the ice and we'll be stranded for a very long time! So, there is no question of taking such a risk and I must do everything I can to try to get the ship out of here as soon as possible. Believe me, there's not a minute to lose."

"What a mess!" Kevin lamented. "What do your meteorologists say about the intensity and duration of the storm?"

"They say," replied Mario, "that the area of depression is quite extensive, that it's moving in our direction at full speed and that we'll be faced with extreme cold and strong winds for at least the next three days... Listen, I think you should go back to your cabin, because I need to steer this ship right now... We have very low visibility and strong swell which means the ship could run aground or hit an iceberg!"

Kevin decided to go back to his cabin. He hesitated to wake Kate. He thought it would be useless. He wondered if he should notify Prosper and Émile immediately but decided to wait until they had been awakened by their alarm clocks.

When she awoke soon afterwards, Kevin explained the situation to Kate, advised her to go back to sleep as the zodiac trip would not take place and warned her that he was going off to talk to Prosper and Émile about what to do next. The three men gathered in Prosper's cabin.

"What exactly did Zampeze tell you?" asked Prosper.

"He said that a huge weather disturbance, with strong winds and a massive drop in temperature, was heading to Paradise Bay, that it would be too dangerous to leave the boat here because it could get trapped in the ice pack that was likely to form and that it was urgent to take the Thetis Adventurer to a safer area. He said he couldn't even think about taking a zodiac out under these conditions, and I think he's right given the terrible weather outside."

"It's really unfortunate" Prosper regretted. "We were so close... At the same time, I think Zampeze's decision is entirely justified: Let's not forget that we're in Antarctica, one of the most inhospitable places on the planet, where we must bow to the power of Nature... I imagine that the Thetis Adventurer isn't likely to return to Paradise Bay any time soon, at least not on this cruise... Do you have any idea of the route he now intends to follow?"

"For the time being," Kevin said, "he's heading for King George's Island in case the persistent bad weather forces our cruise to a stop."

"I'm afraid the only option for us is to bide our time and wait for the Thetis Adventurer to arrive at King George's Island" Prosper said. "From there, we'll call Hans, have him pick us up by helicopter and take us to his base, from where we should then be able to make our way back to Paradise Bay as soon as the weather conditions allow."

"So, really," Émile intervened, "it doesn't change much. I mean, that was always the plan. We were going to go to Paradise Bay with Hans from his base at the end of the cruise anyway."

"What's changed," Prosper replied, "is that we weren't able to pinpoint exactly where we might dig. So, the expedition with Hans is likely to be longer and harder work. Hans' boss on the base might not take too kindly the fact that we need to use their helicopter for longer than expected."

"I hope," Kevin added, "that, since he swore he recognized the bay and its beach, Émile will be able to identify the right spot without too much difficulty. So, this setback might not be too big a deal."

"Gentlemen," Prosper concluded, "There's only one thing we can do. Wait and hope! I suggest we all go back to bed and meet again at around eight for breakfast."

During breakfast, while the ship was being strongly rocked from side to side and serving oneself at the buffet required real balancing skills, Mario came to announce to all the passengers that the weather conditions had forced him to change the itinerary of the Thetis Adventurer. He advised everyone not to venture onto the deck, where the temperature had dropped to minus twenty degrees Fahrenheit. Nobody seemed overly bothered by this announcement, expecting rather harsh weather conditions in Antarctica. On the contrary, most of the tourists, confident in the performance of the Thetis Adventurer and the navigational skills of its captain, were simply having fun with the fact that it was just so difficult to walk around the ship as it was tossed about in the furious swell.

However, optimism and good humor gave way to panic when, at

around eleven, everyone realized that the ship seemed to be struggling to move forward and that her bow was coming continually up against a resistance very different from that of the waves they'd gotten used to. Suddenly, a voice echoed throughout the ship.

"We're stuck in the ice!"

Having heard the scream, Kate rushed to the cabin window and shouted for Kevin to come and join her.

"Come and see this quickly! The boat is caught in the ice pack!"

They were both speechless: As far as the eye could see, in front of, behind, and to the sides of them, lay an immense white expanse, undulating imperceptibly and fully imprisoning the Thetis Adventurer. They were diverted from their haze of disbelief by the sound of an alarm, followed by an announcement over the loudspeaker. All passengers were invited to an emergency meeting with Captain Zampeze, which would begin fifteen minutes later in the conference room.

Prosper, Émile, Kevin and Kate found themselves at the appointed time in the conference room, among hysterical passengers, shouting in every language imaginable. Mario Zampeze appeared and, after having difficulty restoring some calm, made his announcement.

"Ladies and gentlemen, as you've witnessed, the Thetis Adventurer is currently immobilized. When you cruise at Antarctic latitudes, this is something that can happen at any time. The weather here is very changeable and a temperature drop of a few dozen degrees is enough for the sea to quickly transform into ice floes. I understand that this must seem alarming to many of you, but I want to reassure you: You are not in any danger! Of course, I've already reported our situation to the rescue teams, who will soon either come with an icebreaker or, if that option isn't feasible, evacuate you by helicopter. So, please, don't panic! The trickiest part in these circumstances is waiting. On-board staff will organize activities so that you can still continue to enjoy your time with us. You can play various games, watch movies, and when the ice pack is strong and thick, you'll even be able to get off the boat to stretch your legs, exercise and, if you like, learn to fish through the ice! Once again, I ask you not to worry and to keep your cool, which shouldn't be too difficult since it's currently minus twenty out there! Do you have any questions?"

A forest of arms rose up and, with great patience, Mario invited the person sitting right in front of him on the first row to ask a question.

"How long are we going to be stuck here until help arrives and how far are we from where we started out?"

"We're just under five hundred nautical miles from King George Island," Mario explained. "I can't tell you exactly when help will arrive. If an icebreaker manages to pass without too much difficulty, it could reach us within three to four days…"

Someone else didn't even wait for Mario to give him the floor and shouted:

"This is outrageous! How could you not know that this weather disturbance was on its way and take us to an area where the risk of being caught in the ice pack was so high! You're going to hear from my lawyer because I'm going to file for incompetence and dangerous behavior!"

Mario wasn't surprised to be held responsible for this perfectly unpredictable and uncontrollable situation; many tourists, totally unaware of the real risks of a trip in Antarctica, often felt the need to name a culprit as soon as something didn't go as they expected, and on a boat, the culprit can only be the captain.

"Sir, I understand your frustration," Mario said calmly. "The only thing I can assure you is that this weather disturbance developed very suddenly, that I was only informed of it when it was too late to do anything about it, and that I obviously never wanted to expose my passengers to any risks. I repeat that this type of incident is always a possibility on a cruise in Antarctica…"

Mario invited another passenger to ask his question.

"By turning around and blocking the boat in the ice for several days, you've cut our cruise by at least half and now we won't be able to visit all the interesting sites we were promised! We've paid a lot of money for this trip and it seems that you'll only be able deliver a very small part of it! How do you intend to compensate us?"

"Sir," replied Mario, "I'm only the captain of the ship, my priority is to get you safely back to King George Island and I just can't answer that kind of question. If you believe you're a victim of financial loss, you will have to make a claim with your travel agency or your insurance company."

A woman was next to come forward.

"Since the boat stopped, I've noticed that the temperature in my cabin has dropped! Does this mean that there'll be no heating? Is everything broken like on the Titanic? If so, what should we do to avoid freezing to death?"

"Don't worry, Madam," replied Mario, unable to repress an irresistible desire to laugh, "we have plenty of fuel to ensure an excellent level of heating for a very long time and no one will freeze to death! If the heater isn't working perfectly in your cabin, report it to a crew member who will send you a technician to fix the problem."

Another woman then asked her question:

"I would like to remind you that today is Christmas Eve. Normally on this type of cruise, there's always a festive dinner in the evening. Will you, in addition to ruining our cruise, also deprive us of this?"

Mario was beginning to get sick of these people. They were only concerned about their food, comfort and money, and unable to cope with the fact that cruises near the South Pole in minus twenty degrees might expose them to more risks than sailing on the Nile in the summer. He replied quite abruptly to this woman that she should speak to a member of staff and that the sole purpose of this conference was to answer the most serious and urgent questions.

Someone else, seemingly outraged by Mario's attitude, went further still.

"And if this mess goes on indefinitely, is there enough food on this boat and how long can we survive?"

Mario sighed and answered dryly.

"I can assure you there is more than enough food on this boat, and you will certainly not starve to death!"

There were still lots of arms raised and Mario had to give the floor to another person.

"And if there are medical emergencies, or someone needs surgery, is there a medical team on board that can take care of that?"

"Yes, sir," Mario patiently confirmed. "We have someone on board trained to deal with all kinds of medical emergencies. I won't lie to you and say that we have a sophisticated operating theater, but I can assure you that no one ever died because of lack of medical care on this ship! I think I can take one last question and then I'm afraid I'm going to have to close this session. The gentleman in the back row, go ahead, ask your question!"

"My name is Aymeric Verhaeren and I'm a journalist for CNN. Originally, I was here to do a little report on tourism in Antarctica. As a result of this incident, I plan to change the subject of my report. I think my bosses are going to like this. I'm about to send them videos of the boat caught in the ice pack and I'm hopeful that we'll hear about the Thetis Adventurer's setbacks on tonight's news! I think that this is likely to reassure passengers. Once CNN has shown the images of our misfortune, everything will be done to speed up sending us help!"

Aymeric's speech was greeted with a round of applause and many people rushed towards him, hoping that they could be filmed and perhaps broadcast on television. Mario took the opportunity to slip away.

Prosper invited his companions to sit around a table so they could think through their next steps, well away from the horde of tourists now busy harassing the crew with their most trivial questions or buttering up Aymeric to get the opportunity to appear on television.

"Did you hear that lot with their inappropriate questions? The only thing that worries them, while Captain Zampeze is struggling to get them out of an extremely critical situation, is their Christmas Eve party, their food and their money! The hardest part isn't that the boat is trapped in the ice floe, it's having to deal with this army of freaks!" exclaimed Kevin.

"Émile, were the passengers of the Thetis Adventurer like this when you took that cruise with Monique last year?" asked Kate. "If they were as stupid as this lot, I bet you didn't have much fun!"

"You know," replied Émile as if apologizing, "fortunately we didn't experience this type of incident last year. Everything went very well, and we didn't pay much attention to the other people on board."

"Well," Prosper said, "this unexpected event may not be as dramatic for us as it seems. I'll ask Hans to pick us up here, on the ice floe, with the helicopter as soon as the weather conditions allow. That way, we won't have to wait for the Thetis Adventurer to return to King George's Island and we'll save some time. The only problem is that we're going to have to continue to be confined with these people on this boat until Hans arrives. And I don't know how long it's going to last… How do you think we can make it through unscathed?"

"Maybe we could play Scrabble" suggested Émile. "Monique and I did just that during the downtime on the ship last year."

"Why not participate with those other morons? I mean, the crew will be organizing games for everyone!" exclaimed Kate in horror. "I'm sorry, but Scrabble, Monopoly, card games and all the rest of it just isn't for me. Personally, I have no problem reading in my cabin."

"I totally agree with Kate," Kevin added. I think I'll lock myself and read in our cabin too. You're out of luck, Émile! You are surrounded by misanthropic intellectuals who don't need others to fill their inner void. Unless Prosper is a fan of board games?"

"Unfortunately for Émile," Prosper smiled with false regret, "I'm like Kate and Kevin. Nothing satisfies me more than being alone with my studies and my scientific reports. That being said, if Émile's mental health requires it and if it is the only way to ensure his survival during this ordeal, I'm willing to give it a go. What do you say Émile? Are you able to spend some time alone reading or watching TV? Or do you absolutely need the company of other people?"

"Oh, I think I can go without board games for a few days" said Émile. "What bothers me the most is being locked up inside. If I could go out on the deck once in a while, I'd be fine. But the captain gave us a definite no on that."

"Listen, as well as staying in our cabins, we have another big problem and his name is Aymeric" added Kevin. "He's a shithole! And for his CNN scoop, he might try to film or photograph us, if it's not already done. We're not exactly incognito if our faces are plastered on every screen across the globe."

"Actually," Prosper replied, "I'm not worried about this Aymeric doing his report. First of all, I find it reassuring that Aymeric really is a journalist for CNN rather than a secret agent working for I don't know whom. I thought he might be here to cause trouble for us. Secondly, being on the international news for a few days isn't a big problem either. Because when we have our hands on the stele, that is to say in a few days' time hopefully, we'll be doing everything possible to get people to talk about us! Remember that our friends back at True Archaeology are planning to launch a press conference followed by a major communication campaign as soon as our discovery of Civilization X on Antarctica has been confirmed…"

"There you go, Émile" said Kevin, "Prosper just found you an occupation: If you get bored, you can always go play in front of Aymeric's camera!"

On that note, they ordered aperitifs while waiting for lunch to be served. After the meal, during which it was plain to see that there was definitely no shortage of food on board and that they were still a long way from ration tickets, they went and locked themselves in their respective cabins for the afternoon, while the storm outside showed no signs of abating..

27

THE FLIGHT OF THE KON TIKI

Massachusetts that day was also almost as cold as the South Pole and giant flakes of snow had been falling since the day before. Dana Kahn, wondering if it would be safe to take the road that weekend to her parents' house in New Jersey as planned, turned on the small television set in the kitchen to watch the weather channel. But the excited presenter was focused on a news item rather than the usual maps and forecasts. Dana looked at the red banner that was continuously scrolling at the bottom of the screen: *Dramatic Christmas for a hundred tourists trapped in the ice pack in Antarctica.* She then watched images of a ship stuck in the ice, on the deck of which an individual wrapped in his large parka was struggling against fierce winds to explain the situation to the spectators. Dana turned the volume up so she could hear what he was saying. A commentator was speaking:

"Aymeric Verhaeren, let me remind our viewers that you're a CNN journalist and that you were on an Antarctic cruise aboard the Thetis Adventurer when the ship got stuck in the ice. Can you tell us the circumstances?"

How awful, Dana thought. *Those people must be so scared.*

Aymeric explained on camera that a major weather disturbance had surprised the Thetis Adventurer as it had been anchored alongside the Antarctic coast, that the outside temperature had dropped sharply by several dozen degrees and that the ocean, previously ice-free, had quickly turned into a huge impassable ice pack. He said that the ship couldn't break free of its ice prison and that they didn't yet know when the emergency services would be able to evacuate everyone on board. A montage was then shown of the captain, crew members and a number of passengers making the best of the situation inside the ship. Dana couldn't believe her eyes: She thought she recognized Kate Von Tardy's face! She screamed out towards the office where her husband was busy at work:

"Sam, come quick! Come and see this! This is incredible!"

"What's going on now?" Samuel replied sullenly from his study. "What do you want me to come and see? I have better things to do than watch TV."

"Come quickly!" insisted Dana. "Kate is on TV right now! You absolutely have to see this!"

As soon as his wife mentioned the au-pair girl, Samuel couldn't help himself. He joined Dana in the kitchen, where she was standing, her eyes glued to the screen.

"Look," said Dana, "I hope they'll play the right sequence again. They're doing a special report on a cruise ship caught in the ice pack in Antarctica and I'm sure I saw Kate among the passengers. Here you go! There! Look! Don't you think that looks like Kate?"

"God, you're right!" Samuel shouted. "That's her! What the hell is she doing on that boat in Antarctica? That's unbelievable! And that little old man next to her is Émile! God, now it all makes sense! What a bunch of pricks! So, they were in cahoots!"

"Sam, can you explain to me what's going on? Who is this Émile? And why are you calling him and Kate pricks?"

"Émile," Samuel explained, "is the guy who found that precious stone that was in my safe. When I did my little investigation, I learned that he'd been in touch with those bastards at True Archaeology and that it was those guys who'd stolen the stone from me. I was told that Emile was planning to return with them to Antarctica to undertake extensive excavations; that's where the stone was found, you see. What I wasn't sure about was that our au-pair, Kate Von Tardy, must have helped them! It was probably Kate who let the thieves into our home and told them where my safe was. I'm glad they're in this mess! I hope they freeze to death and we never hear again from Kate, Émile, and those True Archaeology freaks with their damn Civilization X!"

"Don't you think it's a little excessive to wish them such a horrible end?" Dana reacted, taking offense. "The goyim already consider that *an eye for an eye, a tooth for a tooth* is horribly barbaric. What would they think if they knew that you wanted these poor folks to die like that? After all, these people have never done anything but take back what belonged to them!"

"You know very well that I don't care what the goyim think" Samuel replied nastily. "You know what? The cost of the damage caused to me by those bastards runs to several million dollars! Anyway, even if they end up being rescued, I'm still going to have my revenge: they'll be immobilized in the ice for a long time and they won't be able to search for anything down there! The True Archaeology nutties are going to have to wait a long time to uncover the remains of Civilization X! I think I'll phone my old buddy Jeff Fishman from TOTEXX to share the good news with him!"

Samuel left Dana in the kitchen and went back to his study to calmly make his call.

"Jeff? This is Samuel Kahn. Have you seen what's happened in Antarctica? It seems our friends are in dire straits!"

"I don't know what you're talking about" Jeff replied.

"I'm surprised your spies haven't already told you" Samuel said ironically. "That's all they're talking about on TV! Émile Delaporte and his partners at True Archaeology are on board a ship in distress! They're all stuck in the ice at the far end of nowhere! I recognized Émile as soon as I saw him on the screen. That Antarctic expedition of theirs is turning into a total nightmare! I have the feeling that their crazy hopes of making the archaeological discovery of the century have just been dashed!"

"I'm not sure I share your optimism" Jeff replied. "I rarely watch television and I was certainly not aware of any boat caught in the ice. But my informants have told me that the small group has already recognized the site of Émile's discovery. I can even tell you that it's called

Paradise Bay and I know the exact latitude and longitude. I also know the identity of all the members of their team. You may be surprised to learn that your former au-pair girl is with them!"

"I'm not at all surprised," Samuel argued, "I saw her on TV. But, let's get back to the chances of success for Émile, Kate and others. Even if they saw the site from their boat, how can they bring back any artifact now that they're immobilized in the middle of the ice pack?"

"How do you know that they don't already have it in their hands? To my knowledge, their group was supposed to be taken ashore yesterday in a zodiac…. Having said that, I must admit that I still don't know if they actually managed to do that… But even if they didn't, I don't see what could prevent them from going back there once their current problem has been solved."

"I can see" admitted Samuel in a disappointed tone "that you're very well informed and there's not much I can really tell you… I think we'll leave it at that. It would probably be inappropriate for me to wish you a merry Christmas and a happy New Year, given the circumstances… So, I'll just say: talk to you later!"

As soon as he'd put the phone down on Samuel, Jeff quickly called Rachel.

"I'm sorry to bother you, but I've just been on the line with Kahn. He told me that the boat our people are on is in danger, immobilized in the ice floe off the coast of Antarctica. Did you know about this? I hear that's it's on every TV channel. What the hell is your Aymeric guy doing?"

"Sorry," replied Rachel, "but Aymeric's last call was twenty-four hours ago and I don't know what has happened since then… I haven't turned on my TV for quite some time, so I didn't know about your ice pack story… Look, I'll call Aymeric and get back to you."

After hanging up, Rachel dialed Aymeric's cell phone.

"Hello, Aymeric, this is Rachel. Weren't you supposed to call me back? What exactly is happening on your boat? Apparently, the Thetis Adventurer is on TV here!"

"Ah, Rachel, I was just about to call you" Aymeric said. "But you know, it's crazy right now! The ship was caught in a sudden and dramatic storm. The sea has started to freeze all around us, and we have been trapped in the ice pack for ten hours now. It's quite dreadful! Everyone is terrified and we don't know when the help will come! It's like hell on board! I made a short video montage and did a webcam interview for CNN. For me, this is the opportunity of a lifetime and I couldn't let it just pass me by. I hope that after my contribution, I'll be able to get a permanent position with CNN!"

"Look Aymeric," snarled Rachel, "your job at CNN is all well and good, but that's not what I'm paying you for! Before you went and played the hero on television, you could have called me to keep me informed!"

"I'm sorry about that" replied Aymeric in a falsely apologetic tone. "But these were extenuating circumstances. When I accepted your offer, it was about a pleasure cruise, not a trip to hell where I might freeze to death! It seems fair that I get some compensation for the enormous risks you've put me through!"

"All right, let's not talk about it anymore" Rachel said in a conciliatory tone. "So how was the zodiac trip to Paradise Bay?"

"It didn't take place because of the weather" Aymeric explained. "The captain decided to leave the area in the middle of the night. But as you already know, the early departure didn't do much good because the bad weather caught up with us."

"So," deduced Rachel, "they'll come back empty-handed! I'm going to have to change my plans a little bit at TOTEXX... No need to panic... Anyway, that's my problem... What else, Aymeric?"

"I think," Aymeric said, "that the next step will be that help will come, either an icebreaker or helicopters; but it won't happen for three or four days. Until then, I suspect that we'll all just be confined to the Thetis Adventurer. It's going to be pretty depressing."

"Well, good luck with that, Aymeric!" Rachel said. "Have fun with CNN... And above all, call me right away if anything interesting or unexpected happens. Talk to you soon!"

***

At Benson Castle, the television broadcast of Aymeric's report on the misadventures of the Thetis Adventurer aroused great emotion. The newscasters were using the most worrying qualifiers to characterize the incident and even going so far as to consider the possibility of a horrible end for the hundred or so tourists trapped in Antarctica's ice. When she recognized Émile on the screen, Monique was overwhelmed by hysteria, accusing Dorian and Edwina, who were watching TV with her, of sending her husband to an awful death with their ridiculous expedition to Antarctica.

It took a lot of composure and patience for Edwina and Dorian to bring her to her senses.

"Calm down, Monique!" Dorian implored. "You can see that Émile is alive and well. This isn't the best news for sure but this type of incident has happened in the past and everyone has escaped just fine. The rescue services have already been alerted and the passengers will more than likely be evacuated very soon. Don't get taken in by the way the journalists report events. They always exaggerate."

"And listen," Edwina added, "Émile is not alone! We saw Kate there with him. Kevin is a resourceful young man whose main mission is to ensure your husband's safety. Plus, I know Prosper more than anyone and he is not the kind of person who lets himself fall at the first hurdle. I'm sure he'll find a solution! If he hasn't called me yet, it's probably because the situation doesn't seem particularly alarming to him…. Why don't we try to call them now?"

Edwina dialed Prosper's cell phone number. Of course, either because the bad weather was disrupting communications or because the satellite's capacity was saturated, it took ten attempts before Prosper finally picked up.

"I wanted to wish you a Merry Christmas," Edwina began, "but I get the impression that it's not really been plain sailing for you on the Thetis Adventurer! Dorian, Monique and I got really scared watching TV earlier. It's all about your ship being caught in the ice! How are you and what exactly is going on?"

"Merry Christmas to all of you at The Manor!" exclaimed Prosper, obviously not in the least affected by the misadventures of the ship. "It's true that we're not having much of celebration here, but it's not really a major catastrophe or anything. We've been immobilized in the middle of the ice since yesterday. The main problem is that we've been stuck on this boat with all these dumb tourists. They're completely freaked out and don't know how to behave properly. But other than that, there's really nothing to worry about: The good news is that, just before this incident, we spotted the bay where Émile discovered his stone last year and so we know about where to dig. The other good news is that I was able to reach Hans at his base and he'll pick us up by helicopter as soon as the weather permits, normally within two or three days!"

"I see that you're not all that bothered by the weather business" Edwina said. "In fact, you seem more motivated than ever! I'm so pleased! Could you reassure Monique? She's been devastated since she saw her Émile on television. Let me put Monique on the phone. Bye, my love."

"Hello, Professor! So, how is Émile?" asked Monique.

"He's in great shape!" Prosper declared. "Your husband is a real champion! He has already led us straight to the site of his discovery and the little setback we are currently experiencing has had no impact on him in the slightest. I can't put him on now, because I'm in my cabin and I think he's being interviewed by the reporter who's on board with us. But I'll tell him to call you as soon as possible, if that would make you feel any better. Merry Christmas by the way!"

"Thank you very much, Professor, you have really reassured me!" concluded Monique, feeling grateful and relieved. "Merry Christmas to you too!"

"You see Monique," Dorian continued, "I told you so! It's all just media frenzy. The more dramatic it seems, the bigger the audience… I was sure that with Prosper, Kevin and Kate at his side, Émile was perfectly safe."

***

Three days passed in status quo. The weather around the Thetis Adventurer remained gray, windy and icy; the routines of the passengers on board the ship had stabilized, punctuated by meals, board games organized by the crew and periodic announcements from the captain.

Aymeric conducted interview after interview, filmed everything he could that would keep people in front of their TV sets around the world, and negotiated his future promotion within CNN. Kate, Kevin, Émile and Prosper, locked away for the vast majority of the time in their cabins, seemed totally indifferent to what had happened to the Thetis Adventurer and its occupants. On the evening of the third day, although the outside temperature remained extremely low, the storm stopped, and the sky began to clear. Captain Zampeze was very pleased to announce that the cessation of strong winds and improved visibility would allow for the arrival of helicopters. He asked everyone to remain calm when they saw them approaching, to wait quietly for their turn to leave the ship and to accept that the sick and the elderly would be evacuated first.

Despite these instructions from Mario Zampeze, the arrival of a helicopter the following morning caused a riot on the Thetis Adventurer. A large number of passengers rushed to the deck, each trying to convince the crew to give them a place in this first helicopter.

Through the loudspeaker, Mario ordered every single one of them to return to their cabins immediately, explaining that only four pre-identified passengers would be allowed to board this particular vehicle. He stated that other helicopters were on their way and that all passengers would have the opportunity to be evacuated that same day, if not on the first flight, then on one of the following. So, there was no reason to fight!

This announcement only caused renewed aggression on the part of passengers. They wanted to know who these four people were and why they had been chosen to leave first and weren't shy in shouting about it. Mario knew, following discussions with Prosper, that the first helicopter, sent by a nearby German base and not by the regular rescue services, was only to take Prosper and his three companions aboard. He went down to Prosper's cabin to validate all the practical arrangements for evacuating the small group, so that the risk of confrontation with fellow passengers would be minimized. It had been decided that Kate, Kevin, Émile and Prosper would discreetly make their way to the engine room one by one, while crew members would take their luggage separately. From the engine room, they would have to use an external ladder that would take them to the ice floe at the foot of the ship. From there, they would proceed as quickly as possible to the helicopter, climb on board and then disappear into the sky before the other passengers even had time to understand what was happening.

Kate, Kevin, Émile and Prosper scrupulously followed the evacuation plan as agreed with Mario Zampeze. As the other passengers rushed onto the deck, the group, one by one, left their cabins and discreetly entered the engine room where two crew members were waiting to help them use the ladder that had been installed beyond a door opening onto the outside. Kevin, who went down first, reassured everyone by testing the strength of the thick layer of ice under his feet and confirmed to Émile, who was following behind, that he was in no danger. Kate and Prosper in turn jumped onto the ice floe. Standing now at the stern, they were not yet visible to the other passengers on the deck at the bow. As the group walked across the ice floe towards the helicopter and those people remaining on the ship eventually caught sight of them, all they could do was watch helplessly.

Hans immediately recognized Prosper for had been an active member of True Archaeology for a few months and greeted him near the helicopter with a hug. He then briefly greeted the other three team members and helped everyone get on board. The luggage, brought by the two crew members, was placed in a compartment under the seats. Finally, Hans sat at the controls and started the aircraft, while the two crew members ran back to the Thetis Adventurer.

"Welcome to all aboard the Kon Tiki," Hans said. "That's the name of the helicopter and also what we call the base."

"Kon Tiki, it's a very good name," Prosper said. "If memory serves, Kon Tiki was the Inca god of lightning? And it is what Thor Heyerdahl named the raft on which he set out across the Pacific to demonstrate that South America could have been originally populated by the Polynesians."

"With any luck," Kevin added, "Kon Tiki will now allow us to prove that the Sumerians came from Antarctica!"

As the helicopter rose above the ice floe, Kevin, realizing that among the mass of passengers clinging to the deck of the ship, some seemed to be screaming insults and making threatening gestures, couldn't help giving them the middle finger through the window. He was really quite pleased to be getting away from the Thetis Adventurer and its herd of cattle tourists, ready to tear each other apart as soon as they felt a little hard done by. Kevin was also able to distinguish, at some distance from the herd, Aymeric's silhouette filming their departure…

When the helicopter was out of sight, Aymeric rushed to his cabin to call Rachel.

"Hey Rachel, this is Aymeric. I have some interesting news for you. Your four friends have just left the Thetis Adventurer. A helicopter came to pick them up. The captain told me that they were evacuated to a German base fairly close to here. They must have connections. Everyone else here is still waiting. Apparently, more helicopters from King George Island are expected to pick us up later today. So, your birds flew away, and I won't be able to keep an eye on them from now on."

"Thank you for letting me know," said Rachel. "Obviously, they know people in the right places. If they have access to a German base in Antarctica, if they have a helicopter at their disposal, there's nothing to stop them from going back to Paradise Bay, probably in the next few days…. Well, I know what I have to do now, I really don't have a choice… Aymeric, I think your mission for me ends here. You did a great job! I hope you won't be hanging around much longer on that boat and that the rescue services will turn up quickly. It's onto warmer skies for you!"

"You know what?" confessed Aymeric. "I'm in no hurry to get out of here. In fact, I'm very happy to have been involved in the drama of it all because it has allowed me to earn my place at CNN. I think I'll stay here until the last passenger has been evacuated. Obviously, my viewers are still very keen on finding out the outcome and I'm the only one who can get pictures of it for CNN… and they can then sell the rights to all the television stations in the world…"

"I'm delighted that my little assignment has turned out so well for you," said Rachel. "Good luck, Aymeric! And let's keep in touch!"

Rachel immediately called Jeff Fishman.

"Hello Jeff. Let me give you all the latest developments. Our friends in the South Pole are pretty well organized it seems. They have contacts on a German base who came to pick them up by helicopter. So they were the first to be evacuated from the Thetis Adventurer. They're probably now going to stay at the German base and I imagine that in a few hours they'll quietly return with their helicopter to Paradise Bay, where they'll have more than enough time to dig up their precious antediluvian stele… So, I suggest we activate the plan B, but first I want to make sure that you have no objection."

"They're good at this!" Jeff exclaimed. "Nothing ever stops these guys… First, that moron Émile escaped Kahn's killers, now the whole troop manages to survive the Titanic shipwreck thing… I see no other option than to throw out everything we've got at them… Are you ready on that front? When do you think we can start?"

"The story is ready to go," Rachel confirmed. "The contacts I have at the major newspapers and TV stations are ready to trigger their media Armageddon as soon as they receive my green light. I thought January second would be the best date for this bomb to hit. And it'll make quite an explosion, let me tell you! It will be our New Year's gift to Green and the rest of them at True Archaeology!"

"Perfect!" Jeff approved. "They won't see this coming. Even if they find their damn stele and the remains of El Dorado, they'll be preaching in the desert, or better yet, they won't even be able to preach at all! Rachel, you have *carte blanche* to do what needs to be done. Impress me! I think you're well on your way to being promoted to Senior Vice President…"

"You got it, boss," Rachel concluded. "If I don't see you before then, Happy New Year!"

28

CONFESSION

The helicopter flight to the German base went smoothly. The Kon Tiki landed on a circular spot marked with a large red cross, a few dozen meters from a building sunk into a thick layer of ice and flanked by an annex from which an engine sound was coming. As soon as they got off the helicopter, the four survivors of the Thetis Adventurer saw a blond giant with a military air emerge the main building. He welcomed them politely but without much emotion. Hans did the introductions:

"Klaus, this is Prosper Tabellion, Professor and Chair of Archaeology at the University of Strasbourg. These are his partners, Émile Delaporte, Kevin McKee and Kate Von Tardy."

A flash of interest shone in Klaus' steel blue eyes when he heard the name Von Tardy. "Pleased to meet you, Miss. Von Tardy is Germanic, isn't it? I wonder if our two families are related… Allow me to introduce myself. I'm Klaus Lubrecht and I run this base. Welcome to Southern Germany! Hans explained to me that you are here to carry out archaeological excavations! I didn't know there were any interesting ruins to find around these parts, but I would be happy to make our equipment available to you, if you think you could make good use of it."

Klaus turned to the men and shook their hands vigorously. Before he disappeared, he addressed Hans in German to instruct him to show the newcomers to their rooms, give them a quick tour of the base and, most importantly, explain the rules in force.

"Ya vol, Herr Kommandant!" Hans replied, before immediately asking his guests to follow him.

He indicated two small rooms of barely ten square meters, each roughly equipped with two bunks and two chairs, which would serve as bedrooms, one for Émile and Prosper, the other for Kevin and Kate. In front of Kate's dismayed face, Hans felt the need to comment:

"Of course, it's not very comfortable, but there's very little space on the base. And it is rare that we have guests here. You'll only be staying here for a very short time, so I hope you can deal with it…"

He then showed them the rest of the place. Prosper, Émile, Kevin and Kate followed in Hans' footsteps and discovered a succession of tiny rooms cluttered with computers, test tubes and vials of all shapes and sizes, and various devices whose function, related to the oceanographic research carried out on the base, completely escaped them. In two of these bunkers sat, glued to their screens, two colleagues with whom Hans was working during his mission in Antarctica. One was called Ulrich and the other Joachim. The two men barely looked up to welcome their visitors. Further away, behind a closed door, was Klaus' office, but they didn't go in there. Hans then showed them the refectory where all the meals were shared and explained that everyone had to participate in the various chores such as cooking, setting the table and washing the dishes. He then indicated the shower room shared by everyone on the base, which was narrow and Spartan. Finally, Hans ended his tour with what he pompously called his office, which was in fact only a tiny room similar to those of Ulrich and Joachim.

"Mealtimes are very important here," Hans said. "Everyone must meet in the refectory at seven for breakfast, noon for lunch and seven again for dinner. Outside of meals, the researchers who live permanently on the base spend all their time working. Time may seem long to you as you'll be confined here without any particular obligations other than the few chores I mentioned. Since we won't be able to use the helicopter to get to Paradise Bay until the day after tomorrow, you will have to find a way to keep busy. You could read in your rooms, watch television or play games in the dining room, where nothing much happens outside meals."

Kate felt depressed by the prospect of remaining trapped in such a grim place for such a length of time and asked Hans:

"Why should we stay locked up in this awful bunker all the time? Your oceanographic research must force you to leave your offices from time to time, so you must have snowmobiles, or some sort of equipment adapted to the terrain… Couldn't we use your vehicles and go for a look around?"

"I'm so sorry," Hans objected, "but Klaus will not allow you to use our work tools for recreational activities. If you want to venture outside, I can lend you some skis."

"If snowmobiles are banned," Kate agreed, "I'll settle for skis! Who wants to come with me on a ski trip this afternoon?"

Prosper declined. As did Émile. Kevin didn't say no but pointed out to Kate that he had never worn skis in his life and that it would probably be dangerous for him to learn the sport in an environment that was very different from Courchevel or Aspen.

"Come on!" Kate insisted. "It's much more fun and original to learn to ski in Antarctica than in some sanitized resort in the Alps or Colorado! You're not going to leave me alone with the penguins, are you?"

Kevin was easily convinced, and the couple spent the afternoon exploring the desolate surroundings of the base on skis. Hans insisted that they should not go too far from the buildings explaining that they risked disappearing forever into the polar vastness, and so they were content to explore around the base. It was an opportunity for Kate, who had practiced skiing since an early age, to rediscover familiar sensations. On the other hand, Kevin, unable to stay more than ten seconds in an upright position on the two planks of wood that stubbornly refused to obey him, bruised by his repeated falls and exasperated by Kate's hysterical laughter, vowed never to let himself get caught in one of her traps again. This interlude allowed Kate and Kevin to escape the boredom that Émile and Prosper had to endure, locked up in the gloomy and cramped premises of the base. Later, dinner was an opportunity for Hans and his fellow oceanographers to learn more about Prosper's surprising theories about the true history of humanity and to hear that, under the ice of Paradise Bay, the ruins of an antediluvian city, of which Émile had already uncovered a small fragment, probably lay dormant. In return, Prosper and his companions learned a lot about oceanography, the techniques used at the German base to advance knowledge of the seabed, and the dramatic consequences that global warming would likely have on the living conditions of underwater inhabitants. On Klaus' orders at the end of the meal, everyone had to help clean the dishes and put the refectory back in order before being invited to return to their rooms.

Once back in their tiny bunker, Kate and Kevin sat face to face in their little chairs and looked at each other, wondering if they were both thinking the same thing before bursting out with a wild, liberating laughter. Once they'd calmed down, Kevin whispered to Kate, fearing that the thin walls of the room would allow everybody to enjoy their conversation:

"What a mess we've got ourselves into! The Thetis Adventurer was bad enough but this is something else! And to think that we'll have to spend the whole day tomorrow in this shithouse.... I hope we find what we expect in Paradise Bay, because if we've put up with all this for nothing, it's going to be awful."

"I have to admit," Kate said, "that I look forward to returning to normal living conditions. I did my best not to complain on the ship, but this is a little too much!"

"It's a shame we can't go back to Paradise Bay until the day after tomorrow. What are we going to do to pass the time? I've already given skiing a try and I'm not doing it again... Do you have any ideas?"

"Look," Kate replied, "let's try to get some sleep. We'll see things more clearly tomorrow..."

They undressed, each lying in their own cramped cot, turned off the lights and tried to sleep. After about fifteen minutes, the silence was broken by the noise of snoring coming from the neighboring bunkers.

"Are you asleep?" Kevin asked Kate gently.

"No," Kate whispered. "It's not easy with all this noise."

Kevin jumped out of bed, lifted the sheet covering Kate, lay down on top of his wife's body and began to caress her. Kate seemed unusually reluctant.

"Don't you want to? Making love is an excellent remedy for insomnia."

"I am too embarrassed," Kate explained. "I don't want the whole base to hear our frolics! It's bad enough feeling watched when you kiss me in front of that herd of old men, so the idea of them listening while we're having sex makes me feel a bit sick."

"But", Kevin argued, "we're not in a dorm and our room door is locked, so it's not like they can see us."

"I can hear their snoring through the walls," Kate replied, "so they would have no trouble hearing the squeaks of the bed springs!"

"If you can hear their snoring, it's because they're asleep! And if they're asleep, they can't hear us! And anyway, I don't care what they do and think; what I'm sure of is that I can't spend several nights on this base without making love to my wife!"

"Don't push it Kevin!" Kate replied in an irritated tone. "Not here! A little abstinence cure won't hurt you! Besides, there's another reason why I don't want to: I'm claustrophobic. You may not have noticed it, but I felt very bad in the cabin of the ship and yet it must have been five times larger than this horrible room. I'm suffocating; I feel like a big cat locked in a tiny cage at the zoo. In addition, since we left Oxford, everything I have done has been decided by and scheduled by others. I feel like I'm in prison!"

"Believe me," added Kevin, "I've spent some time in a jail cell that looked like this room, so I totally get you."

"What?" Kate said as she pushed Kevin aside and sat up on the bed. "What are you talking about? Did you do time in prison?"

Kevin realized that he had just put his foot in it and remained silent for a moment, hesitating between revealing the truth he had so carefully hidden from Kate until now or inventing a new lie.

Kate encouraged him to spill the beans:

"You know, Kevin, now that we're married, you can tell me anything.

We swore an oath to share everything, for better or for worse; even if you confessed to me that you committed some monstrous crime, I'd still love you. So, please, tell me what happened. Why were you in prison?"

Kevin thought this was probably the opportunity he'd been waiting for to clear his conscience. He loved his wife too much to keep lying to her and he felt as though he had to clean up the past and start afresh with Kate on healthier ground. And didn't they say that the sin confessed was already forgiven…

"You're right," Kevin confessed, "I spent a little time in a cell at Oxford police station. Not long. I wasn't really in prison, but it was just like… Well, my cell was even smaller than this room, I thought I was going crazy. I know all about claustrophobia!"

"But what were you accused of?" Kate asked in a worried tone. "It must have been a mistake if they didn't send you to jail, right?"

"If you interrupt me all the time, it's going to be hard for me to tell you everything," Kevin said with irritation in his voice. "I have more than one thing to confess. So please don't say anything, let me talk and listen to me."

"All right, I'm listening," Kate promised.

"I've lied to you about everything, or almost everything," Kevin said. "The only thing I didn't lie to you about is that I love you more than anything!"

"Stop it, Kevin, you're scaring me," Kate mumbled. "How could you have lied to me about everything?"

"I asked you not to interrupt me," Kevin said. "It's very difficult for me to say all this, so let me tell you everything first and you can ask as many questions as you want when I'm done. Right… I was arrested for a robbery I committed in Oxford. I stole from some very wealthy people while I was in my first year of archaeology studies. Commissioner Murphy, who isn't my uncle Bob at all, offered me a deal: Either he would charge me, convict me and send me to prison for several years, or I would do him a favor and he would let it all slide, which I accepted. The favor was to help Dorian Green, who is not my mentor either as I made out, get back a certain object that meant a great deal to True Archaeology. This precious object was in Professor Kahn's safe in Wellesley. It was the stone found by Émile last year in Paradise Bay. Kahn had stolen it from Émile, who had naively entrusted it to him for his expert opinion on it. So, when I met you near the Kahn house where you were an au-pair, I was on a secret mission for Commissioner Murphy, Dorian Green and True Archaeology. In fact, it was thanks to you that I was able to get Émile's stone from the Kahn's place, because you had the good idea to give me the password… little Marduk. So, I owe you my freedom really. My problem is that I fell madly in love with you and I didn't want to leave you there where you'd probably have been accused of participating in the robbery. I wanted to protect you and take you to England. The only thing I could come up with to convince you to leave Boston with me straight away was the story of my dying mother, which was just another big lie. In fact, I never really knew my real mother very much and I don't even know if she's still alive. It's the same with my father. I was raised in social services' care. I was taken from my parents at the age of six. They were degenerates of the worst kind: I never heard from them again… That's it, you know everything now! I bet you feel sick that you married a loser like me, don't you?"

"You're not a loser!" objected Kate, although she felt quite shaken. "You're my husband and I could never have married a man I thought was a loser. And I understand why you had to lie. I would never have followed you if I'd known what you were doing in Boston and I wouldn't have jumped on a plane so fast if I didn't think your mother was dying. I don't regret following you as it turns out. And so, I couldn't really care less about your past mistakes. But you have to promise me you'll never lie to me again!"

"I swear to you!" Kevin declared. But I have to finish my story, because I don't want there to be any more secrets between us. I managed to take you back to Oxford with me because I lied about my mother. Then I had to convince Murphy and Dorian to take us in at The Manor, which wasn't an easy task because you were obviously not part of the original plan."

"So, they lied to me too, and I guess so did Edwina and Prosper" deduced Kate.

"Sort of," Kevin admitted, "but that's because I begged them to do it."

"I'm actually more cross with them than with you. You, at least, had a good reason to lie: You were in love with me and you didn't want to leave me. But there was nothing stopping them from being honest with me? It's very hard to be lied to... Unfortunately, it's not the first time it's happened to me... I've never told you this before, but the real reason I found myself an au-pair at the Kahn's in the USA isn't because my parents prevented me from going to art school. I left mainly because I was cheated on by my boyfriend who, since I had not yet met you at that time, I thought might one day become my husband. This guy's name was Dick, he was Canadian, and he said he loved me. When I found out he was gay, it was as if I'd just been a joke to him. And I can tell you now, he never touched me. He didn't even kiss me on the mouth. At least, you just confessed your lie. He never stopped lying to me. I found out about his homosexuality by accident. If I hadn't, I could very well have found myself married to him and my life would have become a living hell... As long as you're not lying to me about your love for me, I can forgive you your secrets."

"Really, do you forgive me?" Kevin asked.

"Yes, I do!" exclaimed Kate with a smile. "But watch out! From now on, I demand absolute transparency; I want to be aware of everything. And you really owe me. So please just go back to your bed quietly and let me sleep. There'll be no making love until we're off this base and somewhere decent."

"Harsh... but fair enough," Kevin accepted. "I want to regain your trust, so I'm going to have to pay the high price! Night! And try to sleep well."

Despite their claustrophobia and the snoring from their neighbors, Kate and Kevin eventually fell asleep. The following day turned out to be less painful than they'd anticipated. The weather was as summery as was possible in Antarctica, that is, the thermometer had regained the degrees it had lost during the storm and the sky was a spotless blue. For some obscure reason, Klaus had decided that Hans could only take his friends to Paradise Bay the next day. Prosper therefore used this day of forced rest to go through the action plan for the detection of the stele and the archaeological excavations with his teammates. All went to bed that evening with the exalted feeling that they were on the eve of events of extreme importance, not only for themselves, but for all of humanity....

29

BENEDICTION

At six in the morning on New Year's Eve, after a solid breakfast for which Klaus, Ulrich and Joachim didn't join them due to the unusual schedule, Hans and his four companions left the base to board the helicopter. Hans settled at the controls of the Kon Tiki with Émile at his side, so that he could make the most of the seat with the clearest view and guide Hans as best he could towards their target at Paradise Bay. The helicopter rose into the air, made a long curve towards the shore then flew over the ice floe, skirting the coast to the south. The visibility was perfect, and Hans had no difficulty reaching Paradise Bay. It was agreed that Émile would then point Hans to the most appropriate place to land the Kon Tiki, as near as they could get to where he had found his stele fragment last year. The tension rose a few notches in the cabin when Émile admitted that he didn't recognize much… In Émile's defense, Prosper acknowledged that the bay probably didn't have the same appearance from the air as seen from the deck of a boat. Plus, he'd had only seen the bay completely ice free, whereas now, the ice pack covered its entire surface. Émile also pointed out that he could no longer see the huge colony of penguins that were there last year! Hans, only anxious to put his craft down somewhere as quickly as possible and not particularly bothered about sparing poor Émile's blushes, began to show signs of irritation:

"Wake up, old man! We're not going to spend the whole day admiring the scenery! If you can't do your job, I'm just going to have to land anywhere and I don't care how many miles you are from the target…"

Prosper, knowing that putting pressure on Émile would only inhibit him and make him even more confused, asked Hans to leave the bay, then to approach it again but fly more slowly and as close to the ground as possible, in order to simulate the approach aboard the Thetis Adventurer. He calmly reassured Émile, asking him to concentrate on the appearance of the peaks surrounding the beach and to think back to what he had seen straight ahead of him when the zodiac had taken them from the Thetis Adventurer to the beach. At the same time, Prosper handed Kevin and Kate the prints of the photos Émile had taken during his trip, so that they could shout out if they recognized anything.

Hans agreed to maneuver back to the open sea, then to enter the wide bay again flying as low and as slowly as possible. Émile's heart was racing; it was clear that the success of the expedition depended largely on his ability to recall exactly what he'd experienced a year earlier in Paradise Bay and the idea that he could be held responsible for its failure terrorized him. Kevin studied the appearance of the mountains surrounding Paradise Bay and compared them with the photos. He noted that the zodiac had probably landed much further to the right, compared to the direction the helicopter was going in. After confirming this with Prosper and Émile, they all agreed to direct the helicopter further to the right and Hans changed his course accordingly. Émile shouted out in excitement.

"There! It's there! : I recognize that beach there! It was overrun with penguins last year. I remember climbing that slope to take close-up photos."

"Émile," asked Prosper, "when you approached the penguins, where exactly were you coming from? From the right side of the beach? Or the other side?"

"I am pretty sure I came from the right," said Émile, "I mean, from the south. I remember thinking that I was lucky, because I wasn't against the light. It's better when taking photos."

"And how many meters do you think you covered between the zodiac and the penguins? How long did it take you to get there?"

"It wasn't far," replied Émile. "I remember that I started taking my snaps very soon after we landed. I'd say a maximum of three hundred meters."

"Hans, can you put us down on the beach, about three hundred meters from the bluff?" asked Prosper.

"I'm going to go and fly around the target first. Maybe Émile will recognize some other details."

The helicopter regained some altitude, turned forty-five degrees to the right just before it reached the beach and then performed a wide circle around the selected landing area. Émile looked at the mass of mountains surrounding the beach and shouted out again.

"It's right there! I'm sure of it now! When I walked away to pee before returning to the zodiac, I headed that way and I had the impression that there was a passage further away that looked as though it crossed that barrier. There! Look! You can see there is a passage!"

Satisfied, Hans plunged the helicopter towards the target and down into a space about fifty meters from the shore. It was almost nine o'clock, the weather conditions were perfect, and the helicopter landed safely at the chosen location on the pebble beach of Paradise Bay.

They all immediately jumped out of the helicopter and grabbed the backpacks containing their equipment. Prosper began by comforting Émile, whose face was still flushed with the anguish that continued to hold him: After all, what if he was wrong? Until the stele was actually found, there was no certainty that this was the right place...

"Émile, are you feeling okay?" Prosper asked. "You'll have to excuse us for being a little rough with you on the chopper. We're all on edge, which is normal given the stakes. I trust you completely. If you felt like you recognized something, it's because we're in the right place. If you want, rest for a few minutes. Let us know when you feel ready."

"There's an offer I won't refuse!" said Émile. "I'm going to walk a little bit. I feel stiff."

Émile moved away from the rest of the group and did a few stretching and breathing exercises before returning to the group.

"There, I feel better. It's all the stress! It's not easy to handle at my age."

"Well," Prosper continued, "I suggest we have a little snack before we start. Kevin, would you mind getting us the coffee flasks and the cakes I left on my seat in the chopper?"

After the brief coffee break, Prosper gave the signal that they were to set off.

"This is how we'll proceed: First of all, Émile, you will explain to us everything you did on this site last year, showing us exactly where you went between the time you got off the zodiac and the time you got back on it. The aim is obviously to locate the most probable place of your find. Then, all five of us will place ourselves in a line four meters apart from each other and progress from here towards the place indicated by Émile. Those at the end of the chain will have to place beacons using rollers to mark the perimeter of the explored surface. If we don't find anything, we will explore the areas adjacent to the one already explored, until we find the stele. Questions?"

"Do you have any idea what it looks like," Kate asked. "I suppose that the body of the stele is buried in the ground and that the only visible part is the edge. What might it look like? Are we allowed to move the peebles to see what's underneath?"

"Good question," Prosper said nodding. "I recommend that, at least initially, we avoid moving anything. Normally, the stele should be flush and so the pebbles won't be covering all of it. We will only start moving them if the first three areas give us nothing. As for what we're looking for, remember that the stele is made of black diorite. The edge of the stele won't look like the rest of the stones, neither in terms of its color or geometry. The pebbles of the beach are grayish or whitish and their shape is rounded. The stele should have a rectangular or at least an angular shape. Above all, its black color should stand out from everything around it."

Émile began to recount every move he'd taken the last time he'd stepped foot on Paradise Bay.

"As soon as we got off the zodiac, Monique and I headed towards the left, where there was a huge colony of penguins. I remember that we ventured quite far into the middle of the colony. At first, we were scared that the birds would attack. But when we realized that they were not aggressive towards us and were fine with us approaching, we got a bit bolder. I took hundreds of pictures and in total must have been here for nearly an hour. Then we went for a walk at the foot of the cliffs, which we walked along from the north, beyond the penguin colony, to the south. We could see the zodiac and Monique, who was tired, decided to return to the shore, while I continued alone for another five hundred meters. That's when I had the impression that there was a sort of passageway a little further, but I didn't have time to walk all the way over to have a look. I remember that I had come quite far, because Monique and Captain Zampeze had to shout and wave at me wildly to tell me that I had to get back to the zodiac. That's when I had to pee. I remember being very embarrassed, because I couldn't see any place to hide at first and everyone, including a Finnish tourist who had come to walk nearby, could see me. So, I went up to the cliff and finally noticed some rocks behind which I could sort of hide my modesty. After relieving myself, that's when I hit my stone. I was trying to cover my urine tracks with pebbles."

"Émile, that's perfect!" exclaimed Prosper. "It must be quite close to the side of the cliff then, which means we're going to be able to narrow down the search area considerably. There's no need to start so close to the shore. We'll start much higher up, say fifty meters from the cliff. And we're looking for scree or a pile of stones a little higher than the beach floor. We also know that the area is approximately equidistant from where the penguins were on the left and the passageway on the right. All right, I think we can start!"

They all headed for the cliff that surrounded the beach, formed the line as described by Prosper and began their treasure hunt.

The first area they explored, carefully examining each stone, proved to be empty of anything interesting. Prosper then proposed examining the next section to the left of the first one, but it was also without success. The group then moved to the right and again found nothing. Almost two hours had passed, and the morale of the troops was starting to wane.

Kate could not repress her disappointment:

"It's like looking for a needle in a haystack! I have a blurry vision from looking at these damn pebbles! Maybe we could take a break? "

Prosper, realizing that his team was becoming increasingly pessimistic, suggested breaking for lunch. The small beacons that had been installed at regular intervals around the areas already inspected would later make it very easy to locate the next sections. So, they all headed back to the helicopter from which Hans took out a bag containing sandwiches, cheeses and dried fruits for their lunch as well as flasks containing tea and coffee. Everyone ate in silence, without much enthusiasm and feeling worried by the lack of results and the thought of leaving Paradise Bay empty-handed at the end of the day…

Prosper broke the silence.

"I know that this morning has been frustrating and that the temptation to give in to discouragement is pretty strong. But we must stay optimistic and motivated. The stele has to be somewhere near here, and I guarantee we'll find it! Personally, I remain convinced that our strategy is the right one and that we must continue like this, section after section. We still have at least six hours ahead of us, so we can explore this entire beach if necessary! We'll find it! That being said, if anyone thinks we should change our strategy, I'm ready to discuss any proposals. Do you have any suggestions?"

"I wonder," Kevin suggested, "if we shouldn't move along in a south-north direction instead of west-east. I mean, instead of exploring from the middle of the beach up to the cliff, we could explore areas perpendicular to those we inspected this morning, starting with the highest area at the base of the cliff and starting from that passageway."

"Why not?" said Prosper. "If everyone agrees, I have no objection. The only problem with that strategy is that we know that Émile never ventured as far as that passageway; so, it would force us to explore a lot of ground pointlessly. But at the same time, starting at the base of the cliff and moving along its entire length could also save us time. What do the others think?"

"I think it's a good idea," said Émile, "because I seem to remember that I was quite close to the base of the cliff when I found my stone. So maybe we're wasting our time looking in the middle of the beach."

"Perfect" Prosper stated. "If no one has any objection, we will adopt Kevin's method from now on. The most important thing is to keep the faith! We will not leave here without finding what we're looking for! So, let's finish lunch and get back to work in twenty minutes or so."

Kate, who had not touched her sandwich and had contented herself with a portion of swiss cheese and a handful of raisins, decided to use the twenty-minutes to see what the passageway into the cliff looked like. Plus, she needed to relieve her bladder, which she felt was about to explode.

"Have you finished lunch already? Aren't you having coffee? Where are you going?" Kevin asked her as she set off.

"Listen," Kate replied in annoyance, "you could hardly call that crappy little sandwich lunch. Also, that infected sock juice wasn't what I'd refer to as coffee either. If anyone asks you where I'm going, just say you don't know…" And she continued on her way without stopping.

She decided to walk along the cliff face to the south. Unlike the portion of the beach they'd already covered, the base of the cliff was strewn with scree blocks, making it rather difficult to walk at any speed.

Finding this stele is going to be impossible, she thought.

She chose a spot that was partially hidden away before unhooking her big parka, dropping her pants and squatting down. She felt a great relief as the vast amount of urine left her body.

It would be funny to have pissed in the same place as Émile last year, she thought as she adjusted her clothes. *After all, he told us that he'd hidden himself as best he could and that's exactly what I just did…*

Just in case, she carefully examined the ground she had just watered copiously, as well as the few meters between herself and the cliff face.

No luck, it would have been too much of a coincidence! She thought after a few minutes of unsuccessful inspection, before resuming her walk.

The entrance to the passageway was still quite far away and she'd probably have to return to the rest of the group near the helicopter, especially since the terrain was now becoming more and more rugged… She just didn't have the time to get there and decided to turn back. She was now scrabbling over the scree which was crumbling under her feet and causing her to feel unsteady. She had barely walked ten meters towards the helicopter when her left foot slipped, she felt a ligament in her ankle tear and screamed out in pain:

"Damn it! Damn rock! " she shouted loud enough for Kevin to hear from the beach below and rush to join her.

As he reached her, Kevin noticed that Kate was sitting on the floor and massaging her ankle with a grimace on her face.

"Do you think it's broken or is it just a sprain?"

"I think it's just a sprain," Kate sighed as her face contorted with frustration. "But it's very painful. I won't be able to help you this afternoon."

"Don't worry about it" Kevin reassured her. "The main thing is that you didn't break your leg! That would have been a problem as I don't think they're equipped on the base to handle a fracture properly and I don't know how many thousands of miles away the nearest hospital is!"

"Well, help me up and get me back to the chopper," Kate begged.

"Here, hold on to my arm. How does it feel when you put your foot down?"

"I still can put my weight on it, but it's pretty painful."

"Do you mind if I take a look at your ankle? I'd like to see if it's swollen or purple."

"Of course," Kate replied. "But it's not going to change much."

As he knelt down to inspect Kate's ankle, Kevin's eyes were drawn to something glistening on the ground. To Kate's surprise, Kevin turned away from the ankle and started frantically scratching at the stones and soil beneath him.

"What the hell are you doing?" Kate snapped. "Are you looking at this ankle or what?"

"You won't believe this!" Kevin yelled. "You're one hell of a lucky woman!"

"Oh, yeah? I feel lucky," Kate replied sarcastically. "I can't walk, and my husband thinks I'm lucky! I'm jinxed, you mean!"

"Guess what you fell on?" Kevin continued, laughing loudly.

"Look, Kevin, that's enough!" Kate said. "I'm not going to stand here listening to your delusions. I'm in pain!"

"You *are* going to stand there," Kevin said. "Because guess where you're standing? On the stele, my love!"

"No!" Kate shouted in disbelief. "Stop messing with me! Are you kidding?"

"Not at all!" Kevin confirmed. "Here, look! That's black diorite. And this is the other end of Émile's stone! This is amazing."

"Wow!" yelled Kate, her eyes widening. "Now I see it… I think you're right! I found the stele!"

They threw themselves around each other's necks and kissed each other passionately. From the helicopter, Prosper, who had just looked at his watch and was about to give the signal to return to work, saw Kate and Kevin's entwined silhouettes and wondered what could have excited them so much, to the point of risking delaying the rest of the team.

"Kate! Kevin! It's time to get back to work!" he shouted, cupping his hands around his mouth to help the sound travel. "We're all waiting for you!"

Kevin screamed back at him, using the very same hand gesture:

"No! We're waiting for you! Get up here now and don't worry about getting back to work!"

Followed by Hans and Émile, Prosper hurried to join Kate and Kevin. When he saw the looks on their faces, he knew that they'd found the stele.

"You've got it, haven't you?" heh asked, before he'd even reached them. "Let's see!"

Kevin reached down to the ground at his feet.

"There! I think that's it! We've got Kate to thank! She had the bright idea of spraining her ankle in just the right place!"

Prosper was about to rush to the object to examine it but held back and took the time to inquire about Kate's condition:

"Is it true, did you hurt yourself? Not too serious, I hope. Can you still walk? Do you want us to get the first aid kit from the chopper and put some anti-inflammatory ointment and a bandage on you?"

"No, there's no need," Kate assured him. "I'll take care of it tonight when we get back to the base. I don't think it's too serious, it's just painful when I walk, but it's bearable. Anyway, I consider my sprain a blessing! We've found the stele!"

"Actually," Prosper muttered. "I think it's a miracle… When you said earlier that we were looking for a needle in a haystack, you were right; but we should have known we could rely on the help of the gods!"

He turned to Émile and beamed:

"So Émile, this is where you peed last year, isn't it? We're going to have to wear gloves to clear the stele, aren't we?"

Émile, not sure whether Prosper's remark was meant to be humorous, felt obliged to apologize:

"I didn't do it on purpose! But I don't think there'll be any bacteria left after a year…"

"Émile, I'm kidding!" Prosper clarified. "Even if you pissed on it yesterday, it wouldn't stop us getting our hands on it! All right, no more jokes, let's gently release it. All of you, step back a moment because we first need to take pictures."

Prosper took a multitude of photos, from the ground in the middle of which the blackish edge of the stele protruded, to the immediate surroundings, and then to the neighboring landscape in every direction. Finally, he distributed various tools from out of his backpack, and explained everyone's roles. Hans had to dig with a pickaxe about fifteen inches from the object; Émile had to, from the small trench drilled by Hans, trowel away the earth and stones up to four inches from the stele, Kevin had to knife away the last layer of debris covering it, and finally

Prosper had reserved for himself the most delicate and crucial task: To allow the black diorite and the characters engraved on it to appear through the use of a brush. Kate's mission was to take the measures requested by Prosper and to take regular photos documenting the progress of the excavation. It took them four hours of meticulous and arduous work to clear about two feet of stele. Prosper said then that they could stop there for today as it would be impossible to clear the entire monument in just one afternoon. All stood back and contemplated the fruit of their labor. The top of a large stele, 65.4 inches wide according to Kate's measurements, rounded at the zenith, partially fractured and covered with engraved characters, lay there before them. It was astounding.

Prosper made a ceremonial announcement.

"Lady and gentlemen, you have just allowed humanity to take a gigantic step towards a better understanding of its origins and history. You have in front of you a stele dating back at least five thousand years, perhaps more, which most certainly marked the boundary of a great city built very close to here by what True Archaeology calls Civilization X. As you can see, this stele is in an exceptional state of conservation: The engraved inscriptions are extraordinarily legible and include not only cuneiform characters evocative of ancient Sumerian but also signs similar to Egyptian hieroglyphs and other types of glyphs resembling the Easter Island rongorongo. The deciphering of this text will most certainly demonstrate True Archaeology's theories and, at the same time, the serious errors of the Establishment of Archaeologists and Official Historians. I also find it fascinating that its width is 65.4 inches, which is very close to two megalithic yards; as you may know, the megalithic yard was, according to some researchers now qualified as heretics by the Academic Establishment, a standardized unit of measurement used by the builders of Stonehenge. In short, you've just made the archaeological discovery of the century and are on the way to becoming world celebrities!"

All the members of the team had listened religiously to Prosper's speech and remained silent for a moment as they contemplated their stele. Kate couldn't hold back the tears, which she quickly wiped away for fear of her companions mocking her. Prosper interrupted the moment:

"Well, we'll be able to go back to the base now. Nevertheless, before leaving, we will have to ensure this masterpiece is protected. We've just exposed it to the elements. I brought some plastic sheeting, so we're going to cover it and put most of the excavated material back on top of it, and then we'll wedge it all in with a pile of large stones. I have a little True Archaeology flag here, which should guarantee us the ownership of this find in the unlikely event that someone discovers it before we return to complete extensive excavations."

After following Prosper's instructions, the group set off for the helicopter feeling euphoric. Kate barely needed Kevin's help to cover the short distance, as the joy of the success of the mission seemed to overshadow the pain in her ankle. Once the equipment was carefully tidied up and everyone on board, Hans took off and prepared to head for the base.

"Hans, before leaving Paradise Bay," Proper asked, "could you try to fly over that passageway we saw south of our find and see what it leads to on the other side of the cliffs? Let's not forget that the stele is supposed to mark the entrance to a city, and I wouldn't be surprised if it lies behind those cliffs."

Hans started a U-turn and positioned the helicopter towards the entrance of the passageway. It was quite narrow and enclosed on either side by very steep walls. Rather than flying his aircraft into the narrow gorge, a maneuver far too dangerous given the overall level of his flying skills, Hans decided to climb high and pass well above the mountain range surrounding Paradise Bay. No one regretted this decision because it turned out that the mountain barrier was not very wide and that, once they'd passed it, they discovered a huge, roughly circular circus, surrounded in the distance by majestic snow-covered peaks. The bowl was uniformly white, covered over its entire surface with a thick coat of ice. Hans suggested flying around it, which he thought represented a perimeter of about forty miles and which was therefore perfectly feasible without depleting their fuel reserves.

After a few minutes Kate started yelling:

"Look, over there, in the middle of the plain, they look like pyramids!"

They all looked in the direction indicated by Kate and also started shouting out in amazement.

"You're right," Kevin confirmed, "it's not easy to make them out in this blinding whiteness, but there are several pyramidal shapes! They look high compared to the rest of the ground. I think I see three of them."

Hans decided to shorten his tour and dive towards the center of the basin and the possible pyramids.

"We can definitely see something there", Émile said with a hint of doubt in his voice, "but it could be small mountains… maybe volcanic cones in the middle of a gigantic caldera."

"I think," corrected Prosper, "that they are indeed pyramids or ziggurats. Look at the regularity of the sides and the angles between the faces. Three natural formations like that would be very unlikely. It's not surprising that these types of monuments would be here. It's the heart of the city! Too bad there's all this ice, because the site must be absolutely amazing. This could very well be Plato's Atlantis!"

"The problem is the layer of ice. Freeing these monuments will require years of work… All we have to do now is hope that global warming will come to our rescue!" Kevin joked.

They took a lot of pictures and, after flying over the center of the bowl several times, resigned themselves to leaving this bewitching place to return to the base.

30

THE DISCOVERY OF CIVILIZATION X

Klaus, Ulrich and Joachim were there to welcome them when the Kon Tiki arrived, as if they'd anticipated the success of their expedition to Paradise Bay.

"So, did you find what you were looking for?" asked Klaus in a tone that was very much unlike his usual coldness.

"Klaus," Prosper replied with a broad smile, "thanks to you and the availability of Hans and your helicopter, True Archaeology has managed to unearth a stele that testifies to the existence of the remains of Civilization X. If you're interested, we can show you the pictures we took later. But right now, we're all exhausted and need a hot shower!"

"Of course," Klaus agreed. "Rest, freshen up and let's all meet for dinner. Shall we say exceptionally at eight? And there'll be no cooking for you tonight! It's New Year's Eve and we have prepared a little celebration for you guys! We can't wait to hear all about your discovery."

Kate, Kevin, Émile and Prosper returned to their rooms. This time, they barely even noticed the narrowness and discomfort of the place. They took turns taking a shower in the small bathroom, which the previous days had only inspired disgust, but which now, after their exhilarating day at Paradise Bay, seemed almost luxurious to them. Kate applied a good dose of anti-inflammatory ointment to her ankle and wrapped it in a bandage, before slipping on some sneakers instead of the black pumps she would have preferred to wear on New Year's Eve.

Exceptionally, she took this small inconvenience lightly, considering the fabulous discovery that her sprain had allowed the group to make.

At eight, everyone gathered in the refectory, which Klaus and his colleagues had decorated with red and gold garlands for the occasion, and which also no longer had the gloomy and sinister appearance of the previous days.

Klaus looked very proud when he pulled out of the fridge a magnum of *Brut Impérial Moët et Chandon* and popped the cork:

"Cheers to the explorers!"

He served everyone, apologizing for not having proper flutes on the base, before proposing a toast to a new year that was shaping up under the best auspices.

Prosper chose this moment to offer Klaus the eighteen-year-old bottle of Single Malt he'd had in his suitcase since leaving Oxford. Klaus hadn't expected such a gift and was obviously moved. He hugged Prosper warmly and thanked him:

"Thank you Prosper and thank you to the entire True Archaeology team. You know, life on the base is usually very monotonous and, I have to admit, often boring. Your presence during these few days has been like a breath of fresh air. It really is a pleasure for us to be able to celebrate the New Year with you! "

Prosper decided to mark the occasion in his usual style:

"On behalf of my colleagues and friends at True Archaeology (and I would like to include in this category Hans, our wonderful pilot), I formally want to express our infinite gratitude to Klaus, Ulrich and Joachim, for having welcomed us into their home, despite all the inconvenience this may have caused them due to the limited space and the many constraints imposed by the environment. Without their help, we would never have been able to carry out our research. We will not fail to mention their names publicly when the time comes. True Archaeology now holds the indisputable proof that what it has consistently affirmed since its foundation is true: A long time ago, there was indeed a great primordial civilization at the origin of all known ancient civilizations. Until the middle of this year, we were still hesitating about the exact location of the cradle of this great primordial civilization. We believed we might discover traces of it in Antarctica, but we also considered the depths of the Amazonian forest or the Gobi Desert. And then, this summer, Émile showed us his stone and the Antarctic theory then became a matter of course. We are now convinced that Civilization X, either had its epicenter in Antarctica at a remote time when the continent was ice-free, or was able, thanks to a very advanced level of knowledge and technological development, to establish a great city in Antarctica, whose pyramidal constructions we saw today. You can imagine the shock that this discovery is going to cause. It's clear that the so-called experts of the archaeological establishment will have a lot to answer for and that certain historical and religious dogmas, built on sand, will collapse. So today is a great day: This find is equivalent to the Rosetta Stone, or the Gate of Ishtar, and is therefore a treasure of inestimable value. But this day is just the beginning of a fabulous adventure. There is an entire great city under that ice and we will have to come back very soon to explore it. Above all, we will have to communicate to the whole world. We will have to face the pack of our detractors who will no doubt do everything they can to try to save their credibility and status. The coming year will give us the opportunity to meet again and will bring us great triumphs but also great trials! Thank you again and happy New Year everyone!"

A thunder of applause exploded in the refectory. They then sat down to enjoy their meal. To everyone's surprise, Klaus had found a way to obtain some *foie gras* and had cooked a huge turkey. At the end of the main course, they had a raspberry tart, accompanied by small glasses of Lorraine brandy, to the delight of Kate and Prosper, who were both from that particular region of France.

They then sat together in front of the widest computer screen available to look at the dozens of photos taken at Paradise Bay, adding their comments and anecdotes on the day's progress to the projection.

Finally, Prosper suggested setting up a video conference with The Manor in Oxford. After some technical difficulties, Klaus managed to establish a link with Edwina, Monique and Dorian.

"Can you see us?" asked Prosper. "We see you very well from our side."

"Yes, we see and hear you perfectly," Edwina confirmed. "So, how are our explorers? And how far are you along in the mission?"

"Except for Kate, who has a sprained ankle," Prosper explained, "we're all in great shape at this end. It's mission accomplished! We've got our hands on what we've been looking for! We found the stele!"

Everyone at The Manor cheered.

"So? Does this stele seem to you to be what we thought it was? What inscriptions does it contain and were you able to start deciphering them?" Dorian asked.

"Look, I didn't really have time to think about the meaning of the text on it," Prosper replied. "The only thing I can tell you at this point is that it's completely covered with signs. At first glance, I get the impression that there isn't only Sumerian cuneiform; we can also distinguish hieroglyphics of the early Egyptian type, and other signs that could well be rongorongo, as on the artifacts found on Easter Island. I'm going to e-mail you all the pictures we took, and you can have fun deciphering it all! One thing is for sure, it's a stele similar to those that mark the boundaries of the ancient cities of Egypt and Mesopotamia. And not only did we dig up the stele, but we were also able to fly over the city. Unfortunately, it is almost completely covered with ice; however, we spotted three pyramidal structures in the center. So, for me, there is no doubt about it! We've just proven the existence of Civilization X in Antarctica!"

"This is wonderful!" exclaimed Dorian, obviously very moved. "Congratulations to the whole team! Prosper, do you think I can announce this? Or does it seem premature to you to organize the press conference that we planned?"

"It's not premature in the slightest," Prosper confirmed. "Actually, I think it is urgent. We had to leave the stele where we found it because we're not equipped to remove it entirely from the ground and bring it back with us. The sooner True Archaeology can launch a proper excavation campaign and return to Paradise Bay with everything we need, the better. It will take us several days to get back to Oxford, so please don't wait until we get back before you tell the press. The pictures are explicit enough for you to tell the whole world about Civilization X!"

"All right," Dorian agreed. "I'll summon everyone on the second of January! This is going to be their big New Year's scoop! I hope you'll be able to watch the television that evening, because it will make a lot of noise!"

"Prosper," Edwina intervened, "you said that Kate has an injury? It's not too bad, is it? Can she still walk?"

"Thank you for worrying about me, Edwina," Kate replied. "You're the only one! The others can't think about anything but their stele and Civilization X. Actually, I'm kidding. I'm already over the worst of it, and it is thanks to this that I literally fell on the stele; so, I consider it a blessing!

"And what about you, my darling? How did you manage?" asked Monique in French. "What an adventure!"

"I'm doing well," replied Émile. "Of course, I have some aches and pains from being out in the cold and digging for hours. But the main thing is that the rest of my stone has been found!"

"That's right," Prosper agreed. "Let us never forget that all this is thanks to Émile! Monique, your husband is a real hero! And he'll soon become as famous as Brad Pitt, so expect next year to be full of emotions!"

"It comes as no surprise to me," Monique said. I always knew that my Émile had hidden talents, that's why I married him!"

"Anyway, Monique, I can tell you that he has been really missing you this whole time," Kevin said. "You made him the man we know today, no doubt!"

"I don't know if that's true," replied Monique with false modesty, "but in any case, I'm very proud of him!"

"Well," said Prosper, "we're going to have to bring this call to an end because our hosts here at the base might start getting impatient. We wish you all a happy New Year and an excellent press conference for Dorian in two days!"

"Happy New Year!" everyone shouted, and the video conference was terminated.

31

ARMAGEDDON

About twenty journalists responded to Professor Green's invitation and arrived at Benson Castle to participate in the press conference two days later. An extraordinary archaeological discovery was supposed to be revealed to them at eleven that morning. There were representatives from the main English newspapers such as *The Daily Telegraph, The Guardian* and *The Sun,* and also of some major foreign newspapers, such as the French *Le Monde,* the German *Der Spiegel,* the Italian *Corriere delà Serra* and the Spanish *El Pais.* Several British television channels were also present; Kimberley Cosby, the star presenter of *Challenges,* who had recently hosted a program on True Archaeology, even came in person.

Dorian had spent the first day of the year preparing for this event with Edwina. Dorian was convinced that this press conference would be child's play, as the exercise seemed much less delicate than his interview with Kim Cosby for *Challenges.* After all, he would be in charge of the show and the questions would be centered exclusively on the nature and circumstances of True Archaeology's discovery. There'd be nothing particularly difficult for him to manage. Dorian had finalized a memo that he would simply read and whose text, which would be distributed to all the journalists present at the end of the conference, was as straightforward as he could make it.

True Archaeology, on the basis of many archaeological, historical and linguistic arguments and to solve the many deficiencies of official history, has always affirmed that there was, long before the oldest known civilizations such as Sumer and Egypt and at the origin of the latter, a great primordial civilization that was technologically highly advanced. True Archaeology has called it Civilization X. Until now, there was no absolute proof of the existence of Civilization X. Today, this proof exists. True Archaeology has just discovered a stele engraved with signs that could be precursors to the cuneiform writing practiced at the beginning of Sumer, Egyptian hieroglyphics and other not yet perfectly deciphered writings. In addition, True Archaeology believes it has located a large ancient city whose stele marks the entrance.

What gives this discovery its extraordinary character is where it took place: a location far from everything and where it was traditionally assumed that ancient man had never been able to set foot, a continent now completely buried under the ice… Antarctica!

Clearly, the men who built the city that True Archaeology has just discovered in Antarctica could only have done so at a time when the continent was ice-free, that is, according to climatologists and geologists, no more recently than seven thousand years ago. They must have had very advanced scientific and technological knowledge. It is clear that the history of humanity and the beginnings of civilization will have to be completely revised. The discovery of Civilization X will undoubtedly make it possible to explain a certain number of phenomena that have remained mysterious, such as the pyramids of Giza, the ruins of Tiahuanaco, Stonehenge and the Nazca lines. True Archaeology intends to initiate, as soon as technically possible, an extensive excavation campaign in Antarctica, in order to deepen our understanding of Civilization X.

At eleven sharp, Dorian stepped out of the main entrance of Benson Castle and stood in front of the group of journalists gathered at the bottom of the stairs. A forest of microphones stretched towards him, while camera flashes began to go off left, right and center.

"Ladies and gentlemen," began Dorian, "Thank you for coming in such large numbers to learn the details of the exceptional archaeological discovery that True Archaeology has just made and to be able to communicate this revelation as widely as possible to your readers and listeners."

All of a sudden, the screaming sirens of two police cars rushing into the driveway of The Manor diverted the journalists' attention and forced Dorian to stop speaking. The cars arrived a few feet from the front steps and two uniformed police officers appeared, accompanied by two plainclothes individuals who rushed towards Dorian, holding out their Scotland Yard badge.

"Mr. Dorian Green? You're under arrest! Please come with us!"

Surprised exclamations sprang from the crowd of journalists as cameras continued to click. Dorian remained open-mouthed for a few seconds but recovered quickly.

"Gentlemen, there must be a misunderstanding. Can you explain what's going on?"

"You've been accused of a serious crime," said one of the inspectors. "I suggest you follow us without making a fuss. You'll be able to see a lawyer as soon as we're at the station."

"But this is outrageous!" Dorian protested. "I haven't done anything wrong! What exactly am I being accused of?"

"Do you really want me to say it in front of all these journalists?"

"But, sir, I have nothing to hide!" exclaimed Dorian. "I demand to know what I'm wrongly accused of!"

"Well, if you insist," mumbled the policeman. "It's charges of a sexual nature that are being brought against you… with minors."

Dorian became pale, felt his legs bending and, as if paralyzed, allowed himself to be handcuffed and dragged to the back of one of the police vehicles into which he was pushed with force.

The journalists rushed behind Dorian and the police officer. Dorian could hear their insistent questions and the constant noise of the cameras:

"What more can you tell us about these accusations? Who are the victims? When did this case against Father Green begin? Where did the acts take place?"

Dorian collapsed into tears as the car started and he was whisked away to the New Scotland Yard building in London. Edwina and Monique had simply watched in helpless amazement as the nightmare unfolded.

After rushing inside and closing the doors on the journalists who wanted to question them, Edwina and Monique collapsed into the armchairs in the small living room. Edwina had to explain what exactly happened in French to Monique, as she could not understand a single world of the previous exchange in English. She then continued in French:

"What the hell is this all about? This is ridiculous! This whole pedophilia thing is nonsense! I can guarantee you, Monique, that Dorian is totally innocent! Poor thing, doing this to him on a day like this is just monstrous!"

"Yes," Monique stammered, "he didn't even have time to talk about Antarctica! That was some press conference! I'm so glad Émile wasn't here to see it!"

"What can we do to get Dorian out of this mess? I don't understand why Scotland Yard is handling this case. We'll have to go to London to see him. It would have been easier if they'd taken him to Oxford police station, to our friend Murphy's... I have to call Prosper to get his opinion!"

"I'm not sure calling Prosper is a good idea! What do you want him to do about it from the South Pole? There's no need to panic him and the rest of the team. The later they learn of this disaster, the better for their morale! If I were you, I'd wait for his next phone call before letting him know..."

"You're probably right," Edwina conceded. "I don't want to worry them. But I must go to see Murphy. He'll know what to do."

Edwina left Monique, quickly put on a coat and drove to the police station, where she rushed into Commissioner Murphy's office.

"I'm sorry to barge in on you like this, but it's an emergency! Are you aware of what just happened during the press conference at The Manor?"

"No! What happened?" Murphy asked worriedly.

"Some police officers from Scotland Yard came to arrest Dorian!" explained Edwina. "He's being charged with pedophilia! Dorian was about to announce our discovery at the press conference, when, suddenly, in front of all the journalists, he found himself handcuffed and taken off to Scotland Yard's headquarters!"

"What?" exclaimed Murphy incredulously. "But this is dreadful! I don't suppose you were given any details about the indictment or the accuser?"

"No, of course not," Edwina confirmed. "The only thing the inspector said to Dorian, who didn't understand what was going on and was loud and clear about his innocence, was that he was going to be charged with pedophilia."

"Oh, my God! Poor Dorian," Murphy despaired. "He must be going out of his mind. Okay, let's try to stay calm; one thing is absolutely certain: Dorian could never have done that. Never. I think I know Dorian very well. He's a straight guy, with a very high sense of ethics and morality; the very idea that there are pedophiles in the Catholic Church repels him... We've talked about it! So, his accuser or accusers are lying and it's all a setup. The real question is who is behind it and why... Well, I think I have an idea. I think it was the same people who tried to get rid of Émile, or at least to prevent him from going back to Antarctica. Seeing as they failed with Émile, they decided to attack Dorian, probably to ruin his reputation and that of True Archaeology. The timing is very suspicious. The very day Dorian was about to reveal the vestiges of Civilization X in Antarctica, he was arrested and made to look like a monstrous criminal and so the public would forget everything he had to say! I'll tell you what I think: Kahn, who is in no position to set up such an operation himself, is working with a powerful industrial group with interests in Antarctica for whom the discovery of archaeological remains there would be very frustrating! These people are capable of doing anything to protect their profits. And they are specialists in public relations campaigns, as they say, which most of the time are just intended to brainwash people and spread misinformation."

"But if that's the case, what can we do?"

"We're going to get Dorian out of this mess" Murphy said. "I will contact my colleagues at Scotland Yard to find out exactly what's going on. Then I'll pay a visit to Dorian and advise him to hire one of the best lawyers in England, who happens to be a very good friend of mine. Then we'll prove that this whole thing is a setup, that those behind it probably bought the false testimony of some poor sod, and that Dorian didn't commit any crime of the sort! Finally, when Dorian is out of the clutches of Scotland Yard, we make the bastards behind this scandal pay and restore Dorian and True Archaeology's good reputation."

"I'm glad you're so confident" Edwina sighed. "Do you really think we can trust the police and the judicial system?"

"How could a police commissioner not trust the system? Of course you have to trust them! In any case, I trust Dorian! I know he's innocent and I'll do everything I can to prove it!"

Edwina thanked Bob warmly and left for Benson Castle where Monique was waiting impatiently for her.

"So, what did Commissioner Murphy say?" asked Monique.

"I'm glad I went to see him," Edwina said. "He thinks it's all just a setup, like those odd things that happened to your husband just before you came here to The Manor. He's sure Dorian is innocent and he's confident he'll be able to get him out of the situation pretty quickly!"

"Well, you see, there was no need to worry our great adventurers unnecessarily!" added Monique, whose only concern seemed to be her husband's comfort.

"Look," said Edwina, who was quite annoyed by Monique's self-centered attitude, "if you don't mind, I'm going to go rest in my room; I really need to be alone to clear my head a little."

Once in her room, Edwina laid on her bed, played the recent events over again in her head and thought about how to proceed. She wondered if she should not visit Dorian, as the presence of a faithful friend by his side during this ordeal was likely to bring him some comfort; however, she thought that Dorian was the kind of man who preferred to have as few witnesses as possible to his humiliation. She concluded that it was better to wait until Murphy had time to sort things out and develop a strategy. Her visit could then be part of a combative and optimistic plan, rather than appear as a demonstration of pity and commiseration.

She also thought about what to do with the other members of the

True Archaeology steering committee. She concluded that it was urgent to bring them together, on the one hand to inform them of the situation before they learned the sensational version delivered by the media and on the other hand to prepare them to be harassed by journalists in the coming days. However, Prosper's prior approval was required before such an initiative could be undertaken.

Edwina thought that perhaps she didn't need to wait for Prosper's agreement to immediately contact Emma Coffey who, although not a member of the steering committee, had become a very active member of True Archaeology and was now very close to Dorian. Talking to Emma was all the more desirable because Edwina was hoping of calling on her goodwill to relieve her of a burden that was becoming more and more painful every day: Monique Delaporte. Edwina had had to really control herself a few moments earlier in order not to put this woman in her place. She felt that Monique had no good qualities, was focused on herself, indifferent to the distress of others, and only concerned, even under these tragic circumstances, about her husband's fate. Having Monique constantly on her back at The Manor, having to endure her inane chatter all day long and being obliged to speak with her in French had become absolutely unbearable to Edwina, especially with what had just happened to Dorian.

"Hello, Emma, this is Edwina. Something terrible has happened to Dorian and I could use your help!"

"Oh, really?" Emma said, surprised. "His life isn't in danger, is it?"

"Not in the physical sense", Edwina replied, "but psychologically, it is, yes."

Edwina told Emma about the aborted press conference, Dorian's arrest and Murphy's hypothesis about certain people trying to tarnish Dorian's honor and reputation.

"My God, this is terrible!" exclaimed Emma. "I can't even imagine for a second that Dorian might have engaged in that kind of abomination. Mr. Murphy is certainly right. It can only be some sort of slanderous campaign to prevent him from talking about Civilization X. But what can I do to help?"

"Emma," Edwina explained, "you know that we felt obliged to have Emile's wife Monique stay here with us for the duration of the Antarctic expedition. But I must confess that things are difficult at the moment and Monique's permanent presence has become intolerable. I have nothing in common with this woman and her silly thoughts about everything and nothing wind me up the wrong way. I'm afraid I'll lose my self-control at some point and end up throwing her out of my house, but I'd rather not go to that extreme. Would you be willing to take her off my hands now and again until her husband gets back and then we can gently send them both back to where they came from?"

"Of course, no problem," Emma promised. "She can come and stay with me at the library in the afternoons. If you want, I could also take her out to dinner with me once in a while. I understand the issue. I don't think Monique is a bad person, but I noticed that she has a gift for making inappropriate and often hurtful remarks. I don't think she's all that bright and she has no awareness of that. In fact, she has a ridiculously enlarged self-image!"

"Emma, I don't know how to thank you," Edwina confided in a grateful tone. "This really is a massive help. We're getting an action plan together for Dorian. I'll be validating it on the phone tonight with Prosper and will keep you informed. Expect to be invited to an urgent meeting any day now."

Pleased that she had partially solved the Monique problem, Edwina dozed off on her bed until the phone rang and woke her with a startle.

"Ah, Prosper," sighed Edwina. "You have no idea how happy I am to hear from you! How are you?"

"Everything's fine here," said Prosper. "We've left the German base. Hans just dropped us off with his helicopter on King George's Island. From here, we'll be taking a small plane to Ushuaia and then to Buenos Aires and finally London. We should be home in two days! So, how was Dorian's press conference? Have we already become the archaeological heroes of the twenty-first century?"

"This is going to come as a bit of a shock..." Edwina announced in a trembling voice. "The press conference was a nightmare! The police came to arrest Dorian before it had even started. I regret to have to tell you this, but Dorian didn't have time to mention your discovery. I'm sorry, but as it stands, you and your team are still the only ones who know about the existence of the stele."

"What?" Prosper gasped. "The police arrested Dorian? But why?"

"Oh, I don't know if I can tell you that on the phone," replied Edwina in a mortified tone. "I'm so embarrassed and it's so unfair…"

"Go ahead, please," Prosper insisted. "I have to know! He's my friend!"

"A police inspector told Dorian that he'd been accused of pedophilia," Edwina revealed.

"Pedophilia?" yelled Prosper. "But that's dreadful! How can anyone accuse Dorian of something like that? This is totally false! I'd stake my life on it."

"That's what Murphy thinks, too," Edwina confided. "He believes that this whole story is a setup, a smear campaign launched by people who want to discredit Dorian and prevent True Archaeology from revealing the existence of Civilization X in Antarctica!"

"Well, whoever these people are, they've made a grave mistake!" Prosper said in a combative tone. "We'll prove Dorian's innocence and clear his name. And trust me: The whole world will hear about our find. If not through Dorian, it will be through me or Kevin or any other member of True Archaeology. No one can shut us up, you hear me!"

"I'm not really worried about Civilization X," Edwina continued. "Of course, everyone will find out about your discovery at some point. Right now, what concerns me is Dorian and what we can do to get him out of this mess."

"Did you say Murphy was on it?" Prosper asked. "I trust Bob to get to the bottom of all this. I'll see him as soon as I get back. What a nightmare! This really is not what we need! Everything was going so well. We were just about to celebrate our feat with the whole world. And now it's all ruined by this disgusting slander. What a mess!"

"I'm sorry to spoil the end of your expedition," Edwina apologized. "One other thing: I think we need to get the committee together as soon as possible to inform them of the situation and to plan what comes next. What do you think?"

"You're right," Prosper agreed. "I want everyone together in three days' time. I'll probably be back by then. In the meantime, call all the colleagues who don't know what's going on yet."

"Okay," Edwina confirmed. "I also wanted to tell you that I've already notified Emma Coffey. In my opinion, we should bring her on board. She was deeply involved in the preparations for the expedition, she's good friends with Dorian and she really is a woman you can count on."

"Good idea," Prosper agreed. "We're going to need unfailing support in the coming days!"

"I'm so sorry to have nothing but bad news for you," said Edwina. "Have a safe journey back. I'll see you soon!"

Prosper, visibly upset, slowly returned to the table where he had left Kate, Kevin and Émile while he made his call to Edwina, in the small terminal building on King George Island where they were waiting for a flight to Ushuaia.

"I have something very unfortunate to tell you. I know it'll ruin your mood and I'm sorry for that. We've all been so thrilled, and we'd hoped to be able to celebrate our success with dignity, but I'm afraid things aren't going to pan out that way. I've just learned from Edwina that Dorian was arrested by the police at the beginning of his press conference and that he was unable to talk about our discovery with the journalists that were there… I'm going to explain everything. But before I do, I need to tell you that I'm convinced that the accusations against Dorian are totally false and that he is absolutely innocent of the crime for which he's been accuse. It is all a big lie. Right: Dorian has been charged with pedophilia!"

"That's horrible!" Kate cried. "Who would dare accuse Dorian of such a monstrous crime? This is insane!"

"It's disgusting," Kevin added. "I guess Kahn and his buddies paid a fake witness to take Dorian down and ruin his reputation. It's easy enough. Dorian was a Catholic priest and since, as a result of a succession of very well-orchestrated media campaigns, most people think that all Catholic priests are pedophiles, public opinion will swallow all this without even questioning it."

"Yes, but," Émile dared to question, "what proof do you have that Father Green didn't have a moment of weakness when he was a priest?"

"Émile," snapped Prosper, "a little decency, please! I can't bear for anyone to doubt Dorian's innocence! You don't know Dorian very well, do you? I've known him for more than thirty years. I knew him when he was still a priest and I can assure you that Dorian has never committed any offense of this nature!"

"Well," Émile conceded, "since you're so sure of that, I apologize. But the problem is that it's not me who will have to be convinced, but a jury. And you're going to have to provide incontrovertible evidence that the charges against Father Green are false."

"Trust me, Émile," replied Prosper, "it won't be difficult to prove Dorian's innocence. We'll put an end to this plot against him and True Archaeology. Besides, our friend, Commissioner Murphy, thinks exactly as I do!"

"But then," Émile continued, "if Dorian didn't have time to talk to journalists about our discovery, does that mean that we've wasted our time and that no one will ever hear about the stele and the buried city?"

"Of course not!" Prosper protested. "Let me tell you how I expect things to go… First, Murphy, me and all of Dorian's friends will demonstrate that Dorian is innocent of the crime of which he has been unfairly accused. We'll identify the perpetrators of this slander, we'll make his accusers confess their lies, we'll sue whoever is behind this scheme and we'll ensure that Dorian's honor and reputation are completely restored. At the same time and especially since I suspect that there'll be journalists wanting to interview members of True Archaeology, we'll take over from Dorian and immediately communicate our findings loud and clear. Kevin and I are in the best position to take the lead, but we'll form a battalion of True Archaeology members to take over and spread the good news! Of course, it'll be more difficult than we anticipated, but there's no way Civilization X will remain in oblivion. Humanity must understand that we've not been told the truth about our history and that it is high time to revise the official theories imposed by the establishment. It should not be forgotten, despite Dorian's temporary inability to do so, that there is an urgent need to launch a proper excavation campaign. I know that finding sponsors and raising the necessary funds will not be easy given the bad image that True Archaeology will receive because of this case. I know that the same bastards who are behind this coup will probably do everything they can to prevent us from continuing our excavations in Antarctica, but we must not give up. As soon as I return to Oxford and resume my duties at the University of Strasbourg, organizing the continuation of the excavations for True Archaeology will be my priority. I'm counting on you to continue the fight! Remain optimistic and consider all this as an insignificant additional test compared to our achievement."

At The Manor, Edwina had to force herself to leave her room and have dinner with Monique. She thought that hopefully this would be the last time she would have to go through such an ordeal, thanks to Emma's understanding and the imminent return of the expedition team.

"Do you feel better?" Monique felt compelled to ask. "You've been resting for quite a long time!"

"Please excuse me Monique," Edwina replied curtly, "but I have a terrible headache, and I'm afraid we're going to have dinner in silence tonight. And I really don't wish to talk about the painful event we went through this morning..."

"As you wish! But did your husband call you and do you have any news of Émile?"

"Prosper called," sighed Edwina, "and he asked me to say hello to you from your husband who is doing very well!"

"And what does he say about this pedophilia business that Professor Green is accused of?" insisted Monique. "It makes you think... with all these scandals that have broken out all over the world about Catholic priests..."

"How many times do I have to tell you? I don't want to talk about it anymore! Anyway, Dorian's business is not your concern. Please just meddle in what concerns you, that means your husband's health, his imminent flight to England and then your trip back home to Rueil-Malmaison!"

Monique felt it was better for her not to bother Edwina with her questions and comments anymore and so finished her dinner silently before rushing off to do crossword puzzles in her room.

Edwina, relieved by Monique's departure, decided to take a look at the TV news, anxious to learn how this morning's incident would be reported. Although she had expected it, she felt sick when she saw what was written across the screen as the news started: *True Archaeology scandal: Dorian Green accused of pedophilia.* She recognized Kimberley Cosby who seemed to be almost enjoying commenting on the images of the arrest. Kim strongly emphasized that Dorian Green was a defrocked priest and pointed out that pedophilia was an extremely widespread vice in the Catholic Church, as shown by the multitude of similar cases revealed in recent years.

These journalists are all scavengers, Edwina thought. *Dorian is guilty as far as they're concerned... Not a word about his contributions to the advancement of archaeology and history... Only salacious details and a perverse pleasure in dragging people through the mud... They disgust me!* And she turned off the television.

32

CONSPIRATION

Joseph Taittinger, principal shareholder and chairman of the TOTEXX board, had invited his CEO, Jeff Fishman and Rachel Schwartz, Vice President in charge of communication, to an informal dinner on January ninth at his luxurious property in Preston Hollow, one of the most exclusive areas in Dallas.

Three days earlier, Jeff had assured him that the Kahn case was now settled and that nothing was threatening the ICEBERG project anymore. Jeff had explained the critical role played by Rachel in neutralizing the company's enemies, stressed that the young woman had very high potential and recommended her promotion to Senior Vice President.

"Rachel," said Taittinger, "Jeff has told me a lot of good things about you. It seems that, thanks to you, the Kahn issue is already old news. Remind me again what it was exactly? The only thing I vaguely remember is Mr. Kahn coming to talk to us… Something about the ruins of an ancient civilization that could be found on our exploration site and that would threaten the continuation of our ICEBERG project! I remember giving Jeff carte blanche to deal with the problem as best he could, but I must say that I didn't follow the details of the operation. Tonight, I'm curious to know what has happened since Kahn's visit."

"Sir," Jeff intervened, "if I may, before Rachel explains how the problem was solved, I would like to remind you of the general context. TOTEXX has already invested several hundred million dollars to develop a phenomenal oil field in Antarctica and we expect billions in profits from our ICEBERG project in the medium term, which will ensure the company's financial health for the foreseeable future. This is therefore of paramount importance to TOTEXX. When Professor Samuel Kahn told us about a possible archaeological discovery in Antarctica near our site and therefore a major threat to the ICEBERG project, we decided to take his story very seriously and take all necessary measures to eliminate the threat. You call it the "Kahn issue", but the "Green affair" would be more appropriate. We now know that our real enemy is Dorian Green, founder of a pseudo-scientific society called True Archaeology. Kahn was ultimately of little use other than sounding the alarm, but Green and True Archaeology are obsessed with the idea of a great antediluvian primordial civilization whose traces they believe they have found in Antarctica: This Green is particularly angry about companies like TOTEXX removing archaeological remains that could prove his theories are true."

"If it makes you happy, Jeff, to talk about the Green affair rather than the Kahn issue, I really don't care!" said Taittinger in a caustic tone. "What interests me is to understand how Rachel managed to eliminate the risk to the ICEBERG project."

"Yes, sir. Just one last word, however," Jeff carried on boldly. "Dorian Green, having learned that a French tourist, Émile Delaporte, had found a stone in the area where TOTEXX plans to drill, recruited him and convinced him to return, along with members of True Archaeology, to the site of his discovery, in the hope of finding the remains of what he calls Civilization X. If Green had been able to announce to the general public that he'd found ancient ruins in Antarctica, TOTEXX would have had the greatest difficulties in moving forward with the ICEBERG project. I think these clarifications are important to your understanding of Rachel's strategy."

"Blah, blah, blah, blah..." Taittinger commented, deliberately hurtfully. "Maybe I'll eventually get to hear what Rachel has to say to me? Go ahead, Rachel!"

"First of all, Sir," Rachel said in an obsequious tone, "I want to thank you for your invitation and tell you that I am very honored. I'd also like to say that it was Jeff who helped develop our strategy and I am very grateful to him for having placed his full trust in me to execute the plan. There were three phases to it: one centered on Samuel Kahn, one on Émile Delaporte and the other on Dorian Green. First, we had to understand the role played by Kahn. When we realized that Kahn actually had no control over the situation, we managed to prevent him from blackmailing TOTEXX."

"I apologize for interrupting," Taittinger said in an authoritative tone. "So, you finally realized that Kahn was just a blackmailer! It took you long enough! As soon as I saw and heard the man, I immediately knew that his only purpose was to extort money from us. All his stories of antediluvian civilizations, Atlantis and pagan gods... it was obviously just bullshit! All right, keep going!"

"Sir, you are absolutely right," Rachel continued meekly. "Kahn was hoping to get five million dollars out of TOTEXX! I managed to convince him to give up his ridiculous claims and, in total, we only gave him two hundred and fifty grand in exchange for a certain amount of useful information about Émile Delaporte, the French tourist who caused all our problems in the first place."

"That's already far too much for a crook like Kahn!" exclaimed Taittinger in outrage. "If you'd let me do it, I'd have paid him in kicks in the ass! At least you saved us a few million dollars..."

"The second part of the action plan was much more difficult," Rachel continued. "Clearly, the only person who could lead True Archaeology to the exact location where archaeological remains could be found, was Émile. So, we tried to dissuade him from returning to Antarctica. Unfortunately, all our attempts failed, mainly because True Archaeology removed him from his place of residence in France to True Archaeology's headquarters in Oxford, where he became out of reach."

"Damn it!" Taittinger said. "You should have called on a real professional who would have had no difficulty in eliminating this Émile once and for all... You can't make an omelet without breaking eggs... If you want to succeed in business, you can't have too many scruples: There are more than sixty million insignificant little Frenchmen, while there's only one company like TOTEXX, which serves all humanity and it is infinitely more precious!"

"Nevertheless, I managed to put one of my acquaintances on his trail," Rachel continued, unabashed. "My agent managed to board the same ship as Émile and his three True Archaeology buddies. I soon learned that they all landed in Paradise Bay, very close to our future drilling site. I also learned that they'd received support from a local German base so that they could go there by helicopter and do their excavations quietly. We assumed that True Archaeology would make a significant archaeological discovery in Antarctica and that, if they did, they would quickly communicate their discovery to the general public."

"You're not telling me you believe all this nonsense!" Taittinger said. "Don't give me all that antediluvian civilization crap, tales of a lost city in Antarctica and stories of incredible technological advances made by pagans ten thousand years ago! You haven't seen any evidence of that, have you?"

"I fully agree with you, sir," Rachel replied calmly, with an unfailing sense of diplomacy. "But we needed to avoid the risk of a gullible public believing in a civilization that disappeared under the ice! We didn't want to put TOTEXX at risk and so decided to make a preemptive strike. By ruining Dorian Green's reputation and credibility, and therefore that of True Archaeology, we had a chance to prevent him from being heard and taken seriously by the public. So, I dug into his past and found out that he was a defrocked Catholic priest. I imagine you are aware of the many pedophilia scandals that priests around the world have been met with in recent years. It wasn't too difficult for me to get my hands on a former protégé of Father Green in London. One of my agents managed to convince this unfortunate man, who has since become an unemployed drug addict always on the lookout for money to satisfy his addiction, to file a complaint against Dorian Green for rape. It was then very easy to get the media involved."

"Is your accuser reliable?" asked Taittinger. "He's not going to retract his complaint, is he?"

"It doesn't matter," Rachel argued. "Even if he does, given the slowness of the legal proceedings, the steamroller of the tabloid press will have had plenty of time to do its job, i. e. to ruin Dorian Green's reputation. I can assure you that the image of Father Green as a pedophile is already well established; it will remain in the public's mind for a very long time and it'll take Green several years to clear his name… Do you want me to show you some of the headlines from the international press?"

"I would love to!" Taittinger smiled. "Anyway, whether or not your addict really was raped doesn't make a big difference in my view. I've always been convinced that all Catholic priests were sexual deviants, so I imagine this Dorian Green probably abused a lot of innocent children. We Presbyterians have never been affected by this vice which is an inescapable consequence of the dumb rites imposed on its clergy by the Vatican. Let's see these newspapers!"

"I've brought you a copy of the *Herald Tribune,* a rather conservative English newspaper, which has the story on its front page: *Professor Dorian Green, founder of True Archaeology, accused of pedophilia.* I also have *The Sun,* which is more popular, which says: *True Archaeology Scandal: Dorian Green arrested for pedophilia!* Similar titles can be seen in almost every major newspaper across the globe. Look at the *Washington Post: New case of pedophilia: The founder of True Archaeology under lock and key!* And this is the *New York Times: Father Green, suspected pedophile, arrested at True Archaeology headquarters!* I'm sure you won't be hearing about the archaeological discoveries made of True Archaeology for a very, very long time…"

"My dear Rachel," said Taittinger with a satisfied look, "I see that you've done a remarkable job! Jeff and I agree that you have earned your promotion to the rank of Senior Vice President, retroactive to January first this year. Let's think of this as year one for you at TOTEXX, since the doors of the executive committee are now open to you… Today is the ninth of the first month of the year. We could call it 9-1-1 considering the way you handled this emergency. Don't you think that's a happy coincidence?"

EPILOGUE

- **Joseph Taittinger**, on his seventy-fifth birthday, sold his shares for several billion dollars and retired from the TOTEXX board of directors. He acquired a private island in the Bahamas where he had a sumptuous residence built. He also bought a private jet, so that he could regularly travel to Aspen-Colorado and enjoy his luxurious chalet, or to Dallas where he kept his Preston Hollow mansion.

- **Rachel Schwartz**, barely a year after her rise to the rank of Senior Vice President, was promoted to Executive Vice President. Joseph Taittinger's departure did not affect her. On the contrary, the new Chairman of the Board greatly appreciated the regular face-to-face meetings she privately had with him in the magnificent duplex she acquired at the top of one of the most prestigious buildings in Fort Worth.

- **Jeff Fishman**, following Joseph Taittinger's departure and the reshuffle of the board of directors, lost his job as CEO of TOTEXX. The rumors of inappropriate behavior that were circulating about him prevented him from landing an equivalent position elsewhere.

- **Samuel Kahn**, shaken by Dorian Green's ordeal and guessing at TO-TEXX hand behind the slanderous campaign against him, decided to forget his dreams of easy fortune. He reoriented the main themes of his department of archaeology at Harvard to focus on the search for the remains of a great primordial civilization…

- **Émile and Monique Delaporte** returned to their modest apartment in Rueil-Malmaison and fell back into anonymity. They invested the money earned by Émile for his services to True Archaeology in a small house by the sea in Brittany, near Carnac. Émile found a new passion in the *menhirs* and other *dolmens* in the region.

- **Kate McKee, born Von Tardy**, reconciled with her family, to whom she introduced her husband, Kevin. Happy to be accepted into a real family, **Kevin** decided to move to France. After completing his master's degree at Oxford, he enrolled at the Faculty of Strasbourg to obtain his doctorate and became Assistant Professor of Archaeology there.

- **Prosper Tabellion**, aiming to influence the European Union policy concerning archaeological research, was able to get elected as a Member of the European Parliament for the Green Party. He stepped down from his academic position to focus on the fight to restore Dorian's good name and to advance True Archaeology agenda. Edwina left The Manor to live in Strasbourg with her husband.

- **Emma Coffey** was dismissed by the Bodleian Library, due to her support for Dorian Green during his arrest. She developed into a very active member of the True Archaeology steering committee and became Mrs. Green.

- **Dorian Green** eventually proved his innocence and recovered his freedom. With the support of his loyal friends at True Archaeology, he found a renewed energy to overcome the derision of the academic establishment, convince sponsors to provide the means to launch a major campaign of archeological excavations in Antarctica, stimulate the interest of the media and finally make Civilization X better known of the general public.

THANK YOU

Thank you for reading *Anu Tara Tiki*. If you enjoyed it, please take a moment to leave a review on Amazon, Barnes and Noble, Goodreads, or your preferred online retailer.

Reviews are the best way to show your support for an author and to help new readers discover their books.